RENEGADE HAWKE

A SECOND GENERATION HAWKE FAMILY NOVEL

BILLIONAIRES OF NEW ORLEANS: THE HAWKE FAMILY SECOND GENERATION
BOOK 7

GWYN MCNAMEE

RENEGADE HAWKE

Cover Model: Christopher Jensen; Photographer: Michelle Lancaster

Cover Design: Michelle Johnson at Bluesky Design

Editing: David Michael at Encompass Press

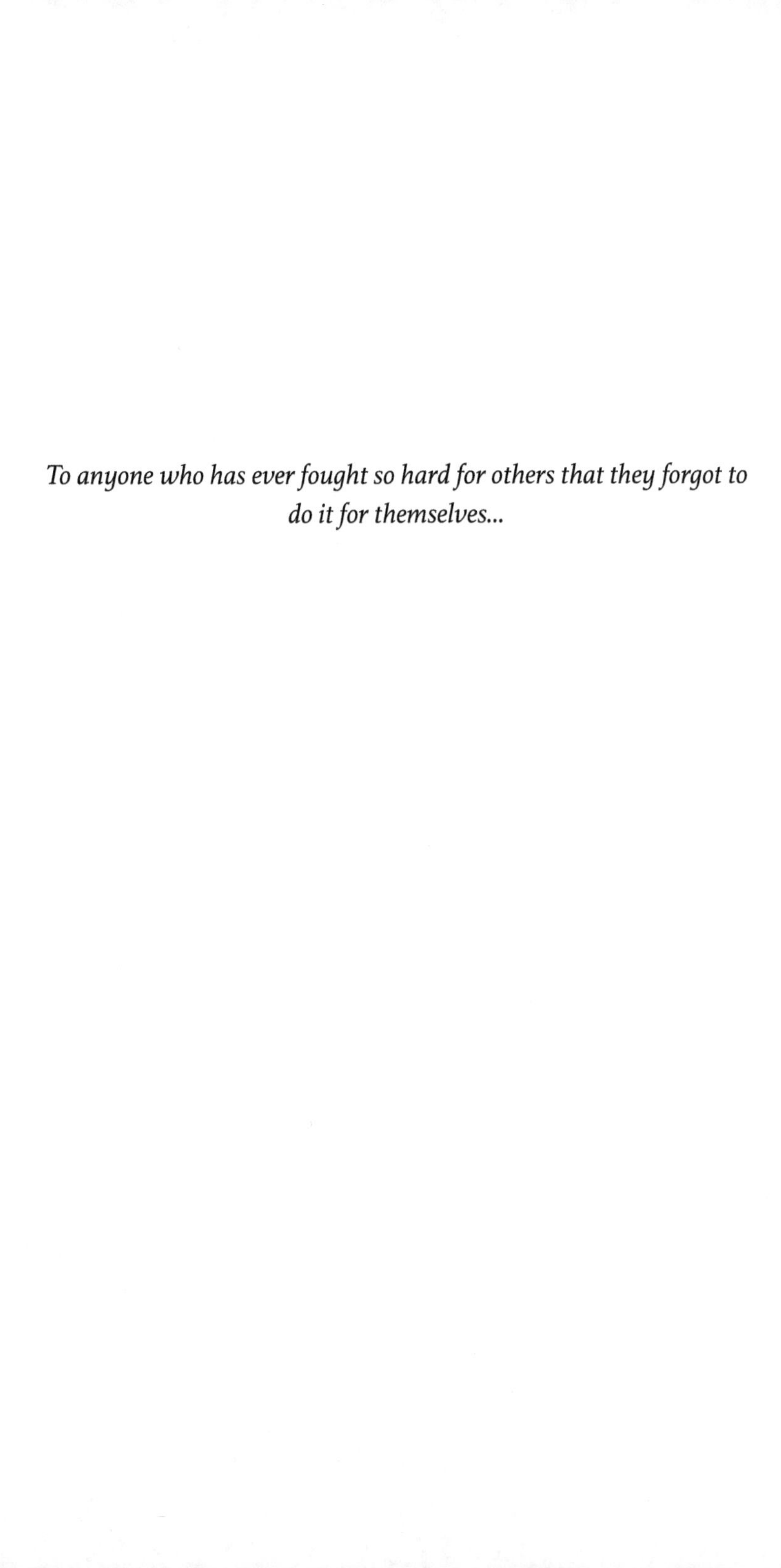

To anyone who has ever fought so hard for others that they forgot to do it for themselves...

HAWKE FAMILY TREE

THE HAWKE FAMILY

Antonia and Sam "The Savage" Hawke

SAVAGE COLLISION

Savage Hawke & Danika Eriksson

Kennedy Hawke

STONE SOBER

Stone Hawke & Nora Eriksson

Isaac Hawke Coen Hawke

TAINTED SAINT

Solomon "Saint" Clarke & Caroline Brooks

Pope Clarke Bishop Clarke

TORTURED SKYE

Skye Hawke & Gabe Anderson

Atlas Anderson Astrid Anderson

BUILDING STORM

Storm Hawke (Matthews) & Landon McCabe

Angelina Matthews Alessandra McCabe

STEELE RESOLVE

Luca "Steele" Abello & Byron Harris

Jude Harris-Abello (ad)

1

BISHOP

The familiar antiseptic scent that desperately tries to cover that of sickness and death fills my lungs. Each breath becomes increasingly harder to take the longer I wait, as if the tainted air is slowly killing me as much as the uncertainty and worry threatens to.

It doesn't help that there's no escaping the cacophony of sounds that always overwhelms the hospital.

Beeping of machines...

Squeak of shoes on tile...

Cries of pain and loss...

All of it permeates my head, making a dull ache form at my temples. I'd also love to blame all of it for the way my stomach roils, but it isn't the smell or the sounds making me feel like I'm being eaten alive from the inside out...

It's guilt.

Plain and simple.

Because this *shouldn't* all be so familiar.

It shouldn't be someplace I'm constantly finding myself.

If I were doing my job properly...it wouldn't be.

That's what it comes down to—if I were actually capable of protecting the people I love the way I'm supposed to, we wouldn't have to be in this hospital.

Again.

But I've failed.

Over and over.

And there is no denying it's why we are here right now...

This is all my fault.

I stand in the hallway peeking into the room where both Jack and Allegra lie in their beds. While Allegra looks far better now than she did at the club, and Jack appears more annoyed than ill, the fact is, they're still *here*. They're still in danger. There are still too many unknowns around what made them so sick.

Isaac and Coen fawn all over them while they await results from the battery of tests Aunt Nora and Pope have run, their distress creating a palpable tension that vibrates through me.

Because I share it.

That feeling that something is just *wrong.*

Since the moment Coen came rushing out of the bathroom at the club with Allegra in his arms and told me she was sick and so was Jack, I knew, deep in my gut, that it wasn't a coincidence.

It can't be.

I haven't believed in those in a very long time, and I'm confident this is somehow connected to Satriano and the diabolical plans he loves to set in motion when it comes to the Hawkes.

A man like him doesn't simply give up the kind of vendetta he's held against us for so long.

That isn't something you just let go.

It doesn't matter that Allegra is his daughter. She may share his blood; she may have been raised by the man; but she made her choice. A very dangerous one. She crossed the invisible line drawn between Satriano and us that is somehow still very real to the other side—to the *Hawke* side.

She betrayed her father.

We all know there will be consequences for that, and I only had one job: to keep them safe and ensure something like *this* didn't happen.

"Fuck!"

I smash my fist against the wall, hard enough to make my knuckles sting.

"If you do that again, you're going to end up breaking it." Astrid's voice cuts through my fog of self-loathing as she steps up beside me and leans her shoulder on the wall, her blond hair cascading over her collarbone. Hawke-blue eyes assess me, searching my face intently. "Seriously. Hitting something this hard isn't the best idea."

"Yeah, well"—I shake out my hand, the sting reminding me all too vividly of my failures and the pain the Hawkes have suffered because of them—"I can't exactly head to the gym now, can I?"

Her gaze narrows on me. "Look, we're all upset, Bishop—"

"Upset?" I raise a brow at her. "I crossed upset and went *way* beyond it a long time ago. I didn't keep them safe, Astrid, I fucked up..."

And I can't even voice the potential consequences of that.

She releases a long sigh. "You don't really believe that, do you?"

"Believe what?"

Astrid's features soften even more, her concern written across her face and the way she watches me. She's always been the most empathetic of all of us, and while that quality is typically a good one to have, when I just want to be left alone and wallow in my guilt, it can be grating. "That it's *your* sole responsibility to keep everyone safe?"

"I mean…yes." I throw out my open hands toward the room. "That's *literally* my job."

She snorts and shakes her head. "No. It isn't. You're one of *many* people who handle security for us. And technically, Saint is in charge of running it. You're just his second in command. If something *did* happen to Jack and Allegra, if someone managed to slip something into their food or their drinks, or whatever else could've caused this, that doesn't mean it happened on *your* watch and that it was *your* fault."

I clench my fists and that ache flares in my knuckles, but I don't mind it. In some strange, masochistic way, I crave it. I need the reminder so I never fail again. "Yes, it does, because if I wasn't there personally, I *should* have been."

Her blond brows fly up. "And what? You're going to taste-test every single thing every one of us eats or drinks for the rest of our lives?"

Well, when she puts it that way, it sounds fucking stupid, doesn't it?

I shake my head, pinching the bridge of my nose in a futile attempt to alleviate the pounding that has moved from my temples to behind my eyes. "I don't know." A long sigh falls from my lips, filled with all the frustration that's coiled inside me with no way to release it. "I just can't believe we're here again…"

It's been one mistake on my part after another.

First, Jack was taken, then the bombing of the Grind, the shooting at the reopening, and the sniper attack on the penthouse that almost killed Atlas and Astrid…

Everyone has suffered, either directly or by watching those we love bleed and lose things sacred to them.

Each of us is scarred in some way.

The woman in front of me certainly hasn't been the same since the shooting. She tries to hide it behind an easy smile or by spending every waking moment she has tutoring our employees or helping anywhere she can at the clubs, the Grind, or elsewhere, but I see it for what it really is—a defense mechanism.

Because she doesn't want to be alone.

She's *afraid* to be…

And there's only one reason for that—*me.*

I release the bridge of my nose and open my eyes again to find Astrid watching me carefully. "You've suffered as much as anyone."

Her lips press into a thin line, her jaw hardening. Something dark crosses her typically warm gaze. It's fleeting, but it's there. And it isn't the first time I've seen it since she was shot and almost died. She continues to fight whatever demons are chasing her and refuses to let any of us help, which is why I thought she of all people would understand. "I know."

"Then how can you be so calm about this? What if—"

She steps forward and grabs my wrists, squeezing them gently. "Don't think about worst-case scenarios. You'll drive yourself crazy." Inclining her head toward the room, she locks her gaze with mine. "They're going to be *okay*. Nora and Pope have run every test under the sun to figure out what's wrong. So, take a breath, all right? And stop hitting walls."

Deep down, I know she's right—that panicking or allowing my distress to show will only make things worse.

I'm here to keep them safe.

I can't do that if my head isn't in the game.

I nod, forcing myself to draw in a shaky breath even though the sting of failure and suffocating panic still battle to control me.

And that pisses me off more than anything about this entire situation.

It isn't like me to spiral, to give in to those emotions that prevent me from focusing on my job, on the task at hand, which, right now, should be tracking down whoever is responsible for what happened to Jack and Allegra.

But this has been building and building with each attack on the Hawkes, each time I fail to prevent another catastrophe, and it's only getting worse.

Get a fucking grip, girl!

Another deep breath helps me regain a bit of my composure, but Pope and Aunt Nora appear down the hallway behind Astrid, and any hope I had to let go of that rising tide of panic disappears.

I immediately tug out of Astrid's hold and rush toward them, unable to wait for even the few seconds it would take for them to reach us to find out what they've learned.

Falling into step with them, I raise a brow. "What's wrong? Are they going to be okay?"

Nora inclines her head to indicate that we should keep walking toward the room instead of stopping to discuss this in the middle of the hallway and issues me a reproachful look.

She's already kicked out the rest of the family and banished them to the waiting room due to their incessant questions and buzzing around, but I refused and stood fast by the door despite her objections.

I failed to protect them everywhere else, but I damn well am not going to leave them unprotected here.

No one has gone in or out of that room unless they were family since Nora and Pope brought them over from the clinic after determining they needed more testing than they could handle there.

It would have been more private.

Easier to control and defend should anyone take the opportunity to attack while we were distracted.

But ultimately, Nora wanted them *here*. Which means that's exactly where I will stay.

She steps into the room first, followed by Astrid, but I grab Pope's arm and keep him back.

"Well?"

He offers me an incredulous look. "You think I'm going to give away confidential medical information to you?"

I glower at him. "This isn't the time to try me, little brother."

Pope stares down from almost a foot above me, fighting a grin. "Call me *little brother* again. I dare you."

The humor in his threat somehow cuts through the tension about to snap me in half—likely his very intention. He knows how wound up I've been since I arrived, and he also understands—as a brother *and* a doctor—that it isn't healthy for me to get like this.

I can't help the twitch of a smile, despite my current distress. "I'll see you in the ring in the morning, and we can put this to the test."

He grins and tugs out of my hold easily, and that tilt of his lips is enough to ease a little of my worry. If they were in danger, he wouldn't be so quick with a smile.

I follow him into the room where Coen and Isaac are already on their feet, each of them gripping the hand of the woman they love tightly.

Matching sets of panicked blue eyes land on Nora.

Isaac swallows thickly. "Mom? What is it?"

She offers a tight smile and glances at Pope, sharing a look I can't quite decipher.

Coen shifts restlessly. "Mom, what's wrong with them? Do you know?"

"We have the results of some of the tests back. Others, we're still waiting on, but given their symptoms, I feel comfortable saying that there's absolutely *nothing* wrong with either of them."

Coen and Isaac's brows both furrow, and Jack and Allegra join them in looking utterly confused.

What the hell does she mean?

Isaac shakes his head. "Mom, I don't understand..."

Nora locks gazes with her eldest. "They've both been exhausted, dizzy, nauseous, feeling off..."

He and Coen nod.

Her eyes drift to her daughter-in-law and then the newest member of the Hawke flock. Jack exchanges an unsure look with Allegra, but it only takes a few seconds for Jack's eyes to widen.

"Oh, shit!" She looks to Nora. "We're pregnant, aren't we?"

Nora can't fight her grin. "You are. *Both* of you."

What?

My breath catches.

Isaac's gaze cuts over to his younger brother before they both drop back down into the chairs beside the beds as if their legs can't hold them up anymore.

I understand the feeling.

Both of them?

Astrid releases a squeal of delight and claps her hands, but Coen's worried gaze sweeps over Allegra, who appears stunned speechless. Her wide gray eyes carry a mix of excitement and deep dread, which I imagine is tied to the situation with her father and what this might mean for it. Isaac shares a look with Jack that is pure, unadulterated joy and adoration.

And suddenly, I feel like I'm intruding on something I absolutely don't need to be a part of.

Because I know exactly what's coming.

They're going to get all gooey and lovey dovey, and I'm going to be the one who ends up throwing up even though they're dealing with morning sickness.

I back out of the room and pull my phone from my pocket, but Astrid hurries after me, following my path toward the waiting room.

She grins, the happy, bubbly energy she used to always have

seeping from her now, completely overwhelming the earlier melancholy when discussing what happened to her. "Where are you off to so fast?"

"I can't be here right now." Not when it feels like the walls are closing in on me. "I'm going to get my dad to stand guard."

"Wait, Bish." She grabs my arm, halting my flight. "You should be *happy*."

I *should* be.

It *should* be a relief to know both of them are only experiencing symptoms of something everyone in the family will be thrilled about, but I can't shake this feeling that more is happening that I'm missing.

"Just because someone didn't do something to Jack and Allegra this time doesn't mean they haven't tried or won't try in the future."

"Bishop..."—she sighs—"can't you relax for *one* second and be excited about the fact that we're going to have new nieces and nephews?"

I try to draw in and release a deep breath to get my heart to stop racing and that vise that's tightened around my chest for the last several hours to loosen, but it doesn't.

Astrid reads my continued distress easily. "You *didn't* fail."

It doesn't matter how many times she says those words to me, it isn't going to make them feel any truer. Especially now that there's another reason to be alarmed when it comes to Satriano beyond the fact that one of his henchmen is now in the city—his daughter is pregnant with a *Hawke*.

"I have to go."

Her eyes widen. "Where?"

"Back to the club."

"Why?"

Everyone will be celebrating.

As soon as Isaac and Coen head to the waiting area and

make the announcement, the Hawke clan will switch over from terrified to ecstatic.

But not me.

The memory of a mop of sandy-blond hair and a man in a leather jacket leaving the club immediately after Allegra got sick flashes through my head, as does Isaac's warning about Michael McDonald arriving in New Orleans.

No such thing as coincidence.

"There was a guy there tonight, before Allegra got sick."

"Yeah?" Astrid's brow furrows. "What about him?"

"He..." I struggle with how to explain to her the feeling I got when I saw him, but words seem to fail me. "I don't know, there was just something *off* about him."

Her eyes darken with concern. "Did you stop him?"

I shake my head. "I had to call Dad, let him know what was going on with Allegra and Jack. The guy slipped out before I could grab him to question him."

"So, why are you going back now if he isn't there anymore?"

"To scour the video footage to try to figure out who he is and why the *fuck* he was there in the first place."

And why everything about him felt wrong.

TWO DAYS LATER
GAGE

Every club has an energy.

A vibe.

Something you feel the moment you step through the doors that makes your heart pump in time to the music blasting through the speakers and that gets fully absorbed into your bloodstream.

It engulfs you and draws you into a different world from the one outside the doors.

The Hawkeye Club is no different.

From the first moment that deep, rumbling bass vibrates through your feet and chest until the moment you walk out the door and it closes behind you, you're enveloped by pure elegance.

A rich tapestry of color, light, texture, and sound that swallows you whole and wraps you in a silky sensual cocoon you don't want to climb out of.

I've spent enough time in enough seedy clubs to know the difference between them and *this*.

What they've created at The Hawkeye Club is so unlike those other places that they aren't even in the same category.

Beautiful surroundings.

Gorgeous women.

The kind of dancers who have talent *and* class, who don't rely on shock value to make money off the patrons. They're actually *good*. The best I've seen in New Orleans, or anywhere else that I've been over the last several years, for that matter.

And this place is locked down tight.

Security at the door, more near the stage, several *big*, muscular men who look like they could break most of the patrons in here in half like a twig roam around in civilian clothes that do little to conceal who they are or why they're here.

They don't take chances when it comes to their girls, and that's something I can appreciate, even if it does make me a little uneasy as I walk in. Most of them pay me no mind as I saunter through the main room and slide onto an empty stool near the far end of the bar, exactly where I was sitting only a few days ago when it all went down.

And when I saw *her*...

My eyes immediately scan the club, barely skimming over the redhead on the pole who has everyone else's rapt attention.

She doesn't hold mine.

Not because she isn't beautiful or talented. She's definitely both those things. But the woman I'm searching for won't be on that stage tonight.

She'll be watching from the wings, standing in the shadows, even though she's far more stunning than any of the girls who get naked and perform.

I haven't been able to stop thinking about the brief glimpse I got of her the other night during all the commotion—or hoping I'll see her again.

But she isn't here tonight.

Just a normal crowd enjoying the music, the show, and a drink. No stunning burnt-umber-skinned beauty watching intently from the wings…

Disappointment hits me squarely in the chest, but I push it away.

You don't need the complication.

It's a reminder I've told myself many times in my life—that getting involved with a woman for anything more than a quick release only leads to heartbreak and pain. And for the most part, I've been able to keep things casual with my entanglements. They never last long, and I make sure they end before something like *feelings* can get involved. But something tells me that staying casual would be impossible given the way my body reacted to seeing *her*.

I've never believed in anything beyond lust at first sight.

There's never been any reason to…

Yet, the moment I saw her racing into action when it was apparent someone was sick, it felt as if I'd been struck squarely in the chest by something far more powerful.

Something that drew me back here tonight when I should have stayed away.

The young bartender makes his way over to me and inclines his head. "Nice to see you again."

He remembers me...

That could be a bad thing, or a good one. Friendly people have looser lips. That means I might learn a thing or two about the stunning woman who suddenly occupied all my thoughts over the past couple days.

I shift in my seat slightly, angling my body so I can see the club better—to watch for *her*. "Thanks."

"What can I get for ya?"

"Whatever IPA you have on tap."

He nods and offers a grin. "You got it."

Without even thinking, I slide my hand into my right jacket pocket and close my fingers around the hard metal there, almost as if I need to feel it to ground myself tonight.

And honestly, maybe I do.

I need the reminder of who I am when things have felt *off* for a while now. It's something I can't put my finger on. An unsteadiness when I'm typically rock solid. Questions when there used to be none. And somehow, I thought coming here and drowning myself in hoppy beer was the answer.

Liar.

That's not why you're here.

That little voice inside my head better shut the fuck up, because I have absolutely no business being interested in that woman.

None.

Yet, my eyes keep sweeping the club for her as if seeing her again will somehow wipe away this feeling growing inside me.

I only caught a glimpse of the other night before I had to duck out, but it was enough to leave a lasting impression. Even from across the large space, even with people laughing, music playing, and everything else happening around the club, her presence overwhelmed everything else. *She* took center stage without ever setting foot on it.

That's how I know she isn't here.

I don't feel that magnetic draw that kept my focus squarely on her when it should have been literally *anywhere* else.

So instead of hopelessly searching, I force myself to watch the girl on the stage. She moves fluidly. Effortlessly. The beat of the music perfectly in sync with the way her body twists and bends.

The bartender sliding a beer over to me refocuses my attention. "Anything else?"

I shake my head. "I'm good."

"You want me to leave your tab open?"

"Nah."

If I need to leave quickly again, the last thing I want is to owe the club money, or to have my credit card sitting unclaimed. It's better to fly under the radar as much as possible.

I grab a twenty out of my wallet and toss it onto the bar top. "Does that cover it?"

"More than. Let me get you your change."

I shake my head. "Keep it."

His eyes widen slightly. "That's like, a ten-dollar tip..."

"Keep it."

I know what it's like to be young and struggling at a job like this where you're really making all your money off tips. And he's a decent bartender. Friendly, talkative but not intrusive, which means now that I have my drink, he'll leave me alone unless I engage him in conversation.

Which is how I prefer it...

To be in control.

Allowing otherwise could be catastrophic.

Settling in, I absorb the vibe, scoping out everyone in the club—their locations, who they're with, what they're drinking, how many they've had, their demeanors and conversations.

I don't even do it consciously anymore; it's just become natural, so ingrained in me that I couldn't stop myself from doing it even if I tried.

Some folks people watch for fun; I do it because not paying attention to those things can lead to dire consequences.

The doors on the elevator on the far side of the club glide open, and my heart climbs into my throat as *she* steps out.

With her long braids tied back in a bun high on her head and shoulders back, she takes strong, confident steps through the club. Her sharp gaze sweeps across everyone, carefully surveying all the patrons, the girls, memorizing where each and every person is and every detail about them—exactly what I was just doing.

I can practically see the wheels turning in her head behind those stunning dark bourbon eyes. She's taking stock of everyone, making calculations, considering where she would need to be and what she would need to do if there were a problem.

Wicked intelligent and calculating.

Only more reason to like the woman—and need to fly under the radar around her.

The corner of my lips curls up watching her work, and I force myself to take a drink of my beer and tear my gaze from her before she catches me staring. Drawing unwanted attention to myself—now or ever—wouldn't be wise.

Not when coming to NOLA is complicated enough already for me.

I sip my beer, watching the woman on stage and the group of men congregated around it. Despite so badly wanting to check to see what she's doing, I keep my focus anywhere else. But I feel the *exact* moment her eyes find *me*.

It would be impossible not to when the hair on the back of my neck rises and heat licks across my skin like a raging wildfire searing across dead treetops. It crackles and scorches through me, igniting something I haven't ever felt before—yearning.

I shift uneasily on the stool and take another long gulp of the cool beer, but it doesn't do anything to help my restlessness.

I'm not used to being assessed like this.

I'm the one who does the assessing...until I set foot in The Hawkeye Club.

Apparently, everything I thought I knew and understood about myself changed the moment I saw her. Decisions I made long before coming here now seem...undetermined. Plans long held...suddenly less certain. A future and end game laid out... now open for play.

The music thrums through the air, and I force myself to watch the dancer who moves in time with the beat rather than looking to see where *she* is and what she's doing.

She's careful, which means she won't make it obvious she's observing me, but the way my skin keeps sizzling, there's no question that's exactly what's happening.

Why?

What caught your interest?

If anything, she should be concentrating on the men near the stage who have been getting more boisterous the longer I've been here. Two of them stumble over, leaving three of their buddies to throw money at the woman on the pole.

One of the men bumps into my left shoulder as he shoves his way up to the bar.

Asshole.

"Heey!" He yells for the bartender with a slight New England accent and a slur that suggests he's a tourist who has likely spent most of the day on Bourbon Street before heading over here tonight. "I need shots." He slams his fist on the bar top. "Tequila!"

My friendly bartender tenses the same way I do. We've

clearly both had plenty of experience dealing with stupid drunks, and these two definitely seem to be somewhere on that scale. Maybe not at the top yet, but well above mid-level.

I slide my hands off the glass, resting them on the bar, and turn to more fully face them.

The bartender looks behind me at someone or something before he inclines his head at the two men, grabs the bottle and the shot glasses, and lines them up. He pours and motions toward the shots. "After this, you guys have had enough for the night."

Good.

They certainly don't need more from where I sit, and the man on the other side of the bar is good enough at his job to see it, too. These two—and their friends at the stage— will be trouble if they don't sober up or make their way out of here—*soon.*

The bigger of the two of them, whose slicked-back jet-black hair shimmers under the lighting where he stands beside me, narrows his eyes at the bartender. "We're fine."

Disdain coats his pronouncement.

The bartender shakes his head. "We reserve the right to cut you off at any time."

With a scoff, his friend who has the build of a wrestler and the sneer of someone used to getting his way glares across the bar. "Cut us off?"

They each grab a shot and take one, then slam them down.

The one with the black hair turns from the bar just as one of the girls walks by. He reaches out and snags her by the wrist, dragging her over to him with a lecherous grin that tightens my hand into a fist. "What about you, sweetheart? Do *you* think we should be cut off?"

Her eyes widen slightly and dart to the bartender, and I glance toward the security guard at the door as he starts to make his way over.

But I can already tell he's going to be too late.

Shit.

The D-bag's free hand travels toward the girl's almost bare ass, but before he can grab her, I'm up from the stool, slamming my elbow into his face and knocking him back.

Blood splatters across his face and shirt, and his yelp of pain fills the air as I tug her away from him and his buddy.

My arm moves around her waist, and I pull her to me, putting myself firmly between her and the assholes. With her protected against the bar, they can't get to her without coming through *me*.

And that sure as hell isn't happening.

Before she can say anything or even react, my arm is pulled from around her waist and jerked behind my back as I'm shoved to the floor.

My chest hits the tile, all the air rushing from my lungs as someone pins me down with their knee between my shoulder blades, twisting my shoulder and wrenching my arm violently.

Fuck…

Warm breath flutters over my ear, and a light jasmine scent floats over me, stilling any reaction my body wants to take against the attack. "What the *fuck* do you think you're doing, touching one of the girls?"

Holy hell.

It isn't the voice of the big burly guy who stood at the door that rings in my ears; it's the voice of a fucking angel with an impressive submission hold.

2

BISHOP

I drive my knee harder into the upper back of the man I have pinned on the floor and wrench his arm even harder behind him, knowing the type of strain I'm putting on his shoulder and the agony he must be in.

Relishing it.

Using all my leverage to make it even *worse.*

This fucker thinks he can touch one of the girls which means he's going to learn a lesson in what happens when you do...

Straddling his hips, my entire body weight on him in a kimura hold, he's completely at my mercy.

And I can't wait to hear him *beg*.

They always do.

But unlike so many other troublemakers I've forced into submission, he doesn't fight it.

No bucking and flailing to try to throw me off like most people would if they were in his precarious position.

He calmly glances over his shoulder at me the best he can, and one Cerulean blue eye meets my gaze. The corner of his mouth twitches, but instead of a cry of agony or an angry demand that I get off him, his body starts to vibrate beneath me with strained *laughter*.

"Damn, woman. Most men I know can't pin me like that. *Impressive.*"

This smug motherfucker...

I lower my mouth to his ear and snarl, my fury only growing at his unusual response to the situation. "Nothing about this is funny, you asshole."

He continues to chuckle lightly, despite my weight pinning him down and the discomfort he must be in due to the strain on his shoulder and arm. "Oh, I disagree."

The shuffle of footsteps and click of heels beside me draws my attention up, and Jade grabs at my shoulder, her eyes still wide and darting around us. "Bishop, stop! He was trying to help me." She motions behind her to two men being shoved out of the club by the doorman. "Those two were being creeps. This one was *protecting* me."

Well, shit...

Everything happened so fast, and I briefly looked away from this man at the bar and was watching Honey on the stage and keeping an eye on the rest of the rowdy group at the front of it.

All I saw of whatever went down over here was the man under me with his arm around Jade and her looking terrified...

And apparently, I completely misread the situation.

Fuck.

I loosen my grip on the man's arm and slowly release him, starting to push up onto my knees. He deftly rolls over beneath me before I can get to my feet and stares up from the floor as if I didn't just take him down embarrassingly easily and try to rip his shoulder out of socket.

Absolutely mesmerizing blue eyes lock with mine, and a full-blown grin curls his sensuous lips set in a stunningly handsome face with high cheekbones and a strong jaw covered with dark blond stubble.

My breath hitches slightly, and I swallow through the tightness in my throat. "I...guess I owe you an apology."

They don't come to me easily. Something about being reminded constantly as a child that I shouldn't always rush to apologize just to resolve an issue unless I am truly in the wrong has made them more difficult as I've aged. But there's no debating I am wrong now.

And that fucking stings.

He shrugs nonchalantly, his broad shoulders moving under me in his black leather jacket in a way that sends a buzz of awareness through my body. "No apology necessary. You can pin me like this any time you want."

That grin of his only grows, as does the heat now coursing across my skin the longer he assesses me and looks at me like *that.*

Shit.

I quickly scramble to my feet and step off him, retreating slightly to give him room but also to put space between us so I can get my shit together. Because staring at a stranger like *that* is *not* having control.

The longer I look at him, the more it feels like I'm spiraling faster and faster, losing my connection to the things I pride myself in, the ones that keep me so grounded to this life, this job. My ability to remain passive and unaffected.

If I were being polite, I would offer him a hand to help him to his feet, but I don't trust myself to have skin-to-skin contact with this man.

Not when I just reacted like that.

Not when I know exactly who he is...

The same man who was here the other night. The one who set every nerve in my body to attention the moment I laid eyes on him. The one who screams *danger*, from his black leather jacket to the tattoos visible in the open V of his button-down shirt and that sly grin that continues as he slowly pushes up from the floor to his full height, towering over me at least a foot.

He leans in, and his warm breath flutters across my cheek. "I wasn't joking, by the way. That *was* impressive. It takes a lot to get the drop on me, let alone to keep me on the ground." Somehow, he shifts even *closer*, until I can feel all that hard muscle pressed against me and the scent of New Orleans air, leather, and something warm and spicy fills my breath. "And I wasn't joking about wanting you to do it whenever the mood may strike you."

The mood...

Heat flares in my gut and between my legs, and I press them together to stop the dull ache and throb starting there.

There isn't any question what he's referring to.

The innuendo isn't even thinly veiled.

He's flat-out propositioning me after I put him on his ass.

And my body seems to *like* it when I should want to throw this arrogant prick out onto the street, not into my bed.

Apparently, I've gone far too long not taking care of my own *needs* if it's this easy for him to get under my skin.

I tilt my head up to meet his heated gaze, willing myself not to display outwardly any of the ways he's affecting me physically. "That *won't* be happening."

One of his sandy-blond brows rises slowly. "Whatever you say."

But there's something about the look in his eyes that tells me he doesn't believe me, and I'm not so sure I do, either.

Some sort of strange electricity buzzes between us.

Something I don't like.

Something I absolutely don't trust.

Trust is *earned*, and it isn't something I give away cheaply.

Just because he protected Jade, that doesn't make him some sort of hero. It doesn't erase that initial unease I had when I saw him the other night, even if it did turn out that Allegra and Jack are both fine. It doesn't alleviate any of my concern where this handsome stranger is concerned.

I clear my throat—and hopefully, my thoughts—and take a step back, freeing myself from his entrancing gaze and his scent so I can draw in a breath without being overwhelmed by it.

Alex approaches, motioning over his shoulder toward the door. "They're gone."

"Good."

"I told them they're banned for life."

I nod, relieved he took care of *that* situation while I was dealing with *this* one—the man who still watches me intently with a penetrating gaze and that tiny smirk playing at his lips. "I'll make sure we pull images of them from the video and show the photos to all the staff."

Alex nods, then heads to the stage to talk to the other men who were with them, while the rest of the club quickly returns to normal, the excitement finished.

Jade whispers a "thank you" to her savior, then disappears into the back to take a few moments to gather herself together before it's her turn on stage.

Our girls aren't used to being manhandled by the patrons. Incidents like this *don't* happen frequently at any of The Hawkeye Club locations—if at all. Because we demand better than that; from our security, from our customers, from ourselves.

Just one more failure on my part...

Instead of seeing this coming, I stepped out of the elevator too distracted by my conversation with Savage and Gabe about the potential threat the arrival of Satriano's man in town might pose.

I haven't been able to stop thinking about it since the night Allegra and Jack were rushed to the hospital. Haven't been able to stop seeing all these puzzle pieces I can't *quite* fit together even though they appear to be from the same board.

With the opening of the second Hawke Hotel tower happening so soon, I can't shake this tension and feeling that something bad is just on the horizon. But that isn't an excuse for letting *this* happen on my watch.

If this stranger hadn't jumped in and helped Jade, things could have gotten much further out of control before Alex or I could have intervened.

And I never would have been able to forgive myself.

I might not even be able to now...

The man who stepped up when I failed continues to watch me carefully, as if he's waiting for me to do or say something more, and there's plenty to say.

Not only have I had a bad vibe from him since the moment I set eyes on him the other night, but reviewing the video surveillance only frustrated me more. Because he somehow managed to spend *hours* in the club without his full face ever appearing on screen.

Almost as if he planned it that way...

And even *if* there's an innocent explanation and I'm being paranoid where he's concerned, we can't have people believing it's their responsibility to act as security and get involved in incidents at the club—that will only lead to more problems.

And this man is trouble enough.

I approach him again, trying not to squirm at the heat emanating from his blue eyes that only burns hotter when I draw up right in front of him and they rake over me from the top of my head down to my booted feet. "While I appreciate your help, please leave protecting the girls to us."

The corner of his lips twitches. "You take your job very seriously."

Crossing my arms over my chest, I narrow my eyes on him. "Of course, I do."

"And just how did a beautiful woman like you, who can put a man my size on the floor so easily, end up working at a place like this?" He spreads his hands wide. "Your talents are wasted here."

I know it's meant as both a compliment and sexual innuendo, but it's the apparent dig at the club that makes my hackles rise. "My family owns the place."

"Really?"

I nod.

One of his brows rises. "I thought the Hawkes owned it?"

It's an innocuous question, but there's something about the way he asks it that makes my fists clench at my sides. Preparing to defend them and myself if necessary. "They do."

"So...you're a Hawke?"

I swallow thickly, letting that question play in my head for a moment, because it's a loaded one. They're as close to me as my family by blood, but I don't bear the name or look anything like them. That's something that has always been evident yet never important to anyone in the Hawke brood.

We *are* Hawkes—by birth or by choice, no matter our skin color or the last name on our driver's licenses.

"Yes..."

Even though I've failed them too many times to count recently, they somehow still trust me to protect their investments. To protect *them*. Because they love me and have faith in me even when I don't have any in myself.

"They *are* family."

He nods slowly, then shifts to step around me and make his way back to his seat at the bar, but he pauses with his shoulder pressed against mine to lean in until his lips feather over my ear, sending a little shiver through me straight to my core. "The offer still stands. Anytime you want to pin and straddle me again, I'm more than happy to let you."

My knees waver slightly, and that *heat* I could see in his gaze rolls over me like licking flames. Though *he* appears unaffected by this electric charge coursing between us.

Bastard...

Men like him—beautiful and confident, arrogant and cocky—are basically waving a giant red flag in the air.

I don't need any red flags in my life.

He brushes past me and returns to his stool, sliding onto it and immediately grabbing his beer to down the rest of it. His Adam's apple bobs with his heavy swallow, and as he sets the empty glass on the bar top, his hand trembles slightly.

Maybe not *so unaffected?*

It could just be from the adrenaline of the situation, but the way he surreptitiously reaches down and adjusts his cock behind the zipper of his jeans makes me smirk.

I shouldn't be so pleased by that revelation...

Red flags, Bishop.

Red fucking flags.

Tommy hustles over with a new beer for him. "On the house. I saw what happened. Thanks for the help."

Hell.

Now everyone's treating him like he's a hero.

I can admit, in that moment, maybe he was a bit heroic, but there's something about him that just doesn't feel right. That hasn't felt *right* since I saw him the night Allegra got sick.

There's too much power in his body.

Too much strength in his frame.

Too much confidence in the way he looks at me.

A cunning I can see swimming in that blue gaze.

I need to keep an eye on him.

We all do.

That means I might have to play nice with him, even though every instinct I have is screaming to stay away—for both of our protection.

GAGE

It takes all the willpower I possess to stay seated on the stool and not look over my shoulder to see if the stunning woman who made my cock hard by pinning me to the club floor is still looking at me.

But I don't have to *see* it.

I can *feel* her intense gaze sweeping over me.

Taking me in.

Assessing me.

Analyzing every little move I make.

I reach for the new beer the bartender brought me, willing the tremble in my hand to go away, and take a long sip of the cool liquid, hoping that it might calm my libido and my racing heart.

Because damn...

I never thought getting taken down like that by a woman could be so fucking hot, but with her—*good God*—I almost came in my pants the second I realized who was straddling me and wrenching on my arm.

The pain she inflicted only made me harder and more interested in the woman I should be avoiding, who made it very clear she doesn't trust me and isn't interested in anything I have to offer.

Except maybe my exit from the club and her life.

Which would be better for both of us.

I sense her approach, my entire body stiffening in anticipation, and the stool next to me scrapes against the floor before she takes a seat on it.

It's a true struggle fighting the grin that pulls at my lips.

She didn't walk away...

Maybe she couldn't.

The same way I can't seem to stay away from the club—or *her.*

She motions toward the bartender for something, and he brings over what appears to be soda water with lime for her. Slender dark fingers with short nails painted a deep red wrap around the glass, but she doesn't take a sip, peeking at me out of the corner of her eye. "This isn't your first time here."

I slowly turn my head toward her.

It wasn't a question.

She noticed me the other night, too. I wasn't merely imagining her intense gaze on me, and that should make me want to leave even more than the attention that's already been drawn to me tonight.

But that jasmine scent wraps around me with her this close and prevents me from moving.

"No"—I shake my head—"it isn't."

Her fingers drum against the glass lightly, matching the beat of the music thumping through the speakers. "You were here a few nights ago."

I nod. "I was. That was my first time."

She raises a dark brow. "How'd you find us?"

Fate...

Good. Bad. Or otherwise.

Fate seems to have brought me to this place at this time, knowing she would be here.

I allow the grin to spread across my lips. "I asked around for the best club in New Orleans, and I was told that The Hawkeye Club was the only place to go."

She nods slowly, her head tilting slightly, as if she isn't quite sure she's buying my explanation and might be able to see the truth if she looks at it from a different angle, even though I deliver it as smoothly and confidently as possible.

A moment passes where something unspoken passes

between us—an acknowledgment that she suspects I'm lying and I know it.

She finally lifts the glass to her lips and takes a sip. "So, what do you think?"

"About what?"

"The club."

I grin, never looking away. "It's beautiful. Fantastic vibe."

"And the girls?" She tries to keep it out of her voice, but there's a tension there, something I can't quite place. Surely, not jealousy. "What do you think of them?"

I keep my eyes locked on her stormy dark bourbon ones. "There's one I'm *very* interested in."

She dips her head, averting her gaze, and takes a much longer sip of her drink before she clears her throat. Her slender yet muscular shoulders and arms tense as she scans the club.

The incident certainly got her worked up, but this seems like something else. A rigidity and unease that goes far beyond two drunk men getting a little handsy with a stripper.

"You seem to be on edge tonight. Is something going on?"

Her head whips in my direction, her eyes hard, suspicious, and maybe even annoyed. "You mean besides the fact that one of my girls got grabbed by a total creep and I didn't get here fast enough so you had to step in?"

And there it is...

The *real* reason she's upset.

I smirk, turning slightly on my stool toward her. "That really rubs at you, doesn't it? That I took care of the situation before you could."

She presses her lips together in a firm line, her jaw tensing.

A chuckle slips out before I can bite it back, and I take another sip of my beer, never tearing my eyes away from her. "It does." I set the glass down on the bar top and lean toward her. "It really bothers you that someone else stepped in."

My observation causes her to shift on the stool. "My father has run security for the Hawkes longer than I've been alive."

"And that means it automatically becomes your job?"

Drumming her nails on the bar top, she releases a long sigh and shakes her head. "No. I wanted it to be. I could have gone to law school or been a doctor like my brother. I had the grades for it, but I stayed in the family business."

Why?

She's clearly intelligent, focused, driven—and the type of student who had grades good enough to get her into those types of schools. Yet, after experiencing the way she took me down so easily tonight, I can see how it may have been the right career move for her to work with her father.

That move was effortless, and on a man who has at least fifty pounds and a foot on her, she made it look like child's play.

This woman is a force of nature, like a fucking hurricane that can't be brought to submission by anything or anyone.

She will always come out on top and be in control.

Or at least try to be.

And tonight, she wasn't.

For those few moments it took that fucker to grab the dancer and for me to intervene, she wasn't doing what she's best at; she wasn't doing her job. Or, at least, she thinks she wasn't. But I know she was keeping an eye on the other three guys near the stage, watching out for the girl on the pole. And it's impossible to watch, let alone be in, two places at once.

My chest tightens, and a dull ache forms there watching her struggle with what she sees as a failure.

I lean back, giving her some space as she shifts uneasily in her stool, trying to gather herself back to the stoic, controlled woman she undoubtedly typically is.

A new song starts, signaling a change in dancers on the stage, but I don't even so much as glance in that direction. The only woman in this entire place that could hold my interest is sitting beside me right now.

She releases a long, slow breath, and her shoulders straighten, as if she's rebuilt that wall of strength that only moments ago had cracked. Staring into her drink, she swirls it aimlessly but peeks at me again. "So, are you new to town?"

Apparently, we're done talking about what went down tonight and the relationship she has with the Hawkes.

I nod. "I am."

"Will you be staying for a while?"

There's the slightest dip in her voice, something someone else might not have noticed, but it's the kind of thing I always pick up on.

A tiny fissure in that wall she's rebuilt—or at least, attempted to.

But if I mention it, she'll bolt and shut down completely.

I shrug as nonchalantly as I can, trying to keep my expression neutral. "That depends."

Her gaze shifts over to meet mine. "On what?"

"On how some things play out..."

"What sort of *things*?"

"My job, mostly, but also something personal..."

That beautiful umber skin darkens even more on her cheeks, the only sign this woman is ever likely to give me because it's one she can't control.

She didn't miss the fact that I meant her, but the real question is what she will do with it.

It would be better for us both if she ignored the flirtation, pushed away this spark between us and wrote it off as something not to explore.

I hold my breath, waiting for her to act. Waiting for her to make the decision to slam the door shut on me so that it won't remain in my hands that seem desperate to hold it open.

She considers me for a moment, and for a split second, I see a glimmer of interest in her eyes that makes me think she might bite.

But it's gone just as quickly.

Replaced by a steely resolve I don't like being on the opposite side of.

Casually, she brings her drink to her lips again, and I can't help but focus on the way her throat moves as she takes a sip from it.

Fuck.

My palm itches to wrap around her smooth dark skin, to feel her gasps of pleasure rumbling beneath it.

I shift on the hard stool, trying to relieve some of the tension building in all the wrong places.

She sets the glass down and runs a fingertip around the rim. "What do you do for work?"

"I fix things."

Her dark brows rise. "What kinds of things?"

"I'm a mechanic."

Those intense eyes automatically dip to my hands.

I hold them up, showing her all the calluses. "Mostly motorcycles, but I love to get my hands on anything with an engine."

This woman's runs fast and hard.

She vibrates with the kind of power that's always been an aphrodisiac for me, and she doesn't even seem to know it. Her bottom lip disappears under her teeth for a second, and when she releases it, she flashes me a little half-grin that does dangerous things to my willpower.

"And what else do you *do*, besides work on engines and hang out in strip clubs?"

I chuckle low. "You make that sound like a bad thing. I'm giving your family business, aren't I?"

Her eyes darken as they lock on me. "Is that the only reason you're here?"

There it is.

The question she should be asking, what she's been wondering about since the moment she saw me the other night.

She doesn't trust me.

Not even a little.

I slide on the stool, moving closer to her until my knee brushes against her thigh. The music thumps around us, and I lean in so she can hear me over it while also ensuring no one else walking by might. "I noticed you the other night, too."

Her back stiffens. "Did you?"

Nodding, I slant even closer. "All these women you have on the poles, dripping with sex, making men tremble and fall to their knees for a single second of attention, but the only one who drew *mine* was you."

"Really?"

The disbelief in her voice hangs in the air between us.

An unspoken challenge permeates her question.

I raise a brow. "Want me to prove it?"

She mirrors a raised brow in response, and I chuckle, moving in until my lips ghost over her ear.

"You were standing in the northwest corner of the club, watching everything and everyone, taking stock, sizing everyone up, including me." Her breath hitches. "You were wearing a steel-gray T-shirt that showed off all of your beautiful skin and muscles that I imagine you earned doing something like martial arts. Probably Jiu-Jitsu, given the hold you put on me." She stops breathing completely. "You had on a pair of dark jeans that clung to you like they were painted on, and all I could think about was tearing them off you."

I pull back slightly to see her half-hooded eyes locked on me, her lips parted slightly, as if I stunned the breath right out of her.

A second passes.

Another.

Then she lets out a rush of air from her lungs and quickly looks away.

She clears her throat and takes a sip of her drink. “Point proven.”

I chuckle and down the rest of my beer, then slide off the stool and toss another twenty on the bar.

The bartender approaches and shakes his head. “I told you it’s on the house.”

I incline my head toward him. “That’s for you. See you next time.”

She rises off the stool beside the one I just vacated. “You’re leaving?”

“I have somewhere to be.”

The tiniest hint of disappointment crosses her face. “You didn’t even tell me your name.”

“You didn’t ask.”

An annoyed huff slips from her lips, and she crosses her arms over her chest again, as if she needs the protective barrier it creates. “Well, I’m asking now.”

“Gage.” I grin at her. “Gage Newhart.”

I turn to walk toward the entrance, knowing full well I’ve failed in my effort to keep my attraction to this woman under control.

“You’re not going to ask mine?”

Her question stops me in my tracks, and I twist back and wink at her.

“I already know it.”

Before she can say anything else, I stalk out of the club, forcing myself not to look back.

3

GAGE

Dark clouds billow overhead, threatening to release their haul on New Orleans, soak me, and slicken the pavement under the tires of my Harley, making what I had hoped to accomplish today far more difficult.

But it's irrelevant at the moment.

I sit on my bike in the parking lot, tucked against the side of the building.

Concealed.

Where I can wait.

And *watch.*

I wouldn't mind the rain, though. If it does begin to fall, it would almost come as a relief. A gift from the sky that might melt away some of the tension and frustration building inside me. It might bring some clarity, help break through the fog of uncertainty that has settled over me and that I can't seem to escape from.

There's something about it that always calms me.

The smell that permeates the air...

The sound of it hitting the glass of a window…

The feeling that God is washing away all the filth in the world…

That He's giving us a chance to start anew.

To make better choices.

To live better lives.

To be who we're *supposed* to be.

But I'm not sure I know who that is anymore.

I haven't for a while now.

Everything went haywire so damn fast. The only option I had was to come to New Orleans. To start over here and see if it would open doors to me that had previously been closed.

It should have been relatively easy.

If it weren't for one thing.

One person.

Bishop Clarke.

A complication I never saw getting in the way of my intended goal.

I don't understand it. Can't control it. Don't have the faintest fucking clue what to do about it. All I do know is that no matter my intent to stay far away from one particular place when I climbed on my bike today, I found myself pulling up across the street from The Hawkeye Club and settling in the shadows here.

My booted foot bounces wildly as I watch the building with the logo of the giant hawk wing above it.

Patrons entering and leaving.

Security stepping out to scan the parking every once in a while even though they have a whole slew of cameras around the exterior and interior.

Time ticks by slowly.

Seconds.

Minutes.

Half an hour.

An hour.

Nothing changes save for the darkening color of the sky and the rumbles of thunder that roll through the air now.

The angels bowling...

That's what Mom always told me when an incoming storm made me uneasy as a child, but now, those sounds bring different memories. Ones I try to push away to the back of my mind, but they always seem to come back at the most inopportune times.

I squeeze my eyes closed for a few seconds, breathing in the air that already smells like rain, and when I reopen them, it's with renewed focus on the club and what I'm doing here today.

Something stupid.

What is it about her that makes you do stupid things?

I've been asking myself that question for days now. Each time I do, I come up with the same answer—*everything.*

It isn't just that she's beautiful.

She's also intelligent.

Fierce.

Strong.

Loyal.

All the qualities I've always wanted in a woman and thought didn't exist. Somehow, they all do in that one feisty package, and after what happened last night, I fear I'm a goner when it comes to Bishop Clarke. That I'll continue to make stupid decisions where she's concerned.

It's the only explanation for why I've been sitting here despite the incoming weather, ignoring the warning rumbles and occasional flashes of lightning that have started to streak the sky.

Each one charges the air.

Raises the hairs on my arms under the leather of my jacket.

Heightens the tension as I continue to wait.

I almost give up a dozen times. My hand has reached for the

key to start it up, but each time, I let it fall away, unable to follow through with it. Because something drew me here today.

After what feels like an eternity, they start to arrive.

The Hawkes...

One after another, flashy cars and expensive SUVs pull up and park in the spaces reserved for the family. They climb out, disappearing into the club that also houses offices on the second floor.

Over the course of twenty minutes, half a dozen of them enter.

Clearly some sort of family meeting happening.

But the person I came here hoping to see hasn't made an appearance yet.

I almost ride away.

Almost give up hope.

But then *she* pulls in and parks her black Escalade.

I hold my breath waiting for her to get out. By the time she climbs down from the high cab, my chest burns, and the rush of air I let out sounds so loud to me that I swear she will hear it all the way from over there, turn, and find me watching her.

It's all in my head, though.

Nerves I *shouldn't* have.

Not anymore. Not after all these years. Certainly not over a damn woman.

Her toned, muscular body moves fluidly—*confidently*—as she stalks toward the club, her long braids swinging behind her as tugs open the door. She pauses for a moment before she enters, her head tilting slightly, as if she can sense she's being watched.

I freeze, keeping my body pressed to the old brick, protected somewhat by the slight overhang that casts a shadow over me even under the dark sky.

She scans the street. Once. Twice. Her gaze lingers for a moment on the line of family cars. Then she disappears inside.

Thank fuck.

If she had seen me, I'm not sure what I would have done. How I would have been able to explain why I was lingering here, watching her like this. She would never believe that something deep in my chest drew me here today. That I hadn't planned on coming this way at all when I left the shop.

Given how she reacted to me last night, chances are she would have me facedown on this rough concrete before I even had an opportunity to *try* to explain.

My feet itch to follow her, to see if I can get her to sit down with me again at the bar, but I force myself to pull away from my hiding place beside the building instead.

No good would come from going in after her today—or *any* day, really.

The fact of the matter is, Bishop is a distraction I can't afford.

Now or ever.

I tear down the street, speeding away from The Hawkeye Club and whatever Bishop might be doing in there with the rest of them and heading toward the center of all the nightlife in town.

The sky finally unleashes its torrent, water cascading down in sheets that make the street slick yet somehow allow me to draw in breaths easier than I have in days.

It brings flashes of clarity.

Maybe coming here was a mistake...

I never imagined finding myself in a place like New Orleans, a city with so much history—good and bad—with so much liveliness, color, and sound.

It hits me from all sides as I weave through the streets.

The sounds of jazz bands floating out of propped-open bar doors.

Bright murals painted on ancient brick.

Revelers out enjoying everything despite getting soaked in the process.

Some dance in the rain—spinning around Jackson Square with grins on their faces and their bellies full of Cajun cooking and specialty drinks designed to lure the tourists in for a night of excess.

It's easy to see why the Hawkes didn't set up anywhere near Bourbon Street or the French Quarter. Their bars, their restaurants, their clubs, are all purposefully located in parts of the city where someone won't just stumble in drunk.

They attract their clientele other ways—through their reputation alone. That's what draws me away from the tourist traps and toward one of the most popular Hawke establishments.

The Grind bustles this evening, people moving in and out, sipping on their coffees and other drinks under umbrellas. Because of the rain, the tables on the sidewalk in front of it remain empty, but on a sunny day, they're no doubt packed with customers enjoying the spot.

I pull over and pause outside it, watching everyone inside through the rain-fogged windows.

Despite it nearing dinnertime, the place is bustling, as is the bookstore and art gallery across the street. I scan the windows of Hawke's Novel Idea where people move about, picking up books from shelves and reading the backs to determine their potential entertainment value.

Even though I shouldn't, I turn off the engine, swing my leg over, and jog across the street to enter the shop.

Warm air hits me the moment I step through the doors, and the jingling bells above my head alert the tall blond man behind the counter to my arrival. He tips his head toward me in acknowledgement but doesn't approach to make a pushy sales spiel.

I wander around the space, moving from the new popular

fiction sections back to the far corner that houses the classic literature.

My gaze tracks over the familiar titles until it lands on a maroon cover with two simple words on the spine—*Catch 22.*

That's what it feels like my life has become.

A series of decisions that, despite my best efforts to change the outcome, each lead to the same place—where I stand right now. Caught between duty, obligation, and convoluted feelings that aren't becoming any clearer even when I force myself to consider them.

I pull the book from the shelf and stare at the cover for far too long, remembering the other times in my life that I've read it and never imagined finding myself wrapped in a situation that feels so similar to what Yossarian faced.

One massive clusterfuck with no way out.

All I can do now is try to survive it, or die trying.

I bring the book up to the counter, and the man behind it offers me a smile, his warm blue gaze tracking over my soaked head, wet jacket, and water-logged jeans.

"You look like you walked here."

Grinning, I motion toward the front window. "Close. Rode my bike."

He winces, eyeing the motorcycle parked across the street. "Maybe a bad call tonight."

I chuckle, handing him a twenty for the book. "I don't mind the rain. It cleanses everything."

His brow furrows as he wraps the book in two plastic bags, trying to get them as tight and secure as possible. "Huh. I've always thought that, too." He hands the package over to me with a smile. "I hope you get this home dry. It's one of my favorite classics."

Unfortunately, mine, too.

Inclining my head in thanks, I smile. "I'll keep it safe."

I slide the book into my interior jacket pocket, then step back out into the storm, hustling across the street to my bike.

As soon as I have the engine roaring again, I pull away from the curb, making my way farther down the street, past their steakhouse restaurant, another one of their bars, then I shoot across town to scope out The Hawkeye Club Two and Three.

With almost a hundred businesses under the Hawke Enterprises umbrella, I can see how they've grown so powerful here. Money grows power, and they sure have a fuckload of it.

All their establishments seem to be so well run, so well loved and cared for, so well protected.

I couldn't help but notice the security at every location. The black SUVs parked outside and who did a very shitty job of looking inconspicuous...

Of course, I know what to look for.

Bishop wasn't joking when she said that making sure everyone was safe was her job and her highest priority. Even when she isn't with them, she's doing it. But there are so many of them now, it would be impossible to keep track of them all, to make sure that every single one of them is safe from every single threat.

My chest tightens with that thought, and I rev my engine and pull away again. By the time night starts to descend, my phone buzzes in my pocket, and I pull over and take it out to read the text.

We need to meet.

I scowl at it.

Not tonight.

The rain begins to taper off, but getting home and getting

dry is my main priority. Not dealing with the devil on my shoulder.

Now. Don't forget who you work for.

I grit my teeth and stare at the message for a few moments, trying to sort through the feelings raging in my chest.

I've never been particularly good at taking orders. A fact that got me into trouble more times than I can count. Most of the time, I'd rather go with the flow, figure things out for myself and take action only when I find it necessary.

But that isn't the nature of the job.

A job you willingly took...

"Fuck..."

I fire off a reply text.

Fine. I'll see you in an hour.

Because he's right.

I have to remember who I work for and why I'm here.

I can't throw it all to the wayside because I'm attracted to Bishop Clarke, because her passion for protecting the Hawkes is admirable.

Do your job, Gage.

It will be painful tonight.

He won't like what I have to say.

It's why I've been putting off this meeting for as long as I already have. There are only so many ways to avoid facing the situation, and I can't come up with new excuses anymore.

This is going to be a very long, very painful night filled with those decisions that all lead me back to the same inevitable internal conflict when all I want to do is go back to the club to find her.

BISHOP

"So, what do we do?" I pace Savage's office, tugging on the hair tie on my wrist as I try to work through the dilemma that's been plaguing me for days. "Postpone the opening of the second tower?"

Everyone in the room stares at me as if I just suggested razing it instead of merely bumping the date until we have a better handle on what's going on, until I can be confident we can do it *safely* and *securely*.

I look from Savage to Dani, then to Gabe and Luca, and finally, Mom and Dad, waiting for someone to agree with me that it might be a good idea, but the hard set of everyone's jaw and wide eyes tell me I'm not going to get much support on this.

Not that I expected it.

My meeting with Savage and Gabe yesterday about the same issue went absolutely nowhere. They wouldn't even consider my suggestion to postpone. I don't know why I thought having anyone else here might actually change the result.

Maybe because my head has been swimming to places it doesn't belong since Gage walked out of the club.

Warm blue places filled with heat and passion that are nothing more than a distraction I can't afford.

Not when there are dark places swirling with chaos, pain, and uncertainty that need to be my focus.

Satriano...

Michael McDonald...

I can't wrap my mind around proceeding with such a huge, public event when there is one massive threat and an even greater unknown out there. "You all really want to go ahead when we know Satriano flew in one of his top people and could be bringing in more?"

Gabe runs a hand back through his thick, blond hair that's starting to go gray at the temples. "Like I told you earlier, we're trying to track down this Michael McDonald guy, but he's basically a ghost. We can't find any information on him, and he vanished after he landed here. All we have is the photo and information from his passport, which is likely all fake. Even the photo looks doctored, like he was in disguise."

He's right.

I've seen it.

And something about it is just *off* in a way I can't put my finger on.

His hair, too dark. His eyes, too green. His skin, too pale.

The man in the passport photo might actually be Michael McDonald, but it certainly isn't what he looks like now.

Which makes finding him even harder, even for the experienced people we have working for us and our connections who are digging into every dark corner they can find looking for him.

I pace in front of the windows on the second floor of the club, unable to sit still, the storm raging outside perfectly echoing the tumultuous current coursing through me. "We have less than a week. What if we don't get eyes on this guy? What if he came in because Satriano has *plans* and wants to make a public statement? You know we can't trust that man."

Everyone nods.

We may not all be on the same page about how to handle the situation, but we can all agree on *that* point.

Dad pushes off the wall where he was leaning and walks over to place his large hands on my shoulders. "You know as well as I do that if we canceled our plans every time there was a threat, we wouldn't have a business anymore."

I scowl at him and his logic that is far too *logical.* "I know, but this just…feels different."

Attempting to explain it to him or anyone else in this room is like trying to explain how you can feel an incoming storm. The charge in the air. The energy that feels "off." That's how I've felt since Atlas threw that fight, and it has only gotten worse since Allegra left him behind and joined us. Couple that with the arrival of Michael McDonald in town, a man Allegra says worked for her father and who has mysteriously been absent for over a year…it feels more like a hurricane brewing.

I slide out of Dad's hold and resume my pacing. Not wanting the placation or the reminder that there isn't much we can do without more information. "I don't know how to explain it. But I have a *bad* feeling…"

A massive understatement.

But it's all I can say.

Luca looks from Savage to Gabe, then to Dad before coming to rest on me. His dark eyes hold sympathy and understanding. If anyone would understand the mind of a man like Satriano, it would be him. "It wouldn't be the worst idea to wait until we at least have eyes on this guy. Satriano has been silent for far too long. This feels like a move for McDonald to come *here* after being MIA for a year and a half."

Mom shakes her head, exchanging a look with Dani. "It would be a PR nightmare to have to retract all those invitations to the grand opening. I wouldn't do it. It'd kill all the momentum we have with the hotel and casino."

"And Satriano could kill *us*."

Luca's dark words cut through the room, silencing everyone.

Savage glares at him. "Really, Luca?"

The former mob boss shrugs, his perfectly tailored suit jacket clinging to his broad shoulders. "When everything went down with Allegra, we knew that we'd be poking the bear by protecting her and bringing her into the fold. We also told him we'll never partner with him. If he can't get us on board with some sort of business agreement, then what other option does he have than to remove the competition?"

Who are about to open another major portion of the lucrative business he wants a piece of...

I point at him. "You're the one who told us to never partner with him."

Which pissed him off more.

Luca nods. "You shouldn't. But I also think you're right to be nervous. We haven't heard from him in months, and it typically doesn't end well when he disappears. When he reappears, it's usually with a bang."

Savage's jaw locks, and a muscle there tics. The memories of what has happened to the family over the last few years because of that man have left all of us scarred—none more so than him.

Sitting at the head of the family, Savage takes every wound suffered by anyone onto himself, when it really should be *me* who bears that burden.

He put his trust in me to protect everyone.

It isn't his fault I failed.

Only my own.

Dani steps up behind his chair and rests her hand on his shoulders, rubbing gently, trying to calm him before he explodes.

He looks to Gabe. "Postpone. Yay or nay?"

Gabe shakes his head. "Nay."

Savage looks to Dad next, who gives me a sympathetic look but shakes his head. "No."

Mom releases a sigh. "Sorry, sweetie, but no."

Savage's gaze finally meets Luca's, and he stands stock-still for a few moments, considering all the options available before he shakes his head. "No." He offers me an apologetic look that does nothing to ease my annoyance at his sudden flip. "But only because I ultimately think that giving *anything* to Satriano only grows his ego and his belief that nothing will ever be beyond his grasp."

I throw up my hands. "Am I the only one who feels like I'm just waiting for the other shoe to drop? It's been one thing after another for years, and now both Jack and Allegra are pregnant. What the hell do you think the man's going to do when he finds out his grandchild is coming and is going to be a Hawke?"

Everyone shifts restlessly.

The question has been on *everyone's* mind since we learned that there wasn't technically anything medically *wrong* with either of them.

No nefarious plots that made them ill.

No poison or other means of hurting them physically.

Just the Hawke sperm going to work creating the next generation.

And one of them also carries Satriano's blood.

Gabe shifts restlessly. "All we can do is keep pushing our sources and hope that one of them comes up with something useful on McDonald or Satriano." A ding sounds in his pocket, and he reaches in and pulls out his phone. "Speaking of which..."

He scans the screen, his jaw hardening.

Shit.

That doesn't look good.

His eyes darken as he reads the message. "Shit."

Savage raises a dark brow. "What?"

Gabe lifts his head and meets his best friend's gaze. "That was a text from one of my contacts in Europe who is familiar with Satriano and his group over there from before they moved here."

My frustration starts to boil over waiting for him to tell us whatever he's learned. "And?"

Hard green eyes sweep from Savage to me, and when he's like this, I truly see the lethal sniper he once was still living in his gaze. He's pissed. And worried. Bordering on murderous. "He says Michael McDonald is a munitions expert. Specifically...explosives."

The word sends a shiver down my spine as flashes of what happened to The Grind flicker through my head.

Flames shooting into the night.

Charred wood.

Broken tile and ceramic.

The smell of smoke clinging to the air.

Utter devastation.

The destruction of something Angelina worked so damn hard to create.

"Fuck." I scrub my hands over my face, then scan the room again. "Anyone want to rethink that vote we just had?"

Everyone exchanges uneasy looks, but Dad shakes his head. "We go forward with it. We have bomb-sniffing dogs that can check the entire hotel tower, and we don't allow anyone—and I mean anyone—within a hundred yards of the property unless they're on a very short list and they've been quadruple checked. Nobody we don't already know will be there, and we're going to scour everyone's backgrounds just as a safety precaution."

I grit my teeth, fighting the urge to argue with him, but I know I'm not going to get anywhere because they're right as much as they're wrong. If we keep caving, if we cower in the face of this vague threat that Satriano poses, we will never get anything done.

We won't have any businesses left to run before too long.

And the Hawke Hotel and the casino are our future.

Assuming things continue to go well, plans to expand on the entire Gulf Coast are already sketched out and front and center in everyone's minds. The only hiccup is Satriano and the fact that he has been buying up competing properties behind our backs for God only knows how long without us even knowing about it—and the fact that he might resort to violence to ensure he comes out on top.

The unease in the room matches what currently wraps tightly around my spine, and Coen and Allegra appearing in the open doorway doesn't help, given the nervous look both of them wear.

Luca narrows his dark gaze on them. "What are you doing here?"

Coen ushers Allegra in ahead of him with a hand at her lower back. "We just got a call that you need to know about."

Allegra swallows thickly, pressing a hand over her still-flat belly that won't stay that way for long. "It was my dad. He said 'congratulations,' and he 'can't wait to meet his first grandchild.'"

Ice floods my veins, making my vision blur for a moment as I clench my fists at my sides. "How the fuck does *he* know you're pregnant?"

She shakes her head, sending her dark hair flying around her face as unshed tears shimmering in her eyes. "I don't know." The typical warm gray there darkens slightly with her growing fear. "But he's hacked medical records before, right?"

I exchange a look with Dad.

Gabe shoves his phone back into his pocket with a muttered curse. "He has."

Savage watches the newest member of the Hawke family carefully, and even though his shoulders are tense, he keeps his voice level when he finally asks the question we are all wondering. "Do you think this means he's going to show his face again?"

Allegra bites on her bottom lip and glances up at Coen, who wraps his arm around her shoulders protectively. "He might. Family's always been the most important thing to him. Like I told you before, this all started because of his brother's death and because he justified it saying he was doing it for me, to secure *my* future. Even though he told me he's cutting me off for choosing Coen, this baby changes things for him. I know it does."

Savage's jaw hardens, and he offers a slow nod. "That's exactly what I'm afraid of."

4

FOUR DAYS LATER

BISHOP

Today should be a huge celebration.

This land that holds the second Hawke Hotel tower was once owned by Falcon Enterprises. Controlled by a man who was our sworn enemy. We feared him. We fought him. Now, I can't imagine Cass not being one of us.

Opening this tower should feel like putting the final nail in the coffin on everything that went down with him and all the bad shit that happened when we thought Falcon was behind the attacks on us, but instead, I'm more on edge than I have ever been.

From up on the dais, I survey the gathering crowd in the lobby.

Shockingly, my suggestion that we move the festivities completely inside because it would be easier to manage was taken to heart. I hadn't been sure it would be. It meant severely limiting who is here—even more so than we had already decided to. But at least in the tower itself, we have control.

Unlike the groundbreaking for the main hotel when anyone could've taken a shot at us standing out in the open.

I often wonder why Satriano *didn't* that day...

It would have been the perfect opportunity to attack us—when we were distracted and concentrating on the festivities. When he did show up, everything was over, almost as if it were a taunt about the fact that he *could* have easily done much worse and didn't. Another statement that we weren't truly safe anywhere.

Which only makes me more certain something is going to happen *today...*

Adding this second tower is the final step in finishing off the Hawke Hotel and the first in building what will hopefully be our empire of them across the Gulf Coast—maybe beyond it.

A direct competitor of the man who seems to have his foot on our throats.

It's the ideal time for him to remind us of that fact.

My stomach churns as I pace and continue to search the crowd from my raised position, looking for signs of anything amiss, while the rest of our security team does the same. Stationed at each entrance, mingling with everyone gathered to celebrate with us, watching our backs when we'll be busy smiling for the cameras.

Even with literally dozens and dozens of skilled guards scouring every inch of the place, it still feels like we're *missing* something.

Dad's gaze follows me as I pass him where he stands next to Mom on the dais. "You can stop."

I shake my head. "I can't."

He grabs my arm and pulls me beside him, dipping his head to whisper in my ear. "I've been doing this job for longer than you've been alive, Bishop, and I'll tell you one thing—it'll eat you alive if you let it."

"I'm *fine*, Dad."

"No"—he shakes his head—"you're not." A long sigh slips from his lips, filled with parental love and frustration. "And you haven't been for a while. You're not the only one who feels like they failed."

My back stiffens as I glance at him, finally drawing my eyes away from the sea of people for the first time since they started arriving.

He holds my gaze. "After what happened to Ben and Storm, you don't think I felt like a failure?"

The mere mention of the tragedy that shook the Hawkes so intensely over thirty years ago intensifies the pain I carry for the man I never even met. Echoes of the agony the people I love so much suffered then still reverberate today. Apparently more than I realized because looking into Dad's dark eyes, I can see his distress even now.

"With everything that's happened the last couple of years on top of that..." Shaking his head, his eagle-sharp gaze sweeps over the crowd briefly before returning to me, as if even while trying to lecture me, he can't turn off his instincts either. "I get it. I really do, Bishop. But I don't want you to turn into me."

"What do you mean?"

He's one of the best human beings I know.

An incredible father, husband, friend, and protector of everyone he loves.

He's everything I strive to be.

"Don't let *this* be your whole life, sweetheart." He sweeps a large hand out toward the lobby. "I have your mother to keep me...grounded. To prevent me from over-analyzing everything and falling into some deep, dark hole of guilt every time something doesn't go the way it's supposed to. Every time I feel like I've failed, your mom reminds me of why I fell in love with her by refusing to let me fall prey to that need to punish myself. What do *you* have? *Who* do you have?"

I scowl at him, but he's right.

Nothing.

No one.

Those are the answers to his questions.

No amount of time spent in the ring with Atlas, tied up on the Jiu-jitsu mat, or out on the range firing off rounds can do for *me* what Mom does for him. She does *ground* him. She is his lifeline in a sea of uncertainty. And lately it's felt like I'm floating around aimlessly, unable to grasp onto anything that will help me feel like I'm not drowning in my failures.

It's my duty to protect these people. Not just because it's my job, but because I *love* them. Any injury to them is like a blow to me directly.

And it's been so long since I've done anything for me, since I've been able to actually relax and enjoy myself without wondering what I am forgetting or who might be in danger if I take one second to think about myself that I can't even remember when it was.

"After we get this Satriano stuff sorted out, I'll take a vacation, Dad. Go back to Jamaica and see everyone there, or something like that. Until then..."

Leave it alone.

That last part goes unsaid because I would never want him to think I don't appreciate his concern for my well-being, but I can't be worrying about *him* worrying if I need to unravel Satriano's sinister plans before he strikes again.

He offers me a smile that tells me he doesn't believe for a second that I'll actually take time off, then leans down and presses a kiss to my cheek. "Stop making excuses and do it."

The man has always known when to push me and when to let things go, and as he walks away toward where Savage and Gabe wait to start the welcome speech and where Mom now chats with Dani, eyeing us like she knows exactly what he was saying to me, I know this was one of the moments he knew pushing would only make it worse.

At least this is almost over.

Only a few more minutes until the official ceremony, which Savage promised to keep brief, then we can clear a lot of these people out of here; the mayor, the news crews, all the friends and business associates we invited. Even though we limited the guest list, it's still hundreds of people crammed into the lobby.

Too many people.

Too many dangers.

I shiver and resume my pacing...

And watching.

People mill about, excited chatter filling the massive atrium lobby that Cass, Landon, Storm, Kennedy, and everyone else spent so much time perfecting. They take in the spectacle of the massive chandelier and *ooh* and *aah* over the other art deco designs sprinkled throughout the space.

It's the kind of excitement that should be contagious.

I try to push away the anxiety threatening to overwhelm me, drawing in long, slow breaths. If anything did happen, I can't risk having a shaky hand.

Steady.

My heartrate starts to slow, my breathing following suit, and I almost convince my body that there isn't any reason to be worried when a flash of blond hair in my peripheral vision draws my attention.

Before I have a chance to turn fully toward it, Pope hustles over. He narrows his eyes on me, immediately seeing how tense I am. "Hey, we're all set. Everything good here?"

I scan the crowd one more time and lock gazes with the head of hotel security. He nods toward me, letting me know that things are as they should be, and I turn to Pope. "We're good."

Saying the words out loud feels like tolling some sort of bell.

Like tempting fate.

Another shiver rolls through my spine, and a member of the hotel security team hustles up to the dais with a box in hand and holds it out toward me.

"What's this?"

"It was just delivered to the front door." He tilts his head toward the main entrance. "I didn't want to let the delivery guy in since he wasn't on the approved list."

"Did you clear the box?"

He nods. "We checked it for explosives, and it was clean."

Somehow, that doesn't make me feel any better about a mysterious box showing up *now*.

I take it and slowly slide off the lid.

Pope shifts closer and looks over my shoulder. "What is it?"

An omen.

Tossing the lid to the side, I reach in and pull out a bottle of champagne—a very, very *expensive* bottle of Dom Pérignon Rosé Gold Methuselah.

Pope grabs it from my hand, examining the bottle. "Who the hell is this from?"

"I don't know..."

It wouldn't be unusual to receive a gift from one of our business connections on a day like this, but this is *quite* a gift.

A small envelope with "*Hawkes*" scrawled across the front in elegant script lies in the plush cloth that securely held the bottle.

My hand shakes slightly as I pass Pope the box and tear open the envelope.

Congratulazioni. Be seeing you soon.
- Damiano

"Shit." Pope's sentiment matches my own assessment of the situation. "Should we tell them?"

We both glance toward the other side of the dais, where the rest of the family waits for the celebration to start with Uncle Savage's speech.

Kennedy whispers something to Cass that has him grinning and pressing a kiss against her neck. Astrid and Danika chat with Atlas and Wren, whose hand rests on her growing stomach, while Stone and Nora are in deep discussion with Isaac and Jack. Charlotte and Viviana play with Gio near them who is working to get to his unsteady toddler feet. Storm and Landon talk excitedly with Angelina and Alessandra holding Benjamin in her arms. Meanwhile, Luca stands stoically, scanning the crowd as intently as I have been with Byron by his side.

But it's Coen and Allegra who answer Pope's question for me.

They cling to each other behind the main group. Allegra rests her head on his shoulder, and Coen wraps his arm around her protectively as his sharp gaze takes in every single person in the room.

She's terrified.

So is he.

And they have every right to be.

Her father isn't to be fucked with, and that's precisely what we've done—over and over again—by interfering with his plans and refusing his demands. Now that he knows his first grandchild is on the way, there won't be any stopping him.

I shake my head, shoving the note back into the envelope and tucking it into my pocket. "No. It'll only upset them. It can wait until after the ceremony."

Pope's brow furrows. "Are you sure?"

I'm not.

They'll be pissed I didn't tell them this was delivered when they do find out, but I can't do that to them today. I can't destroy this brief moment of joy for everyone.

It doesn't seem to be an immediate threat.

If Satriano wanted that, he would have personally brought it and made a show of trying to get to us. Plus, I'm confident we have this place locked down tight, so he's not getting in here, even if he wanted to.

"Fuck Satriano and fuck the champagne." I point toward the bottle in Pope's hand that costs as much as some people make in a year but might as well be trash considering where it came from. "Go stick that somewhere no one else will see it."

He doesn't hesitate to hustle down the ramp at the back of the dais, and I watch him use his access card to disappear into the security room along the far wall.

I'll deal with it later.

When Pope reappears, he gives me a tight smile and retakes his position next to Allie on the dais. Benjamin immediately raises his arms for his father, and Pope scoops him up and whispers something that has the baby giggling.

Despite how unsettled I am by the gift, a smile pulls at my lips. Because Pope finally has his own family. Even with everything going on around us, even when he's at the beck and call of a man like Satriano to maintain this false "peace," he's happy. And that's all I've ever wanted for any of them.

But my smile fades quickly...because Dad was right.

I don't have anything.

Nothing but this job and this gut feeling that, if I ever fuck up again, someone else is going to pay the price for it.

And I can't let that happen.

I won't.

GAGE

Savage smiles from his place in the center of the dais, his true joy spread across his face as he holds a microphone, taking in the crowd. "I won't keep you waiting any longer by rambling on about how excited and proud I am that we've finally reached this moment."

His gaze drifts to his family behind him briefly, landing on every member lined up for the celebration, before returning to everyone else in front of him.

"You've already heard about all the hard work, sweat, and tears that went into this space. So, let me wrap up by saying thank you again for coming to celebrate this monumental day with us. Please enjoy touring the new tower. And don't forget to step across the street to play some table games or eat at one of our fabulous restaurants at the main Hawke Hotel!"

I clap along with those surrounding me as he retreats from the front of the dais to join the rest of the Hawkes.

Aside from thanking his daughter and son-in-law, as well as his sister Storm and her husband for their work on designing and building this place, the Hawke patriarch kept things relatively short and sweet.

Probably because he knows this place speaks for itself.

Soaring twenty-five floors above us, the massive panes of glass allow all the Louisiana sunlight to flow in and reflect off the massive chandelier that falls all the way from the top to directly above us.

It is truly stunning.

A piece of crystal art that looks more like it belongs in the Louvre or some other gallery rather than a hotel.

But I wouldn't have expected anything less from the Hawkes.

The main hotel and casino across the street are just as beautiful. Just as opulent and over-the-top extravagant. The entire space glows with a vibrancy and welcoming warmth that I can't imagine anyone could resist.

A flame to lure in the people of New Orleans and get them to let down their guards and empty their pockets on the tables and at the machines.

It's been a tremendous success, and just like with their other businesses, I can see why.

They don't cater to the drunk revelers who only come down for Mardi Gras or to get plastered on Bourbon Street. They attract a higher-end clientele, both here and at the clubs, bars, and restaurants that make up their empire. They know what it takes to truly succeed in business—sophistication and style.

It's impressive in a way I find few things are these days.

Except *her.*

Bishop has been front and center during the entire presentation, standing guard on the raised dais, watching everything like the killer hawk she is. Hunting in the crowd. Not missing a thing.

And despite my best efforts, that includes me.

I felt her eyes on me once.

Only for the briefest of moments.

But long enough that familiar heat spread through me, along with the heavy weight of regret I always carry when it comes to her.

When it comes to *this*—my inability to stay away from her no matter how many times I tell myself I will.

She slowly makes her way down to the main floor and out into the tower lobby—like a panther on the prowl for her prey. With her dark head of braids twisted into a bun at the top of her head today, I'm able to follow her for a while before she disappears into the milling crowd.

As soon as I lose sight of her, the itching desire to follow moves my feet in that direction.

I slowly make my way around the edges of the lobby, keeping my eye on everyone and everything in the tower.

Memorizing the layout. Assessing weaknesses. Preparing myself while searching for her again.

"Looking for someone?"

Shit.

Her familiar voice freezes me in my tracks, and I glance over my shoulder to find her somehow behind me even though I kept my back to the exterior wall almost the entire time.

How the hell did she do that?

She raises a dark brow, arms crossing over her chest, tapping her booted foot impatiently as her eyes sweep over me with a penetrating scrutiny that feels like an equal mix of sexual appraisal and stark threat analysis.

I allow a grin to curl my lips as I turn to face her fully, unable to fight it when this woman is so fucking impressive in just about everything. Sneaking up on me isn't easy, yet she makes it look like child's play. "You, actually."

The second brow meets the first over leery bourbon eyes. "Really?"

Taking a step toward her, I nod. "Really."

Her lips twist. "That's interesting because I don't remember you being on the guest list. How'd you get in?"

The sharp edge in her voice raises goosebumps on my skin.

This woman won't hesitate to slice and dice me with something far more dangerous than her mouth if she found me to be a threat. And the longer she looks at me, the more she seems to see me as one. Yet, I take another step toward her, making room for a group of chattering people to walk past us—and giving me any excuse to get closer.

Any other woman might have backed away, might have recoiled slightly at just *how* close I've gotten, especially given her unease at my presence. But not Bishop.

She stands her ground, glaring up at me with intense darkening eyes full of wariness that grows the longer we stare each other down.

Smart girl.

She has every right to be wary.

If she weren't, I'd actually be concerned.

I shouldn't be here, shouldn't have been able to get through her wall of security, just like I shouldn't be able to get under her skin the way I do.

She hates both those truths.

Offering a nonchalant shrug, I grin despite the glower she continues to direct at me. "I charmed my way in."

Her lips press together, her jaw tightening. "Bullshit. Our security's tight. Tell me how you got in."

The tension has her practically vibrating.

And damn if I don't want to see her unleash all of it.

At me.

Something tells me it would be fucking beautiful to witness...

I slide in a little closer, dipping my head until her jasmine scent fills my breaths. "If you really must know, I walked in the front doors."

She flinches as she drags her head back so she can search my face. "How did you get past security?"

Reaching behind her, I place my hand on the wall so I can lean in, so I can test her limits and see just how much she's willing to withstand before she snaps. "I know you think you have this place locked down tight, but I have a secret for you."

Her throat works a thick swallow. "What's that?"

It's important she listens to me, that she heeds this warning, so I pray her distrust of me doesn't make her disregard it.

"No one and no place is ever one hundred percent safe or secure."

Those stunning eyes of hers somehow darken even more, the warm bourbon almost disappearing completely in the depths of her skepticism and suspicion. "And how does a *mechanic* know that?"

I grin at her. "Because I haven't always been a mechanic."

Her eyes flair wide. "And what were you before?"

The edge in her voice makes me suspect she's already tried to find out. If I were her, the second I gave my name the other night, I would have run a full background check and done as much digging as I could.

Which means she's probably very frustrated right now with what she's been able to learn.

"Bad fucking news. I got into quite a bit of trouble in my misspent youth. Boosting cars. Stealing. Those days are long behind me, but I learned a lot of invaluable skills and painful truths that have come in handy in my reformed years."

"I bet."

The coolness emanating off her does nothing to quell the heat I feel with our bodies this close. It has nothing to do with the crush of people making their way past us or the warm sunlight streaming in the atrium. This warmth somehow just *exists* when we're in the same space, sharing the same air, even when she's trying to ice me out.

"What are you doing here, Gage?"

Fucking hell...

Hearing my name from her lips tightens my chest as a much lower part of my body hardens, and I step in another few inches until my chest brushes hers. "I came to see what all the fuss was about. Everyone's been talking about the opening."

Bishop stands absolutely still, not reacting to our proximity or me invading her personal space. With her stuck between me and the wall, we both know she could grab my arm beside her head and have me down on the floor in a millisecond to free herself if she wanted to, but she doesn't budge.

She knows what that would mean—surrender.

And this isn't a woman who ever surrenders.

She stares me down, challenging me, *daring* me to move even closer. "Have they?"

I tilt my head and examine her, searching for a crack in the armor I can pry at. The warning I just gave her was very real, yet she appears unfazed by it, by *me* being this close. Simmering unease continues to bubble within her, but she keeps herself calm rather than lashing out with accusations against me when she has nothing but her instincts to back her up.

"You don't trust me, do you?"

Her brows rise slowly. "Should I? I don't know a single thing about you."

"Of course you do. I've already told you lots of things."

More than I should have.

But this woman knows the right questions to ask.

"And how do I know the things you've told me are real, that they're the truth?"

I don't bother to fight my grin at the way she just proved my point about her perfect intuition. "Because I've been told I'm a shitty liar."

She doesn't miss a beat. "You're lying right now."

Good God...

It takes everything in me not to kiss her right now. Not to grab her face and drag her lips to mine. Not to devour her here and now despite the way she just saw right through me. *Because* of the way she just saw through me.

That makes this even more dangerous.

I *should* walk away and never look back.

I *should* take my own advice to never let anyone distract me.

I *should* keep focus where it belongs.

But I can't look away from her.

"You're right, Bishop. I am lying. But it's not about what you think. I did come to see what all the fuss is about, but my real reason for being here today?" I tip my head until my nose brushes her soft cheek, that heady jasmine scent making my already semi-hard cock throb. "Was because I wanted to see *you*."

She tenses again, and when I pull back, she offers me an incredulous look that screams she doesn't believe a word that just came out of my mouth.

But both reasons for being here are true.

One was just a stronger pull than the other.

"Bishop!"

Someone calls out her name, and the voice bursts the invisible bubble surrounding us that made it feel like we were the only two people in the damn room.

She shakes her head slightly, as if she was just freed from it too, and glances behind me at someone, then starts to step forward to get around me but freezes, returning her gaze to mine. "What is it you want? You've been hanging around the club, now you show up here. You must *want* something."

"I would've thought that was obvious at this point."

Without waiting for her reply, I push off the wall, turn, and walk away, weaving my way through the remaining crowd, her scent still filling my lungs and my cock still straining against my jeans.

By the time I step out into the fresh New Orleans air, it's too late.

I made a mistake coming today. Seeking her out and thinking I could do it without her noticing was arrogant, risky, and downright foolish.

She's too observant.

Too smart.

Too cunning.

That woman won't give me an inch when I want to take it *all*.

Pushing her harder could massively backfire.

Or it could give me exactly what I need.

5

ONE WEEK LATER

BISHOP

The rain that's been falling off and on for days comes down in a full-on deluge now, my windshield wipers barely able to keep up with it as I turn the final corner toward the gym.

Most people would have taken one look at the weather and stayed in bed.

This early, the sun barely peeks over the horizon, fighting to break through the storm clouds, the day not even truly started yet, but the last place I want to be is back under the covers.

I'm buzzing to get in the ring with Atlas.

Dad may have been right about needing something *more*, but for now, I have to work with what's available. And lately, tearing into Atlas in the ring has been the only way I've been able to work out any of the frustration that's been overwhelming me.

He craves it as much as I do.

Needs it the same way.

I'm the only one readily available who can get even close to giving him any sort of competition, though the boys will never concede that. Their egos won't allow it—even with the split lips, bruises, and stitches they've received from Atlas when he's holding back considerably for their sakes.

There won't be any holding back today, though. At least, not from me.

The past two weeks have pushed me to my breaking point. After the scare with Allegra and Jack, then the incident with Gage at the club and his reappearance at the opening, not to mention the shit I received when everyone found out about Satriano's "gift" and the fact that I hid it from them, I am ready to kick some ass and have mine kicked, too.

Sometimes, it's the only thing that allows me to sleep.

Without the sheer physical exhaustion, I lie awake at night, wondering what Satriano might be doing at that very moment. And when I do manage to doze off, it's to nightmares filled with explosions, blood splatters across sidewalks and tile floors, and visions of the people I love in hospital beds…

Or worse.

Last night was one of those nights, which means I'm itching to get in the ring before I have to head into work and face the fact that we still have *nothing* on Satriano or McDonald that might lead to an end for that uncertainty.

I pull to the curb in front of the gym behind Atlas' SUV and catch a glimpse of a motorcycle parked in front of it. "Who the hell is that?"

Since Jimmy passed away, the only people who come this early are Wren and Atlas. If he lined up a legit sparring partner, he would have told me to make sure I came even *earlier* to watch and help assess.

Plus, who the hell rides a motorcycle in the rain?

Shutting off the engine, I glance through the tinted glass windows of Wren's pilates studio to see if the owner of the bike might be in with her. She moves around preparing for her first class that starts in thirty minutes, but it doesn't appear that anyone is in there with her.

The windows of the gym are too fogged from the humidity to see much, which means Atlas is already hitting the heavy bag hard this morning.

Hopefully he's ready for me...

Grinning, I snag my bag from the passenger seat, climb out, slam my door, and tuck my head down to race into the gym through the downpour. I yank open the door, rush in, and shake free some of the water clinging to me, letting the door close behind me.

The familiar smell of leather, sweat, and the polish that Jimmy always used on the gloves fills my nose, and I lift my head, taking in the space that's more like a second home—or third, after the club.

Atlas bounces on his toes in front of someone in the ring who has their back to me...

Colorful swirling tattoos spread out across a vast expanse of skin glistening with a sheen of sweat under the overhead lights. Muscles bunch and flex with each movement, making the ink come to life.

The guy is big—as big as Atlas—and last I checked, we didn't have anyone who came here to spar this size, but with the headgear on and his back to me, it's impossible to make out who it is.

Atlas pays me no attention and takes another swing at his opponent, who ducks and weaves, sneaking in a blow to Atlas's right side.

Damn.

That isn't easy to do.

Something I know from a *lot* of personal experience.

Atlas just grins at him, flashing his mouthguard. He circles away, still light on his feet, seemingly unaffected by the blow. But I can see that this guy hurt him. Anyone who didn't know

Atlas as well wouldn't see that slight twinge when he takes his next swing, but I bet he'll have a hell of a bruise after this match.

They go at each other again, a flurry of jabs and hooks as I move in closer, entranced by the way his opponent moves so fluidly, as if he were born in the ring.

Who the hell is this guy?

I don't even notice Astrid until she pushes away from her spot on one of the benches and approaches. "Hey, I didn't know you were coming in this morning."

She offers me a partial hug, but I can't tear my eyes away from the ring.

"Who in the hell is he sparring with?"

Astrid glances in that direction. "Oh! I'm not entirely sure. The guy came in super early this morning and spoke with Atlas while I was over with Wren, then they got suited up and climbed in."

Odd.

It isn't like Atlas to let someone walk in off the street. And he certainly wouldn't get in the ring and go like *this* with just anyone. There's too big of a risk of hurting his opponents, even if they aren't going at one hundred percent.

He wouldn't ever put anyone in that position.

He knows better.

Or at least, I thought he did.

Atlas lands a right hook that sends his opponent's head snapping back, but instead of the typical reaction to taking a hit from Atlas "The Hurricane" Hawke, a familiar deep chuckle fills the gym and I freeze.

Astrid narrows her eyes on me, squeezing my shoulder. "Bish, what's wrong?"

I slide out of her hold and circle the ring until I can get a better view of both men, and my heart seizes when a familiar face appears opposite Atlas.

Gage?

What the hell is he doing here?

I let my bag slide off my shoulder and to the ground with a heavy thump that finally draws both men's attention away from each other and toward me.

Atlas's eyes widen slightly, but Gage just grins, a red mouth guard flashing as he inclines his head toward me. As if he's been *waiting* for me to arrive and for this very moment.

That smug bastard...

Atlas approaches my side of the ring and spits out his mouth guard into his glove, leaning against the ropes. "Hey. I wasn't sure you were coming in this morning. I would've waited for you"—he tips his head backward toward Gage—"but I found a fun sparring partner."

Fun.

That's certainly an interesting word to describe the man.

"Yeah?" My gaze dips over to Gage, and I do my best to appear unaffected by his sudden appearance in the place I come to blow off steam—when he has been the source of a lot of it himself. "Where'd you find him?"

Atlas shrugs, the movement causing his muscles to pull at the massive scar on his shoulder that came courtesy of yet another one of my failures and almost ended his boxing career. "He came in this morning and explained that he's new to town and was looking for somewhere to train."

I gape at my cousin, who has apparently lost his damn mind. "And you just *let* him?"

It isn't like Atlas to risk an unknown opponent in sparring.

With the type of power he has, he could kill someone with a single blow if they weren't prepared and built to withstand it.

Gage certainly has the size to take on Atlas, but presuming he would know what it takes to step into the *ring* with the man who holds the middleweight belt is a huge and dangerous leap to take.

Atlas grins. "Apparently, he fought WCAP a few years ago."

Of fucking course, he did...

I narrow my gaze on Gage, who offers another half-grin as he starts to make his way over to us.

It shouldn't surprise me, really. The first thing I did when Gage gave me his name at the club the other night was to run a background check on him. A basic check didn't bring up much, though, save for a birth certificate from Virginia and a record confirming he was in the Army at some point but no longer active duty.

Knowing he served explained a lot.

The initial vibe I had of him and how he carried himself. The way he handled those assholes at the club so easily. The instinct to protect Jade in that situation even if it wasn't his place.

If he fought WCAP, that means he was a damn good boxer when he served—with a potential to compete at the Olympic or even pro-level. That never happened or the background check would have come up with more information on him.

Which means something interfered with his plans.

That gives me somewhere to start digging, another clue that might help me unravel the mystery of why he's really here.

Atlas pushes off the ropes and motions to his opponent. "Gage Newhart, this is my cousin, Bishop Clarke."

Gage spits out his mouth guard and winks at me in a way that makes my entire body go molten—with a strange combination of hellfire and sexual heat. "We've met."

Astrid's eyes widen slightly as she looks between us. "You have?"

He waits for a moment to see if I'm going to offer an explanation. Maybe he's holding open the door for me to describe our run-ins or the fact that I've expressed my distrust of him. But even though I don't completely trust the man, he hasn't *actually* done anything wrong or suspicious.

The fact that he got into the opening and I still don't know how says more about how I failed in creating the security plan than it does about his motives.

And Atlas appears thrilled to have him in the ring.

I won't shatter that unless there's a very good reason to.

When I don't offer an explanation to Astrid's question, Gage nods. "I was at the club."

Her warm blue eyes flash with the most excitement I've seen from her in a long time. "Oh, really?"

The smirk he offers me makes me wish I were standing in the ring with him right now. I would wipe that right off his face before he even had a chance to get his guard up. "That's where I learned about this place. From your bartender..."

"Oh, cool!" Atlas swipes away sweat from his face with his forearm. "I'm really glad you stopped by."

"Don't tell me you're done?" Gage asks the question playfully. "You could push at least one more round."

Atlas shakes his head. "Nah, but I have to save some for her." He tilts his head toward me. "And trust me, she's worse in the ring than you. A total hellcat."

Gage's lips twitch as he fights a grin. "I don't doubt that for a second."

Astrid laughs. "Did you know that on top of being a killer on the canvas, she also has a black belt in Jiu-Jitsu?"

What the hell is she doing?

The look she gives me tells me I should be thanking her for talking me up, but all I want is for her to shut her mouth and stop acting like she wants us to make a love connection.

Gage bites at the Velcro on his gloves and rips it off—one then the other. "Again, that doesn't surprise me."

It may not surprise him, but the fact that he's *here* at all sure as *hell* surprises the fuck out of me. This man somehow got into what should have been an air-tight secure event and now just waltzed into the gym where Atlas trains and talked his way into the ring with him.

Who the fuck does that?

This man, apparently.

He definitely has an *agenda* that I can't figure out.

I follow him from outside the ring as he walks around to the other side where his bag rests on one of the benches. Astrid leans in to talk to Atlas about something, and Gage climbs through the ropes and hops down, holding out his gloved hands to me.

"A little help?"

I scowl at him because he is perfectly capable of removing them himself now that he got the Velcro off.

They hang out in the air between us for a few seconds before he leans in. "They're going to think you're rude if you don't help me."

Casting a quick glance toward the twins, who are, in fact, scoping us out while they talk, I tug them free a little too forcefully. "You know there's a word for what you're doing, Gage."

His brows rise innocently, but there's absolutely nothing innocent about his grin. "Yeah? What's that?"

"*Stalking.*"

GAGE

"Stalking?"

My bark of laughter carries through the gym, and Atlas and his sister's heads whip our direction, their attempt to sneak peeks at us while pretending not to be interested in our conversation completely blown.

Astrid gives me a little half-grin, then returns to talking to her brother while keeping an eye on us in her peripheral vision.

She *definitely* heard Bishop's accusation and finds it as amusing as I do.

But the woman in front of me doesn't find it funny in the least.

Bishop stands with her arms crossed over her chest doing her best to look intimidating—and knowing what she's capable of, she should be—but it will take a lot more than *that* to scare me off.

Especially when I'm certain she feels whatever this is too.

It would be impossible *not* to.

The strange buzz of electricity that crackles between us whenever we're together is a physical manifestation of what I've been feeling inside since that first night at the club.

And how she's acting now feels more like a defense mechanism than actual anger at seeing me again.

She may not fully trust me, but she's also attracted to me.

That pisses her the fuck off.

Giving her my most innocent smile, I shake my head. "I'm not stalking you, Bishop."

"Oh, yeah?"

I tug off my helmet, tossing it into my bag before leaning in toward her slightly, not even caring that I am dripping with sweat. "If I *were* stalking you, you would never know it."

Instead of being shook or frightened by my half-joking statement, Bishop stands her ground yet again and merely raises a dark brow. "Pretty confident in yourself, aren't you?"

You have no idea...

Confidence has never been my problem.

Mine lies in my self-control—or lack thereof. Standing here right now being a prime example of that.

Each time I see her, I promise myself it will be the last, yet I can barely make it a week without finding an excuse to be in her orbit.

I shrug as I turn away to dig in my bag and grab a towel to wipe off the sweat trickling across my brow and down my chest. Bishop's gaze follows the movement, her eyes tracing over the ink covering my pecs, stomach, and arms, taking in every dot of it with rapt attention until they finally fall to where the V of my abs disappears into my boxing shorts.

"My eyes are up here, Hellcat."

Her head whips up, her eyes narrowing and flashing with that fierce anger I've seen before and somehow crave. "What'd you call me?"

I smirk at her. "You heard me."

She scowls, pointing a finger squarely in my chest. "*You* don't get to call me that." Her finger whips toward Atlas. "*He* barely gets to call me that while keeping his head. You sure as hell won't."

Chuckling, I retreat a step, instantly missing the feel of her skin against mine—even if it was only one fingertip.

I snag my T-shirt and tug it on over my head. "You are a feisty one, aren't you?"

Her hackles only seem to rise more at my observation, but I don't mean it in a bad or condescending way.

Far from it.

Bishop's fire and the way she's constantly throwing everything back at me only makes this little game of ours more fun. I push and she pushes back harder. It's nearly impossible to walk away from the enjoyment it brings me, even if it does drag danger along with it.

I run my hand through my sweat-soaked hair. "If you want me to stop coming to the club, or here to work out, all you have to do is ask and I will."

The twist of her perfect lips tells me she doesn't believe me. "That easy, huh?"

I throw my bag over my shoulder and nod. "That easy."

While flirting with Bishop has become a favorite pastime, I also know it would be far better for both of us if I stayed away. Her asking me to do just that would make it a much easier proposition. Because as it stands now, I keep drifting toward this woman despite the current of sanity flowing in the opposite direction.

Her gaze shifts over to where Astrid and Atlas are watching us intently. She inclines her head toward the ring. "He any good?"

Atlas leans on the ropes and laughs. "I'm kind of terrified to answer that question."

"Why?"

He scoffs. "Because I'm afraid you'll kick my ass if I tell you yes."

She scowls at him, then turns back to me. "I won't keep you from coming to train with my cousin, because this is his career. I don't interfere with that. But..."

I knew there was a but coming...

"But what?"

There are so many things she could ask of me, that she could demand, and most of them, I would probably do without even thinking about it.

She releases a little sigh, averting her gaze and shifting on her feet as if whatever she is refusing to say makes her uncomfortable in a way I haven't seen her yet. "Just..."—she throws up a hand dismissively—"never mind."

Whatever she was about to demand still sits on the tip of her tongue, and she shifts uneasily, wincing, as if holding it back physically hurts her.

I lean in, disregarding the fact that I stink from the workout and the twins are still watching us. Because something tells me she won't say it when they might hear. "But *what*, Bishop?"

"Just..."—she glances toward me, then away again—"stop looking at me like that."

There it is.

Heat flares through my blood, my cock stirring to attention with the admission underlying her words. That the way I look at her is actually getting under her skin.

"Like *what*?"

Bishop presses her lips together firmly, her hands fisting at her sides. If steam could shoot out of someone's ears like it does in the old cartoons, it would be from hers right now.

She hates that she admitted it. Despises the fact that she's given me *anything* that might spur me on. But the longer we stare at each other, the longer I wait for her response, the more confident I become that she *is* going to break.

When it finally comes, it's because she glances over at Astrid and Atlas and realizes they're watching us and she has to do *something*.

With a huff, she leans closer so they won't hear. "Like you want me to pin you again."

I can't help the smirk that pulls at my lips. "*That* I can't promise you. I told you I'm a bad liar." And I would most certainly be lying if I said I was going to stop looking at her like that, or that I don't still mean my offer. I wink at her again. "See ya around."

She watches me walk over to Atlas and Astrid but doesn't make any move to follow.

I hold out my fist to bump with Atlas.

He grins at me. "Thanks, man. That was a great workout this morning."

"Anytime. You have my number now. Give me a call and we can set up a schedule."

Being the same weight class as Atlas means that we can actually spar in a way that he can't with people in his family. Based on what he told me before we started in the ring, the

Hawkes have a long history with the sport and have all spent time in here at some point. But none of them give him the type of competition he needs—save for Bishop.

This is the perfect opportunity to get in a good workout *and* work out some of my frustrations.

Hopefully often.

Though, the main source of one of them stands staring at me and watching me carefully from the other side of the gym right now, so maybe not.

Astrid smiles, leaning against the side of the ring. "It was nice to meet you, Gage."

"You, too."

Shifting a little closer to me, she drops her voice so only Atlas and I can hear. "Can I ask...what's with you and Bishop?"

I raise a brow, pretending not to know what the hell she's talking about when it would be clear to *anyone* in the same room with us that there's tension. A lot of it. "What do you mean?"

She laughs lightly. "Come on now. I've known that woman my entire life, and she has been rattled ever since the moment she walked in here and saw you, so spill."

Rattled.

It's a good word to describe it, but I want Bishop more than just rattled.

I want her to give in to this attraction. Allow this tension to pull her to me. I want her to *want* to pin me again, in a very different setting.

Not that I would tell her cousin any of that.

"We had a little run-in at the club the other day, and I don't think she liked it very much."

One of Astrid's blond brows rises. "Why is that?"

"Because I stepped in to help one of the girls."

They both wince and Astrid nods. "Yeah, I could see how that wouldn't sit well with her. She's under the impression that it's her sole responsibility to ensure everyone with the name Hawke on this planet remains safe."

I nod. "I kind of gathered that."

Atlas reaches up and rubs at the massive scar on his shoulder from when he was shot. The newspaper articles and news broadcasts gave a lot of details of the attack, enough to know that Astrid almost died from her wounds, too.

I can only imagine how Bishop must have felt after that...

"Was she with you guys when..."—I incline my head toward his hand, and it freezes—"that happened?"

Astrid's back stiffens, and the color fades from her face as she clears her throat and glances away. She shifts on her feet, pressing her hand over her abdomen as if she can still feel the wound there.

Clearly uncomfortable discussing the shooting, she keeps her gaze diverted on anything but me, which is completely reasonable considering I'm a stranger and it was likely the most traumatic event in her life.

Atlas shakes his head. "She was downstairs in the building lobby and chased after the gunman but couldn't find him."

"That must have been very frustrating for her."

He nods, his hand falling away from his shoulder. "You have no fucking idea."

I think I do.

It's clear Bishop has a sole focus. One thing she allows herself to think about day in and day out. And that's her responsibility and her role in the Hawke family.

Her protective instinct is so ingrained that she doesn't know how to turn it off, doesn't know how to stop worrying, even now.

She doesn't trust me and is running through all the potential reasons I would have to be here, all the ulterior motives. Making a threat assessment and planning what action she would need to take to secure them if she needed to.

That shouldn't be so fucking hot.

It should be a warning to put as much space between us as possible.

But just like a moth drawn to the flame, her fire and spark light up my world in a way that prevents me from doing anything but walk straight into the conflagration. Damn the consequences.

Even now, I have to force myself to keep my focus on Astrid and Atlas and not allow my eyes to drift over to her. "Well, thanks again, guys."

Atlas grins. "I'll call you. We'll do it again soon."

"Perfect."

Because something tells me I'm going to be needing that kind of release and relief from the conflict raging in my head and heart.

With my bag slung over my shoulder, I move toward the front door and the rain outside that's finally starting to let up.

And it's getting harder and harder to do without looking back at her.

6

TWO DAYS LATER

BISHOP

The sun is just starting to set as I pull into the Hawkeye Club and park in the area reserved for the Hawkes.

All the other spots are empty.

As they should be.

Everyone else is enjoying a night off. A break away from daily stress of their jobs and the uncertainty that continues to surround us.

I could have gone to Mom and Dad's place instead of staying at home alone. Dad's invitation to come have some of his famous jerk chicken with them, Pope, Allie, and Benjamin was tempting.

But ultimately, I just couldn't do it.

No matter how much I hyped myself up, I couldn't go and be the fifth wheel again. I couldn't bring myself to show up, sit with them around that table, watch how happy they are together despite the fact that at any moment, Satriano could make good on his warning that he would be seeing us soon. At any moment, Michael McDonald could surface with a bang.

Days have turned into weeks since we first learned of his arrival in New Orleans, yet we're no closer to discovering where he is or what he's doing here.

And everyone else just goes on with their lives as if living under this cloud is normal.

Like it doesn't keep them awake at night the way it does me.

So I couldn't go there tonight. I couldn't sit and pretend. But I also couldn't spend the night on my couch, either.

Because you can't take a night off.

You've never been able to.

Even before Leonardo Satriano appeared in New Orleans all those years ago and fucked up our lives by coming after Jack, I always found myself restless on my nights off.

Unable to relax to read or watch a movie like a normal person would.

I couldn't last more than an hour before I'd find myself driving to one of the clubs to just feel...useful.

And since the *other* Satriano arrived, it's only gotten worse.

Most nights, I don't even last ten minutes.

Tonight, it was more like five. Five damn minutes after I got back to my place after meeting with Gabe and Dad to discuss the current status of our investigations, I was changing and turning around to come here and have a drink at the bar.

Anything but champagne...

Satriano's "gift" and note continue to keep me awake at night as much as the nightmares do. There was no way I would have slept tonight even if I had stayed in.

So, I might as well be here.

I sigh at the absurdity of my life lately.

How I've become this machine that doesn't sleep, barely interacts with anyone other than those I need to for work, and only thinks about one thing—what it will take to remove that fucker Damon from the face of the earth without bringing down the might of his entire organization on us in retaliation.

Of course, that would require *finding* him first.

So, one baby step at a time.

But those baby steps are becoming agonizing.

I turn off the engine, open the door, and step out onto the familiar pavement. Though it finally stopped raining last night, the scent of it still lingers in the air and clings to the grass surrounding the club. I inhale deeply, pulling it into my lungs and holding it there for a moment.

That fresh, clean smell carries so many good memories with it. Ones I so desperately need now of easier times. When we weren't always on edge. When I wasn't living every moment wondering when the other shoe would drop and trusted the people in my life would protect me from the dangers of the world beyond our little bubble.

Splashing in puddles with Pope...

Dancing in the rain with Astrid, Kennedy, Angie, and Allie...

A smile pulls at my lips remembering how muddy we would be when we walked back inside. But we never got yelled at for it. There were never any reprimands for destroying our clothes or dripping water across the floors of the various Hawke houses. If anything, it made everyone happy to see us so carefree. They lived to give us that feeling, to have childhoods free from the tragedy and strife they all suffered at some point in their own lives.

I can't even remember the last time I felt like that.

Well before either Satriano arrived.

Maybe before Dad accepted that I wasn't going away to college and wanted to stay here and work with him instead. Before he showed me what protecting the Hawke empire truly required. Before I took some of that burden off his shoulders. Because before that, I was still living in ignorant bliss about all the threats.

They may have primarily been from business rivals back then rather than mob bosses, but they still existed. And now, there's no going back to that time or place when I could relax and just enjoy life without the constant worry for everyone around me plaguing me at every moment.

No matter how badly I may want that for all of us.

Releasing the breath burning in my lungs now, I turn toward the building, intent to grab a drink, chat with the staff, and keep an eye out for any troublemakers so it feels like I'm at least doing something.

But the rumble of a motorcycle engine approaches, growing louder until a Harley pulls into the lot. Even before it rolls up behind my SUV, I recognize the bike and the black leather jacket stretched across the shoulders of the man on it.

Gage tugs off his helmet and shakes out his sandy-blond hair, offering me a grin and a heated assessment that might as well be a flashing neon sign that says "pin me." Apparently, my request the other morning was for naught because this man has zero intention of stopping that *look*. "Bishop..."

Hell...

The way he says my name only makes it worse.

Smooth.

Sexual.

Like he's making love to the word the same way he would my body if I let him get his hands on me.

I tense as he shuts off the engine, anticipating his approach and the way my body will inevitably react to his proximity. Because as much as I try to deny it to myself, there's something about this man that drives me mad—in the worst and *best* ways.

The quiet that settles over us makes me hyper aware of how still the night is. No cars passing on the road. No patrons coming out from the club. Just the two of us staring each other down in a parking lot, waiting for the other to make a move.

Self-preservation finally wins.

"Remember that word I used to describe you?"

Another panty-melting grin spreads across his face. "This is just a happy coincidence. I was hoping you'd be here."

Coincidence.

One of the reasons I've never believed in them is because people use that word to cover up calculated moves. But then again, the chances he *would* find me here are pretty high considering how much time I spend at the club.

Forcing myself to give someone like Gage Newhart the benefit of the doubt is painful when I've spent my whole life being taught to question everything and never accept things at face value.

It's the only way to protect what we've built and bled for.

I don't know what game Gage is playing, or if he truly is only inserting himself into my life because he's interested in me.

The more I try to dig into his background and military record, the more roadblocks I hit. But there's some part of me that's curious. A part that *needs* to know what he really wants. That part that can't deny my attraction to him.

"Why were you hoping to see me?"

He leans against the handlebars, a spark of mischief flashing in his blue eyes. "Because I want to take you somewhere."

The idea of going *anywhere* with Gage is equal parts thrilling and terrifying. Little girls learn at a very young age not to trust strangers, to never go anywhere with one, and I've always been the most skeptical of the Hawkes when it comes to earning trust.

But there's just something about this man that draws me to him.

Not because I trust him.

Not because he's impossibly handsome.

Definitely not because he's a shameless flirt who often crosses the line of what's socially appropriate.

It's the instinct to keep him close—that it's somehow important that I do.

He's either completely genuine and the first man I've actually been interested in for a very long time, or he's a talented conman with an ulterior motive I haven't uncovered yet.

Friends close and enemies closer...

I raise a brow at him. "Where do you want to take me?"

He grins, waggling his eyebrows playfully. "It's a surprise."

Everything about this man is.

Each time I learn something new, it gives me another piece to the very messy puzzle. I don't have enough to create a clear picture yet, but if I go with him tonight, that may change.

I may actually discover what it is Gage Newhart *really* wants, but I am not above making him work for it. "I'm not a big fan of surprises."

He chuckles low and shakes his head, sending the silky blond strands falling over his forehead. "Somehow, I knew that, but I think you'll like *this* one." His gaze sweeps to the front door of the club. "Do you have to go in tonight?"

"No."

His grin grows, and he holds out a hand, palm up. "Then let's go."

It would be easy enough to say *no.* To just walk away and return to my original evening plans of sitting at the bar. But with his eyes locked on me like this and his hand extended in offer, climbing on the back of his bike and discovering what Gage Newhart has in store for me—and maybe what his ultimate goal is—is far too tempting to ignore.

I approach him cautiously and slide my hand into his. Rough callouses scrape against my skin, sending a little jolt of heat searing through me, awakening something I long ago buried. Something I've ignored and actively pushed away. Something I've refused to allow myself because I know it can never happen.

There isn't any room in my life for what everyone else has.

My focus can't be pulled away from protecting the people important to me.

I can't have a relationship beyond a few fun hours with someone.

So this *longing* has to go.

Easy to say but much harder to actually accomplish when he squeezes my hand and steadies the bike for me like a true gentleman.

I swing my leg up and over the seat, settling in behind him while trying to keep some space between us.

He glances back at me. "Do you know how to ride on one of these?"

Offering an incredulous look, I laugh. "Do you really have to ask that?"

Another cocky grin spreads across his face, and he motions toward one of his saddle bags. "There's another helmet in there."

I reach in and snag it, releasing my braids from the bun so I can settle it on my head.

He pulls his back on and glances over his shoulder at me, his eyes swimming with so much promise that the stupid feeling I'm trying so hard to fight flutters in my chest. "You better hang on."

Shit.

I didn't think this through all the way.

It's been years since I rode on the back of a bike instead of driving it myself, and having to press my entire body to his is a *very* bad idea.

But it's too late to chicken out now.

If I did, Gage would know why, and I refuse to give him that satisfaction.

I shift forward until the cradle of my hips presses against his ass, my thighs alongside his, and wrap my arms around him. Flattening my palms on his chest, I have to fight the urge to dig my nails into him. Hard, taut muscle lives beneath the leather, and images of him sweat-slickened in the ring with Atlas flash through my head so vividly that I instantly regret my decision to accept this invitation.

The way he moved...

How those corded muscles bunched and flexed so fluidly...

Each swing and jab perfectly timed and accentuating his perfect physique...

Heat pools where my hips press against him, and when he fires up the engine, the low rumbling vibration beneath us does nothing to help convince me that getting on this man's bike was anything but a very big mistake.

He tears out of the parking lot and onto the street, the roar of his acceleration filling the early evening air.

The powerful, deep, resonant growl of the motor somehow soothes some of the regret I'm feeling about my current position.

It's far better than the alternative.

Silence always makes me nervous.

Like the whole world is holding a collective breath and waiting for something.

As we weave through the streets, making our way across town, the sound and vibration help relax away some of the tension I had when I arrived at the club.

But a new source of it sits directly in front of me.

Where is he taking us?

A thousand different possibilities float through my head the farther and farther we move from the club, but when we turn onto City Park Avenue, my breath catches.

City Park?

With the sun going down and darkness starting to descend, people are filing out, done utilizing one of the best public spaces in all of New Orleans.

Somewhere I haven't been in ages.

Mom and Dad used to bring us out here to feed the ducks and walk the trails, but it's been years since I've set foot in the park. Since I've taken any time to enjoy *anything*, really.

That regret tightens my chest as Gage pulls the bike into a parking spot and shuts off the engine, holding out a hand for me to grab to climb off.

The same shiver of awareness ripples through me at the skin contact, and his grip lingers a few extra seconds after my feet are on solid ground, making it impossible to look at him without heat spreading across my cheeks and between my legs.

What is it about this man that puts me so on edge?

That question rattles around my head as he removes his helmet and shakes out his hair, the blond locks flying around his face, then holds out his hand for mine. I unbuckle it and pass it over to him, and he opens his saddle bag on one side, puts mine back in, then sets his on the seat.

"What are we doing at the park?"

He fights a grin as he climbs easily from the bike and opens his other saddle bag. "You'll see…"

God, I really hate surprises…

Anything unknown ties my stomach in knots, especially now. Yet, it isn't just *that* fluttering there. There's the anticipation of what else might happen. The hope that I'm wrong to suspect ulterior motives.

He pulls out a black bag that conceals whatever's inside of it, and I narrow my eyes on him.

"Have I mentioned I really hate surprises?"

His grin spreads as he turns to face me and invades my personal space, backing me into the bike. "You have, but I think that's something you're going to have to get over."

"Why's that?"

"Because I love them, and I like seeing you like this."

"Like what?"

"Not in control."

I gape at him.

"You're a control freak, Bishop." He offers me a smug look that I instantly want to wipe off his pretty face. "I don't think *anyone* would fight me on that fact. And sometimes, you just have to let go."

Just have to let go?

He says it as if it's the easiest thing in the world. Maybe for him it is. With his smooth, affable disposition, quick smile, and calm demeanor, Gage doesn't seem the least bit aware of the dangers I live my life trying to build up defenses for.

I shake my head. "That's never going to happen. When I'm not in control..."

Shit.

Shit. Shit. Shit. Shit.

I suck in a sharp breath, not finishing that statement.

The last thing I want to do is acknowledge that he's right.

He already has an inflated ego, and conceding that I am a control freak and can't stand not being the one commanding the ship would only make him more unbearably smug.

But as he narrows his eyes on me, there's a tenderness to his voice that wasn't there a moment ago. "When you're not in control *what*?"

Along with the change in his tone, his gaze shifts from playful and soft to a darker, more intent assessment that makes me squirm.

This man sees far too much, and despite all the reasons I shouldn't trust him, the sincerity with which he looks at me now, the genuine concern in his eyes is enough to make me *want* to answer.

"People get hurt, okay?"

Not just any people.

My people.

The sympathy in his gaze breaks me, cracking my chest

wide open, and I have to look away, off toward the vast expanse of green grass and shimmering water of the lake in City Park beyond it so he doesn't see the unshed tears I'm willing away.

GAGE

Hell...

I've never seen Bishop like this.

She may have been rattled when she found me at the gym, but now, she's *shaken.*

Seeing her like this almost makes me regret teasing her about it.

Almost.

But the truth is, Bishop is a control freak. She needs to manage and direct everything around her because she believes that's the only way to keep people safe.

And I *know* that feeling. I understand it...and how dangerous it can be.

I give her a moment to collect herself, allowing silence to linger between us until I can't bear to see her suffer alone anymore. Tentatively, I reach down and slide my hand into hers, squeezing it gently before I tug. "Let's go."

She releases a long, relieved-sounding breath at being given a reprieve and lets me lead her into the park.

It's different at night.

Calmer.

Even more serene.

Without people picnicking, riding bikes, throwing Frisbees, rowing boats across the water, the beauty of the place in the quickly fading light takes center stage.

Which is exactly why I chose *here.*

Bishop needs some serenity. Some calm. A break from all the tension that she always carries.

We make our way toward Langles Bridge in silence as the sun continues to dip lower into the horizon, extending the long shadows of the massive trees.

I finally pause at a grassy area tucked behind one of the large old oaks.

Bishop glances around us. "Here?"

Nodding, I hold up the bag I pulled from my bike. "I brought us a picnic."

A bark of laughter bubbles up from her chest, completely natural and unexpected, as if she's releasing panic she's been holding onto since she climbed onto my bike. "A picnic?"

I reach into the bag and pull out a checkered blanket. She watches me carefully as I set down the bag on the grass and spread out our seating area. "Go in there and pull everything out."

Bishop pulls her bottom lip under her teeth, worrying it for a moment before she snags the bag and reaches inside it. She pulls out the bottle of Pinot Noir and raises a dark brow. "Wine?"

I grin as she goes into it again and comes out with a French baguette and a container of cubed cheese.

She laughs lightly, the sound so unusual from her that I genuinely take a moment to enjoy the ease of it. "You're serious?"

Settling on the blanket, I cross my booted ankles and lean back on my hands to stare up at her. "As a heart attack."

Bishop glances around the darkening park, then down at me. "Why?"

I pat the blanket beside me. "Because it looked like you needed a break."

That brief second of unguardedness I got from her slips

away instantly, replaced by her typical defensive look of mistrust. "I don't."

I keep my gaze locked on hers, hoping she won't turn and run when I speak this truth. "You really, really do." Holding out a hand, I curl my fingers in invitation. "Join me."

The moment of hesitation is enough for me to hold my breath, but she eventually steps forward and slides her palm into mine, allowing me to tug her down.

She settles next to me on the blanket, but she doesn't relax.

I'm starting to wonder if it's even *possible* for her to anymore —or if she *ever* really did at any point in her life.

Her spine stays rigid, her body tense, as if she's ready to bolt at any moment.

And she might be.

The look she gave me in the Hawkeye Club parking lot when I rode in should have made me turn right around, and I almost did. But then I got close enough to see the exhaustion on her face. The dark circles under her eyes. How *frayed* she looked. As if she hasn't slept in days. And I knew I was right in my assessments of her.

Bishop will forgo taking care of herself and her needs in order to ensure everyone else has theirs met, in order to secure the safety of those she loves.

Even now, out here in the park, with nothing but the sounds of the crickets, frogs, and other animals coming out at dusk surrounding us, she's still somewhere else in her head. Still wrapped up in the concerns that plague her when she's in her protector role.

I lean in and feather my lips across her ear. "Relax."

She flinches slightly at the contact, or maybe at the word that represents something she struggles with so much.

It takes her a moment before she inhales a long, slow breath, then releases it, but almost instantly, her shoulders relax slightly, a bit of that tension floating away.

A small victory to be celebrated.

Because Bishop Clarke will not give up *anything* easily.

Especially not something personal that might show she's human.

My entire purpose in bringing her here tonight was to get her out of the environments we've been in together previously. Places where she feels obligated to be on-guard at all times, watchful and tense. Bring her somewhere completely free from the threats she's seemingly worrying about, and that's as breathtakingly beautiful as she is.

I reach over her and snag the bottle of wine, twisting off the cap.

She raises a brow. "Twist top?"

Laughing, I set the cap beside me. "It's good. I promise."

"Did you bring glasses?"

I bring the bottle to my mouth and take a sip of the sweet and tanniny liquid, then grin at her. "Do we need them?"

The corner of her lips twitches, as if she's fighting a smile she doesn't want to give me, but she accepts the proffered bottle and takes a sip of it herself. "I can't say I've ever sat in the park and drank wine straight out of the bottle before."

"Really?" I raise a brow. "'Cause I do this every weekend."

Bishop laughs so hard she actually releases a little snort, the sound carrying through the night air. She slaps her hand over her mouth, her eyes widening with sheer embarrassment, but I reach up and pull it away, wrapping my fingers around her slender wrist.

"Don't." I squeeze gently, bringing the top of her hand to my mouth and pressing my lips to soft skin there. "That was adorable."

Her breath hitches, and she tugs her wrist from my hold, rolling her eyes. "Fuck, don't say that. The last thing I want to be is *adorable*."

"Why not?"

I genuinely meant it as a compliment, but the way Bishop purses her lips, she seems annoyed, like she would rather punch me than sit here with me right now.

"Do I really have to explain it to you?"

"Apparently..."

She releases a long sigh that carries far more than just annoyance over the "adorable" comment. "You know I help run security for my family."

I nod.

"So, does looking 'adorable' really fit with someone in that position?"

"I mean..."—I shrug—"they're not mutually exclusive. You can be a total badass who pins me to the ground in a split second and takes absolute control of the situation and still be adorable as fuck."

She sure fucking is.

Bishop offers me an uneasy look, like if she had a choice, she'd rather be anywhere but sitting here with me on this blanket under the darkening sky in this beautiful park.

I've seen that look so many times from her over the short time we've known each other. It's pretty clear what's going on in that head of hers right now.

"You don't believe a word I say, do you?"

She takes another sip from the bottle, averting her gaze. "Honestly? I don't know."

At least she's being honest.

It would have been easy enough for her to lie, for her to tell me she believes me when I know she doesn't get whatever it is she's looking for from me, but the fact that she was willing to tell me the truth suggests she at least *wants* to trust me.

Somewhere, deep down, she doesn't want to bicker and have the push-pull sometimes contempt-laced interactions we have in the past.

That's a massive step in the right direction as far as I'm concerned.

I won't push her for more at the moment.

The only way to get Bishop Clarke to trust me is to earn it.

That takes time and patience.

I snag the container of cheese and tear it open, then rip off a hunk of bread. "Hungry?"

She shakes her head. "I ate."

I pop the food into my mouth and chew, waiting for her to make the decision about how the rest of our night is going to go.

Her gaze stays locked on the water for so long that the sun fully sets, plunging the park into darkness.

When she finally glances at me again, I take that as an opening.

"I really suck at this, huh?"

Her brow furrows. "At what?"

"The whole spontaneity thing..."

The tiniest smile pulls at her lips, and aside from the earlier laughter, I think it's genuinely the first time I've seen a reaction from her that wasn't all-out contempt—at the very least, mistrust—when looking at me. "No." She scans the dark park again. "This is actually pretty nice."

"Wait a minute, was that a compliment?" Her head whips back toward me, and I grin widely. "Maybe I'm hallucinating—"

She shrugs at me with a full-blown smile this time, and it completely lights up her entire face.

Gone are the dark circles under her eyes.

The deep lines she worried into her forehead disappear.

All I see is a happy—and amused—woman for the first time since I met her.

"It was definitely a compliment, but don't let it go to your head."

"I won't."

That's a lie.

It was a big win. Hopefully, a massive step forward in whatever this is that's happening between us. Maybe it's too much to hope for that, but something seems to shift between us.

A lightening of the air.

Her eyes continue to move over the park, from the huge grassy areas, to the old bridge and the water sparkling under the almost full moon that is out tonight. "Why here?"

She hands me the bottle, and I take a sip.

Breathing in the fresh air scented with cut grass, flowers, and the water, I hold it in my lungs for a moment before I answer. Wondering how much I should reveal to her when she's always so quick to believe I'm lying. "I much prefer to spend my time outdoors, if at all possible."

"How come?"

I swallow thickly as years of memories cascade through my head, some good, some bad, until I land on one. The one that always comes up when I'm in places like this and that always draws a smile across my face. "My dad used to take me camping when I was little. It was our bonding time. The only real time I got with him."

"How come?"

"He was in the military. Deployed a lot. Then he went into foreign service and was busy at the various consulates. So, when I did get to spend time with him, it was extra special."

Bishop offers me a sympathetic look, and I know she's moving around the various pieces of information she has about me and adding this new stuff to it, trying to create a clearer picture. "I'm with my dad, and basically the rest of my family, every day. Always have been."

"You say that like it's a bad thing."

"No, just..." She twirls one of her long braids around her finger as she considers her response. "We have a very complicated relationship. Not just me and my dad, but all of us Hawkes. And it only seems to get more complicated as the years progress."

"What makes it complicated?"

She shrugs. "Life, I guess. We grew up. We have different lives, different experiences and priorities."

Something dark passes over her eyes, and I push up until I'm fully sitting and tilt her chin toward me until she's forced to meet my gaze.

"No matter how complicated your relationship with them might be, I know for a fact that they all love you and appreciate what you do for them."

"How could you possibly know that?"

"Because I've seen them in the club and at the opening. I've seen the way not only your family members, but all the employees, look to you. They know who always has their backs and best interests at heart."

For a second, Bishop appears ready to argue with me, but I brush my thumb across her bottom lip slowly, and instead of looking away like I expect her to, or pulling free of my hold, her eyes stay locked with mine.

"You can't be everyone's savior all the time. Bishop." The words burn coming out of my mouth, old pain laced with new. When they were said to me, I was lying in a hospital bed, trying desperately to get out of it, to get back to work, to my team. I didn't want to hear those words, and neither does she. "You know that, right?"

She tries to look away, but I hold her chin firm, making her gaze stay locked with mine.

Unshed tears shimmer there, and that's when I know I've hit a nerve.

I've said exactly what she needed to hear but also didn't want to.

That bottom lip of hers quivers. "You say that like you know from personal experience."

More memories flood my head. Mistakes of the past. Things I wish I had done differently. Things that would have changed so much for so many people.

"I do. I lost a lot of good friends over the years."

"Deployments?"

I give a sharp nod, willing those memories to go back and stay buried where they belong. This isn't about my past or what I lost, it's about what she will lose—*herself*—if something doesn't give. "Sometimes, bad things happen to good people, and there's nothing we can do about it."

"But—"

I press my thumb across her lips again, mesmerized by how soft and kissable they are. "I worry about you..."

God knows I do it far too much.

It's a complication I never wanted. But I never saw her coming. Never expected to be hit square in the chest with this feeling the first time I saw her at the club.

Like we were kindred spirits.

Like I could see *her* and she could see right through *me*, too.

Bishop tenses. "Why in the world would you worry about me? You barely know me."

"I know enough. I've seen enough to understand that you take care of everyone else, even if it's to your own detriment."

She flinches again, as if that truth physically hurts her.

Maybe it does.

Her entire life is wrapped up in playing this one role, in being this specific person for her family, and that doesn't leave room for her to think about what *she* needs or wants.

The sound of crickets and frogs in the lake and all the other animals that come out at night fills the air, and the tension between us thickens.

I tip my head closer, still holding her chin, still keeping her in place. "I think it's time you let someone take care of you."

She doesn't pull away.

Doesn't retreat.

Her gaze continues to hold mine as I lean in and press my lips to hers.

I expect her to tense, to jerk free, but she doesn't. She accepts my kiss and responds in kind, her mouth moving over mine.

Tentatively at first.

Exploring.

Seeking.

Allowing me to do the same until her hands come up to my chest and slide inside my unzipped jacket.

Her touch, her eagerness that matches my own spurs me to deepen the kiss, gliding my tongue across her lips. She opens for me, a tiny little moan in the back of her throat enough to make my cock ache and press against the confines of my jeans.

I roll her onto her back on the blanket and tug away, just far enough to allow myself to breathe. "Will you let me do that, Bishop? Will you let me take care of you?"

7

GAGE

She stares up at me from under impossibly long, thick lashes with dark, uncertain eyes, as if my question somehow confuses her when what I'm asking should be obvious.

This entire time, since the moment we met, it should have been obvious what I wanted—to be *this* close. To have her under me and trusting in me enough to allow me to show her how good it can be to let go.

I brush my fingers across her lips again, wanting so badly to take them with another kiss.

But not until she answers me.

Not until she tells me with words what she *really* wants.

"Tell me, Bishop. Can I?"

She tries to hide behind this impenetrable wall she puts up around herself, around her heart, but I see it there—the need, the desire. To be touched. To be loved. To be *seen* and know she's more than just her job.

It matches my own.

She's just too afraid to admit it.

Too afraid to give in to the attraction that's been sparking between us since the moment she pinned me to that floor. Too afraid that everything I've told her might be true.

I dip my head closer, giving her every chance to say no, to push me away, to tell me to get lost, and I pause with my lips a mere hairsbreadth from hers. Prepared to stop. Ready to admit defeat where breaking through to her is concerned. But she closes the distance between us and presses her lips to mine.

The kiss is harsh, greedy, like she's desperate for what I'm offering or terrified that she'll realize what she's doing if she gives herself even a moment to think about it.

But Bishop isn't the type of woman who does anything she isn't one hundred percent on board with, which is probably what's really scaring her.

How real this feels.

How much she *doesn't* want me to stop.

She runs her hands through my hair, her mouth moving against mine as she shifts under me, trying to press her entire body to mine. I keep a tiny bit of space between us, holding myself up and away from her, but there's no hiding my hard cock digging into her upper thigh, the way my body responds to having her this close.

"You haven't answered me, Bishop." I lick along the seam of her lips, and she groans and digs her nails into the back of my neck. "I want to hear you say it. I want to hear you say 'yes.'"

More than *want* it.

I *need* it.

To confirm she knows exactly what I'm asking for and that she's freely giving it to me with not just her body, but her mind, too.

Because that's where she's trapped.

In her own head.

This idea that she has to be *one* thing and one thing *only*.

She gasps as I drag my free hand down between her legs to cup her there, and her hips arch up to grind against my palm. "Yes."

It's such a simple word, only three tiny letters, but I know that her saying that took a massive amount of courage.

She's always taking care of everyone but herself, always thinking about other people, what they need instead of what she does. But this moment is about her. Only her and what I can do to make her soar.

I press the pad of my palm to the apex of her thighs, and she rolls her hips up again, releasing a tiny mewl at the friction it creates in exactly the right spot.

God, that sound...

My blood heats. My hands itch to touch every inch of her skin. My cock aches to be buried inside of her. And I so desperately want to strip her bare and bury my face between her thighs right now.

But while we may be alone out here at the moment, someone could come walking by at any second, could interrupt us and steal this little sliver of time that we have, and I won't risk that.

The threat is enough to make us frantic.

Knowing it has to be fast.

I fumble with the button on her jeans but manage to pop it free and pull down the zipper. Before I can slide my hand in, she reaches to her hip, lifts her shirt, and grabs a gun from a holster.

The sudden appearance of a firearm should give me pause, but the fact that Bishop is carrying doesn't surprise me in the least.

I would have been more surprised if she weren't.

She sets it beside us on the blanket, and now that she's moved it, I can glide my hand along her hot, smooth skin, spreading my palm out across her stomach and dipping my fingers lower.

Bishop bucks at the contact, grinding even harder against my hand when I reach lower. I capture her mouth with another searing kiss, matching her desperation with my own.

She moans, her hands clinging to the back of my head, her nails digging in there, that small, sharp bite of pain enough to make me crave even more, to need it, and when my fingers finally find her core, it's a glorious epiphany.

"Christ, Bishop." I groan against her lips. "So fucking wet."

I slide a finger easily into her, her body contracting around it the same way I wish it were my cock. It throbs, demanding to be there. But I won't give in to that desire.

Not here.

Not now.

Not tonight.

She clings to me like I'm the only thing keeping her from floating away. Maybe, in this moment, I am. I've forced her to admit things tonight that she might not have been ready to face, and she has looked so lost that this dark park might have been the perfect place for her to completely disappear. But I refuse to let her hide from me or from herself.

Not now.

Not *ever.*

I thrust my finger in and out of her slick heat slowly, grazing my thumb across her clit in a lazy rhythm that has her hips thrusting to meet me, trying to force me to move harder and faster.

And I can't deny her that.

I match her rhythm.

Sharing breath as I devour her mouth and she fucks my hand relentlessly.

My thumb swirls rapidly as I slide a second finger into her. Her back bows toward the stars now speckling the night sky with a gasp. I take her mouth again. Desperate to capture every little sound she makes and consume them. To keep them inside me forever knowing this moment won't last that long.

Her body trembles under mine.

She's close, so fucking close.

Bishop tears her mouth from mine, tipping her head back, and I graze my teeth along the column of her extended neck.

She finally snaps.

Her cunt pulses around my fingers, her hips arching, her mouth falling open on a sharp cry.

I capture it with another kiss, swallowing down her pleasure as it ripples through my own body.

Good God...

Teeth gritted, I use every ounce of my willpower to hold back my own release. Because when I do come, it's going to be inside this woman. Nowhere else.

She rides out her orgasm with her body arched into mine, and it's the most beautiful thing I've ever seen.

Bishop coming undone under the stars.

Her total escape from *everything*.

Fuck yes.

I'd give anything to know how to make this moment go on forever. To find a way to help Bishop break free from all the things that weigh her down. To ensure she can float away on a cloud of sheer bliss indefinitely.

But it has to end.

All good things do eventually.

A sad reality that I had hoped might hold off for a few more moments.

When she finally starts to sink down, I pull my fingers from her body and slip them into my mouth, licking off every bit of her release.

Her eyes flutter open in time to catch me doing it, and her already labored breath hitches. "God..."

I chuckle as I brush a kiss across her parted lips. "You can call me that if you want to."

She shoves playfully at my chest, the touch making me crave even more of it. Without the barrier of my shirt between us. With *nothing* but her skin against my own. "That's not what I meant."

"I know." I grin, loving how relaxed she looks in this moment. "But I mean it."

Her eyes soften to the warm bourbon color I could drink down all day but rarely see. This is how they look when she isn't worrying, when she's let go of being the Bishop she thinks she needs to always be and allows herself to be the one she wants to be. The one she deserves to be. "I'd rather just call you Gage."

"That works, too."

And hearing it again—my name from those beautiful lips—makes me simultaneously wish I had never met this woman and that I could spend every waking moment with her.

BISHOP

Something changes in Gage's gaze.

The warm, welcome depths of his blue eyes suddenly shift to something darker. Something harder.

Like he's shutting down, shifting away, and then he does so physically, moving back slightly and putting some space between our bodies.

I immediately miss the heat, the weight of him on top of me, that leather and spice scent of his invading each breath.

A chilly breeze floats over me, and I shiver as I reach to

zip and rebutton my jeans before anyone who might be out here randomly strolls by and discovers what we've been doing.

Holy shit, Bishop...

Gage clears his throat, then reaches back and grabs the bottle of wine and takes a long pull from it, offering it to me as he swallows.

The mood has changed.

The balmy night air now feels cold, raising goosebumps all over my skin.

Reality comes back in a rush.

I scrub my face with my hands, trying to figure out how the hell I just let that happen. When I reopen my eyes, he's holding the bottle out in front of me, and God knows I need it to try to help me make sense of it all.

How did I go from being suspicious of this man to coming on his hand?

The answer isn't clear, but the little flashes he gave me of himself tonight somehow coalesced into a completely different view of him. And the way he seemed to see right through me left me feeling exposed and raw.

I snag the bottle from him, focus on the water, and take a huge drink.

The heavy tannins and sweetness of the red wine splash against my tongue as the vision of him licking my release off his fingers flashes through my head.

My pussy throbs, my clit pulsing in a way that has me shifting to try to relieve some of the pressure.

This was a mistake.

I don't know how I let myself get swept up in the moment, in the attraction between us, when I know damn well that the last thing I need right now is a distraction dressed in leather. Especially when there was this sudden change in him the moment it was over.

An awkward silence falls over us, and Gage glances at me out of the corner of his eye.

"What?" I raise a brow at him. "Why are you giving me that look?"

One corner of his mouth curls up into a half-grin. "Just trying to figure you out."

I shake my head. "There isn't anything to figure out."

The last thing I want is him trying to root around in my head any more than he already has tonight. In such a short amount of time, he's unraveled so many things that have been tangled up inside me for so long that it's terrifying what he might do if given another opportunity.

"Oh, I beg to differ." He accepts the bottle again. "There's a lot going on inside that head of yours."

"And what about you?"

He raises a brow. "What about me?"

"I've been trying to figure *you* out. But I don't know anything about you."

Tonight he's told me more than I learned through any of my research into his background, and even without him explicitly saying it, I know he's seen things that no one should have to. Experienced similar traumas to the ones I have, just in a different setting.

His jaw hardens. "You know enough."

There's a finality in his words.

A definitive statement that says I won't be getting anything else out of him tonight.

That only adds to the frustration growing inside me like a festering weed that couldn't be eradicated by what just happened—no matter how damn good it was.

The night air continues to chill, and the sounds of the animals by the lake fill the silence between us as we pass the bottle back and forth several times.

We allow the tension to rebuild, but this isn't the same

tension that made us lay down on this blanket together. It's the one that's been plaguing us since I first saw him—that lingering question that I can't shake.

Finally, I can't take it anymore. "What are you doing here?"

Gage raises a brow. "The park?"

I shake my head. "No, New Orleans."

"I told you." He stares ahead at the quiet lake, the moon reflecting off its surface giving it an almost ethereal glow. "Work."

"Yeah, but you also told me you're a mechanic, and you can do that anywhere, so why New Orleans?"

He swallows thickly. "I've always loved New Orleans. All of Louisiana, actually—the food, the people, the culture." Finally, he glances over and gives me a little half-grin. "After I retired from the Army, I moved around a lot. Never really had a place to call home. So, when the opportunity presented itself"—he shrugs—"I came here."

I nod slowly. "That makes sense, I guess."

"You guess?"

Fiddling with the edge of the blanket, I attempt to process how I've felt around this man since the moment he appeared in my life. There isn't any reason to believe he isn't exactly who he appears to be, or that he isn't here for exactly why he says he is. Yet, I can't let go of this disquiet in my heart where he's concerned.

"I'm trying really hard to believe that your interest in me is genuine, Gage."

He flinches, as if the statement physically hurts him. "Why wouldn't it be?"

"Because there are a lot of reasons people try to get close to the Hawkes..."

His back stiffens. "Like what?"

"Their money. Their power. Revenge." That word hangs in the air between us like a bomb waiting to hit its mark. "You wouldn't be the first one to show up and weasel your way in with an ulterior motive."

That's what Cass did with Kennedy and it almost destroyed her. It almost destroyed us. Then Allegra did the same with Coen, using their closeness to spy on him for her father, our greatest enemy.

It would be impossible *not* to be suspicious.

The truth is never as simple as people make it out to be.

It's heavily layered.

Predicated on certain beliefs that themselves could be lies.

After everything that's happened, I don't think I have the strength to face the type of betrayal Kennedy did when Cass came clean or Coen suffered when Allegra did.

I don't know that I'd survive it.

Gage is silent for a few seconds before he turns to fully face me. "The only reason I'm sitting on this blanket with you right now, Bishop, is because I want to be. Because I can't seem to stop myself from wanting to be wherever you are."

The sincerity in his words makes my chest tighten violently around my lungs, making it hard to breathe.

People don't talk like that.

Men don't say things like that to women like me.

I've always been the Tomboy, the one kicking asses instead of kissing them. I've never cared what anyone thought about me or what I was doing with my life. I've ignored the dirty looks from other women, the jibes tossed at me from men who were just insecure because I was stronger than them.

I'll forever be thought of as a renegade for not following the path I *should* have, and I've embraced that. This is who I am and always wanted to be.

Yet, what Gage observed so easily is true. Since I became an adult, no one else has ever really taken care of me because I haven't let them.

I've taken care of myself.

Any sexual connections I had couldn't even be called relationships because they were always brief—hot, hard, and fast flings designed to satiate my momentary needs.

Never more than one or two nights in any one bed and never in mine.

Never opening up.

Never revealing anything about myself that matters.

Because ultimately, the life I lead isn't one that leaves room for someone else.

Gage somehow sees that. Yet, he's still here. Where he claims he wants to be. He *sees* me and isn't scared away.

"Can I ask you something?" His voice wavers slightly, and I wait for him to continue. He takes another sip of the wine before he does. "What would've happened the other night if you hadn't been at the club?"

"What do you mean?"

He shrugs. "If you hadn't been there and that creep had grabbed the girl, what would've happened?"

"I guess you would've intervened and our doorman probably would've put you on your ass, the same way I did, and then kicked you out. Unless he saw the whole thing and knew what you were doing. In that case, he would have thanked you and gotten you a free drink."

He nods slowly. "So, either way, everything would have been handled."

"I guess."

"Meaning they *can* operate without you there."

I lock my jaw because I can see *exactly* where this is going, and it is not a journey I particularly care to take right now.

Gage keeps pressing. "You're not supposed to be working right now, are you?"

"No."

"But I caught you walking into the club."

"Yeah…"

"On your night off."

With a huff, I throw up my hands. "What's your point?"

He offers a little mirthless laugh. "My point is that you have to have something in your life outside of your job. I know they're your family and you care about them, but you hire people to do certain tasks. You delegate. You trust them to do it. And if you don't, you're going to burn yourself out or drive yourself mad trying to handle it all on your own."

His words sting more than they should because I know he's right.

It isn't anything I haven't heard from Dad, Mom, Pope, and most of the rest of the family at some point over the last couple of years especially. But it doesn't mean I want to discuss it with a man who is still a stranger to me.

Ugly truths are hard to face, and knowing I'm going to spend my life alone because I don't know *how* to let anyone else in isn't something I'm ready to stare down right now.

I grab my gun, shove it back in the holster, then push up to my feet and release a heavy sigh. "I appreciate the picnic, Gage, but what I don't need is advice on how I live my life."

"Bishop, wait." He holds up a hand. "That's not what I—"

"It is what you meant. I don't know who the hell you think you are, showing up out of nowhere, stalking me, whisking me away on this…"—I spread my hands out over the blanket—"whatever this is. Just to offer commentary on something that you know nothing about."

He opens his mouth to offer another apology or explanation, but I hold up my hand to stop him. If I let him keep going, any lingering good vibes still coursing through me from that orgasm will be long gone.

"I'll see you around."

Because something tells me he isn't going to just walk away like I am right now.

Not until I explicitly ask him to.

And I don't have *that* in me when my legs are still trembling and my body throbbing from release.

I pull my phone from my pocket and consider which one of the Hawkes to call to pick me up so that I'm not stuck on the back of that bike with my arms wrapped around that man tonight.

8

TWO DAYS LATER

BISHOP

The whine of the espresso grinder fills the air as Angelina works on the order for the woman standing at the counter. She's been doing this for so long that she makes drinks without even consciously thinking about it, going through the motions by rote.

Ang says something to the customer that makes her laugh, then pauses and points through the windows, across the street toward Jude's book store. Probably suggesting the woman make her way over there today, too.

Knowing Ang, she's already convinced her to buy something there before she even sets foot inside.

It's easy for her.

Interacting with customers. Offering a quick smile or story. Sending them off with their drinks to Hawke's Novel Idea so Jude has a steady stream of people wandering in his doors and making purchases there, too.

The Grind continues to be one of the city's favorite coffee spots because of all her hard work and ability to remain positive despite all the shit that has come down on her the last couple years. But sitting here, tucked into the back corner, my mind can't help but to drift back to what this place looked like after the bombing.

A black, charred shell.

Utter ruin.

We weren't sure we should rebuild. Whether Ang would even *want* to after what had been done. But she never hesitated in her mission to ensure Hawke's Daily Grind came back better than ever.

It meant starting from scratch. Rebuilding from the foundation up. It meant months and months of hard work and agonizing reminders of what was lost. But through all the sweat and tears, somehow, we did it. *She* brought The Grind back to life...

Only to have the grand reopening destroyed by Satriano's thirst for power.

My eyes naturally dart to the front windows, to the sidewalk where several small tables stand for customers to use when the weather cooperates.

It's a peaceful, pretty spot, and it isn't unusual to see people sitting with a book from Jude's and a mug with a piping hot cappuccino, enjoying the atmosphere of the quaint, historic street the Hawkes carefully created.

Yet, all I can see whenever I look out there is the blood splattered across the sidewalk—Uncle Stone, Isaac, and Kennedy lying there in it...

A shiver rolls down my spine, and I clutch my drink tighter in my hands and take a sip, hoping my favorite tea might warm those parts of me that have suddenly gone ice cold.

But it doesn't.

Nothing can while sitting in this space today.

Satriano's warning the day of the opening that he would be seeing us soon has rarely left my mind since then. The only times I haven't been thinking about it and worrying about what he might be planning were when I was in the ring with Atlas over the past couple weeks…or lying on that blanket with Gage.

It was one fleeting moment when the world seemed to stand still, when I was able to take a deep breath, when I somehow found blissful release in the arms of a man who then so quickly reminded me of why it can't happen again.

Because of what happened here.

Because my job will always take priority or things like bombing and the attack on The Grind will happen *again.*

"Hello? Earth to Bishop." I blink rapidly and turn toward the voice to find Allie looking at me with raised dark brows. "Where the hell were you?"

I shake my head to clear away the lingering memories as she slides into the chair next to me at my usual table, where I can have my back to the wall and keep an eye on everything and everyone in the café. "Sorry, I was just thinking."

She blows out a huff that sends her hair flying off her forehead. "Well, you looked catatonic."

Just lost in the memories…

Apparently, more so than I realized because two familiar faces now stand at the counter talking with Ang.

"When did Kennedy and Jack get here?"

Allie laughs. "Umm. With me." She leans forward slightly to search my face. "Are you feeling okay?"

I turn toward the door to my left that leads to the kitchen and the only other entrance to the café. "Did you come in the through back?"

She nods and I release a little breath of relief.

At least I didn't miss them coming in the front door while staring right at it, but the fact that I didn't see them walk right past me on their way to the counter means I really was out of it.

That can't happen again.

My focus has to stay on the here and now, not trapped in the past.

"Seriously, Bishop, what are you thinking about that has you so distracted?"

I turn toward Allie, who watches me with bright, worried blue eyes.

She's the last one I want to unload my concerns on. After barely surviving the shooting at the condo, and with Pope's "agreement" to help Satriano at the clinic still looming over them, I don't want to cause her any additional turmoil.

Instead, I take a sip of my tea and offer her a smile that I hope conceals the continued maelstrom in my head. "Just work stuff you don't need to worry about."

She narrows her eyes on me. "Do I need to call Pope?"

Shit.

So much for being convincing.

If she thinks I need my doctor baby brother to come check on me, I must be doing a very crappy job at acting normal.

I shake my head. "Don't you dare. Where is he today, anyway?"

It's unusual not to have most of Hawke family members wandering in here at some point in the morning to grab their favorite drinks before heading off to their various offices, but it's been quiet today.

Gabe came through to snag a tray of drinks for everyone who works out of the Club, but I have yet to see anyone else make an appearance for their caffeine fixes.

"It's his day off. He took Ben to the zoo with Isaac, Vivi, and Gio."

"Oh." That explains why Isaac hasn't been in to get drinks for him and Stone. "That sounds like fun. You didn't want to go?"

Allie shakes her head. "I'll be honest"—she gives me an almost embarrassed look—"I needed a day off, too."

I chuckle. "Why do you think I'm never going to have kids?"

"I thought that, too and"—she shrugs—"look what happened."

Point taken.

Allie certainly never planned to get pregnant with Dan's baby.

Or anything that came after it.

His unhinged assault on the condo that almost killed Atlas and Astrid cemented his fate—and further brought Satriano into our lives.

She isn't referring to that last part, but it's impossible for me to separate the idea of having children from all the turmoil that has followed the ones born to the Hawkes.

When Kennedy and Jack approach with their mugs, sliding into the two remaining seats at the table, Kennedy grins at us. "What are we discussing? What's the hot gossip?"

Allie sighs, rolling her eyes dramatically. "Nothing. Bishop's distracted with"—she does air quotes—"'work' and is being boring."

"Gee, thanks."

Kennedy narrows her eyes on me. By far the shrewdest of the Hawke women of this generation, she knows what it means when I'm "distracted by work" and is the least likely to let Allie's comment go. "What do you have to be worried about? The opening went off without a hitch."

I give her a look that tells her to drop it because getting into the status of everything Gabe, Dad, Luca, and I have been doing to try to hunt down Satriano and this Michael McDonald person would ruin what should be a nice, relaxing morning for all of us.

She purses her bright red lips together with an exaggerated huff, then brings her coffee to them and takes a sip. Which offers me the perfect opportunity to segue to another topic of conversation.

One far safer—I hope.

I turn my attention to Jack, who hasn't been out much since her release from the hospital—due to her morning sickness and Isaac's incessant worry about her. He would keep her locked away in their house until the day that baby is born, if he could.

God knows he might have tried if Jack weren't so formidable herself.

"How're you feeling?"

She gives me a tight smile and motions toward her mug. "Well, I'm drinking decaf tea instead of my usual triple shot latte."

I offer a sympathetic look. "I don't think I could survive without caffeine."

With my lack of sleep getting worse and worse as the days continue to drag on with no resolution to any of our problems, copious amounts of caffeine seems to be the only thing keeping me going.

Jack sighs and takes a sip of whatever Angelina made for her. "I mean, it's not bad, but I could really use the caffeine most days. It's hard enough chasing Vivi and Gio now that he's trying to walk without dealing with morning sickness on top of it."

I can only imagine...

My own stomach turns just thinking about it, and I take a sip of my tea as Astrid hustles in through the door and beelines straight for us.

"Hey!" She snags a chair from one of the other tables and drags it over. "Sorry I'm a little late."

Kennedy zeroes in on her. "Where were you?"

Astrid's back stiffens. "Um..." She glances away, waving to Ang behind the counter for her drink. "Just preparing for a tutoring session later."

When she looks back at the table, it's clear she's lying.

Astrid has never been very good at covering her emotions, and the way she squirms confirms all our assessments. She forces a smile. "What're we talking about?"

Allie offers an exaggerated sigh. "Nothing."

The annoyance in her voice makes me fight a grin, but when Astrid's gaze zeroes in on me, my hackles immediately go up.

"Then how about we talk about the hottie who showed up at the gym the other day and clearly had something going on with Bishop?"

Shit.

She's clearly deflecting attention away from herself by throwing me under the bus.

I glare at her as everyone else zeroes in on me with intense focus.

Allie squeezes my arm. "Who?"

Kennedy drums her nails on her mug. "Spill."

Jack nods her agreement. "Yeah, spill."

I swallow the lump in my throat, then clear it and try to appear unaffected as I offer a half-grin. "He's nobody."

Astrid chuckles. "Bullshit. I saw the way that man looked at you."

"Really?" I do my best to sound confused when I damn well know *exactly* how he looked at me. "How did he *look* at me?"

She grins ear to ear as I take a sip of my tea. "Like he wanted to eat you up."

I practically choke on the hot liquid in my mouth and cough but manage to swallow it before I shake my head. "That *isn't* happening."

Then again, I never thought I'd let him shove his hand down my pants in the middle of a public park, either.

Jack shakes her head. "Oh no, you're not getting off that easily. Tell us about this guy."

Allie nods, and Kennedy drums her long nails on the top of the table.

"Don't make me use interrogation techniques on you." She motions toward Jack with a red-tipped nail. "Between what she knows when it comes to torture and what I can do, we'll get it out of you."

They aren't joking.

Unfortunately.

When it comes to getting information from someone that they want kept secret, both Kennedy and Jack are experts.

I release a little sigh and lean back in my chair, running my hand across my face. "He's just this guy who showed up at the club one night. He helped when a dirtbag grabbed one of the dancers, and I may have misread the situation and put him in a kimura on the ground."

Kennedy snort-laughs and presses a hand over her mouth, but Jack, Astrid, and Allie don't bother to conceal their humor at my expense.

Allie barely manages to control her laughter long enough to suck in a breath. "And how did he respond to that?"

My cheeks heat because I could feel his response against my thigh as I straddled him on the Hawkeye Club floor after he turned over under me. "Surprisingly positively."

Astrid nods. "Apparently, because he showed up at the gym like, a few days later."

Jack's brow furrows. "Looking for her?"

Looking for trouble.

Astrid shrugs. "He said he wanted to come spar with Atlas, but the way he looked at Bishop when she walked in, I'm pretty sure he was hoping she'd show up."

"That wasn't why he was there."

And that sounded a little too defensive.

But I'm not used to having the inquisition directed at me. I'm never the source of the family gossip.

I much prefer being on the giving end than the receiving one.

Astrid settles back and shakes her head. "I'm not so sure about that."

I wave them off. "It doesn't matter. There's nothing going on with me and Gage."

Jack leans closer, seemingly entranced by the info, her complaints about morning sickness and lack of caffeine long forgotten. "His name is Gage?"

"Yep."

Kennedy grins, her eyes practically glowing with curiosity. "What does he look like?"

Fucking hell.

Fate must be fucking with me today, because no sooner does she ask the question than the man himself walks through the front door of The Grind.

GAGE

The inside of The Grind is exactly what I would've expected it to look like from what I could see from the street. Bright, airy, artfully decorated with local New Orleans decor that gives it a relaxed yet still upscale feel that makes it inviting.

A dark-haired woman bustles around behind the counter making drinks for a few people waiting by the register, but I only glance at her briefly before I zero in on my reason for coming today—the woman sitting at the back corner table with her eyes locked on me looking like she just saw a ghost.

Okay, maybe not *so inviting...*

At least, not to me.

I had hoped giving Bishop a few days to cool off after the way she left me in the park might have earned me a warmer welcome, but apparently she's still pissed and thinks I was trying to somehow judge her life when all I wanted was for her to take a step back and do something for herself.

Burnout is very real, and Bishop is approaching it fast.

It didn't take long for me to see that, and I can only imagine her family has noticed it and said something, too. Which is likely why she reacted that way the other night.

When something has become your entire life and the people you care about tell you that you have to take a step back, it's hard. When someone you barely know tells you the same thing, it's infuriating.

I know that from personal experience…

All the women around the table with Bishop turn to look at me as I move farther into the café, several sets of eyes widening. The blonde sitting next to her leans over and whispers something that has Bishop blinking and shaking her head slightly before she pushes up out of her seat.

I don't even make it to the counter before she intercepts me.

She deftly blocks me from advancing any farther, setting her booted feet wide to solidify her stance and make herself more difficult to move—as if I'd even try. "What the hell are you doing here?"

Spreading open my hands, I glance around at the customers and raise a brow. "Getting a cup of coffee?"

Bishop scowls, crossing her arms over her chest and puffing it out in a probably unconscious move to make herself look bigger as I tower over her by at least a foot.

She may not have size, but what she lacks there, she makes up for in tenacity and strength. This woman could take down a man bigger than me and can absolutely handle herself in *any* situation without any help. I don't have a single doubt about that after seeing her in action, and right now, it looks like she wants to go to full-on battle with me in her cousin's coffee shop.

"You can get coffee anywhere, Gage."

I grin as I step even closer, purposely invading her personal space to try to rattle her. "I can, but the thing is, I've been looking for this woman who seems to be avoiding me."

Her shoulders stiffen, and her eyes dart away toward the counter. "I'm not avoiding you."

"Oh, really? Then *look* at me."

Her gaze snaps back to meet mine, and I can see how much willpower it takes for her to actually keep it there. She so *badly* wants to run from me again, but lucky for her, I'm not afraid of a good chase, and she has nowhere to go in here without making a scene.

"You ran away from me the other night..."

She swallows thickly. "I did not."

"You *did*." I keep my voice low, not wanting to draw any additional attention to us when we already have such a huge audience. "And I get it, I really do. You didn't like the fact that I called you out on a truth you're not ready to face."

That fiery anger that seems to act like an aphrodisiac for me flares in her eyes. "Who the hell do you think you are, Gage?"

I close the distance between us and grab her arm, knowing full well it could be a bad choice, considering how easily she put my face on the floor at the club. "I'm the man who wants what's best for you, who wants to see more of you, who wants to get to know you better, who wants *you,* but you keep shutting me out."

And saying all that is probably a *really* bad choice on my part.

But it's out there now, hanging in the air between us and thickening it.

Before Bishop can say anything, the woman from behind the counter appears beside us, grinning ear to ear. Out of the corner of my eye, I catch her eyes dipping to where my hand is wrapped around Bishop's bicep. "Hi, I'm Angie. And you are?"

I keep my gaze locked on Bishop, waiting to see how she's

going to react—like the hellcat I know lies beneath the beautiful surface who will flip me on my ass and kick me out, or the woman who laid on that blanket with me the other night in the park and let a crack form in this wall surrounding her for one brief moment.

A second passes.

Another.

When she finally tears her eyes away from mine to look at the woman, I allow myself to do the same.

She watches us with wide eyes.

"Hi, I'm Gage."

Her gaze darts down to where my hand still rests on Bishop's arm, and then she shoots an inquisitive look toward Bishop, likely wondering who the hell she's allowing to touch her like this.

Before she's forced to offer an explanation, I grin at Angie. "I'm a friend of Bishop's."

Friend.

I despise that word.

Not because I don't want to be her friend.

Because it makes what I feel when I'm around her sound so trivial when it's anything but.

If that's all it were, I wouldn't be thinking about her all the time. I wouldn't be spending my nights remembering how amazing kissing her was or how fucking incredible her cunt contracting around my fingers felt, not to mention how she tasted...

Angie's gaze widens slightly along with her smile. "Oh. Wonderful. Can I get you a drink?"

"I'd love a triple shot of espresso."

Her cousin raises a brow. "You want anything in that?"

I shake my head. "Just the caffeine, thanks."

Something tells me I'm going to need it to handle the showdown Bishop seems intent to have.

Angie continues to grin at me, darting her gaze between us a few times before she hustles back around the counter to make my drink.

As soon as she's sure Ang is far enough away again, Bishop leans in toward me. "You get your drink, and then, you get out of here."

I laugh at how deeply serious she sounds, the threat underlying her words. "How come? What if I want to sit and enjoy the space and the pleasant company?"

She scowls again.

Good God, does she look cute when she does that.

For some reason, the more she tries to pretend that whatever this is between us doesn't exist, the more I want to prove to her that it does. Seeing that blaze inside of her ignite each time I nudge her is enough to keep me addicted to the burn of it.

Astrid waves us over to the table Bishop vacated, the big grin spread across her face enough to say that at least *someone* is happy to see me.

Even if it is the wrong woman.

"Your cousin is waving us to the table."

Bishop glances over her shoulder. "Fuck." The word rushes out on a heavy breath filled with the same annoyance as the look she gives me when she turns back. "Come on. But you're leaving as soon as you get your drink."

I release her arm and hold up my hands in surrender. "Whatever you say, Hellcat."

She hisses. "Don't call me that."

Chuckling low, I follow her to the table, completely aware of how all the women seated there assess me the entire way. Their gazes sweep over me, from my boots up my jeans, T-shirt, leather jacket and over my hair that I'm sure is disheveled after wearing my helmet on the ride here.

Bishop reaches her seat and retakes it, leaving me standing facing an entire table of Hawke women. "Girls, this is Gage.

Gage, these are my cousins. Allie, Kennedy, Jack, and you know Astrid. The one behind the counter making your drink is Allie's sister, Angelina."

I smile at all of them, meeting each of their inquisitive gazes, and watch as several try to fight a grin. "Nice to meet all of you, and to see you again, Astrid."

Kennedy leans her elbows on the table, resting her face in her manicured hands, her bright red lips curled in a devious grin. "So, Gage, how do you know Bishop?"

Bishop tosses her a look that could kill—something I'm quite sure Kennedy has seen often given the way she completely ignores it.

"We met at the club."

Jack snorts, eyeing me with cool calculation. "From what I hear, she kicked your ass."

They share a laugh at my expense—all of them except Bishop, who looks ready to either slaughter them with her bare hands or slide under the table to hide.

Maybe both.

I run my hand through my hair and nod. "That she did. And I told her how impressive it was."

Bishop's back stiffens again, that guard of hers seated firmly in place.

Apparently, my compliment didn't land the way I hoped it would.

She's so on edge with me here that she can't even relax enough to accept it for what it was.

Astrid nods. "I'm sure it was. You should see her in the ring. Are you going to come back to the gym?"

"I plan to. Hopefully in the next few days." *If Bishop doesn't kill me first.* "I'll text your brother."

She grins. "I'm sure he'd love to have you around more. Finding someone he can actually spar with has been difficult lately."

I chuckle, remembering what it felt like to get struck by Atlas "The Hurricane" Hawke even when we weren't going anywhere near all-out. "I bet. And I have the bruises to prove that even in sparring mode and not full strength, the man is dangerous."

The Hawke women all nod their agreement, save for Bishop, who sits absolutely still, as if she's holding her breath and just waiting for this to be over and for me to leave.

Allie watches me carefully. "So, other than kick your ass, what do you and my cousin do together?"

Kennedy almost chokes on her coffee with her sputtered laugh, and Bishop appears ready to leap across the table at both of her cousins when Angie arrives carrying my drink.

"Here you go, Gage. A black triple espresso."

"Thank you." I accept the travel cup from her. "How much do I owe you?"

She waves me off, squeezing my arm gently. "It's on the house." A knowing smirk tugs at her lips. "For a *friend* of Bishop's..."

I take a sip of the scalding-hot liquid, the bitterness matching the feeling rolling off Bishop right now.

The good-natured ribbing her family is giving her only seems to have put Bishop in an even worse mood, and I can see why she wanted me to get out of The Grind. She knew this was coming and was trying to intervene before they could get their claws into me—or her.

She glances up at me with a fake smile plastered on her face. "Well, you have your drink..."

Is she really going to tell me to get lost with her family sitting here?

I smirk at her and open my mouth to tell her I think I'll stay for a bit, when the bells above the door jingle.

Bishop's head whips that direction and those bourbon eyes darken immediately, icing over as her entire body tenses. Her hand slides down toward what I'm sure is the same gun concealed at her hip that she had when she was with me in the park.

My gut tightens, and I turn to see what has her reaching for a weapon as a man with slicked-back silver hair wearing a perfectly tailored suit walks in and zeroes right in on the entire table of Hawkes with a smile that's equal parts charming and menacing.

9

BISHOP

There isn't any time to act.

No opportunity to get the girls out through the back door and to safety.

He's already here.

Already approaching us.

The Devil in the flesh.

Everyone at the table tenses as my hand curls around my gun at my hip, concealed by my jacket.

Gage stands just to my right, directly in the line of fire, completely oblivious to the fact that the man approaching us might be one of the most dangerous people on Earth.

Because he certainly doesn't look it.

With his perfectly cut and styled silver hair, immaculately tailored Italian suit, and matching shoes the gleam under the lights of The Grind, he looks like he should be on the cover of a magazine.

But I know what lies underneath the slick exterior.

Pure fucking evil.

The Devil in disguise who uses his charm to hide his sinister intent.

Someone who's willing to do whatever it takes to get what he wants.

And what he wants is New Orleans—and more.

He came here on a revenge mission against the Hawkes, and he's stayed to cement himself as the most powerful crime boss in the Gulf Coast. The only thing standing in his way now is our refusal to bend the knee.

I grit my teeth, fighting the urge to pull my weapon and point it at him immediately, but a quick scan of The Grind tells me it would only cause panic and hysteria for the customers milling about and sitting at various tables casually enjoying a lazy morning.

Something we definitely don't want.

After the explosion and shooting here, it's taken Ang far too long to get things back to running normally. We don't need to remind the public that this place has been attacked twice, or they're going to steer clear of it.

Why tempt fate a third time?

That would ruin her business and permanently destroy her greatest joy in life—running this place.

I can't do that to her, no matter how strongly all my instincts tell me to just *end* him now.

Satriano inclines his head at Angelina, who stands completely dumbstruck behind the counter clutching a coffee mug in her hand as he moves toward the table.

I keep my palm wrapped around the gun grip—just in case he leaves me no other option but to pull the trigger my finger has been itching to for so long.

When Satriano finally stops directly behind Jack and Kennedy and beside Gage, I hold my breath, staring down the man who has caused nothing but pain and anguish for this family for so long.

He offers a warm smile that anyone who didn't know what he was might believe is genuine, but I see the monster that hides beneath it. "Well, if it isn't the Hawke ladies, looking lovely as ever."

His smooth, slightly accented voice floats over us, and any tension that we were all holding only increases ten-fold.

Astrid goes ghostly ashen, her hands fisting on the tabletop. Kennedy turns slightly and glares at him with a stiff spine, her knuckles white with her death grip on her mug. Jack does the same, one hand sliding below the table to rest over her belly protectively.

Of anyone at the table, Allie knows him best. Or at least *knew* him. Back when he was merely Damon, before she had Benjamin, when she was working here and he was still concealing his real identity.

He offers her a soft smile. "Alessandra..." Her name rolls off his tongue so beautifully that it almost sounds like poetry. "*Bellezza,* I do hope your *bambino* is doing well."

She swallows thickly, casting a glance in my direction as if to ask, "What the fuck do I tell this man?" but I don't have the slightest clue what the right move is when it comes to Satriano.

He did step in to help rescue her, Benjamin, Atlas, and Astrid from Daniele Roselli when he came for them, but it came at a price to Pope, one he still pays. It leaves Allie and Pope in a strange and tenuous position with this man that there isn't any clear way to handle. Or a way out of. At least, not yet.

Finally, Allie gives him a curt nod. "He's good."

"*Eccellente*! I haven't needed to call on Pope recently"—he grins—"knock on wood...that's the expression you Americans use, isn't it? Well, it's such a relief to know that I can, at any given moment, and any time of night, and he'll come running to assist."

It isn't a compliment toward my brother or his medical skills.

It's another reminder that he has an invisible hold on Pope, and that he's going to pull on it if he needs to in order to remind him, and all of us, who is in control.

Damiano's eyes sweep over the table again, lingering on Astrid for a few seconds with a tension at the corners of his mouth before his focus moves to Jack and Kennedy. "It's nice to see that you ladies are all doing well."

Kennedy snorts. "No thanks to you, asshole."

She doesn't bother to say it under her breath, just looks the man dead in his eyes as she throws her contempt for him squarely in his face.

I cringe.

Of course she would antagonize this monster.

Kennedy's spitfire attitude has always served her well in her role at The Hawke Enterprises office and as the heir apparent to running everything one day, but when we're facing a man like Satriano, it's more like she's poking a bear who could snap at us any second.

But he doesn't react, just continues to smile at her. "And how is Cass?"

He asks the question so casually in response to her ire, but we all know what it really is: a reminder that Cass betrayed him, that he's on the top of his shit list and that all has most certainly *not* been forgiven between them.

Kennedy plasters on the fakest smile I've ever seen, batting her thick, black lashes at him. "Better than you're going to be in a minute when Bishop gets done with you."

Fuck.

The man's gaze flicks to me and he grins, then his eyes sweep up to Gage standing beside him and just behind me. "And who's your friend?"

Shit.

Gage's hand brushes my shoulder, as if he's trying to give me a physical reminder that he's backing me up.

He may not know who Satriano is or *why*, but he senses the problem without me even having to say a word or look at him.

"None of your business." It's the only answer I can give, because the last thing I want to do is drag Gage into our shit. "What do you want, Satriano?"

The fucker smiles broadly, motioning toward the mugs on the table casually. "I came in for one of those wonderful cappuccinos Angelina makes." He glances over at her behind the counter where she stands stock-still, watching everything unfold with sheer terror racing through her gaze. "Ang, *principessa*, can I get my regular?"

Her hand trembles as she sets down the drink she was working on and gives him a sharp nod. She watches us out of the corner of her eye, occasionally glancing toward the front windows that we all know Jude can see straight through from their condo or the book shop.

If he saw Satriano, he will have alerted the family by now.

Which means the cavalry is on the way.

Unless Jude has his head buried in a book or in his computer, working on his own, or is busy with a customer and missed the arrival of our greatest enemy.

When Satriano turns back to me, he crosses his hands behind his back in a casual move, but all it does is expose the grip of the gun at his hip underneath that perfectly tailored jacket. "I've missed this place." Another sly smile spreads across his face. "Now that I'm back in town, this was my first stop."

Because he wanted to make the threat to the most vulnerable members of the family.

He wanted to prove that he could get to us.

And he did.

Far too easily.

He just waltzed straight in.

The security personnel who escorted all the girls here today remained in their vehicles on the street since I'm in here to guard them, and as I glance at the glass windows lining the front, I can see them watching everything unfold, debating if they should come in or if I have everything handled.

You should have handled it before he even got in *here.*

But I know why they didn't.

The same reason I give them an almost imperceptible shake of my head now.

I don't want to escalate anything, and they didn't want to draw on him with customers around and risk a shootout.

But my hand doesn't leave my gun.

I stare up at him, doing my best to keep my voice level. "Well, as soon as you have your drink, you can leave."

His silver brows rise. "Speaking of drinks, did you receive my gift?"

Kennedy scowls at him. "Kind of cheaped out, didn't you?"

Jesus...

Stop antagonizing him!

I want to scream it at her, but I grit my teeth instead to keep from doing just that.

He chuckles low. "I didn't realize you had such expensive taste. Next time I'll try to do better."

"There won't be a next time." My warning comes out as cold as ice, and his hard, dark eyes shift to meet mine. "You're going to walk out of here, and you're going to leave us alone."

Gage's hand brushes my shoulder again in warning, but I've already said it. It's already hanging out there, and I didn't bother to veil *my* threat, either.

At this point, the game has gotten old and stopped being fun a long time ago, at least from our side. Satriano appears to still enjoy it, though.

He merely smiles again. "Bishop, I've always appreciated how unwavering you are in your desire to protect your family. It's admirable, really."

His gaze flicks to Astrid again and lingers there, and I know what he's thinking. That I failed that night, when she and Atlas were shot, when Allie and her son and Kennedy were all put at risk. How ultimately, it was his intervention that got Astrid and Atlas the help that they needed before they bled out on that warehouse floor because he distracted Dan enough to allow Gabe, Dad, and I to do what we do best and take out the fuckers holding them one by one.

I grit my teeth, trying desperately not to say something that's going to antagonize the man even *more*, and Ang walks over with a to-go cup in her trembling hands and holds it out for him without a word.

Satriano offers her a soft smile and takes it, bringing it to his lips for a sip. "Mmm. Just as I remembered it. *Grazie*, Angelina." He inclines his head toward the table. "It was lovely to see you, ladies. Please give my best to the rest of the Hawkes and let them know I'm back in town."

His gaze sweeps over each and every one of us, pausing on Gage for a second before he turns and walks out as casually as he walked in.

Satriano is the king of making veiled threats, of using simple pleasantries to prove his point, and that's just what he did during the entire conversation.

Anyone seated around us in The Grind would have been completely oblivious to what was happening at our table, that we were seconds away from potentially exchanging gunfire with the man they undoubtedly all thought was incredibly stylish and handsome.

I watch the door close behind him, and our men on the sidewalk step back, giving him a wide berth.

He walks to the curb and climbs into the back of a black SUV that pulls away the moment he's inside.

Gage's hand slides fully across my shoulder, squeezing it tightly. "Who the fuck was that?"

"None of your business."

"Bishop..."

I whip my head around and glare at him. "It's none of your *concern*, Gage."

Not now.

Not ever.

This is Hawke family business.

I look to all the girls, who all appear shaken—none more so than Astrid, who trembles in her chair. "We need to go. All of us." Glancing over at Angie, I give her a tight smile. "Ang, shut down early. It's time for a family meeting."

GAGE

I tighten my grip on Bishop's shoulder as she tries to stand, keeping her down in her seat. If I don't make her stay for one second and explain what's going on, she's going to shut me out completely like she already attempted to more than once.

"Wait, Bishop. What the fuck just happened?"

She glances up at me, her eyes drifting to where my hand rests as if she's debating physically removing it with force. "I suggest you take your hand off me, unless you want me to break your arm."

Fuck.

The look she's giving me tells me it isn't an empty threat.

This isn't the time to test that theory, either.

I slowly withdraw my hold on her as all the women at the table rise to their feet, murmuring to each other in hushed tones I can't hear, but the panic and distress etched on their faces is unmistakable.

Angelina and Allie begin making their way around the café, letting the customers know they're going to be closing down unexpectedly, while the rest of their cousins pull out their phones and start making calls.

"Who was that guy?"

Bishop pushes to her feet, only now pulling her hand from her gun. "None of your business."

"Like hell it isn't."

I didn't mean to say that so loudly, or for it to sound so possessive or so much like an order when Bishop isn't the type of woman who appreciates them, but it's too late to take it back now.

She glares at me, her tight jaw working, but I don't back away, holding my ground and making it impossible for her to move from the table without physically moving *me*.

"It *is* my business if someone's threatening you, Bishop."

And what just went down was *clearly* a threat.

Under all the niceties and forced smiles—from everyone except Kennedy and Bishop—it was one of the most tense standoffs I've ever been a part of. And that's saying a lot considering the ones I've had in my career.

Bishop's fists tighten at her sides, her dark eyes carrying so many different emotions: hatred, annoyance, and a spark of something else I saw that night in the park that she doesn't want to admit.

Fear.

"Are you in danger?"

She releases a huffed little laugh that carries no humor in it. "We're always in danger, Gage. That's the whole fucking point."

"The point of what?"

"My job." She throws up her hands. "Which you keep pointing out I spend too much time obsessing over. But that"—she points to the front door—"is why I have to do my job twenty-four-seven, because at any minute, a threat could just waltz through the fucking door."

"Why didn't you shoot him?"

She recoils slightly. "Are you fucking nuts? This is Angelina's business. And her boyfriend has one right across the street. It's already been blown up and shot to hell. I'm not going to pull my gun in here and shoot that man just because I want to and he deserves it. It would bring a whole hell of a lot worse down on us."

Worse.

Bishop is already walking the razor's edge of burnout trying to protect her family.

The idea of *worse* makes me want to sweep in and take her away somewhere that she can't be touched by any of it ever again. Where she never has to look over her shoulder or worry about protecting so many backs.

I watch the Hawke women cluster together at the counter with Angelina, whispering and glancing toward us and the street. The undercurrent of anxiety rolls off them as customers slowly file out, leaving the once-lively and happy place as quiet as a tomb.

It isn't my place to intervene.

But I also can't just walk away after witnessing that.

How the hell could I?

Scrubbing my hands over my face, I release a sigh. "So, what are you going to do?"

Bishop crosses her arms over her chest. "What do you mean?"

"I mean *now*."

For a moment, it doesn't look like she's going to answer me, but she finally relaxes slightly and nods toward the girls. "Going to go meet with the rest of the family and figure out what the fuck to do next."

"And push me away."

Her brow furrows. "What?"

"You're going to push me away even more now, right? Because you don't want me involved in whatever the hell that was. You're going to use it as an excuse to keep me at arm's length like you were already doing because you were fucking scared."

She opens and closes her mouth a few times, gaping at me, and maybe it isn't the time or place to push her on this, but I can see the truth in her eyes even as she tries to lie through her teeth.

"I'm not pushing you away."

"Bullshit." I raise a brow. "You *literally* ran the other night."

She squeezes her eyes closed for a second and shakes her head. "I don't have time to have this argument with you right now."

When she reopens her eyes, they hold renewed determination and she pushes at my chest to move me out of the way. Of course, I could stand my ground and challenge her further, refuse to budge an inch the same way she is, but that wouldn't get me anywhere. Certainly not where I want to be with her.

I allow her to push me back a few steps, giving her space to move around the table and over to her family. She whispers something to them, and Angelina locks the front door, staring out across the street toward the book shop.

"I have to call and let Jude know what happened…"

The fear and worry in her voice make it crack slightly, and Bishop walks over to her and wraps an arm around her back, urging her away from the front windows.

And now that they're all together, they close ranks completely.

Shutting me out.

Preventing me from hearing what any of them are saying as several of them text or whisper on their phones.

It feels like a massive intrusion watching them handle their family business, but even worse, witnessing their panic and fear and not being able to do something about it makes me feel useless in a way I haven't in a long time.

I scrub my hands over my face and shove them back through my hair.

Fuck this.

Of all the stupid things I've done in my life, stalking over to Bishop right now might be at the top of the list, but I do it anyway and grab her arm, tugging her away from the girls.

"Let me help you."

There isn't any way to keep the plea from my voice. No way to hide how desperately I need her to say yes.

She locks her gaze with me, holding it steady. "You don't want to be a part of this fight, Gage."

"You've seen me in the ring. I like to fight."

That's one thing she absolutely should have learned about me in the brief time we've known each other.

I will *not* back down from a challenge or a threat.

Bishop shakes her head, sending her braids flying over her shoulders with the sheer force of how hard she does it. "This isn't about wanting to fight, it's about needing to, and that's a totally different thing. You don't *need* to."

"I've been in more firefights than you can count. I've taken bullets and been blown up on two different continents..."

She recoils slightly at my confession, but I'm not telling her this to brag or try to somehow get her to feel sorry for me. I'm telling her so she understands that I *won't* just walk away from this.

"I'm not afraid of the danger, Bishop, but I am afraid that eventually it's going to crush you; this need to be the one who solves the problem and protects everyone. It's going to get you killed."

Her jaw hardens, and she wears the same look she did the other night before she left me alone on that blanket, but Astrid steps over to us.

"Sorry to butt in to what is clearly a private conversation, but maybe he's right, Bishop."

Her head rolls toward her cousin. "What?"

Astrid shrugs. "Maybe you should consider bringing him in to meet your dad and Gabe. To join the security team."

Bishop doesn't even take a second to consider the suggestion. "He has a job."

Her cousin glances at me. "What do you do?"

"I'm a mechanic, but I own my own shop. I make my own hours. If you need help, let me help."

For the love of God, let me help.

I may not be able to convince Bishop on my own, but with Astrid standing right here, clearly on board with bringing me into the fold, it has to be harder for her to say no.

Bishop weighs the options for a moment before shaking her head. "I don't like it."

I dip my head low, close to her ear, so Astrid won't be privy to what I'm about to say to her. "Of course you don't, because it means you're going to have to be around me even more, but put that aside and think about your family. Think about what having someone else who's trained and skilled on your team could do for you."

It's the best argument I can make.

Simple.

Straight to the point.

And maybe a little underhanded to suggest that not bringing me on would negatively affect her ability to protect her family.

But at this point, I'm willing to say whatever I need to in order to get Bishop to listen to reason.

I know the second she concedes because her shoulders slump slightly.

"This is a *maybe*." She holds up a finger. "And don't get any ideas about what it means *beyond* that." *Meaning us.* "I'll take you to meet my father and everyone else and they'll check you out and make their decision about you."

I hold up my hands. "I'm an open book. And it feels like you've already made your decision about me and it's to cut me out."

Her mouth opens and closes, like she's not sure how to respond when her cousins are standing within ear shot. Instead, she just shakes her head. "We're not doing this now." She motions to the girls. "Let's go."

"Where are we going?"

She holds up her phone. "Emergency family meeting. And I'm warning you, this is going to be tense."

"I can handle tense."

Her brow furrows. "Are you sure?"

"I handled you, didn't I?"

The heat that flares in her gaze almost overpowers the glower she tosses my way before she brushes past me, intentionally bumping her shoulder into mine.

I can't fight a smirk that Kennedy, Jack, Astrid, and Allie all return as they brush past me to follow Bishop out the back of The Grind.

They know I won that battle, but it feels like the war is only just beginning.

10

GAGE

I pull up behind Bishop's SUV at the curb, tug off my helmet, and stare up at one of the most beautiful houses I've ever seen.

Actually, *house* isn't even the right word for it.

Nestled in the heart of the Garden District, surrounded by the wealthiest homes in the entire city, the massive Italianate mansion could grace the covers of an architectural magazine. With a waist-high iron fence circling the property, the imposing white house towers above us, a stunning and intimidating monument to taste...and *money*.

Lots of it.

These people have the kind of money most can't even fathom.

Dad used to call it "*fuck you money*" when I was growing up, and his voice always held a hint if disdain for those who possessed it. Not because he was jealous. More due to the fact that he firmly believed money was the root of all evil in this world.

Though, I haven't seen that with the Hawkes, from what little interaction I've had with them. If anything, they seem down to earth despite their wealth, and are even known for giving millions to charity through the Hawke Foundation annually.

If he had met them, I wonder if he would have held those views.

Bishop steps from her SUV out onto the road, and I climb off my bike and approach her, still staring up at the house.

"Whose place is this?"

She doesn't even look at me when she answers, just slams her door and presses the button on her fob to lock it. "Cass and Kennedy and their daughter Charlotte."

The tension radiating off her only increases as she stalks through the iron gate, up the stone walkway, and toward the massive front door without glancing back a single time to see if I'm following her.

As far as she's concerned, I could have gotten lost on the drive over from The Grind, and she would have been happy about it. Her concession made because of Astrid's suggestion doesn't mean she's fully on board with having me here.

She doesn't like the idea of me helping with whatever's going on with the Hawkes, but I can't just stand by and pretend none of this bothers me.

Seeing how upset she is.

Witnessing how hard she's working.

Knowing that she's going to burn herself out if something doesn't change.

It all drives me forward, even if her entire body language is telling me to get lost. Before she reaches the door, I grab her arm, halting her progress.

I haul her back against me and lower my lips to the shell of her ear, holding her tightly. "Please don't waste your energy fighting me when you clearly have a bigger adversary to focus all this animosity on."

She doesn't really hate me.

We both know that.

The icy front she's blasting me with is just another defense mechanism she's using to keep me at arm's length. To prevent me from getting close.

But it isn't going to work.

Eventually, she'll stop trying, but until that moment comes, all I can do is keep reminding her that I am not the enemy.

Her body relaxes slightly in my hold, but it's the only hint I receive that suggests I may have gotten through to her. Because in the next moment, she's wrenching herself free and opening the door. She steps inside without any announcement of our presence or invitation to me, but I follow anyway, nudging the door closed behind me.

The grand foyer of the mansion is exactly how I imagined it would look. Glistening marble, filigree wallpaper, fresh flowers on a small table, and my eyes immediately cast upward toward the chandelier that hangs in the center of two spiral staircases that lead to the second floor.

Given the excited menagerie of voices coming from our left, the rest of the Hawkes must already be here.

The girls all left The Grind well before us, with Bishop taking great care to ensure their security teams had them protected for the change of venue before she was willing to leave with me.

Now those men patrol the outside of the house, offering at least a modicum of comfort that we'll all be guarded while this meeting takes place.

That doesn't seem to help Bishop relax at all though. She steps into a large living room filled with so many people I can't even take them all in.

All the conversations slowly taper off as the Hawkes turn to face her.

And me.

Dozens of sets of eyes roam over me, taking me in and sizing me up the same way Bishop did the first time she saw me. The women all appear surprised and interested, giving me at least somewhat friendly smiles, but the men just seem utterly pissed that Bishop has brought an outsider to a Hawke Family meeting that was clearly meant to be private.

I've been in some *very* uncomfortable places before, but this feels different. Somehow more dangerous, even though there isn't a single gun pointed at me.

At least, not one I can see.

Bishop glances at me before facing all of them. "This is Gage Newhart. He stepped in to help one of the girls at the club recently."

Some of the tension in the room evaporates, but it's still there, simmering beneath the surface. They've all no doubt heard about what went down that night, which at least gives some explanation for my presence.

"Astrid thought he might be able to help with security, given what just went down today."

The man seated in a plush leather chair in front of the fireplace with jet-black hair graying around his temples who I instantly recognize as Savage Hawke inclines his head toward me. "I hear you met Satriano."

I rub my hand against the back of my neck and nod. "If that was the guy at The Grind today, then yeah."

"Well"—he locks his icy blue gaze on me—"he isn't exactly our favorite person."

A sardonic biting laugh comes from Gabe Anderson—Savage's business partner and best friend, and Atlas and Astrid's father. Though I've seen him at the club more than once, I've never actually spoken to him. "That's a fucking understatement. The man is a menace, one who continues to cut at us like a thorn in our side."

Bishop's shoulders tense, as if she's preparing herself for another showdown with him even though it's been an hour since he walked away from The Grind. "And now he's back in town."

Gabe nods, rubbing a hand across his stubbled jaw. "Which means things are about to get very interesting, and not in a good way."

The man I instantly recognize as Bishop's father approaches and holds out his hand that's goddamn near twice the size of mine. "Saint Clarke. It's nice to meet you."

His harsh grip suggests that he's making an unspoken statement that has nothing to do with the Satriano situation and everything to do with how near I'm standing to his daughter.

Shit.

I hadn't mentally prepared for "meeting the parents" when I offered my assistance, but since her father runs all the security for Hawke Enterprises, it only makes sense that he would be here tonight, front and center of this family gathering.

"You too, sir."

His brow furrows, eyes a shade darker than his daughter's assessing me shrewdly. "What sort of experience do you have?"

I glance around the room and find Atlas, who is the only one of the Hawke men who offers me a genuine smile.

"Well, he can sure throw a fuckin' right hook." He chuckles and pushes to his feet from where he was seated on one of the couches to make his way over and shake my hand and slap me on the shoulder. "We sparred the other day. He fought WCAP."

Saint's eyes widen slightly. "Really?"

I nod, trying not to squirm under the scrutiny of every single person in the room who seems to be taking stock of me —a few who appear to find me wanting if their faces are telling me anything.

"If you were military, then you know how to handle a weapon."

Bishop's father is already mentally preparing my résumé, probably thinking about where they could use me in their security protocol, but saying I know how to handle a weapon is like saying Atlas knows how to throw a punch.

I clear my throat and glance away from Bishop. "I can do more than that..."

Everyone's attention locks in on me even more, but one set of eyes in particular narrows with sharp awareness.

Gabe's gaze sweeps over me again, from my hair down to my combat boots. "Where did you serve? What branch?"

Swallowing thickly, I brace myself for the blowback I'll probably get from Bishop for not revealing this sooner. "I was a Ranger. 3rd battalion, then RSTB."

All the air seems to get sucked from the room with my admission.

Gabe nods but doesn't say anything else.

He was a bit of a legend in the 75th even decades after he retired. One of the best snipers to ever serve with them. And he knows that anyone who was part of the Regimental Special Troops Battalion is more than capable of handling *anything* that might come for the Hawkes.

Though, I'm not so sure I'm prepared to handle what Bishop will say or do when we're alone again. The heat of her stare licks across my skin until I finally glance over at her.

Now that it's all out there, she has to understand why I was so insistent on helping them, why it would be impossible for me to just stand by and do nothing. But the way she's looking at me says that keeping my background from her was a huge mistake she will make me pay for later.

Her father assesses me for another second, his gaze drifting over to the way his daughter looks at me, then he retreats to his original spot near a small brunette woman who must be Bishop's mother. She offers me a tight smile but doesn't say anything, instead taking her husband's hand in her much smaller one.

Atlas clears his throat loudly in the now awkwardly silent room. "Well, now that's settled...let me give you the quick introductions. The one in the chair is Savage, and the tall blond standing next to him is his wife, Danika. They're Kennedy's parents. You now know my dad, Gabe, and the woman beside him is my mother, Skye."

She gives me a kind smile and a small wave while Gabe continues to watch me with the same calculation I would expect any former-Ranger to.

"The one in the corner of the couch is my uncle Stone. The blonde beside him is his wife, Nora. Their sons are Isaac and Coen." He motions toward two very similar looking dark-haired men standing in the corner with their arms protectively wrapped around two women. "That's Giacomina, but we call her Jack."

"We met at The Grind."

Atlas nods. "Right, and Coen's girlfriend is Allegra. She also happens to be Satriano's daughter." He skims over that fact like it isn't probably the most important thing to know, moving right on to the others in the room. "That's my aunt, Storm, and her husband, Landon. You met Angelina and Alessandra, their daughters."

I smile and nod.

He points to the man sitting beside Allie. "That's Pope, Bishop's little brother."

Pope smirks at the description and gives me a little half-wave.

Atlas inclines his head toward a dark-haired man across the room. "Cass is the one beside Kennedy near the fireplace. This is their house. We chose to meet here because it has the biggest living room to cram all of us into."

I snort. "That's probably a good thing."

"Yeah. Well, you're about to learn that family meetings can get a little heated. It's why we keep the littles out of the room when we're doing this. All the kids are upstairs with Cass and Kennedy's daughter's nanny."

Atlas does another scan of the room and stops at the only two people he hasn't introduced. One man sits casually in an armchair, offering a soft smile while the second lingers in a shadowy corner with a glass of amber liquid in his hand.

A shiver rolls down my spine instantly, but Atlas doesn't seem to notice.

"That's Byron and Luca. And that's everyone...except Jude, but he rarely comes to these things."

He was the one behind the counter at the book store the other day—Angelina's boyfriend...

Scanning each face in the room, I get a returned mix of interest and suspicion, but I couldn't have expected anything else.

The Hawkes are notorious for closing rank and keeping their business dealings and family affairs very private. To be let into the inner sanctum, especially on a day like today when they've just been confronted by a man who clearly screams danger to them is unusual and is bound to have people on edge.

All I can do is try to smooth out any feathers I may have ruffled by showing up here. "It's nice to meet all of you. I'm sorry it isn't under better circumstances, but I just want everyone to know that I'm here to help. Any way I can."

Bishop continues to stare at me, her arms crossed over her chest in that defensive posture she loves to take up. Her eyes carry a mix of emotions so potent that diving into them would probably be toxic and deadly, but that doesn't mean I won't try to survive whatever she has worked up for me.

But we have to make it through this meeting first.

Savage clears his throat. "Since we've all had the introduction to Gage, I think it's time we get started. We need to figure out what to do about Satriano...and fast."

BISHOP

I can't concentrate on coming up with any sort of intelligible plan with Gage standing so close to me. That leather and spice scent of his seems to shift through the air and dive right into my lungs, and right now I need to be able to think without remembering what he tasted like when he kissed me in the park.

A damn Ranger?

It explains so much about him—the way he handled himself at the club, the vague statements he made that night in the park, his insistence that he could help us with security—but it also leaves me with so many more questions.

Ones I know won't get answered while we're here meeting with the family.

Or maybe ever.

He had every opportunity to tell me that night, to explain further some of his personal experience when he was talking about the stress and weight of protecting other people. But he didn't.

There has to be a reason...

I walk away from him, making my way over toward the fireplace where I can lean against the mantle near Cass and Kennedy, putting the entire room between us and allowing me to watch him as he takes in the conversation happening around the room.

Dad crosses his arms over his chest, bracing his legs apart and looking every bit as intimidating as I've ever seen him. The fact that Satriano got so close to all of us today rattled him.

Badly. "Our security at all the properties is locked down tight, so we don't need to worry about anything with that regard."

I snort, shaking my head. "Yeah? Then how did he waltz right into The Grind the minute he got back into town?"

He glances over at me. "*You* were there. You would've protected the girls."

"Of course, I would have. That isn't the point, Dad. He just *walked* in. The men who brought the girls over weren't even standing at the door, they were sitting in their cars until he was already inside."

Angelina sighs. "I can't have armed security standing at the door, Bishop. I wouldn't have any customers. It's bad enough the place has already been blown *and* shot up. No one's going to come if they think they're not safe."

That's fair.

And I truly do feel for her where her business is concerned.

It's one of the main reasons I didn't do more when Satriano appeared today, but that doesn't mean we can't do better in the future to ensure none of us ever find ourselves in that position again.

"Your business isn't my top priority, Ang. I'm sorry to say that, but the security of everyone in this room is. And in order to do that, in order to keep everyone safe, we may have to make some sacrifices in some other areas."

Savage presses his lips together tightly and glances at Gabe, then at everyone in the room. "We know Satriano's back, so that frees up some of the resources we've been expending trying to locate him, right?" Everyone nods their agreement. "So, anyone we had on that, let's put on trying to figure out what the fuck he's doing back in town. Where's he staying? Who is he meeting with? Every fucking breath that man takes, I want a record of it, and I want it reported to me. Immediately."

Gabe nods. "He wouldn't be back if he doesn't want something, if he isn't going to make a move."

Coen issues a frustrated growl. "Do we really think that move would be anything other than coming for Allegra now that she's pregnant with his grandchild?"

All eyes sweep over to the woman in question, and Coen wraps his arm around her as she trembles beside him.

Despite how upset she clearly is, she shakes her head. "He won't hurt me."

Coen presses a kiss to his temple. "That may be true, but he's not going to just leave you to raise our baby with the Hawkes, cutting him off completely, either. You know that."

Tears shimmer in her eyes, and she bites her quivering bottom lip and nods. She doesn't want to see who and what her father really is, and the fact that she still loves him and believes he is a different person than the one we know is only going to hurt her in the end.

It will take time for her to come to terms with everything her father has done, what he *continues* to do, but each time he does something like his stunt today, it helps nudge her toward finally understanding what he's capable of.

"Keep her locked up in the penthouse." Gabe's order floats through the air, leaving no room for argument. "She doesn't leave. It's the most secure property we have."

Isaac scoffs. "That's what we all believed before that fucker Dan Roselli had it shot up."

Atlas winces, and Astrid suddenly goes very pale, curling in on herself slightly.

Gabe gives him a hard look. "Well, now it has bulletproof glass, and we've tripled the security in the lobby. No one's getting in or out. We've also installed a separate ventilation system to ensure that nothing like a fire or any gas put into the building vents can reach the penthouse. It has its own exit stairwell. We've done everything we can to ensure it's safe."

Isaac scowls. "Doesn't make me feel any better about it."

Which is one of the reasons he took Jack and their kids and

moved into their house shortly after the shooting. The memories of what happened at the penthouse certainly played a role too, but ultimately, Isaac wanted a place his family could feel safe.

And that wasn't it anymore.

Allie clings to Pope, resting her head against his chest. "What about the rest of us? What do we do? He brought up Pope and his agreement with him. He's going to come calling at some point."

Not only does Pope have his agreement with Satriano, but Coen agreed to play for him in any tournaments he demands to pay him back for the money lost due to Atlas' fight.

Just because he hasn't come to collect yet doesn't mean it won't happen.

Everyone knows it, too.

The reprieve we've had has come to an end.

Those vague threats we've been so worried about with Satriano MIA don't feel so vague anymore, knowing the man is in town along with one of his henchmen.

An eerie silence settles over the room because it's become very clear that we don't really have a plan to deal with him.

Gage watches all of it, gathering what information he can, but without all the particulars of what's gone down with that man over the years, there's no way he can fully grasp the situation. Still, the gears are turning behind his blue eyes.

I look from him to Dad, then to Gabe, Stone, and Savage. The men who have always stood at the head of this family. Yet no one has offered any sort of solution that will end this, once and for all.

"What do we do?" It's the question all of us are asking ourselves, but apparently, I'm the only one willing to voice it. "Do we take him out? Have we finally reached that point?"

They all look to me, and the man who's been standing silently in the corner shakes his head.

Luca steps forward, one hand shoved in the pocket of his suit, the other holding a glass of bourbon. "No. I've spoken with many of my contacts in Europe, where he was lurking before he moved over here, and if we take him out, his entire organization will come down on us with all the force they can muster. It won't be good, and they won't stop until a river of blood runs through New Orleans. Hawke blood..."

Kennedy scowls at him. "Then what the hell do we do, Luca? We sit and wait for him to make a move? I feel like that's all we've been doing for years."

Me, too.

There has always been a reason to hold back, to allow that man to keep breathing when each breath he takes only causes us more pain, but we've reached a breaking point. Or at least, I have.

"We're not just sitting." Gabe pushes off the edge of the couch where he's been leaning, making eye contact with everyone in the room. "We'll get people trailing him, and we're already looking into this McDonald guy. As soon as we know what they're up to, we can move."

I throw up my hands. "Move how? If we're not going to kill Satriano, and we're not going to partner with him, then what the fuck options do we have?"

"We find leverage." Savage's voice cuts through the tension, and his eyes zero in on Allegra. "You're right about what you said, Coen. About him not just walking away from his grandchild. So, we use that."

Coen snarls at him. "The fuck we do! You're not using my baby to negotiate with a fucking monster!"

Allegra flinches, tears rolling down her cheeks.

Savage holds up his hand, and Stone looks from his brother to his son.

"He's right, Coen." Everyone looks at Stone and waits for him to expound upon what he just said. He twirls his cane in his hand, staring at it. "He won't walk away from his child any more than any of us could, and now that he has a grandchild..." He offers a slight shrug. "We need to meet with him. We need to figure out if there's a way that we can get him to back off whatever plans he has. And we use his access to Allegra and the baby as a means to negotiate."

"Dad"—Coen's voice breaks—"you can't be serious!"

Isaac looks to his younger brother. "The truth of the matter is, you have something he wants, and this might be the first time that's ever happened since we've been facing him. We have to seriously think about how to handle this, but from where I'm standing, I don't see any way we make it through this without some sort of negotiation and concessions."

He flicks his gaze to me, then to Dad. "Until then, you keep the security tight. On everyone. And Allegra stays in the penthouse. We'll figure out what he wants, beyond his grandchild, and we see what we can give him without any of us suffering."

That's the key that not everyone in this room seems to understand, or maybe they just don't want to accept it because the reality is too painful.

Satriano lives to make the Hawkes suffer.

He likes to watch us squirm and bleed.

And he's going to milk every fucking drop from us before this is all over.

It would be so easy to simply take the man out, to lie in wait and put a bullet in his fucking head and end all this. It's what I've wanted to do for a long fucking time. The only thing preventing me from acting has been Luca's insistence that Satriano's organization would step up to avenge him in a way that would put us at just as much risk—if not more—as we already are under the man himself.

It's all one giant quagmire there is no way out of.

And I feel like I'm drowning in quicksand...

My eyes drift to Gage, the only one in the room who hasn't

been affected by what Satriano has done. His tense gaze travels over all of us and then meets mine, and I see the resolve there.

He told me he couldn't sit back when there was a threat, and now, I know he won't walk away.

Even if I ask him to.

He isn't going anywhere.

11

BISHOP

What the hell am I doing?

I follow Gage's motorcycle up the cracked driveway of the small, two-story building. The word "mechanic" across the top of the garage door, barely visible in peeling paint, is the only sign that this must be his shop.

And apparently where he lives, too.

He climbs off his bike, pulls off his helmet, sending his golden locks flying around his face, and manually rolls up the garage door, then glances back at me as if making sure I'm not going to drive away.

Fuck.

His blue eyes pierce me even from there. The windshield doesn't offer me any protection. The intensity of his gaze still raises goosebumps across my skin.

I grip the wheel tighter, my foot still depressing the brake while I debate making a run for it.

Why the hell did I agree to follow him back here?

Deep down, in the places I don't like to think about, I know why.

Because I was a hot fucking mess after that meeting, and he wasn't going to let me just walk away when he could see how shaken I was by what we discussed. By what is coming.

Even more so, I agreed to come because he would've followed me if I hadn't to ensure I was all right, and I do not need that man knowing where I live any more than I need to hear his thoughts about my work ethic.

If I try to leave, he'll just come after me.

It's what he was trained for. Laser focus. Completing tasks. Hunting down people. Ensuring his target doesn't slip away.

Especially now that he revealed he was a Ranger, I understand his earlier quip about me not knowing it if he *were* actually stalking me. He certainly possesses the skills to stay in the shadows, to remain undetected, even by someone as observant as I am, if he really wanted to.

But Gage has been very direct and public about his intentions with me.

The only thing clouding it has been my inability to accept him at face value. That nagging feeling that he's keeping things from me. But tonight, he was forced to drop some of that façade.

What's holding you back, Bishop?

He watches me now from the open garage door, my headlights shining directly on him, illuminating his broad, muscular frame and the set of his shoulders that suggests he absolutely *will* drag me back here kicking and screaming if I leave before he says whatever he needed so badly to say in private. Or he'll try, at least.

Now that I know what type of training he's had, it would certainly be entertaining to try. But there isn't any point fighting it tonight.

I don't think I have the energy to. This lack of sleep and

constantly being on edge has frayed my nerves more than I ever knew possible. It feels like teetering on the edge of an abyss, which I am one exhausted misstep from falling into, with shaking legs.

The arms of the man standing in front of me would be a much better option.

I release a long, heavy breath and throw the car into park, shutting off the engine. He finally looks away and moves his bike inside while I climb out and slowly follow him into the historic building.

Given the ancient brick and peeling paint everywhere I look, I would guess it must have stood here for at least a hundred years. Big enough to hold two vehicles at a time, it currently houses his Harley that he just rolled in and another bike up on a stand. A long table filled with tools stands along one wall near a door in the corner, and a set of metal stairs leads up to a second-floor loft.

The smell of motor oil, gasoline, and metal permeates the air, along with a hint of the leather and spice scent that Gage always carries with him.

I move toward the bike up on the rack, examining the frame lines and the old, rusted tank. "Is this an Indian?"

Gage's brows rise as he nods. "It's my current project."

"What year?"

His lips twitch, as if he's fighting a grin. "You think you can guess?"

I run my fingers across the tank. "If I guess the year correctly, do I win something?"

"Maybe."

He leans back against a counter behind him, watching me take in everything I can see in the dim lighting provided by a single overhead bulb.

"Well..." I glance up at him. "It's a Chief." He grins. "I'd say it's a '47, but it might be a '48."

His grin grows, as does the heat emanating from his appreciative gaze. "Impressive. But I shouldn't be surprised. Everything about you is."

My cheeks heat at the compliment, and I look away from him, concentrating on examining the repairs he's done to the bike. "You don't have to do that, you know."

"Do what?"

"Constantly compliment me." I peek at him over the bike. "I have good self-esteem."

He barks out a laugh. "Believe me, I know you do, but that's not why I do it."

"Why, then? Because you're trying to get in my pants?"

He raises a blond brow and wiggles his fingers. "Wasn't I already in them?"

Hell...

My pussy throbs at the memory of him getting me off in the park, and I press my thighs together to try to ease the ache without being obvious about it. "That's not what I meant."

He smirks and pushes off the counter to move toward me. I stay frozen in place, watching him approach like a deer caught in the headlights of a Mustang Fastback barreling down on it. He rounds the bike, and I turn so it's at my back and I'm facing him.

Bad idea.

Gage slowly cages me in so I have nowhere left to go, my butt bumping the bike stand. He captures my face in his palm, the rough callouses brushing against my skin, sending a little shiver through me. "Do you really not know why I always say you're impressive?"

I thought I did.

Men aren't generally very hard to figure out. They're usually motivated by one thing and one thing only. But staring into his warm blue eyes, there is far more than just sexual attraction and need burning there.

He tilts my face up toward him. "I tell you you're impressive because I am *constantly* in awe of you, and apparently, I really suck at expressing that with words."

Could have fooled me...

I don't even know how to respond to that, or really to anything Gage says or does because he doesn't fit into any of the boxes I've always shoved other men into. Boxes that served their purpose and then were easily tossed away when I was done with them.

His thumb brushes lazily over my cheek, sending another shiver through me. "God, I would love to fuck you right here, up against this bike." He leans in, feathering his lips over mine. "But for what I have planned, I need something much sturdier."

Jesus Christ...

My knees start to give out, but I lock them, keeping myself upright because I refuse to do anything embarrassing like collapse into this man's arms. Instead, I force myself to take a breath and meet his gaze with one I hope doesn't make me look like the quivering, needy mess I'm becoming. "What do you have planned?"

He grins. "Come upstairs with me and I'll show you."

It's the type of invitation I normally wouldn't refuse; a handsome man who's clearly very talented with his hands, and probably would be with everything else, is offering me a night in his bed. One I desperately need to work out all this tension.

But something holds me back from immediately jumping on his offer.

The fact that I was *right*.

Gage Newhart has secrets, things that he was keeping from me.

"Why didn't you tell me about being a Ranger?"

His hand freezes on my cheek. "Because it wasn't relevant to any of the conversations we were having."

I narrow my gaze on him. Though he's technically correct,

he had plenty of opportunity to reveal something that was such a major part of his life and molded him into who he is today. And he didn't. "Is there anything else important I need to know?"

He shakes his head and leans in, his warm breath fanning across my cheek as he makes his way over to my ear and presses his lips to it. "At the moment, all you need to know is that the plans I have will be quite beneficial to you."

That throbbing heat returns in my core, and he presses against me tighter, until I can feel the hard line of his cock on my leg.

Shit...

I swallow thickly, trying to gather some semblance of self-control that seems to have fled the moment he touched me.

It's pathetic, really.

How quickly I melt into him.

I hate that he affects me like this. That I seem to lose all sense of command over my body when I feel the scrape of his callouses along my skin or the brush of his lips over mine.

No one has ever done that before—made me forget myself and the world around me like this.

It simultaneously makes me want to shove him away so I can flee and drag him even closer so I can experience everything he's promising. So I can have a taste of that kind of freedom, even if only for one night.

I slide my hands inside the unzipped sides of his leather jacket and across the white T-shirt stretching over his hard chest. "If I come upstairs with you..." He raises a brow, waiting for me to continue. "I want you to promise me no more secrets."

Gage searches my face for a moment. "That goes both ways, Hellcat."

I shake my head. "I haven't kept anything from you."

He leans in and nips at my bottom lip. "We both know that's a lie, but I'll let it go for now."

Just like I'm going to let the *Hellcat* thing go for now, too. Because this time, when he said it, the flare of heat through my body wasn't anger. It was the driving need to touch him and have him touch me that I've felt since I pinned him to the club floor.

He reaches down and grasps my hips, lifting me easily to wrap my legs around his waist. My pussy centers directly along his hard length, and I groan at the sensation and instinctively roll my hips against it. He sucks in a sharp breath, then presses his lips to mine, kissing me long and slow and deep as he pulls away from the bike and stalks across the shop to the metal staircase.

Somehow, he doesn't even break stride or stop kissing me as he climbs each tread and steps up onto the second-floor loft.

I don't have any time to examine our surroundings because he stops after a few more steps and lowers me down onto his bed, his mouth still moving over mine greedily. My fingers delve into his thick, silky hair, the juxtaposition of it on this man made of so much hard, unyielding muscle enough to make a needy little sound slip from my lips.

He quickly captures it with his searing kiss that leaves me breathless, but then he pulls back and stares down at me.

The gleam in his eyes sends my heart stuttering.

A wicked grin pulls at his perfect lips. "Now, about those plans..."

GAGE

Bishop's pupils dilate, the black encroaching on the shimmering bourbon around it as she stares up at me and shifts restlessly where I have her pinned to the mattress.

I grind my hard cock between her legs and a stifled groan

slips from her lips that she can't contain, despite the obvious attempt to bite it back.

Even now, even like this, she doesn't want to let go, doesn't want to admit how good it feels. Or maybe she can't. Maybe she's spent so long denying herself everything that she's forgotten how to accept what's being freely given to her.

And that's all I want to do tonight—give her everything.

If she'll only let me.

She's too stubborn. Too lost in her own head. Clinging too tightly to the control she thinks she needs over everything in her life.

Not tonight.

After that meeting, seeing the way Bishop was left reeling, I knew what she needed.

Relief.

A release.

To be shown how good it can be to relinquish the control that she clings to so goddamn tightly that it's going to strangle her.

The fact that she even agreed to come home with me tonight proves how rattled she truly was, how off-kilter she's feeling after her confrontation with Satriano today. Because there wasn't much fight in her. There may have been a flicker of question when she was sitting on the driveway, facing the prospect of coming inside and committing to *this*, but it fled as quickly as she could have if she truly wanted to.

Which means she *wants* to be here.

She wants *this*, even if there are parts of her that will fight giving into it.

I feather my lips over her ear and nip at the sensitive skin behind it. She bucks against me, and I ghost a kiss over that spot, then suck gently, making her bow up into me.

"Ever since that night in the park, I've been dying to get my mouth on you...*everywhere.*"

She issues a low whimper, and I grin as I pull back far enough to stare down at her fully. That tiny noise is enough of a concession to tell me she's on board. Her chest heaves with labored breaths, the anticipation already riling her up more than I've ever seen her.

I trail my fingers along the waistband of her pants, but I pause when it hits her holster. "Your gun..."

Her lips curl. "I don't think we'll be needing that."

"Oh, I don't know..." I pull it free and examine it with a grin. "It could be fun."

She laughs as I set it on the nightstand, then return to where I really want my focus.

All on *her.*

Bishop lifts her hips in offering. Deliberately slowly, I pop the button and drag down the zipper, making her wait, making her watch each agonizing movement. She lifts her ass so I can grip the denim and drag the black jeans down her legs. I tug off her boots, letting them fall to the floor, then remove her pants and socks, leaving her bottom half in nothing but a thin strip of dark-blue fabric that barely hides the exact place I want to be right now.

My mouth waters to taste more of her, to coat my tongue in her sweet, delicious release again.

I gently drag my finger up across the damp fabric, and her hips buck again. "You're wet, Bishop."

She lifts her head off the mattress and meets my gaze, but before she can open her mouth with some smartass retort, I shift up her again and capture it with another searing kiss. As much as I love arguing with her and getting her riled up that way, *this* way is so much more fun.

For both of us...

Bishop moans into my mouth, greedily playing with my tongue, warring for control as I slide my hand up under the hem of her shirt and tug down one bra cup. My fingertips find her nipple taut, and when I tug on it, she gasps against my lips.

"Just...what is it...you have planned, Gage?" The words come out stilted on a gasp as I twist the hard peak. "Torturing me?"

That *wasn't* my plan.

But I'm not sure she'll see the distinction between that and giving up control to me here.

Something tells me she's never done it, never allowed someone else to take the lead in giving her pleasure.

And that's a fucking shame.

A mistake that has to be remedied.

"I'm going to show you how good it can be when you give someone else control." Her body tenses under mine, and I drag my head back to find her eyeing me warily. I lazily brush my thumb across her nipple, making her twitch as I gaze down at her. "You're wound too tight, Bishop. You're desperately holding on to control of things that are far beyond yours, and letting yourself obsess like that will only drive you into the ground. Let me take control tonight. Of this." I pinch her nipple. "Of you." I brush my lips across hers again, tentatively, trying to get her to ease the tension in her body that has her wound like a bow string. "Please."

It won't be easy for her.

I knew it the moment I told her she needed to follow me home tonight. But I've never shied away from any mission in my life, and she's the best kind of challenge. The kind that has a glorious reward at the end of the effort.

If I can only get her to let go and trust me...

Bishop's gaze wavers between uncertainty and interest. The same war raging there that so often does between us. One I hope to win tonight.

I feel the exact moment she gives up the fight.

She sags back against the bed, that tension releasing as she kisses me hard, sliding her fingers through my hair and tugging at the strands. If she has any lingering reservations, she's locked them away in a place that is no longer interfering with what's happening between us.

Exactly what I've been praying for since the moment we met.

For her to open up, for her to trust, for her to *want* and accept what I have to offer. For her to let me keep her safe.

I groan into her mouth as my cock twitches against her, fully on board with this plan. My eager fingers release her nipple long enough to grasp the hem of her shirt, tug it up and off, and unhook her bra so I can free her breasts and see her fully exposed.

Christ, she's just as beautiful as I knew she would be.

All smooth, silky dark skin and toned muscles she's earned through hard work and dedication that I know cost her in other places. Like her lack of social life and her inability to let go and just enjoy anything.

But that won't happen tonight.

I refuse to allow it.

She will only be thinking about *one* thing—how damn good it all feels. Otherwise, I've failed completely at my mission, and I fucking *hate* to fail.

I slide to my knees at the edge of the bed as I pull off my jacket and toss it behind me, then drag her over to me. Looking up at her, I find a hint of trepidation in her warm gaze. Trailing my hands up her inner thighs, I watch the goosebumps appear on her skin. Feel her shudder restlessly. "Have you even let the men you've been with do this? Or is it just quick and hard to ease the ache?"

The flash in her eyes tells me I'm right.

Any sexual partners she's had never would've been allowed to do this, even if they wanted to.

It's too intimate.

Too time consuming.

Too *real.*

Too much of the things that Bishop doesn't want or doesn't think she can have. All the things she *deserves* so much to have.

I nod slowly at her non-answer, because she knows I can read her like a book and can see the truth in her gaze.

But tonight, she doesn't get to control her pleasure.

She doesn't get to have it fast and hard so she can take what she wants and then run. That doesn't work for me—now or ever—and by the end of the night, she won't ever be satisfied with that kind of sex again.

I trail my fingers up her thighs and grasp her thong. One rough tug on it easily rips the fabric, and I toss the scraps to the side, dipping my head to glide my tongue through her slick core.

Her body arches up off the mattress, her hands clutching the comforter beneath her, and I press my forearm across her hips, pinning her in place, preventing her from moving as I gently lick every inch of her.

The taste of her arousal coats my tongue and makes my cock ache to be inside her, but I refuse to give in to that desire. Not until I've shown her how good this can be; letting go, allowing someone else to find pleasure in giving her pleasure.

I thrust my tongue as deep as I can inside her, and her hips slam up against my arm, her cunt grinding on my face, but I keep her down, hold her steady while I suck and probe. Until she's trembling. Only then do I press a finger into her tight heat.

She gasps, the sound echoing around the lofted ceilings. Her hands shift from the bed into my hair, her short nails scoring my scalp and making me groan into her wet flesh.

"Fucking Christ, Bishop. You taste so fucking good."

I curl my finger and find that spot deep inside her that

makes her hips start to roll and a groan fall from her parted lips.

Those little noises will be my undoing.

I set a slow rhythm, thrusting in and out, dragging my calloused fingertips along her inner wall. Her hips roll harder and faster, trying to buck off the way I have her pinned. But I don't want her in control of this. I want her to allow me to find what does it for her, learn what she needs so I can keep giving it to her again and again.

"Gage..."

My name is a plea from her quivering lips, because she's close.

So fucking close.

I can feel the tiny ripples of her cunt as her body prepares for an orgasm.

God, I want to give that to her...

And so much more.

I flick my tongue across her clit relentlessly, driving her toward it, and another barely audible gasp falls from her open mouth, her head tipped back, neck strained.

She's never looked more beautiful, and when I suck her clit between my teeth, grazing them across that tight bundle of nerves, her scream fills the air. Her body tenses and then convulses, cunt clenching around my finger, her hips desperately trying to move as I keep her in place and force her to take all of it.

I lick and suck and graze my teeth all over her until she's completely wrung out and her hands fall away from my head. Until she sags back with a groan. Until she's completely sated.

But I am nowhere near done.

I could drown in this woman, easily, and not even care.

And that's a huge fucking problem.

12

GAGE

It's impossible to remain unaffected though, when she looks so damn beautiful spread out on my bed, waiting for me, her skin hot with the flush of her recent release, her chest rising and falling rapidly, her glistening cunt spread open.

My cock aches in the confines of my jeans, and I reach for the button and pop it, then drag down the zipper, giving myself some relief.

I shift back up over her and kiss her softly. "Was that so bad, Bishop? Giving over control to me?"

She shudders against me and shakes her head, returning my kiss languidly. A slow, gentle glide of our lips together. Nothing hurried. Nothing forcing her to want to rush through this and run.

"You won't say it though, will you, Hellcat? Won't admit how good it felt for me to take control." Her body tenses slightly, and I nip at her bottom lip. "It's okay. You don't have to. But I need to know, do you trust me enough to let me push it further?"

Her pupils dilate again, zeroing in on me. "How?"

It's a simple question, but the fact that she's even asking it, even *considering* allowing it, is enough to make me almost come on the spot.

I slide back off her to my feet and make my way over to the closet. Her eyes follow my every step, half-lidded but alert.

Curious.

Maybe a bit nervous.

I snag one of my ties and dangle it from my fingertips as I walk back toward her.

She pushes herself up on her elbows, brow furrowing. "What is that for?"

"Fun..."

I nod behind her toward the wooden headboard with the slats that will allow me to keep her hands secured there. Her gaze widens, but what flares in the depths of those bourbon eyes isn't fear; it's heat. Interest. Something I wasn't so sure I would get from her.

For someone whose life is so tied to her need to control everything, giving up even a second of it must be agonizing for Bishop. Yet, she doesn't outright dismiss the suggestion.

Maybe it's the fog of the orgasm still clouding her mind, or maybe that wall has cracked the tiniest bit, enough for her to see through to the light on the other side and what's waiting for her if she only accepts it.

I kneel on the bed beside her and drag the silky material across her bare stomach and up over her breasts, pausing before it hits her mouth. "Well, what do you say? Do you trust me to control this?"

The look she gives me suggests she's going to say no, and I wouldn't blame her if she did.

I've kept things from her.

Important things.

Things she should know.

And she's observant enough to realize that.

But I'm hoping she'll also understand what I'm doing and, more importantly, *why*. Letting go in this setting, allowing me to lead and control it, will take a huge weight off her shoulders that she doesn't know she's carrying.

She hasn't even been able to let go with anyone she's had sex with, and that's a true shame for a woman like her who carries so much raw sexual energy and pent-up tension.

I want to see it snap.

I want to see Bishop Clarke *truly* fly free from the burden of everything crushing her, even if only for a few moments.

If she'll let me...

Bishop pulls her bottom lip between her teeth, eyeing the tie directly in front of her and then glancing back up at me. She searches my face for a moment, as if she might somehow see the answer she seeks if she looks hard and long enough.

Finally, she gives me a sharp nod. "Yes."

I don't think she truly does trust me.

At least, not fully.

Bishop trusts *herself* and the fact that she'd be strong enough to get out of any bonds I could put on her if she really wanted to. Not to mention that even with her hands tied, the Jiu-Jitsu moves she knows could have me at her mercy in only a few seconds if she needed to using her legs alone.

Part of me wants that.

To make her desperate.

To push her to the brink.

I grin at her as I reach for the headboard and secure the tie, then motion for her to shift back.

She crawls back toward me until her head hits the pillow, her long braids spread out across the dark-gray fabric like a dark halo on a woman who is as much an angel as she is the devil on my shoulder.

I trail my fingers across her cheek, down her throat, over

one of her pebbled nipples, along her stomach, until I reach her hand. Goosebumps erupt everywhere I touch, and by the time I wrap the silky material around her wrist, she's trembling.

She reaches out and grabs my wrist with her free hand. "What if I want out?"

"Then I let you out. But it won't be at the word 'stop' because I plan on doing things to you that may make you say that word when you don't mean it."

"A safe word, then."

I grin at her. "Your choice."

She chews on that lip, watching me as she considers her options. Her pulse beats rapidly under my fingers. "Ricochet."

Like how I feel every time she looks at me. As if she's fired straight into my chest and the bullet is bouncing around wildly, slamming into my ribs and lodging in my heart.

I bark out a laugh, and the tiniest smile pulls at her lips.

"What?" She raises a dark brow. "It's something that would never come up in this situation, right?"

"I would certainly hope not. But that's a little too long." I lean down and kiss her again, taking *my* turn to bite that lip of hers that keeps having me imagining what she would look like with my cock there. "We need something short. One syllable. Because you may be breathless..."

She sucks in a sharp breath at my warning, pressing her thighs together in a way that just makes me even more intent to get back in between them. "Umm...then how about we keep it simple? Red."

"Red it is..."

I drop another kiss on her lips, then secure her other wrist together with the first so her palms are together and arms are extended above her head. Looping it through the headboard, I ensure the knot is tight and won't budge. She tugs at the binding, but I know the soft, silky material won't cut into her skin, no matter how hard she might fight it.

Christ, she looks beautiful tied to my bed.

And maybe slightly uncomfortable, but I would expect nothing less from a woman who is used to having her way. Who is used to being in control in every single aspect of her life. Especially this one.

We both know that she still is. All she has to do is utter a single word and I'll release her. But not having to make these decisions. Allowing me to direct her pleasure by securing her hands will give her something she can't get any other way.

Freedom.

I grab the hem of my T-shirt and tug it up over my head, tossing it to the floor with the rest of the haphazardly discarded clothes. Her eyes roam over my shoulders, my chest, my arms, taking in all the ink scattered across it.

Her gaze dips to follow my hands as I shove down my jeans and my cock springs free. They widen at the sight of it and the metal balls traveling up the length. "What the hell is that?"

Fighting a grin, I brush my fingers over them. "A Jacob's ladder."

All the breath rushes from her lungs as she stares at it.

"Trust me, Hellcat. It's for your benefit."

She squirms and presses her thighs together as I grasp my length and stroke it slowly, gliding my fingers across the head to spread the precum there.

Fuck.

It's been so long, and I've wanted this woman since the first time I saw her, even more after getting to know her.

I climb onto the bed and nudge her knees open, fully exposing her to me again. "Are you on birth control?"

"Of course, I am."

"Have you been tested?"

She gives me an incredulous look. "Of course."

"So have I." I lock gazes with her. "So, do I need to grab a condom out of my drawer, or can I feel your hot cunt on my cock and allow you to feel *this* the way it was intended?"

"Fuck."

Squeezing her eyes closed, she shifts restlessly, tugging on the binding. She wants it as badly as I do, to truly feel all of me, and what it ultimately comes down to is how much she really does trust me. If what she said a few moments ago was true, or merely bravado and not wanting to back down from a challenge.

Because I do trust *her*.

Bishop isn't a bullshitter.

She isn't a liar.

She isn't the type of person who would ever go to bed with me and lie about something this important. Her integrity means too much to her. Just like mine used to not that long ago.

Her eyes flutter open and zero in on me stroking my cock. A little groan slips from her throat. "I want to feel you."

Fuck.

Those words are sweeter than any other ones I can remember ever hearing.

I shift closer to her, dragging the head of my cock through her slick core, and she groans, her hips bowing up in offering. That little brush with her heat is enough to make my length throb in my hand.

All it would take is one little thrust to have the head inside her and one, long, slow glide to allow her to know what being with me really feels like. How *good* my piercings will make it for her.

But I brace myself over her, feathering my lips across her breasts and along the column of her neck, to her mouth again, kissing her hard and deep, until she begins undulating under me.

She rolls her hips against mine, urging me to enter her, but

I hold steady with just the head of my cock pressed where she wants it.

"If you thought I was done with you, that I had gotten enough of your taste, you're dead wrong, Bishop. I'm going to make you come at least once more that way, maybe two or three more times, before I finally fuck you."

That's a fucking promise I intend to keep, no matter how agonizing it might be for me...

And her...

She gasps, tugging at her bindings, and I grin against her lips.

"No"—she shakes her head—"I'm too sensitive. Too—"

I release my cock and drag my thumb across her engorged clit, and her hips buck.

"Fuck..." She clenches her teeth, the muscles in her throat straining.

"I'm going to do it, Bishop, until you're a quivering mess and begging me to take you, but remember, all you have to say is one word to make it stop. If that's really what you want."

She groans, because we both know that it isn't really.

My Hellcat is just terrified of the pleasure she knows I'm going to bring her. Of not being the one driving that train.

All I have is an illusion of control, but it's enough in the moment to have her panting in anticipation.

I slide back down and throw her thighs over my shoulders, burying my face between them again. She gasps, rolling against me, and I jab my tongue into her core.

Her thighs tighten around my head, and I groan into her flesh, digging my fingers into her as I hold her steady and lap at her hyper-sensitive clit.

The headboard creaks, mixing with the gasps and moans falling from her parted lips.

It's music to my fucking ears, and I could devour her like this forever, but I know it won't take long for her to explode a second time. Not when she's so primed. Not when I don't give her any quarter.

It only takes a few moments before her body tenses and she erupts again, grinding her cunt against my face as she twists in my hold. Her strong thighs crank on my neck, the best kind of pain caused by her absolute pleasure.

When she sags back to the mattress and her legs release their death grip on me, the headboard creaks again, and I look down at her from my position, her body angled up toward me, her pussy still directly in my face.

I kiss her glistening inner thigh. "What do you think, Bishop? Again?"

She shakes her head. "No. I can't."

"I think you can, Hellcat."

She whimpers, but it only encourages me to dip my head again, and this time, slide my hand up to shove two fingers into her. Her strangled groan and the way her cunt clenches around me proves she can do it. I curl and thrust up into her G-spot, dragging my calloused fingertips there with each retreat while I alternate between flicking my tongue across her clit and sucking it gently.

Over, and over, and over again.

Building her up slowly this time.

I so badly want to see her *truly* come undone, to give her the one thing I know no man ever has.

And I know when it's coming.

She thrashes in my hold, gasping and tugging at the headboard binding until it finally happens. The ultimate release. She squirts, shooting down my throat and coating my mouth and tongue with her addictive taste.

I swallow down every drop, the satisfaction of knowing I did that enough to make me give up my resolve to try to milk another one out of her this way.

Because I can't wait anymore.

I need to be inside her.

It's all I've wanted since the moment I walked into The Hawkeye Club and saw her. And despite all the reasons why it's a horrible idea, I'm not going to stop until she says "*red.*"

BISHOP

My body still pulses from whatever the hell Gage just did to me when he releases my legs from up on his muscled shoulders. He gently lowers them to the mattress and settles over me, slamming his mouth against mine so I can taste my release on his tongue.

Good God that was...

There aren't even any words that can describe it.

It was like my entire body spasmed and released all at once.

My head floats in a fuzzy cloud of pleasure as he kisses me ruthlessly, like he wants to make me come again just from this. And the way the heat builds low in my belly again tells me he probably could.

His cock stays pinned between us, and the cool press of the metal balls that run up either side contrasts against the heat of his body in the most delicious way.

He reaches up and wraps one hand around my wrists, testing the bindings. "You still good, Hellcat?"

I nod, shifting under him restlessly, my pussy clenching and ready even as I struggle to regain any control over my limbs.

"Look at me." My eyes flutter open, lids heavy, and a grin spreads across his face as he stares down at me. "What do you want, Bishop?"

He releases his grip on my wrists and reaches between us to

drag the head of his cock through my core again, and I groan, arching into it. "This?"

I barely have time to nod again before he's pressing into me in one long, slow thrust that feels unlike anything I've ever experienced before.

Absolutely fucking divine.

"Oh, God..."

Those little metal balls lining each side of his length glide against the walls of my pussy, pressing in places I didn't even know was possible, his thick cock stretching me with a beautiful ache. When he's finally fully seated inside me, he stills, tipping my chip up toward him. "Open your eyes, Bishop. Look at me."

My eyelids flutter open again, despite the fact that it's too intense.

This.

Him.

All of it.

I do it anyway because I *want* to see him.

I want to look into those crystal-blue eyes of his and see his desire there. See how good this feels for him reflected back at me as he draws his hips back and then slowly pushes back in, allowing me to feel every damn inch, every fucking ridge created by the piercings and his hot, hard flesh.

"Fuck!" His jaw locks, as if he's struggling to fight the lure of the pleasure coursing through him. "You have no fucking idea how incredible you feel, Hellcat."

I might.

Because this is...

Otherworldly.

My head spins and my entire body throbs with each retreat of his hips and pleasure courses through my veins with each thrust back home.

He grinds his pelvis against my hyper-sensitive clit each time, and I gasp, struggling to drag in air when I'm completely at his mercy and he's making starbursts erupt behind my closed eyelids.

"Open them!"

His growled command breaks through that spinning haze.

I hadn't even realized I had let them drift closed again, but with his hips moving in this slow rhythm, and elegant drag of the piercings against every part of me, I can't process all the feelings.

Frustration. Burning need. Molten desire.

I want him—no, *need* him—to move fast, to go hard.

Whatever this is...it is slow torture. And when I open my eyes to meet his sizzling gaze, I find he seems to be relishing it.

The way his eyes rake over me, the way they flare every time I gasp or moan at the roll of his hips, at the grind of his pelvis, at the catch of the head of his cock at that perfect spot deep inside me that made me lose control earlier.

Sliding his hand up from my chin, he presses his thumb into my mouth.

"Christ, Bishop. Your cunt feels so good. I can't wait to fuck this pretty mouth of yours, too."

I bite down on him sharply as he drives into me harder this time, bottoming out with a grunt and rotation of his hips that has a deep groan rumbling in my chest, forcing me to release his thumb from between my teeth.

At this point, I can't even form words to respond.

Nor do I want to admit how good he feels.

How, even restrained like this, unable to move or touch him, unable to get him to do what I want, it still feels more incredible than any other time in my life.

I wrap my legs around his waist, digging my heels into his lower back, trying to spur him on, but that only releases a dark chuckle from somewhere deep in his chest that vibrates against mine.

"Anxious, are we?"

He raises a brow at me, and the smug playfulness there is enough to make me issue a low warning growl that only makes him slow his pace more.

Drawing his cock languidly from me...

Allowing each level of piercing to drag on its way out until his entire glistening cock rests at my entrance...

Watching me as he nudges only the head back inside...

Toying with me as if we have all the time in the world...

He pushes into me just as slowly, only to repeat the process so many times I lose count along with my ability to breathe.

"Please..." The word slips from my mouth before I can stop it. "Just..."

"Please what, Hellcat?"

I issue another warning growl that somehow becomes a frustrated groan, jerking on the bindings to try to wrench them free, but he just grins at me and continues the torturous pace, freezing again with the head of his cock barely notched inside me.

"Please, fuck me hard, Gage."

He dips his head and captures my mouth in a mind-bending kiss as he rolls his hips and drives deep, holding me there, pinning me to the mattress.

"No." He shakes his head, his thick blond hair falling over his forehead. "I want you like this. I want to savor every fucking second of having you here, spread out in my bed, with my cock deep inside you. I want to hear every whimper, see every quiver, and feel your cunt clenching around me. I don't want this to be over quickly."

Arrogant bastard.

I tug at the restraints, the headboard protesting as he captures my bottom lip between his teeth and nips at it, sending a jolt straight to my already throbbing clit and making my hips buck against his.

He kisses the corner of my mouth, then across my cheek, down my neck, and dips his head to pull one of my nipples between his lips.

Oh, God...

The wet heat suctioning around it makes me bow up off the mattress and into his hard body.

He grazes his teeth along the taut peak, and I gasp, my pussy contracting around him in a way that means I can't hide how sensitive I am there from him anymore.

A calculating chuckle fills the space between us and he laps at it now, flicking his tongue back and forth and alternating between sucking and scraping his teeth along it.

It only makes me roll my hips against him harder, but he doesn't move, just keeps me pinned for what feels like *forever* while I squirm under his oral assault.

When he finally lifts his head, I issue a sigh of relief, only to have him dip it to the other one and give it the same attention.

The same sweet torture.

Motherfucker!

I jerk hard on the bindings, desperate to get my hands free, to get some type of control over the situation, but all that does is make the headboard groan ominously and the silk fabric tighten around my skin.

He continues to play with me, to make me gasp and whimper and curse him silently because I can't manage to get the words out, nor do I want to give him the satisfaction of hearing them.

This man *has* to know what he's doing to me. He's so deliberate. So meticulous in every flick of his tongue, brush of his teeth, and soft tug of suction. And by the time he finally lifts his head again, I'm so soaked and close to coming that the slightest roll of his hips or flick of a finger would probably set me off.

He seems to sense it, too, and I open my eyes to find him searching my face.

"You've done so well, Hellcat."

He smiles at me, and it lights up his entire handsome face, when all I want to do is smack the smugness from it. Then he shifts his hips slightly, just a quarter of an inch, enough for my clit to cry out at the brush of movement against it, but then he stills again. "I think you've earned what you've requested."

I gasp. "What? What's that?"

The words barely come out more than a whisper, and he pushes up and shifts back, dragging my ass off the mattress with his hands underneath it.

"Hard and fast."

He draws his hips back and slams into me.

"Oh!" I cry out, my head arching back, my entire body pulsing as he repeats the move, then adjusts his grip on me to put me in exactly the position he wants me. "*Fuck!*"

Over and over again, he thrusts into me, driving relentlessly all the way, slamming his hips against mine on a harsh grind. Hitting every perfect spot. Demanding I take all of him and giving it to me exactly as I requested.

It doesn't take long for my body to heat and tremble with my impending orgasm, even after three times already.

There's no fighting it.

But he suddenly stops, pausing deep inside me again, and I cry out, my eyes flying open as I look up at him.

"Why'd you stop?"

He pulls out of me, and I can only manage a whimper when I see his glistening dick as he shifts back.

Goddammit.

My pussy clenches, desperate to have him back.

The loss is almost too much to bear.

I feel cold, empty, without the press of his body and his length filling me.

He grabs my hips and quickly flips me, the binding twisting as he lowers me onto my elbows and knees. His strong fingers dig into my waist, and he drives back into me, drawing a strangled groan from us both.

Christ…

He's so much bigger in this position. Spreading me wider. Pumping into me in a punishing rhythm that only seems to grow faster and harder.

His ragged breaths match my own.

My heart thunders against my ribs and blood rushes in my ears.

Every nerve tingles and flares to life.

So fucking close.

When it hits, it blindsides me.

My vision goes dark, then bright white as I drop my face into the pillow, my body pulsing and squeezing around him as he continues to drive into me, pleasure coursing through every part of my body as my knees tremble and threaten to give out.

He slides one hand around my stomach to hold me steady, but then his fingers slip lower and find my clit, swirling around it, dragging out the orgasm, keeping it going as he pumps into me like a madman and finally releases a strangled cry, coming deep inside me in hot spurts.

Fuck…

His fingers stop, my body sags, and I collapse forward, unable to hold myself up anymore. He pants behind me and reaches up to untie my wrists, letting me fall fully into the bed. He collapses behind me and moves my braids over my shoulder, pressing a kiss to the back of my neck.

My lungs burn.

Every muscle quivers.

My pussy spasms.

Gage drags me back against him so I can feel every inch of

his body, hot and slick and still hard as hell pressing between my ass cheeks, those metal balls digging into my flesh.

He doesn't say anything.

He doesn't need to, because he just proved his point.

Letting Gage take control was fucking incredible...

And I hate it.

13

BISHOP

Most women would probably be thrilled to wake in the strong, tattooed arms of a man like Gage Newhart, who just fucked her into an orgasm-coma, but I'm not most women.

After everything he did to me, his hold on me, keeping me pressed against his body suddenly feels too restrictive.

Like I'm being suffocated by all the muscle and that spicy rich leathery scent.

Because you're unhinged.

I let this man tie me up, but having him hold me after sex is enough to make my chest tighten painfully around my lungs.

Too close.

Too intense.

Too intimate.

It's too much...*everything.*

There's a reason I don't do this. Why I don't allow myself to actually care about anyone I'm with. Because it always ends up feeling like I'm going to implode with the weight of what that might mean.

Caring about someone means worrying about them, and I already have enough to worry about to fill ten lifetimes. Maybe twenty now that Satriano is back.

I don't have room for Gage Newhart and his expectations of me.

I can't give him what he wants, and I don't have the energy to try.

Squeezing my eyes closed, I force a deep breath into my lungs, dragging with it that spice and leather that's even more overpowering now mixed with the heady, potent scent of sex.

I force myself to release it slowly, then glance over my shoulder at him to find those perfect lips of his slightly parted, his eyes closed, soft, steady breaths slipping out in his slumber.

Thank God...

Let's hope he's a *really* deep sleeper.

Because I have to get out of here.

I can't spend the night in Gage's bed.

He's just...too damn much.

More than I am ready for or maybe ever will be.

I grab his wrist and start to slowly lift his arm from around me, but my eyes snag on the ink there. If I had ever seen him without that leather jacket on before for longer than a few minutes at the gym, I might have noticed that the tattoos aren't random.

His left forearm bears a list of names and dates etched over an American flag waving in the wind. Bile climbs up my throat at the thought that they're probably comrades who died in combat. If I took the time to examine every inked inch of his body, I'd probably find other images that hold deep, sentimental meaning for him.

Because that's the type of person he is.

He cares deeply for other people.

His cocky charm and gregarious nature cover a man with deep wounds and scars.

I saw them tonight.

Puckered skin beneath the ink on his chest.

Jagged pink lines moving through the words and images.

And those are only the physical ones...

Even thinking about what he must have witnessed and experienced in his years in the Rangers makes that vise around my chest tighten and the bile force its way farther up.

I swallow it down and lift his arm fully off me so I can slide out to the edge of the bed. It creaks slightly, and I cringe, glancing back at him, but he hasn't moved an inch.

After all the work he put in tonight, hopefully he'll be out for a while.

Long enough for me to do what I need to.

I slide off the mattress, my bare feet hitting the old wooden floor, and I tiptoe over to where he tossed my clothes and tug on my jeans, wincing at the stickiness between my legs.

What I wouldn't give for a hot shower right now...

But that can wait until I get home.

Keeping my eye on the bed, I grab my bra and shirt and put them back on, watching for any signs that he might be awake, but that strong, inked chest of his just rises and falls steadily.

Those long, thick, dark eyelashes stay down, spread across his cheeks hiding those warm blue eyes I so easily threw myself into, regardless of how easy it was to drown in them—and him.

Christ, he's beautiful.

Even like this, when he's so vulnerable, his strength radiates from him. All that lean, hard-earned muscle, strong hands and immaculately built body.

The way he took charge of me so completely—that isn't something I've ever let anyone do.

So why the hell did you let him?

That question rattles around my head as I tiptoe over to the small desk against the far wall. I scan the papers strewn across the top—a phone bill, a few receipts for gas and parts for the shop, several other scraps containing random notes of things to remember to pick up at the store.

Nothing of importance.

A photo on the corner of the desk of him with his arm around a slightly older dark-haired man catches my eye, and I reach out and snag it. My eyes drift over Gage's easy smile despite the setting in the background. Clearly taken during a deployment, the man must be one of his military buddies.

One of the men listed on his arm, maybe?

I peek back at him, but he hasn't stirred.

The urge to sneak back over there and examine every spot of ink covering his body tries to pull me that direction, but learning more personal things about Gage won't do anything but complicate my feelings for him even more.

I release a heavy sigh.

Given his background, he probably will be a benefit to our security team, but I don't like the idea of having him around, of having to deal with this electricity and attraction between us when I need to be concentrating on the family and keeping them safe.

It's a distraction.

And distractions open the door for danger I can't let slip in.

Which is why I'm sneaking around his place like a common thief after he just fucked me into oblivion.

I return the picture to its place and tug open the top drawer, rifling through a few random papers and other items but coming up short of anything interesting or incriminating.

Because ultimately, that's what I'm looking for.

I know he has secrets, just like I do, despite what he said earlier about us coming clean with each other about everything. Everyone has secrets. Things they hold close to their chests and never reveal due to fear or embarrassment or guilt.

But the problem is, secrets can get you killed, or someone you love could get caught in the crossfire. Which means I have to find out everything I can about the man I just slept with while I have the opportunity.

I dig through every drawer, then do the same in the small kitchenette in the corner that only tells me he orders in most of the time instead of cooking for himself.

He rolls on the bed, spreading out on his back in a way that makes the sheet he pulled up over us shift to the side and expose his cock. I freeze, holding my breath, waiting to see if he's awake, but he resettles and I release the air from my lungs in a rush.

My clit pulses seeing him like this, and his earlier statement echoes in my head.

"I can't wait to fuck this pretty mouth of yours, too."

Lord...

That man's mouth is as lethal as his decorated cock.

And if I don't get out of here soon, I'll be tempted to climb back into bed with him.

I return to searching his dresser and every other inch of the tiny apartment, but there's nothing here that suggests he isn't exactly who he says he is or that he's lied about what he's doing here or his interest in me.

That should be a relief, but it only makes my gut tighten more.

Because it means he's the real deal.

And men like *that* don't exist in my world.

They can't.

There isn't room for them.

My phone buzzes in my pocket and I wince, scrambling to pull it out as the sound seems to echo through the room.

I glance at the screen.

Shit.

Hitting answer as I bring it to my ear, I slip into the bathroom off to the side of the loft and ease the door partially closed. "What?"

Isaac snorts. "Hello to you, too."

"I'm busy."

"Why are you whispering?"

I peek out the cracked door, but Gage hasn't stirred again. "Because I'm fucking busy."

"Well, get unbusy." His voice loses all humor. "You need to come over to the penthouse."

"Why?"

"Just fucking do it."

He ends the call, and I release an annoyed groan.

So much for my hot shower.

Instead, I have to go see Isaac about whatever the fuck is going on with the reminder and evidence of what I did with Gage—or should I say, what he did to me—still dripping from me.

But if he's at the penthouse with Coen and Allegra instead of at home with Jack, Vivi, and Gio at almost midnight, then something is very wrong.

Sucking in a long, deep breath, I slip out the bathroom door and make my way over to the nightstand to grab my gun and slide it into the holster. I snag my boots and socks and carry them down, refusing to risk the sound they might make on the metal treads.

I freeze with each step I take, watching the bed until I'm so far down I can't see it anymore, then I book it across the shop, past his Harley and Indian, to the small pedestrian door next to the large rolling one.

The few seconds it takes to pull on my socks and boots feels like an eternity while glancing up to ensure he isn't watching.

I scan the dimly lit shop as I lace my boots.

I'd love to search down here, too, given the time, but whatever Isaac called about was urgent. And when it comes to the

Hawkes, urgent doesn't usually mean good. Especially with Satriano back in town.

With one last look to the loft, I unlock the door, then slip out into the warm, damp New Orleans late evening air and fire off a text to Isaac.

I'm on my way, but I'm on the other side of town so it'll be a bit.

He immediately returns my text.

Just get here.

Asshole.

I scowl at it, then I slide my phone back inside my pocket as I rush toward the car. My hand trembles digging for my keys and pressing the unlock button, and as soon as it's open, I slide in and fire it up quickly, as if that big sliding door could open at any moment and Gage might come out and try to do something to stop me.

One look is honestly all it would take…

And that realization is terrifying.

But there's no movement from the building, no sound to suggest he woke, and for some reason, slipping out secretly in the dead of night like this makes what we just did feel even more wrong.

Even as my body sings with the memory of it and craves more.

Gage may offer the Hawkes another line of protection—an asset to our defenses against the kind of ruthlessness Satriano loves to direct toward us—but I'm more confident than ever that I'm going to need protecting from him—and from what he does to my heart.

GAGE

The elevator dings and the doors glide open, granting me access to the second floor of The Hawkeye Club.

I thought entering Cass and Kennedy's house for that meeting last night was like being permitted into the holy of holies, but this is the true inner sanctum. This is where they run the entire Hawke Enterprises empire from. Where the decisions are made. Where their most guarded secrets are held.

Few people are privy to what happens up here.

For good reason.

This type of money and power brings with it lots of jealousy and creates enemies—like Satriano.

The information they provided during that meeting was mind-boggling.

All the threats, the harm that has come to them either at his hand or indirectly because of his actions.

It's no wonder Bishop takes her job so seriously and is willing to go to such great lengths to do it. If she doesn't, these people she loves so much might suffer the consequences. She would never be able to live with herself if anything happened to any of them on her watch, which is why she's *always* on-guard, why she refuses to take time to care for herself or her own needs.

But now, it's my job to help her ensure their safety.

And to ensure *she* doesn't burn herself out in the process.

It all starts today.

I suck in a sharp breath and step out of the elevator, my boots moving almost silently across the polished floor. A practiced skill that has saved my life many times in the past. Voices carry down the hall, and I follow them, well aware that one of the owners of those might not be so happy to see me this morning.

She ran.

Waking up in the middle of the night to a cold, empty bed where her warm body should have been shouldn't have come as such a surprise, given her history, but it still stung more than I'd like to admit.

For some reason, I had held out the stupid hope that she would be in my arms when I opened my eyes.

I thought I had finally broken down that wall and left it so shattered that she couldn't rebuild it.

But apparently, I was wrong.

My chest still stings with that realization, and I rub at it absently as I advance down the corridor.

Saint's deep voice reverberates down to me. "Where do you think we should put him?"

I freeze mid-step before I reach an open doorway on the right and press my back against the wall. A familiar annoyed sigh follows Saint's question. I've heard that from Bishop so many times in the short period that we've known each other that I'd know it anywhere.

"I don't know, Dad. He's too skilled not to utilize, but..."

Bishop's hesitation makes me hold my breath.

But?

Last night should have eradicated any *buts* from her mind. It should have cemented for her that I am here to *help* her. That I would do just about *anything* to make all of this easier on her.

"But what?"

Her father's question hangs in the air, and my lungs burn waiting for her response.

"But I'm not sure we can trust him completely."

A beat of silence lingers, then two, before the sound of chair legs scraping against the floor echoes out into the hallway and I use the noise to release my breath in a rush filled with more pain than I ever expected.

She still doesn't trust me.

Visions of her spread out under me, her body trembling

and pulsing around mine, the way she completely came apart in my arms flash through my head.

"We ran a check on him after the meeting last night. Gabe called a bunch of his military contacts, and he checks out, kiddo. He's got half a dozen service medals, an impeccable record and honorable discharge. There's no reason to think he isn't exactly who and what he appears to be."

I inch closer to the door, waiting for her response again like a damn middle schooler straining to hear if the girl he's crushing on likes him, too.

Finally, she releases another deep sigh. "You're right. I'm just being overly cautious."

"That's your job, right?"

His words carry so much affection and pride, it reminds me of the way I used to hear similar words. How much they meant to me at times when it felt like I was drifting.

I hope Bishop can take them for what they are and accept his sentiment.

"It is my job, Dad. And after what Satriano pulled last night? I just can't shake this deep, foreboding sense of *dread.*"

I freeze, my shoulders tensing and my spine going ramrod straight.

What Satriano did?

Something must've happened after she left my place...

I assumed she snuck out because she wanted to avoid having to face me after what happened between us, because she loves to run, but maybe there was actually a reason for her absence when I woke.

"Let's put him with you today. I want you to take him to all the properties. Everywhere. Show him what security does at each location. Take him to all the residences. I want to be able to use him anywhere we might need to at any given time, and he needs to know how to get anywhere fast."

"Agreed."

The slight hesitation in her voice suggests she isn't fully on board, but my bet is it has to do with her being assigned as my guide rather than what he actually wants me to be shown.

And it sounds like their conversation is wrapping up, which means I can't continue to lurk in the hallway.

I step out, intentionally slamming my boot down harder than I normally would to announce my presence. "Hello?" I take the few steps toward the door, pretending to only notice them as I almost pass by. "Oh, hey. The guy down at the bar sent me up. Said you were here and expecting me."

Bishop doesn't even glance at me, just keeps her eyes locked on something in the corner of the room that's suddenly very interesting.

Her dad rises from where he was leaning against the front of his desk and smiles, extending a hand to me as he approaches. "Good to see you this morning. Welcome to the team, officially."

I return Saint's strong handshake. "Thank you. I'm glad to be here and ready to help in any way I can."

He sighs. "We definitely need it. Bishop will fill you in. I have to go meet with Savage, Gabe, and Kennedy, but I'll catch you guys later."

His heavy footsteps trail out of the room, and Bishop climbs to her feet, rubbing the back of her neck and keeping her eyes anywhere but on me.

She's still wearing the same clothes she had on at my place last night...

My hand twitches, so desperately wanting to reach out and touch her, to pull her up against me the way she *should* have been this morning.

She clears her throat and attempts to step around me, but I wrap my arm around her waist, halting her progress. Her entire body instantly tenses, and she keeps her gaze on the open door only a few feet in front of her.

Her escape route.

But I am not letting her get away that easily.

I dip my head, brushing my lips against her ear. "You're running from me again."

She swallows thickly and shakes her head, still refusing to look at me. "No. I'm not."

"Then what do you call sneaking out of my place while I was asleep?" I press my body tighter into hers, purposely reminding her of the position we were in only hours ago. "Did you really think I was done with you?"

A little shiver rolls through her, and I can't help but grin against her warm skin that still smells like me.

Like sex.

Like everything we did together last night.

Finally, she glances up, and the uneasiness and reservation in her gaze makes my shoulders tighten. "I had to leave. Isaac called. Satriano made a move."

I tighten my grip on her. "Then why the hell didn't you wake me up and bring me with you?"

If she thinks I'm going to believe for one second that she left because of the phone call and it wasn't just coincidental timing, then she's greatly underestimating how well I can read her.

She presses her lips together, struggling with a way to justify leaving without letting me know what was going on, but we both know she doesn't have a good reason.

Other than her fear.

Not of *him.*

Of *me.*

And I know I won't get a straight answer from her if I push her here and now, not when bigger things are at play.

I release a heavy sigh. "What happened with Satriano?"

She glances toward the open door, probably terrified that someone could walk down the hall and see me with my arm on her, but I refuse to relinquish my hold and let her run.

Again.

"He called on my brother last night."

"What do you mean?"

Her eyes meet mine again, the anger and tension there darkening them. "Pope made a deal with him a while back, after he helped us rescue Atlas, Astrid, Kennedy, Allie, and Benjamin from Dan Roselli, that he would treat any of Satriano's men who needed medical care and do it at our clinic so there wouldn't be any records at the hospital. Aunt Nora agreed to assist if needed, too."

"Jesus..."

She gives me a little nod. "Yeah. So, he's forcing Pope to be a mob doctor, and last night, one of his men took a bullet to the shoulder, and he called Pope into action."

"Does that happen a lot?"

"Not particularly, thankfully." She sighs. "But enough that it makes all of us uneasy. Not just because Pope could lose his license for what he's doing, but because every time Satriano does it, it's a reminder that he has that power over us. Over my brother."

I nod slowly. "Did your brother speak to him?"

She shakes her head. "Of course, Satriano doesn't personally deal with any of this shit. He just texted him and said a car would pick him up. Pope got there and the guy was practically dead on the table from blood loss. He was barely able to save him."

"But he did." I raise a brow. "What would happen if he hadn't?"

Her jaw tightens. "I don't ever want to find out."

I relax my hold on her slightly, and she starts to slip away, but I catch her wrist, sliding my thumb across her thrumming pulse. This may not be the place or time to say this, but if she has her way, she's going to ensure she isn't alone in a room with me ever again.

"You can't run from me or hide forever, Bishop. What happened last night wasn't the end of this. It was just the beginning."

If she only stopped fighting it.

Bishop locks her gaze with mine, heat flaring there as I tighten my grip, a very visceral reminder of the way I had her restrained. "You sure have a lot of confidence."

I shake my head. "I just know what I want, and I know you want it, too."

She showed me that last night. By giving herself to me. By allowing me to take control over her pleasure. By gifting me that trust.

Bishop doesn't immediately deny it, either.

I'll take that as another win.

"What I want is to get going, Gage. We have a lot to cover today. I need to introduce you to the Hawke Enterprises empire."

I nod and dip my head again, my lips brushing her ear. "Do you know how fucking hot it is to know that you're going to be walking around all day with my cum still inside you?"

"Fuck..."

She shivers, then tugs to try to get her hand free, and I release it one finger at a time.

A scowl twists her lips. "Let's go, Romeo. It's time you got a crash course on the Hawkes."

14

FIVE DAYS LATER

GAGE

Ducking to the right, I barely avoid Atlas's jab that probably would've hit me straight in the face and knocked me the fuck out if I hadn't been so quick.

He is no fucking joke.

And I know better than to get into the ring with him when I'm not one hundred percent *in it.*

Which means I probably shouldn't be here now.

God knows, I'm distracted by the same thing I have been for days...the same *person.*

She isn't even here, but I can't keep my mind from drifting to her when it should be focused on the man in front of me.

I circle around him, bouncing on my toes, trying to stay light on my feet because the only way to beat Atlas "The Hurricane" Hawke is to never give him a fucking millimeter.

One slight misstep, one too-slow response is all he needs to land a punch that could kill some people.

He didn't win that title belt by being anything but aggressive and deadly.

While this was just supposed to be a friendly sparring match as he gets back into shape to start preparing for his next fight, neither Atlas nor I are good at keeping things casual.

We both have that driving hunger, that desire to win, that need to come out on top, and it's playing out this morning here at the gym. Even without an audience, we both push. We both take any opening we see and exploit it.

It's what I was always taught—not just in the ring but in life. To find your enemies' weaknesses. To use them to your advantage. And apparently so was Atlas, because he's going much harder today than he did our previous times in the ring.

He can tell I'm distracted, and he's making me pay for it.

I try to surprise him with a quick jab to his chest, hoping that moving fast and unexpectedly will allow me to sneak in a few good shots. It lands, but I inadvertently open myself up to his right hook.

His glove slams into my jaw, snapping my head back and making little bright lights explode in my vision. My ears ring. My jaw aches.

Fuck.

That one fucking hurt.

The room spins slightly, my vision switching between black spots and ones so bright they almost hurt to look at, but somehow, I manage to stay on my feet.

Barely.

He mumbles an apology he doesn't mean, grinning around his mouthguard. That should be the signal to stop for the day, but all it does is add fuel to the fire burning in my chest.

The second I feel like I'm not going to fall over, I lunge at him with an aggressive combination, but he manages to pull me into the clinch, stopping me from doing any real harm. He shoves me back, and I circle around, ensuring I never put my back to the corner because that's where Atlas is at his best, where he can pummel you and put you in a place you have no means of escape from.

I've watched enough of his fights to know that, even if I'm still relatively new to sparring with him. But being prepared does nothing against a man like Atlas—a lesson I am learning this morning along with the fact that I may have been a decent fighter in WCAP but facing a world middleweight champ, I feel like a novice.

The man is a machine.

Lightning fast.

Strong.

Determined.

With a literal chip on his shoulder.

Desperate to prove his impossible comeback win after being shot when he wasn't expected to ever fight again wasn't just a fluke.

It absolutely wasn't. Even now, when he's spent months only doing light training and mostly spending time with Wren, he's still a powerhouse.

His ego and willpower fuel him.

My frustration fuels me.

After almost a week of working for the Hawkes and having Bishop avoid me in every way, shape, and form possible, including handing me off to any other member of the family or security teams she can find to help me get my bearings, my aggravation has only grown.

With her. With the situation. With the fact that what I want may be out of reach no matter what I do.

Bishop has buried her head in her work rather than face what happened between us.

It's not that she doesn't have a legitimate excuse. The situation with Satriano and the family is tenuous, at best, and knowing that someone is out there shooting Satriano's men means there's another player, too. Someone the Hawkes haven't been able to pinpoint yet.

And unknowns are something the Hawkes—and especially Bishop—aren't fans of, with good reason.

But it doesn't make what she's doing any less frustrating.

Pushing me away. Leaving rooms when I walk in. Ensuring we're never truly alone so I can't say or do what I really want to —*talk* to her and force her to admit what we both felt that night.

She hasn't even been back to her condo, instead spending the nights at one of her cousins' places with the excuse of them needing "extra" security when it was really about her needing somewhere to hide—from me.

If she knew how I've sat outside on my bike waiting for her to come back out each night, she would throw that "stalking" word at me again.

I hope today will be different, but I'm not holding my breath. Just like I'm not holding out any hope whatsoever that I'm actually going to beat Atlas.

My ears are still ringing, my head still spinning from his blow and the flurry of activity after it when I sense her enter the gym.

Hellcat...

Even with my back to the door, it's unmistakable the way my skin heats and my body starts to prime. Her jasmine scent somehow trickles to me, even over the smells of sweat and leather that permeate the air in the gym.

God, she smells good.

I've been living with that scent for days, unwilling to wash it away from my sheets in case she never comes back. I don't want to lose those memories. I'm not ready to give up on her or us. Not yet.

Somewhere, deep down, in a place she's not ready to face yet, she wants what I'm offering her. She needs it to survive what's going on around her. The weight of it all *will* crush her without it. And eventually, she'll realize I'm right about that.

It might not be now. It might not be tomorrow. It might not even be anytime soon. But one day, Bishop *will* see what she's doing to herself and what she can have with me.

I don't dare look behind me at her now, though.

I can't look away from Atlas for a second, not if I want to keep my head on and my ribs intact, along with all the vital organs beneath them.

We dance around each other a little more, and as I move to the left, I catch a glimpse of Bishop out of the corner of my eye, leaning against the wall, watching us with a mix of something in her gaze I can't determine without pulling my attention away from the threat in front of me.

And *good God*, he moves fast.

So fast it makes the men I fought in the WCAP look like sloths moving across the ring.

He lands a blow to my rib cage that feels like getting hit by a truck and I double over slightly, attempting to retreat further out of his reach. Trying to slip away without conceding defeat when I know he will keep coming.

Bishop's voice cuts through the air before either of us can call an end to it. "I think he's had enough, Atlas."

When it comes to her...never.

When it comes to Atlas...probably.

Her cousin continues to bounce on his feet but holds back the eruption of finishing shots I know he had already loaded up and ready to fly. He glances over at her and mutters, "Who the hell are you, his mother?" around his mouthguard.

I snort a laugh that makes my ribs ache and push up to stand fully with a wince I try to hide before I finally look over at her.

She wears a smug smile that tells me she enjoys watching me get hit, enjoys watching my pain.

Maybe a little too much.

I was right about her—Bishop Clarke has sadistic tendencies. At least where I'm concerned. Perhaps she sees it as payback for tying her to the headboard and ensuring her loss of control the other night.

She pushes off the wall and wanders over to the ring, resting her arms on the ropes as she looks in at us. In a thin tank top and sports bra and adorable athletic shorts that show off her beautiful legs, her braids pulled back in a ponytail, she looks ready for a workout...and cute as fuck. "How long have you two been going at it?"

Atlas spits out his mouthguard and glances at me. "I don't know. An hour?"

Her brows rise. "You've been going that hard for an hour?"

I shake my head. "No, he toyed with me for a while first."

She snorts and nods, her own experience in the ring with Atlas enough that she knows *precisely* what I mean by that. "I'm surprised you can keep up with him."

Did she really just say that to me?

I narrow my gaze on her.

The blow to my ego almost hurts more than Atlas' did, until I see the smug tilt of her lips. I'm not the type to stand by and take it when I know she's egging me on.

I spit out my mouthguard, locking my eyes with hers. "I would think that I've given you no reason to question my stamina."

Atlas' gaze drifts between the two of us and then narrows on me. "What the hell does that mean?"

Oops.

Apparently, my defensiveness may have inadvertently outed my—whatever the fuck this is—with Bishop. That hadn't been my intention, but the glower she throws my way is enough to make me wish I hadn't said it loud enough for him to hear.

Coupled with the comments Astrid made at The Grind the

other day and the looks the family gave me at the meeting that night, he surely suspected something far before I made the verbal slip.

But still, I won't delve into my personal situation with Bishop if she doesn't want him knowing about it.

"Just that I've been working for your family for several days now, and she's seen me and what I'm capable of."

He nods slowly, the partial smirk revealing he clearly isn't buying my explanation. "*Suuure.*"

Shit.

Maybe if Bishop weren't standing right there, I could bring myself to care more and make an attempt to convince him it's nothing, but it's impossible when I'm looking at the woman.

I wander over to the edge and stare down at her, then squat to put myself more to her level. "If you think I need to work on my stamina so bad, why don't you come in here and show me what you've got?"

Her brow rises slowly. "You want to spar with me?"

Atlas chuckles behind me. "Boy, you don't know what you're asking for."

It's meant as a warning.

To anyone else, it might have been one.

For me, it just sounds like a challenge.

I grin, never looking away from her. "Oh, I definitely do."

BISHOP

I must be fucking nuts.

It's the only reason I would be standing in the ring in my gear, facing down the most dangerous man I know—excluding Satriano.

And it isn't Atlas.

It's the one who got me to do things I never thought I would, to give up the one thing I so desperately need in my life all the time. It's the man I haven't been able to look in the eyes since then because he saw too much.

He *knows* too much.

From the first moment we met, I could sense it—his ability to read people. And he had me figured out from day one.

Now, he bounces on his feet, slamming his gloves together and cracking his neck side to side as if he's preparing for a title fight and not just a little friendly sparring.

Because we both know that's *not* what this is.

Not by a longshot.

He has a lot to say that I don't want to hear. I've heard it enough in my own head over the last several days since I left his place.

It's been so insistent that I've almost welcomed the distraction Satriano coming back provided. The excuse to avoid this man and the way he pushes me.

Atlas watches from outside the ring, a grin on his face before either of us have even thrown a punch. Whatever he suspects—and he *clearly* suspects *something*—he also knows there's more to this showdown than we're letting on.

Gage wants to prove a point.

I just want to punch him in the face to wipe away that smug smirk he always wears.

And I'm not waiting around for him to make the first move.

I step forward and swing a hard right hook. His eyes widen, but he somehow manages to duck out of the way so the blow only glances off his shoulder rather than hitting him square in the jaw.

It was close.

So damn close.

I almost had him.

And that fucker *grins*.

He *grins* at me as he lays down a barrage of punches that send me retreating into the ropes. They catch my retreat, but I push off them, shoving my hands against his chest, forcing him back with as much strength as I can muster. But he barely budges.

Because Gage is like a goddamn immovable object.

Especially when it comes to this—to us—because he wants there to be something there and doesn't seem content to walk away with just having had one decent night together.

Who the fuck are you kidding, Bishop?

It was more than decent.

My pussy throbs at the memory, and it is absolutely the worst time to be thinking about it because that nanosecond of distraction is enough for him to jab me in the ribs.

I wince at the impact, but I know it could've been much worse.

He's holding back, just like Atlas does when we spar, because he has a foot and at least fifty pounds on me. Because we're not even remotely in the same class. But what Gage has in size and strength, I make up for in speed.

Plus, the fact that he's holding back only makes me want to fight harder.

I push with combinations that would send most fighters to the mat quickly, but he blocks and ducks and weaves fluidly, dodging my strikes the same way I have been him for days.

This is payback for that.

It certainly seems like it is.

And it starts to feel futile.

I push and push, charging and constantly on the offensive, and he looks like he's barely breathing hard keeping me at bay. Regrouping, I fake a left jab and manage to slip my right arm around to punch him in the exact same spot where Atlas landed the blow earlier.

That does the trick.

He releases a little *oomph* noise and backs off with a grimace that only fuels me to move harder and faster. It might be the only opening I get with him to make *my* point.

I step forward with a combination and feet so fast that he doesn't have time to regain his, and it sends him sprawling out on his back on the canvas.

He stares up at me with wide blue eyes, as if he didn't expect me to take advantage of his misstep, but then I see it there…

The corner of his mouth twitching with his suppressed grin.

Because he *gave* that to me.

It wasn't a mistake at all.

It was intentional.

"You motherfucker."

I mumble the words around my mouthguard, and I don't know if he can make them out or not as he climbs to his feet and circles around me like a goddamn lion on the Serengeti stalking his prey.

He throws a couple light jabs, testing out the distance, watching to see what I'm going to do, waiting for me to act, to move again, because he's letting me lead. Because he knows I want to be in control of every situation, including this one. I want to control the fight. Force him to make mistakes instead of him intentionally making them to give me some false sense of victory.

Gage did it to rile me up.

Because he loves the push back.

He craves it as much as I love giving it to him.

I motion with my gloves for him to come at me, and his eyes flare with a heat I remember from the other night, one that sends molten lava flowing through my veins.

And I charge.

My flash of punches combined with my duck and weave,

the way I circle him, all keep him on his toes. Keep him on the defensive. And even though his reach is far greater than mine, I manage to avoid almost every one of his blows.

A few glance off me, but most barely touch me.

"Is that all you've got?"

He definitely heard that one, because he comes again, so hard and so fast that I finally see what he's really capable of. I can see why that had him fighting in the WCAP.

Shit.

Gage pins me into the corner and spits out his mouthguard, apparently not caring that his perfect teeth or pretty smile might get bashed in.

He dips his head next to mine, low, where Atlas is sure not to hear whatever he says. "I like battling with you, Hellcat, though I'd much rather do it in the bedroom."

The truth is...so would I.

And that pisses me the fuck off.

I raise my knee and jam it straight between his legs.

He barks out a cough and stumbles back slightly. His cup may have protected him from being unable to father children, but it definitely hurt. And given the whistle that Atlas releases from between his teeth, it clearly signals the end of the fight, too.

Atlas slides under the ropes and approaches, his tattooed chest still slick with a sheen of sweat from their match and a wearing a shit-eating grin on his face. "That might be the most entertaining thing I've seen in years."

Gage continues to stay partially doubled over, his breathing hard, eyes narrowed on me.

I spit out my mouthguard. "I won."

Atlas chuckles. "It doesn't count. You cheated."

"We didn't establish any ground rules for this match."

It's a bullshit argument on my part. Hitting in the groin, especially intentionally, is *never* permitted.

He looks to Gage, who straightens and finally approaches us slowly, shaking out his leg as if that might relieve some of the discomfort my blow just caused.

Gage offers me a partial grin. "Bishop always uses everything at her disposal to gain control of the situation, don't you?"

I raise a brow at him, *daring* him to bring our personal business out in front of Atlas and see how I would respond.

He stares at me for a moment, then looks back at Atlas. "I won't hold it against her that she couldn't finish me off the old-fashioned way without going for the low blow. Maybe next time."

It would be impossible to miss the double entendre in his statement.

Gage smirks at me before he holds up his hands for Atlas to help him with his gloves. He never takes his eyes off me as Atlas undoes the Velcro and tugs them off, almost as if he's waiting for me to blow and is afraid he might miss it if he looks away.

Atlas passes him his gloves, then turns to me and grabs my right hand. He grips the edge of the Velcro and tugs it off. I glance down to watch his progress, and to avoid his scrutiny, afraid if I look him in the eye, he will see all the things that have happened with Gage.

That's the problem with growing up so close to each other in the Hawke family. Everyone is in everyone else's business and loves to interject their thoughts and opinions about things that are absolutely not theirs to butt their heads into.

And sleeping with Gage would be something Atlas definitely has opinions about.

Plus, once he knew, so would everyone else. First Wren, then Astrid, and it would spread like wildfire through the Hawke gossip chain until the entire flock was yapping about it and giving me their advice I absolutely do not want.

When I finally chance a glance back up, Gage has slid out of the ring and is walking toward the locker room at the rear of the gym.

Hell.

I shouldn't follow him.

Nothing good that will come from it.

But I'm still seething in a way I can't seem to get a grip on, and I hate the way this man makes me feel.

Out of control.

Of my reactions.

My thoughts.

My damn body.

When he's around, everything is *heightened*. I'm more aware of all the things I normally push to the back of my mind in favor of focusing on what's important—protecting the family.

I don't have the time or energy to deal with him on a daily basis, something I damn sure intend to tell him. Or maybe not, as that would only be conceding the fact that he does have some control over me.

Fuck.

Atlas watches me with a raised brow. "What is *up* with you two?" He motions between the closing locker room door and me. "Seriously. It's like thunder and lightning collide every time you are in a room with him."

I roll my shoulders, shaking out my arms. "Nothing. He just...riles me up sometimes."

Atlas chuckles. "No shit."

The door between the gym and the pilates studio opens, and Wren sticks her head in. "Oh, hi, Bishop." She smiles, and it pulls at the scars on the side of her face. "Babe, can you come help me with something?"

Atlas gives me a long look. "Sure can. For what it's worth, Bishop, I like the guy."

So do I.

And that's the problem ultimately.

I can't like him.

I can't *enjoy* this dynamic we have where he pushes and I push back harder.

I can't *want* more of what we had the other night.

I just...can't.

Atlas slips from the ring and goes to help his fiancée, leaving me alone in the silent gym knowing damn well the man behind all my frustrations is only a door away.

15

BISHOP

Even knowing what a horrific idea it is, I shove through the door to the locker room and storm in, intent on confronting Gage and ending whatever this is now.

Before things go too far.

Before we're so deep down the rabbit hole that there isn't any way to climb out of it.

It's one of the reasons I've avoided him. Because even if I think I'm mentally prepared to deal with the emotions he created by our night together, Gage can still toss one *look* my way and completely unravel my well-constructed defenses.

He can unravel me so easily when I need to stay wound this tight to stay alert and ensure I don't miss anything.

Right now, it's impossible to miss *him.*

Gage stands beside the shower in nothing but his shorts, hands at the waistband, about to shove them down. There's no question he heard me stomp in here, and the door swings closed behind me, *ensuring* he's well aware of my presence. But he keeps his back to me, reaching over to crank on the hot water as if he doesn't have a care in the world while I'm over here fuming.

"You held back!"

The words echo off the metal lockers and the tile, my accusation laced with my frustration and annoyance at more than just the few minutes we played around in that ring.

I may have been intentionally icing him out over the last several days, but it wasn't as if I enjoyed it and didn't spend all that time trying to forget everything that happened between us and everything I gave him of myself.

Gage slowly turns to face me, his face deceptively impassive though his eyes burn with an intensity I only ever saw that night at his place. "I'm bigger and stronger than you, Bishop. That isn't meant as an insult, just an objective fact. You're one of the strongest women I've ever met, and definitely the most skilled, but I won't risk hurting you. Don't take it so personally."

Is he serious *right now?*

I scoff at him. "How am I *not* supposed to take it personally?"

He shoves his hand through this sweaty hair, pushing it off his forehead. "You think Atlas doesn't hold back with you?"

My back stiffens.

Because of course he does.

I'm the only one in the family who gives him even a remote challenge, but I still know it isn't what he's capable of. Not in a fight setting. Not even fucking close. But this is different.

With *Gage*, it's different.

I don't want him to hold back with me. I don't want him to treat me like I'm that *adorable* girl he sat with on the blanket in City Park. I don't want him to look at me like I'm someone he needs to *protect* when I'm perfectly capable of doing it myself. When I *have* to be able to do it for others.

We may need his help right now with Satriano lurking

around town, but *I* don't need him to handle me with kid gloves.

"I don't care what Atlas does. I care what *you* do!"

Shit.

I hadn't meant to say that out loud. I hadn't meant to admit that Gage and what he thinks has suddenly become so damn important to me.

He raises a brow. "Is this what I have to do to get you to talk to me? Piss you off?"

Dammit.

When I came to the gym this morning, I promised myself if Gage was here that I wouldn't let this happen, that I wouldn't cave to this *pull* he has or allow myself to get worked up over anything he did or said.

All I wanted was a good workout before going to *real* work after another sleepless night.

Instead, I'm staring at him standing here almost naked, and I can't keep my eyes from roaming over his sweat-slickened muscles, still swollen and trembling from his exertion. The fact that I can't tear my eyes away from him, and that my body aches for his touch even now, only makes me angrier.

I scowl at him and clench my fists at my sides, otherwise, I might do something stupid like *touch* him.

He nods slowly, as if responding to his own question when I didn't.

A non-answer is enough for him to know he's right. That getting me mad is a surefire way to make me come to him. Which was probably his plan all along.

"I see. Well, in that case, Hellcat"—he shrugs—"you weren't a challenge at all."

Gage gives me his back again, then shoves down his shorts and steps in under the water.

Before I even know I'm doing it, my feet are moving across the tile, and I grab his shoulder, spinning him around to face me as the hot water pelts his back and sprays all over me. "You're *lying*."

He grins, amusement dancing in his eyes, too. "I told you I was a shitty liar." His hands grasp my waist so quickly I don't even realize what he's going to do until he spins me and pins me back against the tile, his mouth a mere hairsbreadth from mine. "God, I love it when you're like this, Hellcat, all fiery and angry. You have no idea how badly I wanted to pin you down in the ring and fuck you right there, regardless of who might see."

I groan as his words light that flame deep inside my core and send heat spreading out through every single fiber of my being. Plastering my hands to his wet chest, I dig my nails into the ink there and try to shift in his hold, to put some space between us. Because with him so close, I can't think. He consumes all the oxygen and prevents my brain from processing things clearly.

But his large body keeps me pressed to the tile.

At his mercy here just as I was in his bed.

"Tell me, Bishop. What were *you* thinking about when we were in the ring?"

Nothing I will ever admit to you...

Because he did that on purpose. He got me worked up and toyed with me in that ring in order to force *this* showdown. And I hate that I walked right into his trap.

I swallow thickly, trying to clear my head of the vivid images flashing through it right now—of the way he tied me up, of how he ate me like a starved man who couldn't get enough, of how he fucked me so slowly that it was like torture, only to finally give me what I needed in the best way possible.

And now I can feel his hard length pressed against my leg, straining and so ready, and my body's primed for him again, my pussy throbbing and clenching for something that isn't there but could be so quickly and easily.

"Did you think about how good it felt to have my cock inside you?"

I shudder and shake my head, refusing to look away even though the longer I stare into his eyes, the harder it gets to attempt to remain unaffected by him and our current position. "No."

He chuckles low, the vibration of his chest against my hands somehow going straight through my entire body and centering between my legs.

"Liar." He nips at my bottom lip, then reaches down to lift my leg and drag it up over his hip so he can press his cock directly between them, in the spot that so desperately aches for it. "You thought about this. About doing it again."

I shake my head again, this time clenching my eyes closed, unable to look into his because I know I'll get lost swimming in them again, just like I did the other night.

He grips my chin with his free hand tightly. "Look at me, Bishop."

Those words snap my lids open again, almost as if they have some magical quality I can't fight.

And fuck, I was right.

The warm blue depths look so inviting. His mouth is so close to mine. His hard cock is pressed so tightly along my core. That scent of his seems even stronger, mixing with his sweat and the clean soap sitting on the ledge beside me.

All of it is too much.

I might have had the willpower to resist him if I continued to stay away and put the very real physical space between us like I have over the last several days, but not like this.

Like this...I'm a goner.

Something has to give.

Something has to snap.

And it's me.

I slam my mouth to his, grinding my hips to give myself the

friction my body so desperately demands. He groans low and deep, pressing against me even tighter as the water continues to beat down at his back. He moves his hand from my thigh up to the waistband of my shorts and starts to tug them down, but I tear my mouth from his.

"Here? Now?"

His brow furrows, his eyes darkening. "Do you seriously think being in the locker room of your cousin's gym is going to stop me from getting inside you right now, Hellcat?"

It's a pointless question since we both know the answer before he even says the words, and I drop my foot and allow him to shove my shorts down. I toe off my shoes, and he grabs my panties in his hand and tugs hard.

They rip off, and just like the other night, the sound of that fabric tearing is enough to make me buck against him. He captures my mouth again as he glides his hand up between my thighs and slips two fingers into me easily.

"Good God, woman." His lips roam over mine. "You're going to get what you want. Hard and fast."

God, yes...

He curls his fingers deep into my G-spot and slides his thumb up over my clit, making me twitch in his hold. "Even though all I want to do is drop to my knees and taste you again...I don't have the willpower to wait today. Not after the way you've been ducking and avoiding me this week."

At the moment, I can't remember *why* I was doing that.

All I know is that *this* feels right.

Giving in to this attraction.

Allowing this electricity he produces to flow through me.

Accepting his touch and his filthy mouth all over me.

He pulls his hand from my core, grasps my hips, lifts me so I can wrap my legs around his waist, then aligns his cock and plunges into me as he pins me back to the tile again.

"Fuck!"

My scream echoes off the tile around us, my head slamming back against the hard surface, but it doesn't give him any pause. He draws his hips back again and thrusts deep, a hiss slipping from between his clenched teeth.

"It is taking every ounce of my self-control not to come inside you right now, Hellcat. What you just did out there in the ring was the best foreplay I've ever experienced in my life."

I groan as he rolls his hips, pressing his pelvis against my clit in a way that makes me see stars behind my closed lids.

Fuck. Fuck. Fuck. Fuck.

This man...

I swallow and gasp, trying to get air into my lungs. "I didn't realize getting kneed in the balls was such a turn on."

He barks out a laugh as he drags his hips back and slams into me even harder.

Fuck.

My body tenses as it takes all of him, as it accepts his relentless rhythm, as it consumes the man I've tried desperately to avoid for the last couple of days because I knew how good this would be. To be with him like this again. Because I understood I was weak where he's concerned.

And the last thing I can afford to be right now is weak.

GAGE

Bishop clenches down around my cock like a vise, her slick heat as scorching hot as the water cascading down on me, and I hiss out a breath to keep from blowing my load straight into her.

I've been so on edge when it comes to her for so long, I'm barely hanging on by a thread.

All it would take is one word from her, one admission that

what happened the other night *meant* something and touched a part of her she wasn't ready to see yet, and I could let it go.

But she isn't ready for that.

What just happened in the ring proves it.

I draw my hips back and plunge in again, bottoming out so deep inside her I can't tell where I end and she begins anymore.

She does it again, clamping her cunt so goddamn tightly on me that it's almost like she's trying to prove a point she couldn't in the ring. Like she's trying to show me just how strong and powerful she really is.

But there isn't any need for that.

I already know.

I've already seen her in action.

It's exactly what drew me to her in the first place.

Because she doesn't cower to anything, doesn't cave, doesn't flinch or give an inch to anyone or anything.

She may be half her father's size, but she's every bit as strong as him, maybe even more so because she does it with such a stunning face that makes some people not take her seriously.

People who underestimate her pay for it, but that is not a mistake I will ever make. Not when we're in the ring. Not when we're like this. Never.

If I do, I'll end up with her knee to the balls again.

Or worse.

"Do you want to hurt me, Hellcat?"

Her eyes flutter open and meet mine, and I withdraw only to slam into her again, drawing a throaty gasp from her parted lips. She nods, her nails biting into my chest. "Yes."

That should act as a warning. A very real one. It means I've pushed too hard, gone too far in what I've asked of her. But I'm not afraid of being hurt—at least not physically.

A little pain is often necessary to complete the mission. And my mission isn't complete where Bishop Clarke is concerned. Not by a longshot.

The brutal honesty from her is a good start, though. And instead of being offended by her admission, I grin, remembering the feeling of her knee driving between my legs. "How badly?"

She sucks in a sharp breath, her darkened eyes locked with mine. "Badly enough that you'll never doubt that I can."

"Oh, Hellcat." I shake my head, rolling my hips as I thrust inside her, grinding her back against the tile. "You have no idea how badly you've hurt me the last few days, do you?"

Her body tenses for a second, as if she didn't anticipate me saying that.

And she probably didn't.

She probably doesn't have any clue how torturous it's been to be so close to her, yet feel like we're miles apart. To not be able to touch her like this. To not be able to taste her or feel her lips moving against mine.

Bishop thinks this is all some game, but she has no idea that it's over. She's already won. All she has to do to claim her prize is admit she needs me and what I'm offering.

Help.

She needs to accept that she can't do it all on her own. That she can't carry the weight of protecting the Hawkes on her shoulders alone and expect it not to break her. There has to be some give, some release, some relinquishment of her need to control *everything.*

The longer she considers my question, the softer her gaze becomes, and I keep pumping into her, slowing my hips, taking the violent intensity of the first few minutes and allowing it to fade back.

But she doesn't seem so ready to let it go.

Bishop squirms against the tile, waiting for me to move

hard again. She clenches around me, trying to urge me to move with her feet at my lower back.

I chuckle lightly. "You know better than to try that, Hellcat. Where does it get you?"

She grits her teeth. "Frustrated."

A feeling I am old friends with.

I hate that she feels this way. So much pent-up tension and aggravation overtaking every moment of her life.

The pang of pain that hits my chest makes me still my hips completely.

I bring one hand up to capture her cheek. "You really can't let go, can you?"

Those beautiful lips of hers part with a retort. Like she has so many other times, she wants to argue with me. She wants to deny it's a problem. All those years of being strong, of taking on the weight of the world around her on her own rather than admit it's too much have made it impossible for her to do what I'm asking of her.

I see the exact second she realizes that I'm right.

I'm sure it isn't anything dozens of other people haven't said to her over the years, but standing here under the water in the shower at her cousin's gym, where anyone might walk in on us while I have my cock buried deep inside her, has made it very clear to her that the only time she *ever* lets go of her death grip on control is with me.

That night and now.

But even at this moment, she tries to cling to the last vestiges of that control like a lifeline.

She needs it.

"I'll tell you what, Hellcat." I grin at her. "Next time, I'll let you be on top."

Her eyes flare, the heat there mirroring that of her cunt squeezing around my cock. It ripples along my length as she shifts, and she grinds down, drawing a low groan from deep in my chest.

Her nails bite into the skin there again, then she slides her hands up into my hair, tugging on it to move my head to the side.

Bishop dips her head to my ear. "You're not ready for that."

Good fucking God.

My balls draw up tight, the tingle of my impending release racing up my spine. "You're playing with fire, woman."

"No"— she shakes her head—"you are."

When she flexes her cunt around me this time, she does so at an angle that causes the head of my cock to catch in that spot she loves so much. I roll my hips back, and it becomes a primal drive instead of the deliberate one it was before.

I slam into her again and again, plunging deep, drawing out harshly, each time demanding she take more and that she give it all up at the same time.

Her heels digging into my lower back, moving with me, forcing me to take her hard for *both* of us, and I drop my mouth to her collar bone, exposed in the wet tank top she still wears. The taste of her skin on my lips and tongue makes me downright feral, and I sink my teeth into the flesh there.

She gasps but doesn't stop rolling her hips to meet mine, doesn't stop the way her body clamps around mine, or how tightly she clutches me to her.

When I draw my head back and see my teeth marks on her dark skin, that's the end of me. My thrusts become as erratic as my breathing. I grip her face in my hand, her hip in the other, and drag her mouth to mine, capturing her scream as her body finally tenses and she comes, just in time for my own orgasm to come roaring out of me.

I don't bother trying to bite back my own scream.

Fuck.

When I warned her it would be fast and hard, I should've

been warning myself, because even I wasn't ready for it. All that tension between us exploding. That was what we started in the ring finishing here.

And now that I've finished inside her, my hips still and she sags, my body pressing her to the wall the only thing keeping her upright. Her feet slide from my back and I grip her ass, keeping her upright, but I refuse to release her face until her eyes flutter open and meet mine again.

A single tear clings to her lashes, and I kiss it away, nuzzling against her—face to face.

"Did I hurt you, Hellcat?"

She shakes her head. "No."

"Have I ever? Even that night?"

Another tear slips free from her eyes, and I wonder when the last time she cried was.

Biting her trembling lip, she shakes her head again. "No. Never. The only thing that hurts is—" She swallows thickly. "Is how right you are. About everything."

She collapses into my hold, burying her face against my chest as a tiny sob slips from her. Sliding my hand around the back of her neck, I clutch her to me, letting the hot water soothe away some of the pain she's feeling now that the dam has broken.

Tugging her chin up, I meet her tear-soaked gaze with mine, hoping she can see how much I mean the words I'm going to say to her. "You won't run from me again. You won't pretend that this is nothing. I know you're scared, but I'll tell you right now, I'm not walking away. And you're not going to either."

She draws in a deep breath, her body trembling as she stares at me from under thick, dark lashes. A flicker of that tenacity darkens her eyes. "I can do whatever I want."

I smile softly. "I know you can, Hellcat, but you don't want to. Not really. Not deep down. You just don't trust yourself to fully open up to me, to show me all the things you try so hard to hide. But I'm going to make sure that you do. I'm going to make sure that you see how fucking perfect you are, what an incredible, badass woman I've got my cock buried deep inside of right now. Even if you're overwhelmed. Even if you're scared. You are *safe* right here. You understand me?"

The Bishop who walked into this gym earlier this morning would be fighting me. She would argue with me and say she isn't overwhelmed, that she isn't scared, because admitting those things would mean conceding she can't do it all alone.

But this isn't that same woman.

She nods—a tiny, almost imperceptible movement of her head—but it's enough to know we've moved beyond the fighting stage, that she's finally ready to let me see the other side of her. The one that lies under the tough-as-nails exterior.

Bishop Clarke is finally letting down her guard.

16

THREE DAYS LATER

GAGE

"Are you *sure* you want to do this?"

The uneasiness in Bishop's voice draws my attention from the cute one-story house we stand in front of in Metairie and over to her beside me on the sidewalk.

I raise a brow. "*Should* I be worried?"

She tears her gaze away from the front door and settles it on me, nervous energy bubbling out of her in a way I've never seen before.

When she stared down Satriano, the man who has ruined the lives of everyone she cares about and continues to be the primary source of all of their problems, she was stone cold. But facing her grandmother's house, she seems terrified.

Genuinely *shaken* at the thought of going in with me.

"You've met the family, Gage, but you haven't seen them in action at a Sunday family dinner. Or met Nana, for that matter."

A laugh bubbles up from my chest and I wrap my arm around her shoulders, pulling her against me so I can kiss her forehead. "I have faced far scarier and more dangerous things. I think I'll be all right."

She shakes her head, looking up at me with trepidation. "You greatly underestimate my grandmother."

It's funny to see Bishop so discombobulated over dinner with her family, and the way she talks about her grandmother makes her sound like Don Corleone.

Smirking, I lean in and kiss her softly, letting my lips linger there because I won't be able to do this once we get inside. Bishop made it *very* clear that there are to be no signs of affection or hints that we're together.

"If she's anything like you, Hellcat, then you're right. She's probably a force to be reckoned with." I raise a brow. "But I managed with you, didn't I?"

Her lips twist into a scowl, eyes narrowing on me in that way she always does when she's gearing up for an argument. "Managed *what*?"

I grin, a dozen different things I could say just to set her off flickering through my mind, but I don't want to start a fight we can't end the way I want to—with my cock buried inside of her again like it was an hour ago.

"I'll tell you later..."

"Later?"

The way her cheeks flush and she shifts restlessly on her feet tells me she caught on to why we wouldn't be having that conversation now, but I start walking up the pathway toward the house just in case she decides to push it.

Her hurried footsteps follow behind until she finally catches up with me on the small front patio.

"Do we ring the doorbell?"

She shakes her head and grabs the doorknob, twisting it and pushing the door in. "No need. We're all family here. There is no privacy and no secrets."

I highly doubt that.

Everyone has secrets.

Deep, dark ones that will never see the light of day. Some that are for good reason. Others that people keep from themselves and refuse to acknowledge.

Until a few days ago, Bishop was squarely in that category, refusing to face the fact that she was hurting herself by carrying so much responsibility and guilt that she shouldn't have to alone.

But our breakthrough at the gym seems to have helped relieve some of that for her.

She isn't an open book, but she's definitely started to talk more about the stress of her job and constant concern over the rest of the Hawkes. That's more than I thought I'd get even a week ago. And being invited to Sunday family dinner at Nana's is a *huge* step—even if Bishop isn't the one who extended it.

This is where it all started. Where Savage, Storm, Skye, Stone, and their sister Star, who passed away, grew up. Where Gabe became an honorary member of the family, and where, one way or another, everyone else was brought into the fold. This is where Savage and Gabe had the idea for The Hawkeye Club, where the empire was born.

Immediately upon stepping inside, a wave of excited chatter and multiple conversations flood the air along with the most delicious, mouth-watering smells.

I've already experienced the Hawkes together at the meeting at Cass and Kennedy's house, but this is different. That dark cloud that hung over all of them then doesn't exist here. Like this space is somehow sacred and protected from any of the turmoil the outside world throws at them.

Charlotte and Viviana run around squealing, and Giovanni, who is barely old enough to walk, crawls after them, then tries to climb to his feet, gives up, and returns to all fours to follow.

Bishop watches them, nudging the door closed behind her. "Don't worry about the little one. Char and Vivi have him."

I wasn't actually worried.

Nothing I've seen of the Hawkes—in their businesses or their homes—suggests they're the type to allow their children out of sight of an adult for very long—if at all.

A blond head pops out from around the corner, and Astrid smiles and waves us in. "Hey, guys. I think we're going to eat in like, five."

"Perfect." Bishop leans in with an exasperated sigh. "That means less time for them to grill you pre-dinner."

"They're going to *grill* me?"

"Ha." She rolls her eyes. "*Grill* is the nice way of putting it. You know all those infamous tortures used during the inquisition and the crusades?" My back stiffens, and I shift uncomfortably as she stares me down. "Well, multiply that times ten, and that's what it's like to be scrutinized by the Hawkes at Sunday dinner."

I release a heavy breath. "Well, at least I'm prepared."

Considering the Rangers trained us for the potential of becoming a prisoner of war, having dinner with people I already know and work with doesn't seem like such a scary prospect.

She gives me a tight smile, backing away from me out of the foyer and toward the sounds of the rest of the family. "Or so you think..."

Well, that's ominous...

Maybe I should have heeded her warnings, given my apology, and politely declined coming tonight. But it's too late to regret it now.

She turns and walks away, completely abandoning me as she disappears into the room Astrid came from.

I slowly follow her, pausing in the entry hall to examine a wall of photos of all the different Hawke children and their significant others. Until I get to the final two pictures.

The only ones that are solo shots—Bishop and Astrid.

I don't know Astrid well enough yet to speculate about why she's still single, but I can understand why Bishop hasn't settled down. She hasn't allowed herself to even consider the possibility of having someone in her life like that.

The job was always the most important thing to her.

It still is.

But I hope that's going to change.

Soon.

Caroline rounds the corner and smiles at me, and when she does, it's easy to see how much of her is really in Bishop. She may have followed in her father's footsteps in terms of her interests and career, but Bishop inherited her mother's smile and genuine beauty. A softness. It's just the side she keeps hidden, that she's too afraid is going to make her look "weak" or —God forbid—"adorable" like I accused her of being.

"I'm so glad you made it!" Caroline approaches and wraps her arms around me for a hug I wasn't expecting, then pulls back and looks up at me, the tiny woman grinning from ear to ear. "I wasn't sure you'd come on such short notice."

I offer a slight shrug. "I didn't have much going on."

I'm not about to tell her that when I received the call I was balls deep in her daughter, or that Bishop tried to steal the phone from my hand to disconnect the call when she realized what I was agreeing to.

"Come, come."

Caroline loops her arm through mine and drags me into the living room, where half of the Hawke family sits or stands around chatting and sipping at their pre-dinner drinks.

All eyes immediately dart over to me.

A few people mutter hellos and give little waves, but I can't help but notice that Bishop has mysteriously vanished already, along with Astrid.

"Where did your daughter go?"

Caroline waves a dismissive hand. "Oh, don't worry about

her. She's probably out back with everyone else playing cards." She covers her mouth partially, as if she's going to tell me a secret. "Nana hates when they play their poker games, but truth be told, she's the one who taught them all to play when they were little."

I laugh. "Sounds about right for this family."

Caroline's answering giggle isn't a sound I've ever heard out of her daughter, and maybe I never will. "I know, right? Do you want a drink?"

I glance around at what everyone else has. "I'll have a beer."

She nods. "I'll grab it from the kitchen. Hang tight."

Abandoned in a room full of Hawkes, I take a minute to scan the warm, inviting space, taking in how relaxed and casual everyone seems—the first time I've ever really seen them like this.

Every day since I came on board to the security team, my interactions with any of the Hawkes have almost exclusively revolved around the continued search for the elusive Satriano, trying to hunt down Michael McDonald, looking into who could have shot Satriano's goon, or triple-checking the security for every family member and business location.

Those conversations were clinical.

To the point and precise, like receiving military orders.

This is different.

Laughter. Smiles. Whispers that draw looks my direction and knowing grins from a few of them who clearly suspect I didn't arrive with Bishop by chance.

Gabe makes his way over to me, arms crossed over his chest, bottle of beer in his right hand. He appears so casual in this environment, far different than when he's in work mode. But I know under the seemingly relaxed exterior that the man who became such a legend in the Rangers still lurks.

Always alert.

Always ready to act if he needs to.

He leans against the wall beside me. "So, how are you liking working for us so far?"

I run my hand through my hair, suddenly nervous next to the man who is most likely to see right through me to the secrets *I* keep buried. The moment my hand drops, I slide it into my pocket, grasping the one thing that keeps me grounded when I need it. "I like it."

The last few days have given me a wider view of the Hawke empire and what it takes for them to maintain it when they're under threat from a man like Satriano, but there is always more to learn.

"You know, I dug into you..."

The hair on the back of my neck rises, and I clear my throat. "I wouldn't have expected anything less."

He nods slowly and takes a long pull from his beer, eyes narrowed on me. "Your superiors had nothing but good things to say, and my son says he likes you."

I laugh. "Umm, I guess that's good, right? Considering that we've tried to punch each other in the face a couple of times."

The tiniest hint of a grin appears on Gabe's lips. "I heard about your sparring matches with him. It's nice to have somebody who can actually keep up with him. I used to be able to, but God knows those days are long behind me. Same with Stone."

As soon as he says the words, his eyes dart over to where Stone sits in a leather chair with a cane resting against the edge of it, courtesy of the man who has everyone so on edge now.

He may not have been aiming for the Hawkes when he took out Christiano Roselli that day in front of The Grind, but the collateral damage was huge...and if what Bishop has told me is true, it may have been planned that way.

Two birds...one stone.

"I hear Isaac, Pope, and sometimes Coen like to get in the ring with him, too."

None of them have been there during any mornings I've been able to go, but it would be interesting to see what they're capable of.

Gabe snorts. "Yeah, but they can't do half of what Bishop can, so it isn't much of a challenge."

I can't fight my smirk.

She is every bit the badass that I've seen her to be, even when it's just with the people she considers family. They all know what she's built of and what she stands for, and even though she doesn't always see it, they accept her for who and what she is.

Just like I do.

Gabe leans in conspiratorially. "If you need to get out of here tonight, just tell me a code word and I can make an excuse to send you to go check on something."

I recoil slightly. "Jesus, you're the second person who has warned me. Is it really that bad?"

He chuckles. "It's really that bad. I don't envy what you'll be facing tonight."

Hell...

Skye and Storm appear from the kitchen carrying trays of food. "Time to eat."

Their call carries out across the room like a dinner bell, and they cross the hallway into what must be the dining room as everyone else starts to trickle that way.

Caroline appears behind them with a beer in hand. "Perfect timing." She hands it off to me and then narrows her eyes on Gabe. "You haven't been scaring him, have you?"

He scoffs. "What? Me? No." But as soon as she walks away, he leans in. "So...safeword?"

I take a swallow of my beer, but it doesn't help the unease starting to fill my stomach and coil around my spine. "Red."

What have I gotten myself into tonight?

BISHOP

Nana's sharp gaze stays locked on Gage and me, just as it has since the moment she was introduced to him—as our new employee—and we sat at the table.

Even as the food is passed around and everyone digs in, enjoying all the regular dishes and the easily flowing wine, she sits at the head of the table, only taking a few bites here and there, watching us as if she's waiting for something.

Maybe for me to run away screaming...

I squirm in my seat and avert my gaze to my plate, cutting another piece of lasagna and popping it into my mouth. At least when I'm eating, I can distract myself from the growing dread that the questions are coming.

After almost thirty years of Hawke family Sunday dinners, I've witnessed enough cross-examinations to know what's coming. It's only a matter of time before *someone* pipes up, and if it's Atlas with his slick comments about how "close" Gage and I are getting, I swear, I won't wait until we're in the ring next time to take him down.

Beside me to my left, Gage helps himself to a second portion of baked ziti with a grin on his face like a kid in a damn candy store. "I know I've said it once already, but this is incredible, Mrs. Hawke."

Nana beams at the compliment. "Thank you so much, dear. It's an old family recipe. And please, call me Nana. Everyone does."

He nods, shoveling another mouthful in and chewing. "Did you grow up here? In New Orleans?"

She bobs her head, offering him a kind smile. "Not too far from here, actually."

"How did you meet Sam?"

Everyone at the table exchanges glances, and I reach over and squeeze his leg under the table, trying to get him to stop asking questions.

All it's going to do is open it up for her to do the same with ones we might not want to answer.

Nana looks wistful as she takes a sip of her wine. "We grew up on the same block."

I release a relieved breath that's all she said, but as soon as I take another bite, I know that door that he cracked has actually been flung wide open when Nana speaks again.

"And what about you, dear?" Her voice is deceptively friendly. "I know you're relatively new to town. Do you plan on staying permanently now that you're sleeping with my granddaughter?"

Gage chokes on whatever's in his mouth, coughing and reaching for his water as I try to slink down in my chair and disappear under the table.

How the hell *does she know that?*

I scan the room, searching for the culprit who must have said something to her.

Everyone at the table seems to be enjoying our embarrassment immensely.

Savage barely fights a grin and exchanges a look with Danika that she passes on to Cass and Kennedy, who can't contain her cackle. Gabe and Skye both smirk, as do Atlas and Wren, who already suspected something was going on and may be the guilty parties.

Though, so did Astrid, but she might be the only one who looks even a little bit sorry for us.

Stone slides his arm across the back of Nora's chair, squeezing her shoulder while they both chuckle. Isaac, Jack, Coen, and Allegra all grin and shake their heads as if they expected this and were just waiting for it to hit.

Landon does his best to hide his laugh by snagging his wine

glass and taking a long sip, but Storm doesn't do as well concealing hers.

Neither do Pope, Allie, or Angie.

The only people *not* laughing are the kids who are completely oblivious and focused on their pasta...

And Mom and Dad.

I steal a glance their way and find them glaring at Nana, but they quickly shift their attention to Gage, awaiting his response.

So am I.

As much as I've fought Gage trying to get past my well-established defenses, the last couple days since we sparred at the gym, since I finally broke and conceded defeat, have been ... good.

Really good.

The best I've had in a very, very long time.

Maybe ever.

Being in his arms, in his bed, somehow, I've managed to sleep more than I have in the previous three months combined. And it isn't just because the man exhausts me with his almost obsessive attention to getting me off.

He seems to intuitively know when there's something weighing on me, when something frustrating happened or when I'm about to spiral. He understands how to distract me from that and give me other things to concentrate on. And he only pushes me to talk about it after, when I've released the tension. When I've let a little bit of that stuff that seems to want to drown me go.

Somehow, Gage just *gets* it.

The thought of him leaving, of him suddenly *not* being here, makes me lose my appetite.

He finally manages to swallow and stop coughing, his nervous gaze darting from Nana to Mom and Dad, then falling on me. "Umm, I do like New Orleans a lot. Especially the people. And I hope to stay."

There's something there in his answer. In the way he keeps his eyes on *me* rather than *her* that makes heat flare in my cheeks.

I have to look away from the intensity of it.

Nana gives him a tight smile and dips her head. "A very diplomatic answer."

He tears his gaze from me and returns the smile, then shoves a piece of garlic bread in his mouth before anything else can be said.

Smart man.

Over the years, the family has been brutal to some of the people sitting around this table for the first time, and I have a feeling it isn't over just because Nana gave him a reprieve.

Savage and Gabe lean closer together, exchanging hushed whispers, and the lack of amusement that was on their faces only a moment ago suggests the topic of conversation is no longer Gage's embarrassment.

Everyone around the table exchanges glances.

Nana doesn't like to discuss any sort of business at the table and prefers to find one person to pick on about their social life instead. Which appears to be me tonight. Something I would much rather avoid, but it may be better than the alternative, given the look Savage and Gabe give Stone and Dad.

It's enough to make my blood run cold.

"Is everything all right?"

Savage glances down the long table to me, and his jaw tightens, a muscle there ticcing. "I just got a text."

For some reason, the food I ate turns to lead in my stomach, and all the conversation at the table dies as all eyes turn to him.

He glances to the empty chairs at the end of the table, where Luca and Byron usually sit, and the other, where Jude occasionally makes an appearance when he feels up to coming to these things.

They're the only ones absent tonight.

I didn't get a chance to ask where Luca and Byron were, but it seems evident that whatever's going on has to do with them.

Gabe casts a look to Angelina. "Jude thought he saw someone prowling around The Grind tonight."

Angie shoots to her feet, her chair sliding back on the hardwood floor. "What?"

Allie grabs her arm, urging her back to her seat. "Don't freak out until we know what's happening."

Ang tightens her grip on the napkin in her hand, but allows her younger sister to pull her down.

Allie typically isn't the one remaining calm, cool, and collected in these types of situations, but becoming a mother and moving in with Pope seem to have been good for her.

Good for all of them.

Pope wraps his arm around the back of her chair protectively. "Is that where Luca is?"

Nana releases a heavy sigh from the head of the table. "You know I don't like this talk at the table."

Savage cuts an apologetic look to her. "I'm sorry, Mom, but this is important."

"That's what you always say."

She pushes back her chair with a huff, grabs her plate, and disappears into the kitchen, unwilling or unable to hear any more family business drama that she does not want to be involved in.

The matriarch of the Hawke family has suffered enough at the hands of people like Satriano and likes to pretend the suffering is done, even when things keep happening that leave all of us devastated—including her.

I worry at her age, her heart won't be able to handle another tragedy.

Savage slides his phone onto the table. "Jude called Luca, and he went over to check it out with one of our security teams while Byron went to Jude's, so he wasn't there alone."

Angie glares at him. "Is he okay?"

The panic lacing her voice slices through my chest, and I must not be very good at hiding my worry because Gage's hand finds mine on top of the table and squeezes.

Jude's anxiety can spiral, and after witnessing the explosion at the café and the shooting, another incident so close to home could easily send him to a very dark place. So Ang's concern is warranted.

Gabe nods. "Jude is fine."

"What about The Grind?"

Savage shakes his head. "Luca couldn't find anything. No one there, nothing amiss inside or out that he could detect."

Angie releases a heavy sigh of relief. "That's good."

He nods. "It is."

Gabe shifts restlessly in his chair. "But..."

She tenses again instantly, as does everyone else around the table. "But what?"

Leave it to Gabe to get right to the point. "We all know how vigilant Jude is, and how he keeps an eye on everything from his place. If he thinks he saw someone that shouldn't have been there, then there probably *was* someone suspicious."

Dad nods. "And we still don't know who took a shot at Satriano's man...there are likely other players in town who may assume we're mixed up with Satriano, thus making us targets."

Pope scowls. "The goon certainly didn't have any idea who shot him, or at least didn't say anything to me. I tried to get as much as I could out of him, but either he was well trained to keep his mouth shut or he didn't know."

My stomach continues to turn. All the research, investigation, and frankly hunting we've been doing trying to track down the various potential threats has been exhausting. And my head keeps coming back to one person who still remains a massive mystery. "You don't think this has anything to do with Michael McDonald being in town, do you?"

Gage stiffens next to me, his hand tightening on mine again. "Why don't Gabe and I go over there, just to check it out and be sure Luca didn't miss anything."

Gabe cuts his gaze to us and zeroes in on where our hands are clasped together. I try to tug mine out from under Gage's larger one, but Gage holds it steady.

Shit.

There's no hiding it now. Not that there really was after Nana's question.

Gabe nods. "That's a good idea. We'll go after dinner. I don't think this is a red-level emergency, do you?"

He raises a brow and Gage shakes his head, but there's something unspoken between them that I can't quite figure out. Probably some secret code they used in the Rangers that the rest of us aren't privy to.

Everyone quietly returns to their dinner plates, but the conversations have suddenly died off, the tones more hushed and reserved, as if everyone can sense the shift in the mood.

I can't say I've ever been happy about any potential danger to any of the members of the family or the businesses, but at least it drew attention away from us for the rest of the night.

Gage leans over, finally releasing his hand to wrap his arm around the back of my chair. "You going to come with us, Hellcat?"

"Of course, I am."

His eyes soften, concern furrowing his brow. "You're really worried about this...it could be nothing."

"You weren't here when it happened. The explosion and attack on The Grind..." I release a heavy sigh as my eyes burn and I fight the tears that want to come. "The Hawkeye Club is our second home, but The Grind is kind of like, I don't know, the heart of it all. And when it was gone, when it was tarnished with blood from Kennedy, Stone, and Isaac, it just felt like everything was wrong. Like the heart of Hawke Enterprises stopped beating." I look up at him, trying not to slip and do something stupid like reach out for him to hold me when I feel so out of sorts again. "And now something else might happen..."

Gage's jaw hardens along with his gaze. "We'll make sure it doesn't."

"You can't promise that."

"No." He shakes his head. "But I'll do everything in my power to ensure that it doesn't."

Somehow, I believe him.

Having him by my side, having a partner capable of defending the Hawkes the same way I do and who is willing to do it with that kind of commitment in his voice makes it really seem possible.

17

GAGE

I thought it couldn't get any more tense than sitting around Nana's dinner table last night with almost thirty Hawkes in attendance and all those intense, discerning eyes focused on me when she asked me *that* question.

But I was wrong.

This room is much, much worse.

Gabe sits on the edge of Savage's desk, whispering with him while Saint, Stone, and Luca have their own private conversation near the windows. Kennedy talks on her phone quietly in the far corner while Isaac and Coen sit on the couch, neither speaking, but the look of pure terror on Coen's face says enough.

Bishop leans against the door jamb, where she's remained ever since we came in this morning for the emergency meeting to discuss what happened last night and to work out a plan.

Well, they *will.*

My only plan is to keep my mouth shut, watch, and listen, to learn what I can without overstepping. It isn't my place to interject myself into this situation unless my role on the security team calls for it.

Hopefully, that won't be an issue, but everyone is tense. And the Hawkes tend to run hot—something I've observed many times in the last several weeks.

I catch Bishop's eyes drifting over to me every few moments, but I do my best to keep my focus on the other people in the room who control the Hawke empire.

Her, I understand. The rest of them are still mostly a mystery to me, and the more time I have to observe them, the more I can learn about how they got here, how they maintain their control over so many businesses, how they've managed to become so powerful and influential and how they—for all intents and purposes—run New Orleans.

And today, I'll find out how they respond to something like what went down last night.

After spending hours post-dinner with Gabe, Saint, Luca, and Bishop scouring every inch of the interior and exterior of The Grind, we weren't able to find *anything* that looked out of place or that suggested anyone planted something on the premises.

That should have been a massive relief to everyone.

But somehow, it wasn't.

Bishop didn't sleep at all once we got back to my place, instead spending the vast majority of the night pacing or reviewing surveillance camera footage we had already watched dozens of times, hoping to spot something that could help us identify who it was on the video.

I can see the exhaustion written all over her face this morning, but she also has that look that tells me if I mention it, there will be hell to pay.

All I can do is sit here and wait for the private conversations happening in this room to lead somewhere because right now, I don't have a fucking clue what the next move should be.

For them, or for me.

Finally, Gabe rises to his full height and scans the room. Everyone seems to sense the shift in the energy as his shoulders tense. Whatever he's about to say, he knows it might not be received well. He glances at Savage before releasing a heavy sigh. "We've decided to call Satriano."

Kennedy lowers her phone from her ear and gapes at him, whoever she was speaking with forgotten. "*What*?"

Bishop pushes off the wall. "Why the hell would you do that?"

Gabe tosses her a look that tells her to stop questioning their decisions. "Because after reviewing that security footage last night, we know someone *was* snooping around. It's either his men, or whoever the fuck shot one of them, don't you think?"

She purses her lips together and crosses her arms over her chest defiantly, but she doesn't have any room to debate that with him.

Those are the only two options that make sense.

Either Satriano sent one of his men to scope out The Grind for *future* action, or someone else did, potentially hoping to catch Satriano there again in the future to take him out. It *was* the first place he appeared after arriving in town, and since he's notoriously hard to locate, it may be an opportunity one of his enemies doesn't want to miss.

No one looks particularly thrilled with the idea of calling him, though.

"We need information." Savage keeps his voice level, trying to regain control over the rising tempers in the room. "The only way to get it is to actually *talk* to the man."

Isaac shakes his head. "I don't like it, either. Calling him and acknowledging his presence and that we need something from him never ends well."

Coen nods, running a hand through his hair. "I agree. I

don't think going to him will help. If anything, it gives him more power over us."

Savage spreads his hands flat across the top of his desk. "We're not going to be sitting ducks anymore. Everyone will keep working behind the scenes, but we have to open up a dialogue if we hope to get any information that we haven't been able to find on our own. And as we've said previously, he now has a reason to want to come to some sort of peace with us that he didn't before."

He glances to Coen.

A growl slips from Coen's lips, his hands fisting as he shifts forward on the couch. "You're not using my baby as a fucking bargaining chip."

His uncle appears unmoved by his distress. "You know how important family is to us, Coen, and we all know how important it is to him, too. It isn't that we're using my future grandniece or nephew as a bargaining chip, it's more like we're reminding the man of what's at stake if he doesn't either back off or help us figure out what's going on."

Stone nods from where he stands beside his boys. "I'm sorry, son, but I agree. We have to make the call. If he understands that an assault on us puts Allegra and the baby in danger, it could play very favorably for getting his agreement to something reasonable." He glances to Luca. "Unless you think differently."

Luca remains stoic, but I can see the wheels turning in his head.

The former mob boss, more than anyone in this room, would know how Satriano thinks, how he works, the type of things he might be planning.

He's the Hawkes' single best resource.

"I don't think there's any harm in contacting him. He's already shown up at The Grind, already made his presence known very intentionally. He did that for a reason, when he could have easily snuck back into town and remained in hiding."

Saint scans the room. "Who should make the call?"

Savage pulls out his phone. "I will. And I'll do the talking."

Everyone nods their agreement, no one willing to question his authority here as he dials the number.

Bishop circles back to her place on the wall near the door, looking as tense as I've ever seen her, and when her eyes cut over to me, I mouth "relax" to her.

All that does is earn me an annoyed scowl from her.

And maybe I shouldn't be doing anything that might antagonize her when she could get me thrown out of this room.

The fact that they even let me in here for this phone call says how much headway I've made in earning their trust.

They want my input. Maybe not on strategy, but at the very least, on the security issues. And something tells me there will only be more of them as we move forward.

Everyone seems to hold their collective breaths.

It only rings twice before Satriano answers. "Savage Hawke. Did you call to welcome me home?"

Savage glares at the phone, as if Satriano can somehow feel his animosity if he tries hard enough to project it. "Something like that. I'm calling because there was an incident at The Grind last night."

"Oh no. Is everyone all right?"

In the slightly accented English, the man's concern almost sounds genuine.

Almost.

"Thankfully, yes. No one was injured. But we have video of someone skulking around the building checking doors and otherwise behaving suspiciously. The security cameras there and around other buildings caught most of it. We weren't able to get an image of the person's face, though. I was hoping you might have some information for us about this."

A momentary pause through the line has everyone leaning forward slightly, anticipating what he will say. "Why would I know anything about it?"

Savage somehow maintains his composure despite Satriano's faux innocent game. "Perhaps it was one of your men. You were just there recently..."

Satriano issues a low, dark chuckle. "I was there for my cappuccino. And to say hello to my favorite family. The last thing I would want to do is cause harm to you or anyone there. Where would I get my morning coffee now that I'm back in town?"

"I don't care where the fuck you get it, just get it somewhere else." Apparently Savage is done playing nice. His normally warm blue eyes have gone icy cold. "Are you saying it wasn't your men?"

"That is what I'm saying, Mr. Hawke."

"Then who the hell was it?"

Savage exchanges a confused look with everyone in the room as we all wait for Satriano's response.

"I don't know why you think I would know that."

"Maybe because one of your men just got shot, and Pope had to save his life at the clinic? Your men ending up with bullet holes typically means you're stirring up shit again, and I don't know how or why we would be pulled into that, but I have to ask if this is at all connected."

Satriano releases a long sigh. "My return to New Orleans does not come without complications."

That makes everyone sit up straighter and those standing inch closer to the phone laid out on the desk.

Complications.

Something tells me that word from a man like Damiano Satriano means something completely different than it does to the rest of us.

Savage clenches one fist on the desk. "What sort of complications?"

"Ones that shouldn't and don't concern the Hawkes."

Coen pushes up from his seat, and Stone reaches out to try to grab his arm but can't get to him fast enough before his son slams his palms on the desk across from Savage, leaning over the phone. "Anything that concerns you concerns the fucking Hawkes now, Satriano."

"Oh, is that Coen?"

Shit.

Everyone in the room tenses.

Kennedy throws a frightened look to Stone and Isaac while everyone else looks to Savage for direction.

Should I get Coen out of the room before he says something stupid?

I start to move toward him, but Luca shakes his head, halting my steps.

Apparently, we're going to let this play out.

"Who else is there with you?" Satriano laughs lightly. "The usual suspects, I presume? Gabe Anderson, Saint Clarke, Stone, my good friend Isaac, and the lovely Kennedy. How about the beautiful Bishop?"

It's my turn to tense as my gaze locks on her. Hearing her name from *his* lips is enough to raise my hackles and make my protective instincts kick into full gear.

"And I would bet my old friend, Luca Abello is there as well…"

Luca's jaw tenses.

Savage clears his throat. "Yes, they're all here."

"Wonderful. Then I'll only have to say this once. If I thought any of my dealings would threaten my daughter's life or that of my grandchild, I would let you know."

"Would you?" Coen barely gets the words out through gritted teeth.

"You think so little of me—"

Coen sneers. "We have every reason to question every word that comes out of your mouth."

"Not about this." Satriano remains stone cold despite the heat and accusation in Coen's voice. "I am glad you called though, because I was hoping we might be able to reopen our discussions about potentially working together."

"That door is long closed." Savage's response leaves no room for argument. "Don't try to reopen it."

Satriano *tsks*. "Oh, well. That *is* unfortunate. And I do have to get going, but I appreciate the welcome home phone call. *Ciao*."

He ends the call without another word, and Coen pushes off the desk, running his hands through his hair almost frantically.

Stone steps toward him, reaching out with the hand not resting on the cane at his side. "Son..."

"Don't." Coen holds up a hand, preventing his father from offering him any comfort. "I can't right now. You all think he was full of shit, right? When he said this has nothing to do with him?"

Everyone nods.

Including me.

The way he said "complications" stays ringing in the back of my head.

Coen scans the faces of everyone in the room, his rising panic evident. "So where do we go from here?"

I don't have a fucking clue.

And I'm not sure anyone else does, either.

BISHOP

Everyone begins to disperse from the meeting, Coen's question still unanswered and undoubtedly lingering in the head of every single one of us, but we weren't going to come to any conclusions when everyone was so worked up.

A cooling-off period was needed.

By all.

Even me.

I stay rooted in my position near the door, watching each and every one of them file out until the only ones left in Savage's office are Gage and me.

He didn't say a word the entire time. Not that I really expected him to. He's new to all this. To all the drama, lies, and veiled threats that come with a man like Satriano.

His job right now is to take it all in, to assess, to back us up when needed, but until then, he knows his place. While I appreciated his attempt to help with Coen when he went off the deep end, I'm glad he didn't intervene.

It only would have made things worse for my cousin, who has every right to be scared for Allegra and their child.

Because God knows I am…

Gage's gaze stays locked on me while I stare out the window, watching the trees sway in the light breeze, the bright sunlight such a cheery taunt when inside here, in this room, everything feels so dark and murky.

A few moments of absolute silence pass before he finally takes the first step and approaches me.

He dips his head, inserting himself into my line of vision, forcing me to look at him. "Come on."

"Where are we going?"

Sweeping a hand out to the empty room, he offers a half-smile. "Like everyone else, away from here. You need a break and some sleep."

Gage's idea of a "break" and "sleep" aren't anything most people would consider relaxing or restful.

I narrow my gaze on him. "I'm not in the mood."

He chuckles. "Not that I would say no, but that wasn't what I had in mind." His fingers slide under my chin, tilting my face up. "Let's go get some lunch like everyone else. Some food might make you feel better. As would a nap. You didn't sleep at all last night."

I don't want to eat.

I don't want to sleep.

I want to track down Satriano and confront him in person. Demand he tell us why he's in town, why one of his men was shot, and who the fuck might've been lurking around our building. I want to force him to come clean about Michael McDonald and any other "complications" that may be arising because of him, even if it means putting my gun to his temple to accomplish it.

But one thing Satriano is very good at is hiding.

His movements…

His plans…

All seem to remain in the shadows despite everything we do to shed light on it. The man is basically a ghost. Appearing whenever it suits him to haunt us with traumatic memories of what he's done in the past. Taunting us with the power he holds because he knows damn well we can't act against him without bringing down the wrath of his entire network.

So, I don't want to go sit and eat, or lie in bed with Gage and pretend none of this is happening…

I *can't.*

That swirling storm of anger and uncertainty that threatened to suffocate me before Gage came into my life starts to swamp the edges of my vision, but he holds my chin steady, forcing me to keep looking into his eyes that remain so warm, so calm, so damn inviting.

He doesn't look away or let me, because he *knows.*

He sees it happening.

And he isn't going to give me a *choice* but to take a step back, breathe, and regroup.

The man is a *pusher*, but it isn't drugs he's shoving down my throat. It's something much more dangerous—he's forcing the self-reflection I've avoided so much because it would mean admitting my intense focus on my training and my job was actually hurting me.

Like I might be doing now...

All it took was one look from him to know it, too.

Dammit.

"Fine." I free myself from his hold and push off the wall with a huff. "A quick lunch. But then I want to meet up with Gabe and my dad again. There has to be *some* way to track down the man at the café. Maybe we can hack the city's street cameras and backtrack him that way. Maybe it would lead us to McDonald and Satriano."

Gage's jaw tightens. "What would you do if you did find them?"

"What the hell do you think, Gage? My uncle might be the one who's a sniper, but I have a pretty damn good shot, too."

He lets out a low whistle. "While I know you do, Hellcat, do you really think executing a mob boss is going to solve the problem?"

No.

I shake my head. "It would make things worse, I'm sure, but it doesn't mean I don't think about it every fucking day."

"As long as it's *just* thinking about it..."

Even though we've only known each other for a short time, the way he's watching me confirms that he's already read me easily. He knows I wouldn't hesitate to pull the trigger if given the chance again, without the risk to innocents like there would have been at The Grind. We can deal with the fallout after—or at least, that's what I tell myself in my head every time I picture putting that man down like rabid dog.

With a frustrated huff, Gage reaches out and spins me toward the door. "Let's go."

He ushers me from the office, down the hallway, and presses the button for the elevator. As soon as it lights up, he wraps his arm around me from behind, tugging me back against his firm body and sweeping his lips across the back of my neck.

The contact sends a little shiver through me, and I instantly regret wearing my braids up in a bun today, exposing that sensitive skin to his wicked mouth.

"After lunch"—another brief touch of his lips—"if you still need to relax a little bit more, we can go with your *other* idea."

The elevator doors slide open, and I glance back at him. "Very funny."

I step forward, putting some much needed distance between us, and he comes in after me, chuckling. But he absolutely isn't kidding about being willing to take me to bed to work out some of the tension.

We both lean against the wall, waiting for it to descend to the first floor, and when the doors slide open again, the music and thumping bass hit us. Fairly empty this early in the day, I still immediately scan the club, looking for anything unusual even though there's security everywhere.

They have it handled.

I keep telling myself that as we make our way toward the front door. Gage's eyes follow mine on one final sweep of the club before we step out into the afternoon sunshine. Because we share the same instinct and inability to turn it off.

A deep lungful of fresh air somewhat helps relieve that anxiety coiling when we were inside, and Gage and I walk across the parking lot to the reserved spaces for the Hawkes where everyone still lingers around their vehicles, embroiled in further discussion.

Seems no one is truly able to take a break...

Savage and Gabe talk with Dad near Gabe's car, while Luca, Stone, and Isaac appear to be trying to talk Coen off a ledge where he stands beside his car, the door already open like he can't wait to get inside and get back to Allegra.

I glance at Gage's motorcycle parked next to my SUV on the far end of the line of vehicles. Even though we were both coming from his place this morning, I had insisted we arrive separately, as if that somehow makes a difference when everyone knows what's going on between us now.

He grins, nudging me playfully with his shoulder. "A ride might do you good..."

I glower at him, and he holds up his hands in defense, a smile twitching his lips.

"On the *motorcycle*."

"Yeah, yeah." That is absolutely *not* what he meant, but I can't help grinning right back at him. "I don't think so. I'm driving."

"Whatever you want, Hellcat."

Isaac's head whips toward us.

Shit.

I didn't realize how close they were standing, and Gage certainly didn't know they were in earshot or he never would have let that nickname slip.

Isaac narrows his gaze on Gage. "*What* did you just call her?"

Shiiiiit.

Gage blushes slightly and rubs at the back of his neck, at least having the decency to give me an apologetic look. "Umm. Hellcat?"

Stone, Isaac, and even Coen all bark out laughs while Luca fights a grin.

The earth could open up and swallow me into it right now, and I would absolutely be okay with it.

Isaac shakes his head. "You really do have a death wish, don't you, buddy?"

Gage grins at him, casting me a knowing look. "I guess I might."

His warm gaze sweeps over me, and he urges me toward the SUV, away from the rest of the family quickly, like he can't wait to escape the embarrassment and scrutiny that just brought on him.

But before I can even get my door open, Luca steps over, the hint of humor that's so rare for him completely faded. "Where are you two headed?"

"Lunch." I force a smile. "Then we'll be back."

To return to the hunt.

The last part goes unsaid, because at this point, we're all exhausted with running around and getting nowhere. But we also aren't going to give up.

Luca nods. "I'm going to call my contacts in Europe again, see if maybe they might have anything on who he's gotten into it with this time. Knowing him, it could be any number of people."

Gage leans against the back door, watching the conversation, one ankle casually crossed over the other. His brow furrows deeply, his lips twisting as he slides his hand into his jacket pocket. "What's his endgame?"

Luca raises a dark brow. "What do you mean?"

"This Satriano guy. He's got hotels and casinos built up all along the Gulf Coast now. He must be making millions. Roselli and his crew are gone from New Orleans, leaving a power vacuum Satriano stepped into. So, what does he ultimately want? *Every*thing? Is it as simple as that?"

Releasing a heavy sigh, Luca shakes his head. "It's never that simple with these types of people."

He would know.

He is one of them.

"It never is." I tighten my grip on my keys. "He seems to want what *we've* built. He wants our reputation, our hard work, our connections and power that's totally separate from his own. That's why I've had this feeling for so long. Why I can't shake it..."

Luca nods. "Neither can I. It's only a matter of time before something happens that's going to set off a chain of events we won't be able to stop."

Gabe and Savage finish their conversation with Dad, and Dad starts to walk toward his car, offering me a tight smile that says we are on the same page about feeling agitated after that call with Satriano.

I return the smile...

And the entire world around us explodes.

18

BISHOP

B*eep.*

Beep.

Beep.

The incessant noise cuts through the heavy, thick darkness I'm swimming in and slowly starts to draw me out of its depths. I groan and try to roll away from the sound, attempt to escape back to the soft, warm, floaty place where I've been, where nothing else existed.

Beep.

Beep.

Beep.

That goddamn incessant beeping...

The dark gray around the edges of my mind continues to eke away.

Beep.

Beep.

Beep.

I draw in a deep breath, about to yell at whoever the hell is making that racket, but as soon as the familiar smell I hate so much registers fully, I know where I am.

The hospital.

There is *nothing* else that smells like it.

Nothing I dislike as much as the scents that cling to everything here.

Why am I at the hospital again?

I search that grayness that coats all my memories, trying to find a reason, but all I find are strange flashes that make my heart lurch in my chest.

What is happening?

It takes far too long for my eyelids to comply with my attempt to open them, but when I do, Mom is staring back at me, her worried eyes wide, the lights of the room glowing behind her like a damn halo.

I wince at how bright they are, blinking groggily to try to clear the spots from my vision.

She releases a relieved breath, squeezing my hand while she swipes away a tear from her cheek with the other. "You're awake."

I nod, groaning as the pain hits me with the movement of my head, throbbing in my temples. Trying to roll toward her only earns me agony in every bone and muscle in my body.

Mom squeezes my hand again. "Don't try to move too much."

God...that hurts...

I reach up to rub my forehead, but the IV line stuck in my arm tugs at the skin, only causing even more discomfort. "What happened?"

Now that my vision is starting to clear more, I can see how red-rimmed her eyes are. She's been crying—a lot. "You don't remember?"

I close my eyes again, wracking my brain, trying to come up with the answer through a cloud of confusing, jumbled sounds and images that won't align in any understandable order.

Meeting with everyone...

The phone call with Satriano...

Talking with Gage...

Morning at his place after being up all night...

Riding down in the elevator...

Arriving at the club...

Stepping into the parking lot on the way to lunch...

"Oh, God..." It hits me suddenly, the same way the blast did. Blindsided. Then blackness. "An explosion."

I open my eyes and Mom nods.

"Yes. You're going to be okay, though." She presses her lips together, swallowing thickly to hide the emotion I can see in her gaze. "A severe concussion. You've been out for a while."

"What's a while?"

All sense of time is gone.

The memories still not lining up properly.

Like they got thrown in a blender and dumped into a glass and now I'm trying to pick out tiny pieces and arrange them back in an order that makes sense.

She glances over her shoulder to look at the clock on the wall, her lips twisting before her focus comes back to me. "Eight hours."

What?

"*Eight* hours?"

My brain struggles to piece together everything, to process what she just told me and the bits of memory.

The bright sunlight...

Gage leaning against the SUV, talking to Luca...

Dad about to get into his car...

Savage, Gabe, Isaac, Coen, and Stone only a few feet away from us...

The world exploding in a crash of light and sound...

"Is-is everyone else okay?"

The way her brow furrows, I can tell that she doesn't want to give me the truth. She wants to hold back, save me from the pain of whatever it is that's too hard to say. "Mom? Is everyone okay?"

She swallows thickly, clutching my hand tightly. "Savage has a few broken ribs and a wicked concussion like yours. He was unconscious for a while but woke up a bit ago. Gabe suffered some physical injuries and hasn't woken up yet, but they've done an MRI and there seems to only be some mild brain bleeding they're hoping will resolve itself on its own."

Oh, God...

"But Stone, Isaac, Coen, and Dad are all fine, just shaken up and sore."

I release a relieved breath for them, but it catches in my chest thinking about Savage and Gabe. "Good. I mean..."

She smiles softly. "I know what you mean."

Warm blue eyes flash through my head...

The affection in his voice when he calls me Hellcat...

"What about Gage?"

Mom glances back toward the hallway, then moves in closer, lowering her voice slightly. "He hasn't left your side since the moment they brought you in. He wouldn't let Nora or Pope examine him anywhere else." She offers me a knowing smile. "He's been standing at the door like your own personal bodyguard even though he was thrown against one of the vehicles and is pretty banged up himself and should be resting. When I'm not sitting here with you, he has been."

He hasn't left your side...

My chest tightens, the ache there more intense, and the burn of tears that's been threatening finally gets too hard to fight.

There's a question in Mom's gaze, but she doesn't ask it.

Everyone knows there's something going on between the

two of us, yet she hasn't probed, hasn't pried. I know that's hard for her, but she also understands it would be impossible for me to talk about it, even if she did ask.

It's always been hard for me to discuss relationship stuff with anyone.

Especially her.

Maybe because I've never truly had one and that's all she's ever wanted for me.

"I'm going to go tell everyone you're awake."

She squeezes my hand, then pushes up out of the chair she was sitting in and disappears out the door I hadn't even realized was open until now.

Gage's tall, broad frame appears inside the jamb instantly, filling it as he steps in and nudges the door closed behind him. His intense blue gaze stays locked on me as he approaches and settles into the chair Mom just vacated with a wince he tries unsuccessfully to hide.

He runs his hand back through his disheveled hair, releasing a heavy sigh, and I can see from the bags under his eyes and the lines around his mouth, how worried he's been. "I thought you'd never wake up."

I force a smile, blinking away the moisture that wants to trickle down my face and give me away. "That would've been rather inconvenient."

A half-grin pulls at his lips, but it looks as painful for him to do as it is for me to witness. "Yes, it would've been."

He leans forward, resting his elbows on his knees and scrubs his hands over his face. Sheer exhaustion emanates off him along with a tense mix of emotions I can't pinpoint.

"You've been here the whole time?"

Keeping his head down, he nods. "Yeah."

I scan him over, searching for any signs of injury. Black stains on his shirt mix with red ones that must be blood, and my stomach twists violently. "You got checked out?"

Gage nods again, finally lifting his gaze to meet mine. "Your aunt insisted. I'm fine. You're the one I'm worried about."

"My mom said I'm okay."

A muscle in his jaw tics, and he clenches his hands together in front of him. "I don't call a severe concussion *okay*."

"It could've been much worse."

"You're right." He bobs his head again, and the intensity with which he assesses me tightens that vise around my chest. "It could've been. And I've seen it. So many guys I served with ended up dead or with TBIs that fucked them up forever in all kinds of ways." He presses his lips together as if he's biting back something else he wants to say and shakes his head. "I don't want that for you. You need to make sure you follow the doctor's orders and take it easy."

I laugh, but then immediately regret it as every muscle in my body hurts and pain stabs at my temples. "Oh, shit."

He shifts forward, reaching for me. "What?"

"Nothing." I wave him off. "That just hurt more than I thought it would. I have a hard time taking it easy."

"No shit." There's absolutely no humor in his voice, only a waver I've never heard before that belies how deeply concerned and shaken he really is. "That's what I'm worried about, Hellcat."

I shift in the bed, trying to get more comfortable which seems impossible, especially under his watchful eye. "I'm sure my brother and aunt, not to mention my mom and dad and everyone else, will do everything in their power to keep me from working too hard."

His brow furrows as he leans in even closer, those warm blue eyes going absolutely icy cold. "Working *too* hard? You're *not* going back to work, Bishop."

I try to push myself up because I am not going to win this argument while lying prone in a hospital bed, but the slightest movement makes pain sear through my entire body and head.

Wincing, I grit my teeth, never getting more than two inches off the shitty mattress.

Gage reaches out and gently presses on my shoulder, forcing me back down. "Exactly my point."

"But with Gabe out of commission, I need to be there more than ever—"

"I'm going to help any way I can. Figure out what the fuck happened."

"What *did* happen?" I close my eyes, trying to replay the events again, but they're fragmented. Missing parts. "All I know is there was an explosion..."

Gage's silence draws my lids open again, and the wary look he gives me makes my blood run cold. "Your mom didn't tell you?"

I shake my head. "No..."

He sucks in a long breath, shoving his hands roughly through his hair. "Gabe's car exploded. You were thrown against your SUV with the force of the blast. I was unconscious for a few minutes, and when I came to, I found you crumpled on the pavement beside me and everyone else in various stages of injury strewn across the parking lot."

"What?"

His large hand comes to rest on my shoulder before I can try to get up again. "We don't know what caused it...the police are still investigating obviously, but my bet would be an explosive device of some kind. This wasn't an accident, Bishop."

Not an accident...

It *wasn't* an accident.

"Someone tried to kill Gabe?"

He nods. "Or all of you..."

"Satriano...Gabe said McDonald was an explosives expert, right?"

Gage glances down at where his hand rests on my shoulder,

sliding it down until he can pull my hand into his. "Please stop. You need to relax right now, not be trying to do the police's job."

"The chief of police is...well, he's worked with us before. He can get us information—"

He squeezes my hand. "Bishop..."

"Maybe he can even get us some of the physical materials to run through private labs—"

Another squeeze. "Bishop..."

My mind keeps racing. "Someone would have had to have known we'd all be there—this was a direct attack on us, and if we can actually pin this on Satriano, we have an excuse to go after him full force."

"Bishop, *stop.*"

My back stiffens.

In all the time I've known him, Gage has never raised his voice to me. He's never deviated from being that calm, reassuring person I've come to know him to be.

Until now.

GAGE

Bishop snaps her mouth closed, her gaze suddenly wary, as if she's seeing someone she doesn't know instead of the person she's been sleeping with.

I didn't mean to raise my voice like that, but she said those words so confidently—*we can finally go after him full force*—that I couldn't just sit here and listen to her spiraling down the rabbit hole she has no business jumping into.

Here she is, lying in a hospital bed looking half dead, yet all she can think about is taking on a dangerous mobster. Even if she *weren't* seriously hurt, I wouldn't stand by and let her run off after him like she wants to.

It's a suicide mission.

Despite what she likes to think, she isn't invincible.

She has to take it easy, give her body and her head time to heal, or there could be serious repercussions. Ones I'm not about to sit back and watch her suffer from, not the way I have with others.

I snag her hand and press my lips to the back of it, waiting for her to try to tug it away, but she doesn't. She lets me absorb that jasmine scent from her skin that somehow calms me and releases some of the tension I've been holding ever since the bomb went off that's only grown since I found her collapsed beside me on that pavement.

"You are not going to do anything, Hellcat. Those of us who are *actually* okay are going to do whatever we need to do to make sure the family's safe."

"Is that why you haven't left?" She raises a dark brow. "Because you wanted to make sure I was safe here at the hospital?"

I don't know how to answer her question.

If I do it honestly, it'll terrify her, but I don't want to lie to her, not any more than I already have. This woman has twisted me up so violently that I can't tell what's wrong or right anymore. Other than how I feel about her.

That somehow feels *right.*

Swallowing through my suddenly dry throat, I squeeze her hand. "I stayed because I literally, physically could *not* walk away from you."

She sucks in a sharp breath, as if my words pained her as much as moving earlier did.

They might have.

Bishop doesn't do well with emotion or accepting it from anyone, and I've done my best to temper my feelings, to wrap them up in our playful banter and try to keep things light, but today changed everything.

"From the moment I woke up and found you unconscious on the pavement, saw the burned-out husk of the car and all the shrapnel and realized what happened, the second I pulled you into my arms, the thought of letting anyone take you out of them was..." I pause, searching for the right words. Ones that won't scare her away. "It was just something I knew wasn't going to happen."

At least not without a fight.

Bishop doesn't respond to my confession, just sits staring at me with wide eyes that give away nothing.

She's usually so easy to read, but not tonight.

Not when I don't think even *she* knows what she's thinking or feeling about the situation or me.

"Nora and Pope told me that you'll probably have to be in here until sometime tomorrow at the earliest, maybe another two days before they release you, to be safe."

She closes her eyes and shakes her head, wincing. "No. No, no, no. I *have* to get out of here. I have to go—"

"No, you don't, Hellcat." I capture her face in my palm, preventing her from further hurting herself. "You're not in control of this, and you have to accept that."

Her eyes fly open and meet mine, and the anger simmering there is directed at me as much as it is the situation. Hopefully, more so the latter.

"Your father and I can handle things with the rest of the security team. We'll get it done, whatever needs to happen, while you recover."

"So, you're going to, what? Try to push me out?"

I shake my head. "No. Try to keep you safe from yourself. Because right now, you're your own worst enemy. You have to be calm. A concussion is a brain injury, Bishop. Your fucking *brain*. This isn't something to mess around with."

"This happened on my watch." Her bottom lip quivers and tears pool in her eyes. She tries to tilt her head away, and I know it's because she doesn't want me to see them, doesn't want me to know that she's about to cry, because she sees that as a huge weakness, as something she shouldn't show, that no one else should see. Especially me. "This is *my* fault."

"No, it isn't, Bishop."

Not by a longshot.

If anyone bears that responsibility it's me, but before I can continue trying to convince her to stop fighting what's medically necessary—and me—the door opens and Pope, Nora, Saint, and Caroline enter.

Nora steps up to the bed. "Are we interrupting something?"

I shake my head and pull my hand from Bishop's cheek, sliding back in the chair, trying to control my thundering heart that was prepared to battle her on this topic if necessary. "Nope. I was just re-emphasizing to her how important it is that she take things easy."

Pope snorts, crossing his arms over his chest. "Like she's going to do that."

Nora purses her lips and looks down at Bishop. "He's right. I don't have to tell you how serious a head injury is, even a concussion. No work, and I mean *none*, for at least two weeks. And then we'll talk about it and reassess."

Bishop grits her teeth and pushes up, shifting back in the bed until she's sitting vertically against the pillows. A move that had to be painful but she's so damn stubborn she did it anyway. "I'm not doing that, Nora. I'm not sitting out when someone just attacked us."

Saint issues a low grumble. "You don't have a choice. Those of us without injuries are going to take over everything. And those of you with them are going to do what the *medical* doctors order."

She scowls, crossing her arms over her chest and muttering a curse under her breath when the movement pulls at her IV line. "Well, then I want a doctor who isn't family and doesn't have a personal reason to issue orders that aren't necessary."

For the love of God...

If I thought this would be any easier with the rest of the Hawkes backing me up, I was clearly wrong.

Nora gives her an exasperated look. "Not necessary? I'm happy to call down the neurologist who reviewed your MRI scan and have him explain exactly what could happen if you push yourself if I have to, but he's currently operating on another patient."

Bishop's breath hitches. "Gabe?"

If it is, it happened very recently, because before I came in here, I was under the impression he was stable.

Everyone else exchanges a look that suggests I've definitely missed something.

Nora draws in a slow breath and then releases it. "Yes. The bleeding intensified. They had to go in."

Bishop's eyes dart to her parents, then back to her brother and her aunt. "Is he going to be all right?"

He has to be.

Men like Gabe Anderson can't go out like this.

It wouldn't be fair.

Life isn't fair.

I don't need a reminder of that today, or ever again.

Nora gives her a tight smile. "Dr. Bankes is one of the best neurosurgeons in the country. He'll take care of him, but you need to take care of you. The more relaxed you are, the more you take it easy, the fewer side effects and the sooner you'll recover, I promise."

"You'll come home with us." Caroline steps forward and grabs her hand, squeezing it. "Your old room is still set up and—"

I shake my head. "No."

Caroline glances at me with a raised brow. "What do you mean 'no'?"

Shit.

Maybe I should have thought this through before interjecting myself into Hawke family politics, but I can't just sit here and pretend there aren't things happening beyond these walls that are also at play.

"She's coming home with me."

Bishop gapes at me. "What? Like hell I am!"

"Listen..." I push to my feet, glancing at Saint because I know he's probably pissed, but likely also the one who will understand where I'm going with this. "Whoever planted that bomb was, at the very least, targeting Gabe and Savage, but probably all of you, right?" No one argues otherwise. "Which means Bishop is in danger..."

Saint nods. "Agreed. We all are."

"So, wouldn't it be better if she recovers somewhere no one would look for her? Where no one would expect to find her? Somewhere not connected to the Hawkes in any way, shape, or form?" I press my hand over my chest. "That's my place. I'm new in town. No one knows me, and they certainly don't know about my connection to Bishop. I'll take care of her. I'll keep her safe. I'll do whatever intelligence work I can from there while you do the field work."

It sounded better in my head than it did coming out, and now I have a whole handful of her family watching me with renewed interest.

Saint stares me down, his arms crossed over his barrel chest, and I can see why he was such a good lineman when he played ball. He's big, he's intimidating, like a wall no one will get through.

I just pray my argument got through to him.

Bishop keeps shaking her head. "No. No. Absolutely not. I'm going home, to my place. Thank you for the offer, Mom"—she squeezes her hand, then releases it—"but I'm not going anywhere but my own bed."

She says it with so much finality that, for a moment, I think everyone might have been swayed.

Saint shakes his head. "No, you're not. You're going to *his*."

"Excuse me?"

"Gage is right." He locks his hard gaze with mine. "Security is going to have to be tight on everyone after this. No one's going to leave their residences unless they absolutely have to. And it's one less place to have to cover if you're with him. He can do work reaching out to our contacts from his place while I run down anything I need to in person, along with the rest of our crew."

"You can't be serious, Dad."

Pope snorts again. "I love it when you two fight, but I'm going to actually stay out of this argument."

Caroline rolls her eyes. "That's a first."

Nora offers me a knowing grin. "I like the idea." She looks to Bishop. "Mostly because I know he's not going to let *you* do anything that you shouldn't be doing."

Bishop looks more and more pissed the longer everyone stares her down, until she finally throws up her hands. "So, I don't have any say in this?"

Saint shakes his head. "No. You don't. As soon as you're discharged, you're going home with Gage."

19

TWO DAYS LATER

GAGE

By the time we pull into the driveway of my place, the twenty minute silent treatment Bishop has given me without even acknowledging my presence has ticked by so slowly that it feels more like twenty hours.

I didn't know time could move that slowly, or that silence could scream in my ears so fucking loudly.

There wasn't any point in trying to engage her in conversation, not when she's been acting like this since the moment everyone agreed the safest place for her was with me.

Two fucking days ago.

Of course, at the hospital, I had the rest of the Hawkes around to engage with and to help keep the silence at bay. We had plenty to discuss, from the initial findings from the police regarding the explosion, to Gabe's recovery, and the new security protocols that involve every vehicle, business, and residence being swept with the same bomb-sniffing dogs they used for the second tower opening before anyone goes near them.

I've stayed busy while Bishop has only spoken with the

girls, cutting out anyone she sees as involved in the conspiracy to keep her locked up.

But now that we're truly alone, the quiet is downright stifling.

She can't hold out forever.

That's what I keep telling myself. At some point, she has to break. It might be a tirade and verbal attack worse than the physical one she threw at me in the ring the last time we shared it, but it would be better than this.

Anything would be.

I put the car in park and turn off the engine, but Bishop doesn't budge from the passenger seat. With her arms crossed over her chest, she looks absolutely ticked off and ready to attempt an escape at any moment.

"So, this is how you want to play it?" I can't even get her to *look* at me anymore, but that doesn't mean she won't have to listen. "I know you're pissed, Bishop. I know you want to go home. I know you want to go back to work. But we all agreed this is the safest place for you."

Finally, her head slowly turns toward me, her eyes narrowing in a way I am smart enough to recognize is dangerous. "*You* all agreed being the key takeaway there. *I* didn't agree."

"Because you are so goddamn selfless and worried about everyone else that you're going to kill yourself. That's one of the things I—"

Shit.

I barely stop myself from saying something *really* fucking stupid that I can never take back.

It isn't the first time. Not even the second or third since she woke up in that hospital. The words I've wanted to say, that have sat on the tip of my tongue somehow feeling like thousand-pound weights, are still there, though. Somehow kept in when every part of me wants to come clean.

Because that wouldn't solve anything.

Baring my soul would only result in an even more pissed off Bishop who would fight me harder every fucking step of the way.

At least she's talking again.

She may be angry.

She may be volatile.

But she's *safe*.

That's what matters.

And I just need to keep reminding myself of that each time my frustration threatens to boil over, like it is now.

I sigh and scrub my hands over my face, then push open my door, step out, and nudge it shut behind me when what I really want to do is slam it.

The cool, damp air and the light drizzle hitting me doesn't do anything to dampen the heated aggravation coursing through me as I make my way around to the passenger side door and tug it open.

Her inability to see, for even one damn second, that we're all trying to protect her is going to make the next two weeks... difficult at best.

She stares up at me now, unmoving. That flicker of defiance across her bourbon eyes tells me she *is* going to resist.

"Don't make me reach in there and pull you out, Hellcat." I shake my head, releasing a sigh heavy with all the weariness I'm feeling after the last several days. "I don't want to hurt you."

It's the last thing I ever want to do.

And it kills me that this *is* hurting her.

Not physically but emotionally.

To her, being kept away from her job after something so catastrophic happened might as well be the same level of torture she warned me about at Sunday family dinner.

She scowls at me. Those lips that are capable of saying such intensely beautiful things and kissing me so fiercely twist in a way that makes me wish I could slam my mouth against hers and wipe it all away, but all I can do right now is wait her out.

The misty rain starts to dampen my hair and clothes and she finally reaches over, unbuckles her seatbelt, and climbs from the car with a defiant huff and a wince she tries to cover by looking down instead of at me.

"Don't call me that."

We're back to that, are we?

It shouldn't surprise me that she's thrown those walls right back up, that it feels like we're back exactly where we started. As far as Bishop is concerned, I've betrayed her by suggesting this arrangement and insisting it needs to happen, by ignoring what she wants in favor of what she needs right now.

Bishop slams her door closed, and the sound seems to reverberate around us like a thunderclap. Maybe because we've sat in silence for so damn long.

I'll take loud and angry over silent and angry any day.

"Thank you." I tug open the back door. "I'll get the bags."

I pull out the two large duffels her mother packed for her and brought to the hospital this morning. With them slung over my shoulder, I motion for her to walk toward the shop.

Her body is so taut, her shoulders so rigid in front of me, that I cringe on her behalf because that can't feel good. I'm still achy from getting thrown against the goddamn SUV during the explosion, and she got it far worse than I did.

Being tense won't do anything to help her recovery, but I'm not sure Bishop is capable of relaxing without being forced to.

She reaches the door and moves to the side to give me room to unlock it. I snag the key, twist it open, and let her enter first. Her eyes immediately drift to the stairs that lead up to my apartment, but before she can even think about trying to ascend them, I let the bags slide to the floor.

The thumping sound makes her turn back, but by then, it's too late.

I slide my arms around her and lift her up as gently as I can before she can object.

"Hey!" She smacks my shoulder. "What the hell are you doing?"

Stalking across the shop past my bikes, I glance down at her. "Carrying you up the stairs."

"I'm perfectly capable of walking."

"I know you are, but it doesn't mean you have to."

Doing those stairs herself would likely cause her discomfort she doesn't need to suffer, plus this gives me an excuse to get my hands on her.

A selfish act on my part.

With her this close, her jasmine scent wraps around me, and she lets out a long sigh, crossing her arms over her chest. But she doesn't fight me or my old on her. Probably because it would hurt too much.

That thought weighs heavy on my chest as I start up the stairs.

Bishop raises a brow. "Are you going to treat me like an invalid the entire time I'm here?"

"Are you going to treat me like I'm an asshole the whole time you're here?"

"You *are* an asshole."

I can't help but grin at her despite the fact that she clearly meant that as an insult. "That is true, but not about *this*. I'm right. And everyone in the family knows it. So just accept the fact that you're going to be here for a couple of weeks. That I'm going to take care of you. And that you're not going to be allowed to work."

All the reasons she's so damn angry with me.

I reach the top of the steps, and she shoves against my chest until I set her down on her feet.

She quickly backs away, annoyance written all over her hard features.

Almost immediately, she starts pacing the small space, just like she did the last time she was here—only she didn't hate me then. She *wanted* to be here. But she had the same nervous energy, the same frustration, only now it's directed partially at me.

Even though I do love restraining her, being her jailer is a completely different animal and not something I would have ever suggested if there were any other way. But the family needs to know she isn't going anywhere and no one can find her.

That means she stays put and I remain the bad guy.

It's okay.

I can handle being the bad guy, but it doesn't mean I don't hate seeing her restless and so filled with anxiety over being kept out of the loop regarding what's happening with the investigation. But her obsessive tendencies would mean she would never heal the way she needs to.

She reaches up and releases the band that's holding her braids up in a bun at the back of her head, letting them spill down over her shoulders as she paces. "I can't do this, Gage."

I lean against the brick wall, crossing my arms over my chest to keep myself from reaching for her the way I want to. "Do what?"

"Do *nothing*. For days, for *weeks*." She throws her hands up. "God, even the last two days have been hell being cooped up in the hospital. And all of you keeping what you've learned from me is only making it worse."

Which we are all *very* well aware of.

But if she knew what we found out over the last few days, there's no way I could keep her here. There's no way I could keep her contained. And I refuse to allow her to hurt herself.

I'll use anything in my power that could prevent it.

I watch her pace the small space between my bed, my desk, and my dresser. She loops her hairband around her wrist and tugs at it as she walks, a nervous habit I've seen her do a hundred times over the last several weeks.

"You need to relax."

I barely manage to bite back the *Hellcat* I naturally want to tack onto the end of that statement.

Even without it, her glare cuts my way, practically slicing me open. "What I need is for you to stop telling me what to do."

I hold up my hands in surrender because if I were in her position, I would be objecting the same way. "Fair enough."

This isn't going to be easy.

We all knew that as soon as I suggested it.

I guess I had hoped that once she got here, in this space where we have shared more than one great night together, that she might allow her guard to drop, even just a little bit. That seems to be wishful thinking.

But this is untenable.

It isn't good for her or her recovery, and that's all I want.

I move toward her, and she eyes me warily but stops pacing. When I finally reach her, I take her face in my hands and tip it up, risking the full force of her fury this close. "Please, let me help you relax."

She swallows thickly, her pupils dilating slightly. "How?"

I know exactly where her mind is going, but there's no way *that's* happening when she's recovering from a brain injury and all the other damage that was done to her body…even if I might want it to.

"I'm going to draw you a bath."

Her sharp laughter echoes through the loft, the sound so unfamiliar from the woman who tries so damn hard to be so damn tough every moment of her life. "A *bath*?"

"I have an old claw-foot tub in the bathroom."

She nods slowly, the motion shifting her smooth skin across my fingertips in a way that makes me never want to take my hands off her. "I know. I've seen it."

"I've never used it."

One of her eyebrows wings up. "Really?"

I shake my head. "I don't think I would fit."

She grins, the first real sign of the ice cracking since we left the hospital. "You definitely wouldn't."

It may be a huge mistake to push right now, but I can't help myself. I dip my head and risk drifting my lips across hers tentatively. "So...you'll be the first one. You can christen it. And the hot water will help with all your sore muscles."

She relaxes slightly against me, and I kiss her again, keeping it slow and gentle. An apology for what I have to put her through written in every brush of our lips. When I pull away, I can see that some of her anger has dissipated.

Her shoulders fall. "Okay, fine."

I grin and drop a kiss on her forehead. "I'm going to go grab your bags. Make yourself comfortable in the meantime."

She wanders over to the bed as I hustle down the stairs and snag her bags, and by the time I'm back up in the loft, she's kicked off her shoes and has made her way into the bathroom.

I set her bags down near my dresser and rifle through them to see what her mom put in them that might be useful. When my hand finds the small bottle of bubble bath in with the bathroom items, I release a relieved breath.

Thank you, Caroline.

In the bathroom, Bishop stands at the sink, staring into the mirror, looking at the bruise along her collar bone from when she hit the pavement.

I step up behind her and trail my fingers over it lightly. "Does it hurt?"

She meets my eyes in the mirror. "Not really."

"Liar." I can see the way she fights a wince every time she moves that arm. It's one of the reasons I suggested she take a bath in the first place. "Let's see what we can do to make you feel better."

Bishop might not admit it, but she needs this right now.

She needs someone to force her mind away from the things that are going to cause her pain. And it might not be a lot, but it's all I can offer her right now that could make being locked out from the investigation bearable, even if only for an hour.

BISHOP

As much as I hate to admit that Gage was right, the hot water feels incredible.

All my tight, sore muscles soak up the heat, slowly relaxing away some of the tension and pain I've been carrying. And while this tub might not be deep or long enough for Gage to fit into it, it's absolutely perfect for me. Almost as if it was built specifically for this moment in time.

I sink even lower into it until nothing but my head and hair piled on top of it rises above the steaming water and bubbles.

Damn bubbles.

When he pulled out that bottle and said that Mom had packed it, I didn't believe him at first, but it certainly wasn't something he would have had just lying around. The fact that she snuck it into my bag raises far too many questions because it's almost as if she had anticipated this moment without ever having been in Gage's place.

We are going to have to talk next time I see her...

About a lot of things.

Including the man who reappears at the open bathroom door with a mug in his hand and a sheepish smile on his face. "I thought maybe you'd like some tea while you have your bath."

I raise a brow at him. "Tea? What makes you think I drink tea and not coffee?"

He smirks and leans against the door jamb, looking far too sexy in a pair of gray sweatpants and white T-shirt that's stretched tightly across his chest and biceps and shows off so much of his ink. "My conversation with your cousin, who owns a coffee shop."

Apparently, I need to have a conversation with Angelina, too, when I'm released from Gage Newhart's little loft prison.

I scowl at him. "Is that what you've been doing the last couple days? Going around and talking to everyone in the family to learn all these secrets about me so you can utilize them against me to get under my skin while I'm here?"

He offers a nonchalant shrug, but the corners of his lips twitch as he fights his grin. "Maybe. Or maybe I just wanted you to be comfortable."

Dammit.

That's actually really sweet and thoughtful.

But Gage always has been.

He may love to push my buttons and get me riled up, but he's never been vindictive or mean or ever said anything that wasn't absolutely true—even if I didn't want to hear it.

It makes it very hard to stay mad at my jailer.

He walks in on bare feet that shouldn't be so sexy and kneels next to the tub, holding out the mug to me. I reach my arm up out of the water, bubbles coating my skin and sliding down it as I take the drink from him and bring it to my lips.

Hell, he even got this right...

Right brand.

One spoonful of honey.

Extra hot.

Exactly the way I like it.

Damn you, Ang.

Combined with the warmth of the water, the hot liquid coating my throat and settling in my stomach helps soothe away even more of the aches.

It's exactly what I needed because I really don't want to take any of the pain medication Aunt Nora prescribed. That shit only clouds my head and my judgement. And while everyone might be trying to keep me from working, keep me in the dark about the investigation into the explosion, that doesn't mean I won't be doing my best to try to get that information. Which means I need a clear head.

Hard enough to do around Gage without narcotics thrown into the mix.

I hand the mug back to him, and he turns and drops onto his ass on the old tile, leaning back against the edge of the tub.

"You're just going to sit there?"

He glances at me over his shoulder. "There isn't anywhere for you to put the mug."

"So, you're going to sit there while I take my bath and hold it..."

"Yep." He settles in, facing away from the tub, toward the small vanity and sink. His hand tightens around the mug almost protectively. "I promise I'll keep my eyes directed at the wall."

Grinning at the chivalry, I reach up and playfully smack the back of his head, making water and bubbles trickle off my hand down his neck and onto his shirt. "Like you haven't seen it all before."

He chuckles, the sound somehow so sexual that it makes me shift restlessly in the water. "True, but I do want to give you privacy, if that's what you want. I can leave this on the floor, but you'd have to lean down and grab it every time and"—he shrugs again—"I just think this might be easier."

"All right."

I don't want to admit that it was kind of lonely in here when he was gone, or that sitting in the water with nothing else to keep my mind occupied, I kept replaying the explosion over and over in my head.

The days, hours, and minutes leading up to it…

What I could have done differently…

What I missed and didn't see…

Each moment of the day it happened…

It's the same mental video that keeps playing in my head over and over again, and it has since I woke in that hospital. At first, the visuals were fragmented. But over the course of the last few days, things have become clearer.

Everything but who did it and why.

That's what plagues me as much as my own guilt over missing something—the not knowing.

Satriano's motivations have shifted over the years, from revenge, to an almost jealousy and desire to manipulate us like puppets on strings. It borders on obsession and turns everything he does into another mystery to solve.

I didn't really think it would be any different here, that the memories or questions would somehow go away with a change of scenery, but it's starting to get harder and harder to pretend I'm unaffected by the constant replayed trauma.

A little company to distract from that could be a good thing, even if the man sitting beside this tub is just as complicated for me as the situation outside this loft is.

I release a sigh and sink back down into the water.

"How're you feeling?"

His voice is so soft, I'm almost not sure I heard him right—or maybe I'm just afraid I did. There's a tenderness to it, a heavy weight of concern that goes well beyond a man who is babysitting his employer's daughter. That brings a new ache to my chest that wasn't there only a few minutes ago. The same one I felt when I found out he hadn't left my side at the hospital.

What the hell are you doing with this man, Bishop?

I'd love to blame the confusion regarding that topic on my concussion and the fact that my brain still feels a little scrambled, but that would be a lie.

I've been a mess where Gage is concerned since the first time I saw him.

His question is so loaded, but I will pretend he only means physically since climbing into this tub.

"Better, thank you."

He toys with the handle of the mug while I relax for a few moments, then hands it back toward me without looking—just as he promised.

I accept it from him, take another sip, and pass it into his waiting hand, careful not to allow our skin to touch. For some reason, the thought of feeling that little electrical charge I always do when his callouses scrape against me is too overwhelming right now.

Having his mouth on me for the first time in days out there almost shattered me on the spot, and I can't fall apart.

"You know I have the medication from your aunt. The pain meds, the muscle relaxers...you should really consider taking them."

I shake my head, even though he can't see me. "No."

"Why not?"

I've already had this discussion with Nora and Pope, and Mom and Dad, who have all spent the last few days trying to convince me that dealing with my injuries without any sort of medications was going to be too painful. But I've had plenty of bumps, bruises, and broken bones in Jiu-Jitsu and boxing over the years that I'm used to not always being comfortable.

I'm not afraid to live with a little pain.

"Because I don't like the way they affect me, how they fog my mind."

He nods slowly. "I can understand that. I've been in the same position and done the same thing. I just..."

The longer it takes him to continue, the more unease starts to creep back into my body.

"Gage, you just what?"

Slowly, he glances over his shoulder at me, his eyes roaming over my face. "I just wanted to make sure you weren't making yourself suffer because you felt you deserved it."

I flinch at his words.

Because he isn't wrong about that, either.

It's true I don't want to cloud my head. I don't want to be stuck in some medication haze. But I also crave the pain in a way I know I shouldn't.

Because it keeps me replaying what led up to the explosion. It keeps me analyzing what I did wrong and what I missed. And that's the only way I can figure out what happened and can make sure it doesn't ever again.

Gage seems to see all of that in a mere glance without me ever confirming it, and I press my lips together and hold out my hand for the mug again instead of responding to him.

If I lied about what he just said, he'd see that, too.

God, I hate how well he knows me.

I hate how he read me like a goddamn open book from the moment we met. How he managed to break through all the walls I've always lived behind and has taken root on the opposite side, and now he's like one of those vines that entangles itself with the brick and can't be ripped away without completely tearing the wall down.

Cracked or not, I *need* that wall.

I take another sip and hand it back to him, and he returns to staring at the wall, probably ruminating about how fucked up I am in the head to be fighting him so hard on everything. But a comfortable silence settles over us and I left my eyes drift closed.

"I used to love bubble baths as a kid…"

His words make me stiffen, and I slowly open my eyes to find him staring down into the mug.

"Where did you grow up?"

I barely know a thing about him other than the few documents we've found and a handful of brief conversations where he's revealed very little. Considering the intimate things I've done with this man, that suddenly makes me feel like a real asshole.

Gage uses his free hand to run through his hair, sending the long, thick locks falling haphazardly around the side of his face. "You know my dad was in the military, so we moved around a lot."

"Was that fun, to live different places, or did you hate it?"

He glances over at me and gives me a tight smile. "I got to see the world at a very young age. Six countries before I was eighteen. I can speak five different languages."

"Really?"

An almost shy grin pulls at his lips. "Really. So, it was pretty cool, I guess, but it meant making connections with people, lasting ones, was pretty impossible."

My chest tightens at the admission and the longing in his voice because I've always had that luxury. I've always lived here, in this place, and been able to have deep, meaningful friendships or relationships, and I chose not to.

Beyond the family, beyond the Hawkes, I've kept everyone out. Locked myself away with my core group because I've always felt like it was my responsibility to watch out for them.

And Gage saw that the minute we met.

He saw right through me to my deepest, darkest needs that are so basic in life.

"Is that why you went into the Army? Because that's what your dad did?"

He nods. "I guess so. It was really all I knew." Clearing his throat, he offers a shrug. "My parents both died when I was in my twenties. By the time I got out of the service, I didn't really have a place to call home."

"Is New Orleans going to be that?"

It's the same thing Nana was asking him at dinner, only now, I truly want to know the answer.

Selfishly, I want him to say that it is, that he won't be leaving, but for someone like Gage who has never had roots anywhere, putting them down might be terrifying.

He finally turns fully to look at me, his blue eyes shimmering with something I can't quite place. "I hope so. I really do."

But I can hear it in his voice, the hesitation.

He's holding something back.

20

FIVE DAYS LATER

GAGE

I step out of the bathroom, towel wrapped around my waist, another in my hand as I rub it over my wet hair.

Bishop reclines against the headboard of my bed, my copy of *Catch 22* open in her hands, but her eyes immediately lift from the pages and land on me. They roam over every inch of exposed skin and dip down to follow the trickle of water rolling down my chest, abs, and into the towel at my waist.

Fighting a smirk, I freeze and give her a second to finish her perusal before her eyes finally flick up to meet mine.

I raise a brow. "What are you doing?"

When I went to take a shower, she was napping, something I'm quite confident she never did before the explosion. If anyone had suggested it then, she likely would have responded by going another round in the ring with Atlas or pinning some unsuspecting sucker on the Jiu-jitsu mat.

But that was *before.*

Now, she's battling exhaustion she can't hide, aches in her

muscles and joints, not to mention the headaches that just keep coming back no matter what we try to do to help them.

Since she refuses to take the medication that might relieve some of it, and I'm not about to force it down her throat, it has meant she's been uncomfortable for days, which in turn has made me miserable watching her suffer.

But the way she's looking at me now, it does not appear she's *at all* uncomfortable.

If anything, she's eyeing me the same way she accused *me* of looking at her that day in the gym—like she wants to pin and straddle me.

My cock starts to harden, pushing against the confines of the towel that does very little to hide my reaction to her wearing one of my T-shirts, sitting casually on my bed, like it's *hers* and she *belongs* there.

It would be, if I had my way.

It's where I want her to stay, far beyond the two-week restriction Nora put on her return to work and her normal life, but I know the second she gets medically cleared, she'll be out of here as fast as she can run.

Given the training she usually does, I bet that's pretty damn fast.

She holds up the book. "I found this in your nightstand."

"Huh..." I return to drying my hair. "So you were snooping?"

Grinning, she shakes her head. "No, I was bored."

My eyes dip to where her phone lies on the comforter beside her bare legs. "Bored or annoyed?"

She scowls, and I know I've read the situation accurately.

It isn't the first time I've caught her trying to wring information from one of the Hawkes. She's made her way through the entire family over the last several days, hoping one of them might have a weak moment and tell her what's been happening with both the investigation into the bombing and their continued hunt for Satriano.

Given how frustrated she continues to be, it's clear she hasn't gotten anything out of anyone, but I have to give it to her for the continued determination and lack of quit.

I don't think this woman even knows the meaning of the word.

"You were texting your dad again, weren't you? Trying to get some information from him?"

She purses her lips together, her fingers tightening around the open book. Her annoyance at being kept out of the loop has only grown the longer she's remained confined here and in the dark, but it's for her own good, whether she likes it or not.

The fact that she continues to have intense headaches and be so sore only confirms the need for more time to recover.

But that doesn't mean I don't feel for her.

I can't even imagine how unsettling it must be knowing someone is out there targeting the people she loves when she is helpless to do anything about it. If I were in her shoes, I would be trying everything to get back into the mix, too.

And seeing her continue to stress about it when she needs to *relax* in order to speed up her recovery makes me feel helpless.

I toss the towel I was using on my hair back into the bathroom so I can crawl onto the bed with her. Taking her face in my palm, I tilt it up toward me. "I know it's killing you to be in the dark about this, but I promise, if there was anything we absolutely needed your help with that someone else couldn't handle, we would come to you—even against doctor's orders." Her jaw hardens, and I run my thumb along it. "Tensing up like that isn't going to help your headaches."

She pulls out of my hold and grabs her phone, tossing it on the bedside table along with the book. Her tongue snakes out across her lips, wetting them as she returns to looking at me like I'm a goddamn snack again. "You're right, it won't. But I know something that will."

Her hand cups my semi-hard cock through the towel, and I groan, slamming my eyes shut against the glorious sensation after so many days of sleeping beside this woman and not touching her the way I so desperately want to.

"Fucking hell, Bishop." I shake my head as she drags her thumb across the piercings that line the top, making my cock twitch in her hold. "No…"

I start to shift back off the bed, out of temptation's reach, but she loops her free arm around my neck and tugs me closer, until I'm practically in her lap.

She strokes my cock that's now fully hard and raring to go, skimming her lips across my cheek. "But I heard an orgasm is good for pain relief."

I grab her wrist, keeping her from doing any further damage to my already frayed willpower. "I've heard that, too. Are you in pain right now?"

Her gaze flicks over to the nightstand and the book on it. "I see where you're going with this, Gage. It's a Catch 22, right? If I am in pain, touching me could relieve it, but if I say I'm in pain, you won't touch me because you don't want to risk hurting me more."

Smart woman…

If I weren't trying so hard to fight how fucking turned on I am, I would show her just how impressed I am that she figured out exactly where I was going with that question so quickly.

Bishop's safety and comfort is my number one priority, even if that means rejecting her and probably facing her wrath for it.

She leans up and presses her lips to mine, the taste of the tea she just drank on her tongue mixing with the scent of the jasmine that always hangs around her, filling every breath I take.

God, it's so hard to resist her when she's like this.

Still, I force myself to pull away, still gripping her wrist. "I know what you're up to, Hellcat."

"What's that?"

I have to hand it to her, she somehow manages to appear confused and innocent even when I damn well know she's one of the most cunning women on this planet.

"You think if you have sex with me, I'm going to tell you something that I haven't already about what's happening."

It's only there for a second, just a brief flicker of distress across her gaze, but it's enough to know I'm right.

"Another very good reason not to do this right now, Bishop."

I shift away, releasing her wrist and trying to put some space between us so I can get a clearer head, but her hand catches the towel and she tugs on it, pulling it free of my waist.

Her gaze zeros in on my very hard cock, the metal piercings glinting under the overhead lights. "It looks like you're very on board with this idea."

"Not when you're hurt. And *not* when you have an ulterior motive."

She pushes up onto her knees. "Just because I have an ulterior motive doesn't mean I don't desperately want you right now. Two things can be true at the same time."

I crawl closer to her and pin her back against the headboard. Gently. Ensuring I'm not pressing her anywhere that would make her sore or aggravate any of the bruises on her body.

"You know how much I like playing games, Hellcat. Especially with you. But I'm not going to tell you anything, and I'm not going to risk hurting you."

The plea in her eyes might as well be a dagger straight to my heart. "It's going to hurt me if you don't."

She says the words so softly that I barely hear them, and I might think they're just a ploy to get me to cave...

If I couldn't see the truth in her gaze.

Bishop *needs* this.

It isn't just about hoping I'll slip and give her some information.

She's feeling out of control again, like everything is happening around her and she's locked away in some castle tower but still suffering the consequences from it.

Maybe she can't admit it out loud.

But it's true nonetheless.

She needs control tonight.

She needs me to give it to her.

And I don't know that I can deny her anything that might make her feel better, that might give her something to cling to when she's spiraling.

I take her face in my hand again, holding it firmly. "I'll tell you what, Hellcat, I will gladly make you come to see if it makes you feel better, but if I think for a goddamn second that it's hurting you, then we're done. Agreed?"

She nods eagerly, and I drop my free hand down between her legs, sliding it up under the hem of my T-shirt and into her panties to find her core already starting to slicken.

"Is this from seeing me come out of the shower?"

Her gaze dips to all the ink on my chest. "I love looking at you. You're a beautiful man."

I can't help but grin at her. "That might be the first time anyone's ever said that to me."

"Really?"

I nod. "Is that why you're with me, Hellcat? Because I'm so beautiful?"

Her breath hitches, and I see fear flash across her gaze as she shakes her head. "No."

It wouldn't have mattered in this moment if she had answered "yes" to that question, but her slight hesitation and that tiny sliver of fear are enough to tell me I'm not alone in feeling that what we have goes far beyond the sexually charged energy between us.

I crush my mouth to hers, *truly* kissing her for the first time in almost a week. She moans, wrapping her arms around my neck and tugging me tighter against her. I loop my arms around her back and roll onto mine, taking her with me, careful to ensure I'm not holding her too tightly.

"Pull off that shirt and come sit on my face, Hellcat."

Her eyes flare wide as she stares down at me, but her fingers find the hem of the shirt and she tugs it up and tosses it over the side of the bed, then reaches down and slides off her panties, throwing them on the floor, too.

Even with the bruises marring her skin, Bishop is the most stunning thing I've ever seen on this planet.

How was I ever supposed to resist her?

I shift down until my head rests on the pillow, and she moves up, placing her knees on either side of my head, settling her glistening cunt right where I want it.

"Christ, Bishop. You have no idea how much I've missed this."

She gazes down at me from half-lidded eyes, her bare chest rising and falling rapidly in anticipation.

"Grab the headboard."

Her hands curl around the same slats I had her tied to our first night here.

"If this hurts at all, you tell me and we're stopping."

She gives me a sharp nod, but we both know she's too stubborn to ever admit that, which just means I have to be gentle with her. Though I'm not so sure she'll be gentle with me.

BISHOP

Fire blazes across Gage's blue gaze, burning away the reservation that's been lingering there, and he slides his hands around to grip my ass and drags me forward, lifting his head to slowly run his tongue through my core.

My hips immediately jerk at the contact.

Fuck...

One simple brush against my skin, and I start trembling.

He kisses every inch of me.

My inner thighs.

My dripping pussy.

My clit.

Exploring in the most sensually slow and methodical way.

Not hard.

Not harsh.

Probing, seeking, licking, and gently flicking the tip of his tongue across me so deliciously that stars explode against my closed eyelids.

I drop my forehead to rest it on top of the headboard as a slow groan floats from deep in my chest.

The intensity that has always existed between us is still there, thrumming through every brush of his lips and tongue, vibrating in the way he sucks so gently on my clit, in the subtle tensing of his hands into my ass.

But it's restrained.

He's restrained in a way he never has been with me before.

It's as frustrating as it is beautiful and terrifying.

This tender, caring side of Gage that he has repeatedly shown me over the past several days has made it so much harder to remember why I tried so hard to avoid this kind of connection.

He tightens his grip on my ass, thrusting his tongue deeper inside me, and my body clenches, wanting more. Needing it. As if he can sense that without me even saying a word, his fingers quickly slip into me, spreading me gently, and he curls them up into that spot that always makes my body convulse.

My hips grind down against his face, moving almost of their own volition, as if I'm not even in control of them anymore.

A gasp falls from my lips as he sucks my clit gently, moving his fingers in a languid, methodical motion.

It builds slowly, a sparking heat centered in my core, that feeling of pressure I've only ever experienced one other time.

With *him*.

And I know what's coming.

That insanely intense rush that will utterly destroy me.

My whole body tenses, and Gage stops immediately, his mouth and hand stilling.

Worried eyes stare up at me. "Hellcat, what's wrong?"

I shake my head. "Nothing." My voice comes out breathy. "I'm just—"

Terrified.

"Don't fight it."

His words echo through my head. But what he's really saying is "*Don't fight me.*" It's what he's been asking for since the beginning, for me to let go and let him in. And I've tried. I really have, but years and years of protecting everyone else and myself make it nearly impossible to fully drop my guard.

"Relax, Hellcat."

It isn't said as an order.

More like a plea from him to do the very thing he's been trying to get me to since we first met.

I know what will happen if I do.

This man will unleash that tidal wave of pent-up pressure that's built up. He will help me release the pain and the frustration and all the volatile emotions tangled up inside me.

If I can only do what he asks.

He returns to his meticulous ministrations, his fingers playing me expertly while his mouth and tongue help build me back up to that precipice he had me so close to only moments ago.

I try to let each and every muscle relax.

The same way they have in the baths he's drawn for me.

Or when he's massaged my sore body every night before we climb into bed together and he wraps his solid, warm frame around mine, keeping me safe and holding me steady through the nightmares that seem to come every time I close my eyes.

But they're not there right now.

All that exists is this pleasure coursing through me and the feeling of the building pressure low in my core.

A dam about to rupture…

When it finally spills over, I come in a hot rush, and Gage groans his satisfaction, swallowing down my release, sucking me dry, licking and flicking his tongue over my clit to drag out my orgasm and make my body pulsate with mind-numbing ecstasy.

The fuzzy, warm cloud of post-orgasmic bliss descends over me, and my legs tremble violently, threatening to give way under me.

I've never felt so completely wrung out.

So fully free.

Gage withdraws his fingers from inside me, and I allow my eyes to flutter open and stare down at him between my legs.

His lips glisten with the evidence of what he just did for me, and he grins. "Feel better?"

I nod, still unable to fill my lungs with a deep enough breath to speak.

"Good."

He reaches up and helps me slide down until I'm sprawled across him, his hard cock pinned against my belly.

All those aches and worries I had earlier have evaporated, replaced by a need for this man that makes me feel like I'm completely losing my grip on all the things I've clung so tightly to all my life.

He kisses me long and slow, the same way he just ate me, and my pussy clenches, my body remembering how fucking incredible it feels to be with Gage in every way.

His hand slides behind my neck, and he pulls back from the kiss slightly, holding me just far enough away that I can't get my lips back on him. "Remember I told you that you can pin and straddle me anytime you want, Hellcat..."

How could I ever forget?

Hearing those words again makes that heat, that need, flare hotter.

Gage didn't know me when he said it the first time, but even then, I knew there was something about this man that was dangerous. I just had no idea the risk was to my heart.

I grab his hands and push them back onto the pillow on either side of his head as I kiss him again. He grins against my mouth, and when I pull back, I raise a brow at him. "Those stay there."

His bottom lip disappears beneath his teeth, as if having me command him the same way he has me has him biting back something he desperately wants to say, but he nods his agreement even though the gleam in his eyes suggests his compliance won't last long.

Honestly, I won't either.

After that explosive release, I'm so primed to blow again that my clit pulses and aches for the friction that will send my flying.

I reach between us and adjust his cock at my slick entrance. He releases a low, deep groan, and I slide down it in a long, slow glide, pressing my palms flat against his colorful chest.

Fuck.

The stretch and the pressure of those goddamn piercings

along the walls of my pussy is so fucking exquisite it makes me gasp.

His body tenses beneath me, every muscle going rock hard. "Fucking hell, Bishop..."

When I finally fully seat myself on him, I grind down and clench around his cock, and what slips from his mouth isn't a groan, it's a full-on feral growl.

His hands find my hips, and my eyes fly open to meet his.

"I told you to keep them up there."

He smirks. "I know, Hellcat, but I can't help it." His fingers dig into my skin. "If this hurts, you have to stop."

I nod, but I know damn well I won't.

My body has ached so much over the last few days, but this is different.

This is the *good* pain.

The exquisite ache.

One I've craved lying in Gage's arms each night.

I push up on my knees until only the head of his cock is still inside me and then sink back down, concentrating on the feel of every inch, each of those little balls that create the most magnificent friction.

He lets me take control, lets me move at my own pace, his grip on my hips only enough to hold me steady and assist with what I want to do when he could very easily take over at any time.

But God, I needed this.

Not just the sexual release, but all the feelings being with him like this brings to the surface.

The reminder that I'm alive.

The faith that there are still good people and good things in this world.

The belief that, in the end, everything will be all right.

All of it is somehow wrapped up in this beautiful man who

lets me ride his cock and control his body the same way he usually does mine.

My nails dig into his chest, and he slips a hand between us, his fingers finding my already sensitive clit. He rolls his calloused thumb against it, and I buck on his length, clenching around it in a way that has a low hiss slipping from his lips.

"Do that again, Hellcat."

I do, clamping tightly on him every time I grind down. Clasping on every retreat. Keeping him wrapped in my pussy like a vise.

But I can't take it anymore.

The slow, torturous pace...

I have to move.

I need it harder.

I need what we had before.

I need to not feel like I'm broken and something to handle delicately.

I ride him harder.

Faster.

He moves with me, his hips rolling up to meet every downward thrust, his hands lifting me easily on my trembling legs. With his head tipped back, his neck muscles straining, he looks so fucking beautiful. Like Adonis lying in this bed.

And he's *mine*.

Something about that word makes my heart stutter and I almost slip, almost lose control over my movements, but Gage keeps us going, pushing the rhythm to a fevered pace.

He's so many things.

Brutal.

Demanding.

Controlling.

Infuriating in so many ways.

Yet also sweet and caring.

Selfless.

So many contradictions wrapped up in one man, and I can't get enough of him.

As much as I've wanted to deny what's been happening over the last several days, no matter how badly I wanted to think it was all just lust, just incredible *sex* that brought about this attraction to him, I now know that's a lie.

I've managed to fall for him and all his complications.

And that terrifying realization is the last one I have before my orgasm slams into me.

He continues to roll his thumb across my clit and pump up into me as my body convulses, my nails digging into his chest, my hips bucking wildly as I come. His grip on my hips tightens, and two harsh thrusts have him emptying himself inside me.

I collapse onto him, and he buries his face in my neck, reaching up to pull my braids free from the bun they've been tied back in. They fall all around us, and he brushes them to the side, twisting my face toward him so he can kiss me languidly.

It's so easy to float in this warm, post-orgasmic haze, wrapped in his strong hold, our hearts beating rapidly against each other, and pretend there isn't an enemy out there after the Hawkes.

Tomorrow, I'll face that reality again.

But tonight, I'm going to fall asleep like this, with my guard down.

21

BISHOP

The soft sound of rain hitting the windows and the roof above me draws me slowly from a deep sleep. That blissful fuzzy darkness clings to my brain for a few minutes, and I stay completely still, luxuriating in the feel of Gage's bed and inhaling his leather and spice scent that clings to the sheets along with the smell of *us.*

For the first time since the explosion, I wake feeling good, my body relaxed and sated. And I actually *slept.*

No nightmares.

No staying up all night worrying about what was happening outside this space.

No fear that I missed something and someone else paid the price for it keeping me awake.

All of it was somehow kept at bay while I slept beside the man who has changed my life so much.

I stretch with a groan and my body protests slightly, but it's so much better than it has been the last several days. Instead of aching, angry muscles, only a dull throb between my legs reminds me of what Gage and I did last night.

A grin pulls at my lips, and I push myself up and scan the loft area.

He isn't in the kitchen or sitting at the small desk, and through the open bathroom door, I can tell it's empty, too. Which means he must be downstairs working on his bike.

That's about all he's done the last couple of days—worked on the Indian or stepped outside for long phone calls with Dad and Luca, and probably dozens of other people he wouldn't tell me about.

I know he must have a computer somewhere down there, too, must be working on whatever tasks they've given him while he's also acting as my babysitter, but he's kept me well in the dark about it.

His promise that they would bring me in if there was something they couldn't handle has given me a modicum of comfort, but I still want more.

I want to be involved.

I want to *help.*

And waking today feeling so much better than I have all week gives me hope that maybe things *will* be different. Maybe I can start getting back to my job, even if only gradually, at first.

Because the Hawkes can't stay locked up and living in fear forever.

The girls are going stir-crazy, and the boys...

Given the texts I've received over the past week, they seem ready to bust out the pitchforks and go door to door looking for Satriano to get this resolved on their terms.

If something doesn't give soon, there may be an all-out Hawke riot in the streets of New Orleans.

Which would be ill advised.

Once I get a handle on what the investigation has uncovered, I'll be in a better position to help, but that requires convincing Gage—and Aunt Nora and Pope—that I'm finally feeling well enough to do it.

That starts now.

I slide off the bed and snag a pair of jeans to pull on under Gage's shirt I slept in. The metal treads of the stairs are cold under my bare feet, but I move as silently as I can to try to surprise him. But the usual sounds of him working on the Indian don't fill the space, and when I reach the bottom step and can see the whole garage, it's empty.

He wouldn't have left me, which means he's outside on a call that he doesn't want me to overhear.

Annoyance tightens my chest, but I try to take a deep breath and release it before I get all worked up over his continued secrecy.

Maybe he just didn't want to wake me up.

That's probably wishful thinking, and I step up to the small pedestrian door and peek out through the old, wavy glass window at the top.

Gage stands near the end of the driveway, phone to his ear and back to the shop, seemingly oblivious to the rain falling on him, his shirt and hair already wet.

As anxious as I am to know who he's talking to and about what, I won't be able to hear anything from here anyway, so I turn back to the shop and make my way over to his Indian that still rests up on the stand.

It really is a beautiful old bike, and it seems that the last several days have given Gage time to make some headway on it.

A few random bike parts lay scattered on the cracked concrete around the base of the stand along with various tools and instruments, and I move past them over to the workbench along the wall to examine the rest of his stuff.

I haven't had a chance to explore down here yet.

He either had me tied up upstairs—literally and figuratively —before the bombing, or I've been too tired and sore since then to wander down here. Any time he was working on something in the main shop while I slept, he would come back up as soon as he realized I was awake.

The old place has a certain charm, even if it isn't much to look at, and I find myself grinning at all the tools that look older than me that must have come with the place.

Other than his bikes and tools, there isn't much else to look at other than the door at the far corner of the main space.

I vaguely remember noticing it when I came in that first night, and with the building layout, it makes sense there would be a small storage room of some sort there, directly beneath the bathroom upstairs.

This door is solid, so there isn't any way to peek inside without opening it, but curiosity gets the better of me, and I need to know what's inside.

I try the knob, but it doesn't budge.

Locked.

Why would Gage keep it locked if he's the only one who's ever in here?

Interest piqued, I go back to his workbench and grab a screwdriver. I learned very early on how to get into places where I wasn't supposed to be, and it only takes me a few seconds to get the lock popped.

I nudge the door open and step into the dark room.

With no windows, it's almost pitch black in here, and I reach to the wall for a light switch and flick it on.

I instantly wish I hadn't.

Oh, God...

It takes a few moments for me to fully process what I'm seeing because my head can't make any sense of what my eyes are taking in.

Walls covered in photographs of all of us...The Hawkes.

Outside the club.

Outside our homes.

Outside The Grind and the bookstore.

Pictures of us driving, walking down the streets in various parts of town, eating at restaurants.

Our entire lives.

Everything we've done and everywhere we've been...

And they go back far longer than I've known Gage.

I step farther in on shaky legs, my hand tensing around the handle of the screwdriver.

What the hell is this?

A low table sits cluttered with all sorts of mechanical parts, and as I start to take in what they are, my heart stops, then starts thundering rapidly against my ribcage.

Blood rushes in my ears.

My legs start to give out, and I grab the edge of the table to keep from passing out on the floor.

Blinking rapidly, I try to clear away what I'm seeing...

No.

It can't be...

"Bishop?"

Gage's voice carries through the open door, and I freeze.

Shit.

His booted footsteps sound on the metal stairs as he slowly ascends, then they pound back down when he realizes I'm not up there.

There's no way to sneak out of here and get that door relocked and closed before he sees me, and there'd be no point in attempting to hide it. I can't ever look at him again without him knowing what I've seen.

I tighten my grip on the only weapon available to me and wait for him to appear in the doorway.

He does almost immediately, his eyes wild and wide, his jaw set hard. His gaze locks on me, trepidation darkening the usually warm waters there. "It isn't what it looks like, Hellcat."

"Don't call me that."

My rage bleeds through my words, making them come out colder than I've ever heard my own voice.

He holds up his hands. "Let me explain."

"There's no explanation for this, Gage. None. Especially this." I motion toward the items on the table, and he flinches and squeezes his eyes closed. "I'm no expert, but I know enough to recognize what I'm looking at. This stuff you have here? These are the components for making a fucking *bomb*."

His eyes fly open and meet mine, and there's a plea in them—one I absolutely cannot fall for.

Not ever again.

"Did you—"

I swallow back the words because I can't even form them.

I can't possibly say them out loud because that would make them true.

It would make everything I thought I knew about this man into the biggest lie of my life.

"Did you make the bomb that hurt my uncles? That hurt *me*? Did you try to kill us?"

His eyes harden to that icy blue I so rarely see. "Would you believe me if I said no?"

Oh, God...

I shake my head. He steps closer, but I raise the screwdriver in front of me, pointing it directly at his chest.

"Don't."

It may not be my weapon of choice, but I know exactly where to shove this to do the most damage, to immobilize him or even kill him. And I won't hesitate to do it if he takes one more step.

"Bishop, please." He keeps his hands up. "Give me a minute to explain."

I circle to the other side of the tiny room, trying to make my way to the door without him intercepting me, but we both know he could easily. The space is tight, and he's taller and has a much longer reach than me.

Only a handful of feet separate us—and stand between me and escape.

Keeping the screwdriver raised, I inch toward the door, my bare feet cold on the old concrete. But it barely registers.

My entire body is numb.

Gage lets me move toward the door, and as soon as I'm close enough, I dash out of it and into the main garage, but I never give him my back because I know he'll take that advantage and use it against me.

That's apparently where his expertise lies.

"Bishop, I need you to listen to me." He lets me get halfway across the garage before he steps out from that side room. "Things aren't always what they appear."

My hand trembles as I hold the screwdriver out toward him. "What did you do in the Rangers? What was your specialty?"

He flinches again. "Explosives. But I didn't lie to you. I'm also a mechanic—"

"Fuck you! You didn't lie to me?" My voice echoes around the room, bouncing off all the metal. "How long have you been here, in New Orleans?"

His throat works a thick swallow. "A while."

"Because of us?"

His jaw hardens again and he nods.

Fuck...

I'm so fucking stupid...

Bile climbs the back of my throat, and I fight the urge to gag because that would leave me open to an attack.

No weaknesses.

Don't let him see it.

I've always known that any weakness can be exploited—in the ring, on the mat, or in life.

I just never realized I'd be dumb enough to allow it to happen to me.

Run.

You have to run.

I back away from him on shaking legs, all the way to the door that leads outside, that leads to freedom, that gets me far away from *him*.

"Bishop, don't go. Let me explain." His voice wavers, his gaze swimming with uncertainty and fear. He watches me grab the knob. "You don't even have goddamn shoes on—"

"I don't fucking care."

I throw the door open and race out into the rain, running and not looking back, the screwdriver still clenched in my fist.

GAGE

Fuck.

Fuck.

Fuck.

Fuck.

Fuck.

Fuck.

Fuuuuuck...

I pull out my phone from my back pocket as I run toward the door after her, pausing inside the jamb only long enough to fire off a quick text.

We have a problem: A huge one.

My hand shakes as I hit send and run out onto the driveway with my heart in my throat.

I scan the street in both directions, searching for any sign of her. The neighborhood of mostly old, rundown service buildings and abandoned properties is silent this time of day.

And completely empty.

Shit.

The falling rain has washed away any potential signs of footprints that would allow me to track her, and she's far too smart not to hide immediately, not to make herself invisible any way she can as fast as she can.

But she can't have gotten far.

She was only a few seconds ahead of me. She's barefoot. And she doesn't know the neighborhood.

Those factors all play in my favor, which is good, because I have to catch her before she does something really stupid.

Which way would she go?

Frantically looking left and right, I wrack my brain, trying to put myself in her position if I had just walked into *that.*

She would go toward home.

Toward safety.

Toward her damn gun.

The vision of her clutching that screwdriver flashes through my head. Her trembling hand. White knuckle grip on the only weapon she had. The fear and hatred in the bourbon eyes that only last night looked at me with such warmth and affection.

No.

More than affection.

Last night changed things between us, and we both knew it. This morning should have been a new beginning for us. A step in the right direction. A step toward our future. Which is why that look of betrayal she just gave me will haunt me forever.

I have to find her.

Convince her to let me explain...

She'll try to find a phone, unless I can find her first. I turn left and race down the wet sidewalk, my boots splashing through growing puddles, sending water flying up and soaking me even more, but it doesn't matter.

Nothing does right now except finding Bishop.

She's terrified, angry, and has nothing but the clothes on her back and the screwdriver in her hand.

The chill in the air makes me shiver as much as the fact that she's out here barefoot, running down the filthy street, looking for anyone she might be able to trust who can give her access to a phone, a way to contact one of the Hawkes.

Time isn't on my side. Once she makes that call, it will be too late.

I check every alleyway.

Behind every building.

Inside the burned-out, abandoned houses half a block from my place.

For twenty minutes, I scour the entire area, but there isn't any sign of her.

Where the hell did you go, Hellcat?

Knowing her as well as I do, I'm confident she ran hard and fast. The fact that her body is still recovering from a severe concussion and weak from the injuries she sustained being thrown by the blast would be irrelevant to her.

Once the adrenaline kicked it, she would have been *gone* and not looked back.

All out until she felt safe.

A middle-aged woman turns the corner ahead, approaching me huddled under her umbrella carrying a small bag from the store up the street.

I jog up to her, plastering on a smile when the gaping hole in my chest where Bishop lived feels like it's stealing my ability to breathe. "You haven't seen a woman run by, have you? Barefoot with long dark braids wearing a man's T-shirt?"

She narrows her gaze on me, her hand tightening on the

umbrella so much that her knuckles whiten. "What makes you think I would tell you if I did?"

Fuck.

I sound like a goddamn scumbag kidnapper chasing after my captive who just escaped my evil clutches. It would almost be funny if it weren't so close to the actual truth.

The woman keeps walking, glancing back at me several times with an intensely suspicious look that tells me she's probably going to pull out her phone and record me, too.

Let her.

It doesn't matter at this point. By the time the cops show up, I'll be long gone. Just like Bishop is...

"*Fuck!*"

My scream rips through the air, but there isn't anyone around to hear it. The woman who had every right to be suspicious of me must have turned down one of the side streets, leaving me standing here with nothing but my regret.

I shouldn't have left her alone in the loft.

I should have known a goddamn lock wasn't going to stop her from getting into that room.

But I got complacent.

I got too comfortable having her in my space and in my life.

I forgot what the fallout would be if she ever discovered what I have been keeping from her.

I let myself believe that those people in that bed together last night were who we really are and not two people who have been lying to each other and themselves.

What the fuck do I do?

Tipping my head back, I stare up at the gray sky and let the cold rain pelt my face, as if that can somehow wash away everything I've done to her. Every lie I've told and every misstep I've taken since I arrived in New Orleans run through my head.

There have been so many.

Most relating to Bishop.

And now it's too late to fix it.

My phone buzzes in my pocket, and I reluctantly reach back and tug it out, glancing at the screen.

Then we should meet. Now.

I start walking back toward my place, still idly searching behind every building along the way, as if she's still going to be here, but it's futile.

Bishop already found somewhere safe to hunker down and make a phone call to one of the Hawkes. She's already told them what she found, and they've already come to the same conclusion she did—that they were my targets.

And she isn't wrong about that.

But she *is* wrong about everything else.

I walk back up the driveway toward the shop feeling numb, like my brain doesn't want to process what just happened, how quickly everything went to shit.

The door still stands wide open, and I step through it and slam it closed behind me, the old glass in it rattling. I lean back against it and drag in a shaky breath, building up the courage I need to follow through with what I'm about to do.

It's the only thing I *can* do. The only chance I have to potentially salvage anything.

I pull out my phone again and hit dial on the number that just texted me.

A familiar voice answers. "Are you on your way here?"

I squeeze my eyes closed against the headache suddenly forming behind my eyes and pinch the bridge of my nose. "No. Bishop Clarke found everything."

"Shit."

"She ran from my place. I'm sure by now, all the Hawkes know."

"This is bad."

Underfuckingstatement of the year.

"I know." I swallow thickly. "I have to go after her. I have to go explain."

"If you do that, you're a dead man."

I know it isn't an empty threat or a warning.

It's just the truth.

But I can't leave things like this.

I can't sit here and wait for Saint to appear and kill me with his bare fucking hands, which the man could do easily. I can't wait for Atlas to show up and pound me into a bloody fucking pulp. I can't wait around to see what the Hawkes would do to me if they go on believing what Bishop does.

Especially after the phone call I was on earlier that provided so much information I didn't know before. It made so many things clear that hadn't made sense, things I would have told Bishop had she given me the chance. But I can't say I blame her for running.

I would have done the same in her position. And now, I have to fall on my sword. "I'm going over there. I'm going after her."

"Don't let your personal feelings get in the way of your job."

"This isn't about that."

It's a lie, of course, and we both know it.

My *personal* feelings have been in the way from day fucking one.

I end the call before he can say anything else or try to talk me out of it, then pull out the battery and SIM card from the phone and crush them beneath my boot.

There isn't any time to second guess this decision.

I've already wasted too much of it looking for her when there wasn't a chance in Hell of ever finding her if she didn't want to be found.

As soon as I hit the top step, her jasmine scent hits me, mixed with the smell of sex and comfort we found together over the last several days. The pain that hits my chest is so intense that I double over, trying to find my breath.

"Fuck!"

I stagger to the edge of the bed and collapse there, burying my face into my hands.

You knew this would happen.

You knew she would figure out the truth eventually, that you would have to explain.

I thought I'd have more time.

I thought I could control it, that I could present it to her in a way that she would understand. But now, everything has blown up the same way Gabe's car did the other day, and there's no way to put the pieces back together.

But it doesn't mean I won't try.

I push up with one last longing look at the bed, then quickly strip out of my wet clothes and put on dry ones.

My eyes rake over all of Bishop's things now scattered around my place so casually. She was comfortable here. She may still have been itching to get back to work, but she had settled in and stopped acting like I was holding her prisoner. She had finally begun to accept that everything I was doing was because I wanted to help her.

But now?

That all looks like a lie to her.

And it feels like one to me.

I tug open the drawer of my desk and snag the keys to the car I keep parked the next block over, then race back down to the shop and into the side room, where I grab one of the burner phones from the drawer there.

Snagging my leather jacket from where it rests draped over the seat of my Harley, I take a second to scan the shop in case I never come back.

It wasn't much, but it became more of a home than I've ever

had anywhere else during my adult life. And that was all because of Bishop.

I tug my jacket on, my hand slipping into the pocket and tightening around the metal there for a second before I step back out into the rain that has now tapered off into nothing more than a mist.

It may have washed away the path Bishop took when she fled from me, but I'm very good at finding people, and there's only so many places she would go, where she would feel safe, where she'd feel protected.

Which means I'm about to walk into the lion's den.

22

GAGE

Hawke Tower rises above me dozens of stories.

Fog and inky clouds hang around the upper floors, blocking my view from the street, but I know what waits in the penthouse.

This is the only place they would have brought her. The most secure and defensible position in their empire. Where they've kept Allegra locked up since it became evident her father knew about her pregnancy and would probably be returning for her.

I knew this is where I needed to come to find Bishop.

And I know what I'll be walking into.

A firing squad...

I tug open the glass doors, and the moment I step into the lobby, four guns are pointing directly at me.

The security team I was introduced to as a coworker not that long ago now stares me down as if I'm the enemy. Because, to them and the Hawkes, I am. Because everyone now believes what Bishop does...

That I was responsible for the bomb.

That this entire time I've been working to infiltrate their family and their organization, just to get close, just to have access to create that pain and chaos.

It doesn't matter that none of it is true.

She believes it is; so will everyone else. Including these men who are paid very well to protect the Hawkes against any and all threats.

I raise my hands. "I'm unarmed."

The huge former police officer who has been put in charge of the Hawke Tower security force steps forward and re-holsters his gun. Hard, distrustful eyes sweep over me as he approaches. Tony has been with them a long time. One of the reasons he's here today, because they trust him.

I held that same trust only hours ago.

But it shattered so badly there's no way to ever piece it back together.

He pats me down to ensure I'm not carrying, then stands in front of me with a scowl that would intimidate just about anyone.

If I care at all about my own safety at this point, I might be more worried, but I stopped giving a shit about that the second I found Bishop in that room. The moment she looked at me like I was a complete stranger instead of the man she so desperately needed last night, I knew there was no point in pretending anymore, no point in anything anymore.

Not if I can't have her.

"I need to speak with them."

Tony snorts incredulously. "What makes you think I'd allow you anywhere near the Hawkes?"

It's a good question. One I would ask if I were in his place today and was told there was a traitor in the security team. A man he himself worked with only days ago.

"Because I have answers they need." I hold out my hands. "You can cuff me."

He raises a brow, examining me carefully for a moment before he retreats to snag his radio from the counter. "Mr. Clarke?"

Saint responds to his call immediately, having no doubt been watching and listening through the surveillance feed since the moment I pulled up outside. "Send him up. *Cuffed*."

Hearing those words shouldn't be such a huge relief, but if he had sent me away, or worse yet, had me taken somewhere remote to be dealt with *another* way, there would have been nothing I could do to try to save them.

To try to save *her*.

At least now, there's a *chance*.

I put my hands behind my back and turn so that he can easily apply the cuffs. He slaps the metal on them. Tightly. Intentionally securing them so the metal digs into my skin. But it isn't anything I haven't experienced before, and the small bite of pain isn't anywhere near what I deserve right now.

All I can do is pray they listen.

Tony grabs my bicep, tugs me into the elevator, then releases me and uses his hand to conceal the keypad and punch in the code for the penthouse, which I'm sure they've now changed since I had the old one.

They're no doubt scrambling to revamp their entire security structure since I not only know it all, but even made suggestions for changes they recently implemented. Everything was supposed to make them safer, which is part of why this guy is glaring at me on the ride up like I betrayed him personally.

But there's only one person I truly betrayed.

One person whose trust I decimated.

Not to mention what I did to her heart...

Fuck.

My chest tightens again thinking about that look on her face at the shop, how quickly I became the enemy and not the man who had just cared for her, who had shown her how incredible it could be to let go of the things she clung to so tightly.

God, I really fucked this up.

I knew this would be hard, but one thing I never accounted for was what walking in and seeing that *look* again will do to me.

Nothing can prepare me for it.

The ding that signals us reaching the penthouse makes me cringe, and my escort grabs my arm again and drags me out and into the hallway that contains two doors: one to the left, one to the right.

Even if Atlas is home, he wouldn't be at his place. They would have told him what happened by now. The Hawke flock will be together, unless they made a decision to limit everyone's exposure—which could certainly be the case.

Saint might have moved most of them to a location I'm not familiar with, some place I could never find.

If he took Bishop there instead of here...

If I'm wrong...

We move to the door on the left, and someone inside opens it for us. Before I can even take a step, I'm shoved forward by a forceful hand on my back. Stumbling, I fall to my knees on the hard floor, barely managing to maintain my balance enough to avoid ending up face-first on it.

But maybe that would have been better.

I wouldn't have had to see the furious eyes staring back at me.

It isn't just Saint. Caroline, Isaac, Stone, Kennedy, and Cass all glare at me from their places around the open living room. But there is only one set of eyes I search for.

Those smoky bourbon ones I love so damn much...

I find them in the back corner, where she leans against the

wall, tucked away near the fireplace as if she wanted to put as much space between us as possible and make *herself* as small as possible.

And it isn't just hatred and anger that burn in her gaze.

It's utter betrayal.

And that's so much worse.

For someone like Bishop, who spent her entire life with walls built around herself and her heart, who helped erect them around her family to ensure they were always protected, finding out the one person she let in has been lying to her is the ultimate treason.

Something you never come back from.

Her heart has been crushed beyond repair, and my own shatters seeing her like this.

Trembling.

Curled in on herself as if she doesn't have the strength to even stand on her own.

Terrified of what she's done to the people she loves so deeply and for whom she sacrificed so much.

The door clicks closed behind me, sealing me in with the people who have every right to want me dead, even though all I've ever done has been to try to save them.

Saint steps into my line of sight, blocking my view of Bishop, an unmovable wall of hostility. "You *don't* get to look at her."

I struggle to get to my feet from my kneeling position with my hands still secured behind me, but I somehow manage it, swaying slightly when I do. "You need to let me explain."

Bishop's father shakes his head, dark eyes flashing almost black. "I don't have to let you do anything."

"Please." I squeeze my eyes closed, picturing that room, how scared she was standing in it. "I know what she saw, and I know what she probably told you"—I glance back up—"but I *can* explain."

It's Caroline who steps forward next to her husband, her arms crossed over her chest. The woman may be tiny compared to Saint, but she's just as intimidating with her current look.

Maybe even more so.

I always thought Bishop took after him since she chose his line of work, but seeing Caroline now, I'm starting to think I was wrong.

This little woman is terrifying.

"We don't need to hear more lies from you, Gage. If that's even your real name..."

I flinch. "It is, but I'm not who you think I am."

Isaac glares at me from where he stands near Bishop beside fireplace and snorts. "No fucking shit."

The hostility is more than warranted.

From all of them.

I so badly want to let my gaze drift over to hers, to look into her eyes while I plead with all of them to listen to me and believe what I'm about to tell them, but if I try, Saint will make sure I don't have the opportunity to offer them the answers they need.

"First, you need to understand something." I cut my gaze from Isaac to Stone where he sits on the couch, then to Kennedy and Cass. "I had nothing to do with the bomb that hurt Gabe and Savage. *Nothing*."

Kennedy sits on a high barstool at the kitchen counter and starts to slide off it, like she's going to come at me, but Cass wraps an arm around her waist, holding her back. "How the fuck can we believe you after what Bishop saw?"

"She's right." I stare down the woman primed to become the head of Hawke Enterprises when her father and uncles finally retire and hope she can see the truth in my eyes. "Everything I had in that room was for making bombs. And I *have* been following all of you for months. But not for the reason you think." I swallow thickly, trying to dislodge the nerves threatening to choke me. "I don't work for Satriano. I don't work for Michael McDonald..."

The words of warning from my call earlier echo in my head, reminding me exactly what's at stake if I continue down the road I've already stepped onto by coming here to offer the Hawkes an explanation.

"If you do that, you're a dead man..."

It doesn't matter, though.

My life stopped meaning anything to me when it became clear that I might lose Bishop forever.

"I'm not the enemy." Even though I shouldn't. Even though I'm risking the wrath of her father, I lock gazes with Bishop across the room. "I'm CIA."

She doesn't react.

It's as if I didn't say anything.

Not a blink. Not a gasp of surprise. Not so much as a *breath* taken.

She just stands there, staring at me but not seeing anything.

Out of my peripheral vision, I catch Isaac beside her shaking his head. "CIA doesn't operate on U.S. soil."

I bark out a sardonic laugh at the absurdity of him actually believing that.

The Hawke attorney is wicked smart. Some of the legal maneuvers he and his father have pulled on behalf of the family over the years are pretty epic. But if he really thinks the government doesn't operate outside the law at times, then he's not as bright as I thought.

"We're not supposed to, but counter–intelligence against non-U.S. natives on U.S. soil happens all the time."

Isaac's jaw hardens, and he casts a look to his father.

Stone watches me from his seat with skepticism darkening his blue gaze. "If you're CIA, then why are you using your real name?"

Under any other circumstances, an agent operating in this

type of capacity would have an elaborate fake identity and backstory that would be backstopped so well that no one would ever find out who he really is, and Stone is intelligent enough to know that.

"Because I could only get into the position I'm in now *because* of who I *really* am."

Standing here, surrounded by Hawkes, knowing what I'm about to say is going to rock them, I wish like hell I had done things differently. That I had stuck to the plan when I arrived in New Orleans instead of allowing my attraction to Bishop to cloud my judgment.

Because now, the truth is coming out, and she might never forgive me for it.

"Michael McDonald isn't just one of Satriano's hitmen. He builds explosives for *anyone* who will pay him. He will take money from any asshole who needs his help." I brace myself for the reaction I know will be coming to my next confession. Something likely to only increase their distrust. "And he's also the man who trained me when I was in the Rangers."

All the air gets sucked out of the room.

Tense silence reins, and Bishop finally reacts, her lips curling down slightly before they go back to being pressed together.

"I am here because I knew he was coming. He's the one who set that bomb, but it wasn't because Satriano ordered him to take out a target."

"What?" Saint shakes his head. "I don't follow."

I didn't either, at first. Couldn't wrap my head around why that bomb went off or why the Hawkes would be targets for McDonald. When it finally hit me, everything made sense and proved just how dangerous the situation really is.

"McDonald is here *for* Satriano, and he wants the Hawkes to do the dirty work for him. He wants to draw you into an all-out war with Satriano."

Caroline throws up her hands. "Why?"

"The most basic human reason—he wants revenge."

BISHOP

Liar.

I don't believe a single word that's coming out of his mouth.

How can I, when everything he's told me has been a lie?

The man standing in front of the door to the penthouse with his hands cuffed behind him is a stranger to me.

A complete fucking stranger who *I* let into our lives.

Who *I* let become a part of this family.

Who I let become a part of *me.*

Fuck.

I squeeze my eyes closed, willing my body not to give out and praying my self-control holds a bit longer so I don't give in to the desire to burst into tears right here and now and never stop crying.

It would be so easy to crumple to the floor like I've wanted to since the moment Isaac and Stone brought me back here after rescuing me from behind that old grocery store two blocks from Gage's place. So easy to surrender to the crippling pain and guilt that want to drag me down into the black abyss that's floating around me.

But I can't right now.

Not when Gage is *right there*, spewing his fabricated excuses for why he did what he did. For why he broke me.

When I open my eyes again, I find him staring at me despite Dad's earlier warning. And it's like looking into the eyes of a monster. Anyone who does the things he did, says the things he said, knowing they were all lies, doesn't have a soul.

Yet, I can tell from the look Dad gives me that he believes

him and that this isn't over. "I think you better start from the beginning..."

Why does it matter?

Nothing he can say will change what he's done. Listening to him try to justify it will only make it worse.

Isaac inches closer, settling his hand on my lower back, offering me the only support he can without physically picking me up and carrying me to one of the bedrooms like he had to when we first got here.

He won't do that now.

Not when he knows how important it is for me to both hear this and to never show Gage what he's done to me.

Keep it together, girl.

Gage nods to Dad's request, shifting restlessly in the cuffs that I hope are cutting into his fucking skin painfully. "You all know I was a Ranger, but what you don't know is that Michael McDonald was black ops. A unit you never would have heard of because it doesn't exist. It's why you've been having such a hard time locating information on him."

A hush settles over the room, and every hair on my arms stands on end.

I don't want to believe anything Gage says anymore, but something about his story feels too real, too personal to be a lie.

"McDonald came in and worked with several people at the 75th on explosive ordinances. He was the best I've ever seen. A true master of his field, and someone very high up wanted to ensure his knowledge was passed down to as many of us as possible. After he was done, he just vanished, as if he had never been there."

Part of me wishes Gage would just vanish.

That I could close my eyes and reopen them to find him gone along with all the memories we created together that I will never be free from.

Almost as if he can sense my thoughts, Gage's gaze swings

my way again, and he swallows thickly. "When I was getting close to the end of my contract and was about to reup, right around the time I was fighting WCAP, I was approached by the CIA. Given my training and the fact that I can speak five languages, they thought I would be a tremendous asset to them. So instead of reupping, I finished out my commitment, then went to do additional training to become a CIA operative. That's when they told me the truth, that Michael McDonald had been on their radar since well before his retirement and their approach to me was well thought-out."

Dad shifts his stance, still keeping himself between Gage and me—a physical wall when the ones I created hadn't been enough to protect myself or any of us. "Why?"

"A bomb used in an attack on American interests in Paris had been linked to him, and they thought that maybe I could infiltrate his organization easily because of our history together." He shakes his head. "But I wasn't so sure."

Isaac shifts beside me, clearly intrigued by the story while furious at the man telling it. "Why not?"

"Because Michael knew who I was at my core and that I would never become a mercenary. He knew I wouldn't help terrorist organizations hurt innocent people, regardless of how much money might be on the table."

I wish I could believe that.

I wish I had confidence that Gage wouldn't do anything like what he's accusing McDonald of, but all of this could be an elaborate story to try to save his ass from the fallout of what I discovered.

Dad doesn't seem to buy it either, shifting his stance in a way that emphasizes his size. An old move he only uses when he needs to intimidate someone. "So, what happened with McDonald?"

Gage releases a long, slow breath, rolling his shoulders under his leather jacket slightly. "McDonald never trusted me enough to bring me in. But we stayed in touch. I kept the line of communication open while I worked other jobs for the company. A few years ago, we heard about Satriano's mysterious resurrection and that he was here in New Orleans...and that McDonald may have been working with him when Satriano operated under different identities in Europe over the past several decades."

Mom examines Gage closely, and I can almost see those reporter instincts of hers kicking in. "If McDonald worked for him for so long, then why does he want revenge on him like you suggested earlier?"

Exactly.

Allegra told us McDonald was a known associate of her father's. If they worked together enough for his daughter to know the man, then it doesn't make any sense that McDonald would turn on Satriano.

That type of hatred has to blossom from somewhere.

Drawing in a long breath, Gage shifts his stance again, clearly growing uncomfortable in the cuffs or under our scrutiny—maybe both. "About a year and a half ago, McDonald was working a job for Satriano in Calabria. Michael had his son along, and things went south. There was an ambush at the location where he was supposed to plant the device. His son died. And McDonald believes Satriano set a trap for them. He blames him for his son's death. McDonald went ghost after that, but he's just been biding his time, waiting for an opportunity to get to Satriano."

Stone taps his cane on the floor, drawing my attention away from Gage and to him. "Why did you come to New Orleans?"

To destroy me.

Gage clears his throat, glancing my way as if in response to my thought. "With Satriano here, that's where the CIA's investigation had to lead. And all the activity in New Orleans with your family in recent years—first Leonardo Satriano's death, then the explosion at The Grind, Christiano Roselli's assassination in front of it, the attack on this penthouse, not to mention the fact that Damiano was spotted at numerous Hawke-owned properties, all led us, and the FBI, to wonder if you were somehow involved with him."

I bite my tongue to prevent myself from lashing out at the accusation.

Mom doesn't care. "Us?" She gapes at him. "You thought *we* were involved with Satriano?"

Absolutely ludicrous.

The suggestion is enough to make my hatred of Gage burn even hotter through my blood.

Gage offers Mom a contrite look. "I was sent here with two goals—to figure out if you were in bed with him or if you were just innocent bystanders, and to determine if I could lure McDonald out of hiding by letting him know I was in town and could help him get to Satriano."

Fuck.

Isaac begins pacing, rubbing at the back of his head. Cass and Kennedy exchange a look, and he keeps his arm around her, ensuring she doesn't go after Gage like she clearly wants to.

Cass scans the room. "Why not just approach the Hawkes?"

Something dark crosses over Gage's gaze. "Because if you were in bed with him, then you'd be just as dangerous as he is. There have been rumors for years about the Hawkes, and debate within the FBI about whether or not you were a criminal organization. If I had found anything incriminating, the FBI would have started trying to make a case against you while we continued to try to deal with Satriano and McDonald."

A muscle in Dad's jaw tics as he glares at Gage. "Have you been feeding McDonald information about *us*?"

I hold my breath, but I can already tell by the fear in Gage's eyes what his answer will be.

"No. I..." His gaze flicks to me. "I couldn't—" He swallows

his words, the plea in his eyes forcing me to close my own. "I've been sending information back to my people and the FBI that you're *not* involved with Satriano, that you're not a threat, and that Hawke Enterprises is a legitimate business entity. I explained that you all got unwittingly wrapped up with Satriano. As far as McDonald goes, I haven't seen him in person since he arrived in town, and I had *no* idea he was going to target you, that he was even aware of the ongoing issues between you and Satriano at all."

Dad crosses his arms. "Why did you have all the bomb making materials?"

"Because I was trying to figure out what he used in the bomb at the club, what triggering mechanism was utilized and the frequency, so I could determine if there was a way to ensure it couldn't happen again. I was trying to develop a way to block the signal in case he sets another one."

It was sophisticated.

In the time it took for me to explain what I had found in Gage's secret room, I convinced Dad to reveal everything they had developed since the explosion.

And that bomb didn't go off randomly.

It didn't go off until we were all standing together right near that car, which means McDonald was watching.

"How did he get to Gabe's car?" Kennedy doesn't sound any calmer than she did earlier, despite the efforts of Cass to calm her. "You are the only one who would've had access."

Gage shakes his head, his jaw hardening. "No, I'm not. Someone on your security team has been paid off by McDonald. I was able to confirm that just today through my handler. He gained access to McDonald's banking records and saw a massive cash withdrawal only days before the explosion. He paid someone. It's the only explanation." He locks gazes with Dad. "You need to gut your entire team. Figure out who McDonald approached. Someone who would've had access to the surveillance feeds who could have cut them or looped them when he planted the bomb."

Dad turns and locks his gaze with mine. "Bishop? Who could it be?"

My legs are trembling, my knees threatening to give out, and not just because we have another traitor in the Hawke house, but because I think I actually believe the one in front of us.

There's a plea in his gaze, a look that begs me to see the truth behind all the lies, even if I *don't* trust him.

"I didn't just join your security team to get close to you. I did it because I know how Satriano and McDonald work, and I knew one or both of them would figure out a way to infiltrate you for their own purposes. I was looking for the spy even before I had confirmation there was one."

"You!"

I can't take it anymore and shove off the wall, stalking across the room toward him with all the fury that's been boiling inside me ready to blow. Stopping just in front of Dad and Mom, I glare at the man who broke through my walls, built me back up, only to shatter me completely.

"You're right about there being a spy. I'm looking at him. I don't care if every single word you just said is true, that doesn't change anything. It doesn't make what you did right, and it doesn't mean any of us could ever forgive you or trust you again."

He flinches at my words.

Good.

I storm toward the door, which unfortunately also means toward him.

"Bishop, what are you doing?" Dad's voice doesn't stop me. "Shit."

He probably thinks I'm going to kill Gage with my bare hands.

God knows I could with the rage simmering inside me.

But that would be too easy a way out for him.

I want him to *suffer.*

Brushing past him without even looking him in the eye, I tug open the door.

"Bishop, stop!" Mom's voice cuts through the fog of anger and hurt. "Where are you going?"

I have to leave before this sob tears from my throat.

Because I refuse to let him see me cry.

I refuse to let him see me fall apart—again.

"Anywhere but here."

23

GAGE

Of all the things I imagined happening after coming clean with the Hawkes, none of them involved spending the day locked up in the penthouse, walking through every fucking second of every fucking day of my life since I first heard their name and reviewing every detail I know about McDonald and Satriano with them.

It was more intense than any debriefing I ever had after any mission for the Rangers or the CIA.

And more emotionally exhausting.

Though, I should count my blessings.

Considering the type of betrayal they felt, I anticipated a much more painful confrontation.

I would have deserved it, too.

But once Saint and Stone made a few calls and were able to confirm at least part of my story with some of their contacts, the too tight cuffs came off and the only pain became the memory of the look of betrayal in Bishop's eyes.

The rage she threw at me as she fled from the condo.

The absolute, utter devastation she tried so hard to hide behind that I could read from a goddamn mile away.

Before today, before *her*, I never would've believed it possible to watch all love, light, and hope vanish completely from someone's eyes.

To see it all disappear only to be replaced by something vacant and stone cold.

But that's exactly what happened.

And even after spending almost six hours debriefing with them, discussing potential next moves, offering what I know to help them finally rid themselves of Satriano, I still don't have anything even close to an answer about how to apologize to her.

We never broached the subject. If anything, they seemed reluctant to bring up what I did to her, either because they feared I would break down or they didn't trust themselves not to beat the shit out of me before they got the information they wanted.

Whatever the reason for the reprieve, it's gone now.

There isn't anything left to discuss tonight, nothing more to be done.

The Hawkes need to decide what they want to do with the information I gave them, and I have to go back to doing my job—tracking down McDonald and Satriano before they can hurt anyone else.

They both pose a tremendous danger to more than just this family, and while my loyalties lie with the Hawkes—despite what certain members may think—I also have a duty to complete my mission.

I may be the only person who will be able to lure McDonald out into the open, and that will likely be the only reason I don't get fired or worse for revealing so much classified information.

But I didn't have a choice.

Not if I wanted to protect them and have any chance of salvaging my relationship with Bishop.

She may not ever understand.

How could she?

She may not ever forgive me.

I don't deserve it.

That doesn't mean I won't try.

The thought of losing her and what we had makes me physically ill, and I've had to stop myself from obsessing about it too much or I might have vomited all over their beautiful furniture and floor over the past several hours.

Now, I have nothing left to distract me from it.

As Saint walks me to the penthouse door, the stern set of his jaw hasn't changed, and anger still radiates off him in waves that threaten to knock me the fuck over.

He's pissed about what I've done.

Rightfully so.

He's angry for his daughter.

As a father, he has every right to be.

But it's Caroline I'm actually afraid of.

She has sat back stoically, letting Saint, Isaac, Cass, and Kennedy control the questioning. Her gaze didn't leave me the entire time, and she absorbed every word I said with the intense attention to details that must have served her well when she was still working as a reporter.

I have no doubt she will help ensure Savage, Gabe, and everyone else who wasn't here tonight gets a full rundown so the entire family is up to speed by the time the sun comes up tomorrow.

Right now, though, her laser-like focus is zeroed in on me, and it's clear she has something to say that she's been sitting on for hours.

She pushes past her husband, placing a hand on his chest. "I'll walk him to the elevator. I need to talk to Gage alone."

Saint offers her a warning look, but she merely waves that hand at him dismissively, as if he couldn't stop her even if he tried. Something tells me he probably couldn't despite their massive disparity in size.

I step out into the hallway and she follows, letting the door close behind her, leaving us alone in the tomb-silent space.

Bishop is long gone.

Where'd you go, Hellcat?

Caroline walks to the elevator with me, her lips pressed together in a way that's so similar to how Bishop does it that it's abundantly clear she's just as much her mother's daughter as her father's. This woman has quiet strength while Bishop's is regularly on display for the world to see, but the same fire burns inside her, the same fierce loyalty and drive to protect her family.

And right now, that means her daughter.

I scrub my hands over my face, waiting for the elevator cab to come up, and she leans against the wall, watching me.

"Tell me what happened with Bishop."

I slowly let my gaze drift over to hers. "It was a mistake. I shouldn't have..."

Wanted her.

Flirted with her.

Pursued her.

Fallen in love with her...

The words lodge in my throat staring at one of the only people on the planet who loves her as much as I do.

"No." She shakes her head. "You *shouldn't* have. But, you *did*." Her voice breaks, and she swallows thickly, working through her own emotion. "And now my daughter is destroyed."

I flinch, my hands shaking as I shove them through my hair and drop my head back against the wall behind me. "You think I don't know that? You think I don't know what I did to her?"

Caroline watches me, waiting for me to offer an explanation beyond that which I've already given the entire family, or maybe for me to promise that I'll stay away from Bishop so I can't hurt her any further.

I can't do either.

All I can do is tell her how torn up I am knowing what I've done to her daughter.

"She'll never forgive me, Caroline."

And she'll never let anyone else in again.

She's going to lock down tight, like a fucking bank vault, even worse than she was before...

Caroline knows it as well as I do.

She nods. "You're right, she won't. But you still have to try." Her words take a moment to register, and when I offer her a confused look, she gives me a tight smile. "Bishop isn't an easy woman. She wasn't an easy child and certainly didn't become any easier as an adult. She's always known exactly what she wanted, who she was, and what she wanted to do with her life. From the day that girl took her first steps, I watched her kill herself to do just that, to follow her father's path, to be the protector for everyone in this family. And you know what it did?" She gives me a genuine smile this time. "It turned her into the strongest person I've ever met in my life. *And* the most incredible one."

I nod. "I agree."

"It also isolated her. She never had the type of relationships her cousins did—no serious boyfriends, no close friendships beyond the family. But she seemed happy, or at the least, content to lead that life, and she never wanted us to broach the subject with her. So, I avoided those arguments."

Her gaze softens, and if I didn't know this woman was furious with me, I might think she actually *liked* me.

"What she had with you was different. It was special. I saw the change in her when you arrived—a good one. You challenged her. You made her see things in a different way. You made her see *herself* differently, and now she's out there questioning everything again. You're the only one who can fix that."

Tears burn in my eyes, and I blink them away. "What if she doesn't let me?"

Caroline offers a slight shrug. "You keep trying 'til she does."

I squeeze my eyes closed as the elevator arrives, the ding echoing loudly in the hallway, signaling the end of our conversation.

Caroline steps in and enters the code necessary to bring me back down to the lobby.

"You still don't trust me with that?"

She shakes her head. "Not on your fucking life."

Grinning at her directness, I step in and turn to face her as she holds the door open. "I'm going to do everything I can to find McDonald and Satriano, to make sure you're all safe."

She nods. "I don't doubt that. But right now, you only need to be worrying about one person, and it isn't any of us up here."

No, it isn't.

The fact that she recognizes that there is no way I will be able to concentrate on anything or anyone else until I've spoken with Bishop only makes my respect for her grow.

She steps back with a tight smile, and the door slides closed.

I sag against the wall, burying my face in my hands. "Fuck..."

How the fuck did this happen?

Because I forgot my mission and fell in love instead.

Was it really only twenty-four hours ago that I walked out of the shower and found Bishop in my bed?

I can still feel her touch.

Her hand gripping my cock...

Lips brushing against mine...

The squeeze of her cunt around me as she found her release...

How completely she collapsed into my arms...

Not just sated, but *happy*.

Content.

She felt *safe*.

How could everything have changed so much so fast? How could I have fucked it up this badly?

The elevator plunges down toward the main floor, and my mind races through everything that's happened.

I have to go and report in. After disposing of my phone and not hearing from me for so long, they will have assumed the worst. I need to let them know that my cover's been blown, at least where the Hawkes are concerned. While I trust the Hawkes not to say anything to anyone, it doesn't mean my higher ups won't pull me the second they learn what happened.

The only thing that might save my job is the fact that I'm their only connection to McDonald. Their only possible *in*.

That's what I'll use when I talk to them, when I beg for my job.

But before that, I have to find her.

I have to at least try to fix things.

And if she doesn't let me, I just keep trying 'til she does.

Those words echo in my head as the elevator dings in the lobby, but I don't immediately move to get out of it.

Where would she go?

When she stormed out of a penthouse hours ago, she was distraught, spiraling, more lost than she ever has been in her entire life.

So, where the hell would Bishop go when she's lost?

Somewhere that feels like home. Somewhere she feels safe. Somewhere she might be able to find some semblance of control when everything around her is spinning out of it.

It hits me quickly.

I know where to find her.

BISHOP

My fist slams into the old leather and the heavy bag creaks and rocks back on the chains. Pain sears through my bare knuckles, but I don't give a fuck.

That's what I need more than anything else right now.

I need the pain in my body to match that living in my chest where my heart should be.

I need to keep going, keep hitting *something* until I drop or the bag does.

Considering that this particular one belonged to Wren's grandfather and has been hanging here longer than I've been alive, my bet is on *me* giving out before it does.

That doesn't mean I won't give it my best shot, though.

I lay down a barrage of punches, pounding the bag over and over again, losing myself—or at least trying to—in the rhythm of the attack.

Even though I've been here for hours, alternating between the heavy bag and speed bag in between bouts of relentless sobbing, I still keep pushing as if I just walked in those doors. As if I had just heard the truth.

Because that agony will not abate.

The harder I go, the harder I want to *keep* going, but I'm not so deep into it that I don't hear the gym door open behind me.

I know who it is before he ever says a word or even approaches.

Because somehow, I *always* know.

I always sense when he's near, and the way my splintered

heart does that stupid flip-flop thing is going to fucking kill me long before Satriano or McDonald ever will.

It's the last thing I should be feeling right now—this intense mix of agony and longing for someone who doesn't exist.

He doesn't exist.

The man I fell asleep with last night isn't real. Every word he said, all those things he did...none of it was real.

It was all some glorious illusion created by a masterful magician. A man who was *trained* in deceit. Whose entire life has revolved around it.

And I walked right into his trap.

I squeeze my eyes closed and suck in a sharp breath as the heavy bag rocks back and forth in front of me. If I keep them clenched tightly for long enough, maybe he'll be gone when I reopen them. Maybe it will all have been some sort of wicked nightmare sent as a warning to keep my heart locked down tight...

But tentative footsteps sound across the gym floor, shattering any hope of that dream becoming a reality.

All that's left is the creaking sound of the still swinging bag, my heaving breaths, the sting in my knuckles, and the blood rushing in my ears.

"I assume you're picturing my face while you're hitting that."

His voice cuts through it all as sharp as the knife that he drove straight into my chest with his deceit.

I open my eyes and catch the bag, only now noticing the blood on my split knuckles. I didn't even feel it when they ripped, didn't even register the injury because I've craved the pain.

It's better than being numb.

At least feeling this pain, I know I'm still alive, that somehow, I survived the type of betrayal that should have been unsurvivable.

That's what drives me to slowly turn to face him. The knowledge that if I don't get this off my chest, if I don't have this conversation, it'll never be truly over and it needs to be.

Now.

Gage stands only a few feet from me, still wearing the same clothes he wore at the penthouse—dark jeans, a white T-shirt, and that damn leather jacket that always makes him look so fucking dangerous and sexy. His hair is a disheveled mess, as if he's been running his hands through it repeatedly, and dark circles mar the skin under his eyes.

He bears a look of utter exhaustion I feel to my bones. "I know you want to hurt me, Bishop." His eyes dip down to my hands. "But please don't hurt yourself."

The laugh that slips from my lips is dark, humorless, filled with so much agony and incredulity that I barely recognize the sound. "That's rich coming from you."

From the person who has hurt me more than anyone else ever has my entire life...

He winces, then glances back toward the door and the darkness that has descended outside. "Are you here alone? Where's your security?"

I rest my hands on my hips, trying to regain my breath for the first time since I arrived. Now that I've stopped, I'm sure I'm going to feel it. Those aches and that soreness that has plagued me since the explosion, that Gage was so good at melting away, will come screaming back now that I've pushed so hard.

"I sent them home."

Gage narrows his eyes on me, concern he has no right to feel flickering across them. "Bishop, why the hell would you do that when you know you're at risk, when you know you're a potential target?"

"Seems the only one who was targeting me was you."

"Fuck." He scrubs his hands over his face and shoves them back through his hair, shifting restlessly in his boots. "I deserve that. But *you* don't." He shakes his head. "You didn't deserve any of this. And I know you don't want to hear what I have to say—"

"Why the hell would I?" I slam my fist into the bag again, sending it rocking back. "It's all been lies from day fucking one. Why would I want to hear a single word from your lying mouth?"

God, that mouth...

It said too much.

Brought me too much pleasure.

And I can't look away from it or the tiny frown he wears when he's usually so quick with a smile.

Stop.

That Gage doesn't exist.

This one is the liar.

His hands twitch at his sides like he's fighting the desire to reach for me, but if this man has any self-preservation instinct, he should know better than to try. "It wasn't all a lie, Bishop. It wasn't."

There it is again.

That deep, believable sincerity in his words that I fell for, hook, line, and sinker, that he was probably trained to use to get people like me to fall for his bullshit.

I should have known better. I should have seen through him. I should have listened to my gut and stayed far away from Gage Newhart.

He shakes his head, holding his hands out, palms up, as if he's offering himself to me and praying I'll accept what I can never give him. "Getting involved with you was never part of the plan."

Another mirthless laugh that borders on hysterical falls from my lips, but it beats the alternative—bursting into tears in front of him. "Bullshit! You came at me from day one. You came *straight* for me and didn't back off until you had me wrapped around your fucking finger."

He takes a step toward me, but I hold up a single finger in warning.

"Don't. You. Fucking. Dare."

If he comes any closer, I can't be held accountable for what I might do.

I don't trust myself where this man is concerned, or maybe about anything ever again.

Gage sucks in a sharp breath. "The plan was always to watch the Hawkes, to search for confirmation of where you stood when it came to Satriano. I had always intended to try to get inside." He shakes his head. "But *not* with you. I was supposed to approach Gabe. Use the Ranger angle to gain his trust. It was supposed to be that simple, but then *you* happened."

I squeeze my eyes closed, unable to look in his warm blue eyes when he tells me more of these lies or I'll risk drowning in them.

"I watched you through a camera lens from afar for months, and I saw how dedicated you were to your family, to keeping them safe. I saw what kind of person you were. And then that night, I went to the club to lay the groundwork and set the approach for Gabe. And I saw you in person for the first time..."

Memories of that night and seeing him at the bar for the first time flicker through my head.

That leather jacket.

The sandy-blond hair.

The way he carried himself that raised goosebumps over every inch of my body.

"And then we *met,* and it was like I was struck by fucking lightning."

I wince this time.

Not because his description isn't accurate but because it's too right.

I felt it, too.

More than once. Damn near every time this man looked at me or touched me. It was a constant buzz that charged through me and kept me energized. He kept me going through some of the hardest weeks of my life.

When I was spiraling, he held me steady. When I was lost, he helped me find home. When I didn't recognize the person I was becoming, he helped me find myself in a way no one else has ever been able to.

And it was all predicated on a lie.

When I open my eyes again, he's watching. He's waiting for something. For me to cry. For me to rage. For me to hit him. For me to do *anything* other than just stand here. But that numbness has returned, that feeling like I'm not even in my own body anymore.

"I know you can never forgive me for what I did, Bishop. You can never forgive me for the lies I told. I don't need you to do that, but what I do need you to do is *listen*."

Gage doesn't deserve a single thing from me except my hostility and hatred.

He doesn't get to make demands of me, not anymore. The days of letting Gage tie me up, emotionally and physically, are gone.

"Why would I do that, Gage?" I shrug, my ability to argue fleeing as quickly as my energy seems to have once I actually *stopped*. "Why would I do anything for you?"

Like I've seen him do so many times, his right hand slips into his jacket pocket. "Because deep down, you know I'm still the person you thought I was."

24

GAGE

Bishop winces at my statement, pressing her hands over her chest, like even suggesting she knows me after what I've done is enough to cause her physical pain.

Maybe it does.

And that's saying a lot.

The blood on her split knuckles and the fact that she's probably been here for *hours,* going relentlessly when she should still be taking it easy and recovering from her injuries, proves just how oblivious she's become to it.

That makes her reaction all that much worse.

Those words hurt her more than anything she's done to her body today.

All I want to do is stalk across the distance between us and pull her into my arms, to hold her steady as she falls apart, to wipe away the tears she's fighting, to bring her back to where we were just last night.

Moving together so perfectly.

Completing each other and giving one another exactly what we needed.

So connected that our hearts began beating in time against each other as we laid tangled in the sheets...

It was the first time in my entire life that I understood what people mean when they say "making love."

We've shared plenty of intimate moments, times when I felt like our bodies were speaking words we couldn't say, but last night was like seeing home for the first time after being away for years.

Only I never had a home before her.

I want that back, but all my touch would do now is disgust her. All I would do is upset her more by reaching for her, by even suggesting she might need to be held, might need to fall apart and *feel* all this before she can start to put herself back together.

So, I hold my ground, my left hand flexing at my side, the other wrapped around the *one* thing that always grounds me when it feels like my life is spinning wildly out of control or the decisions I'm making aren't easy ones.

Seeing the consequences of them now, playing out in front of me like a car crash I can't prevent or look away from, only makes me clutch it tighter.

When Bishop reopens her eyes, they're so dark, so steeped in her doubt that I can barely see any of that smoky bourbon I love to stare into so much. "I don't know who you are, Gage. I never did."

I shake my head. "That's where you're wrong, Hellcat."

"Do. Not. Call. Me. That."

The ice in her words slides over my skin and seeps into my blood.

That's what she thinks I am—ice cold. An uncaring, unfeeling piece of shit man who used her and lied to her, when I never told her a single thing that wasn't true. I *kept* things from her that she sees as lies. But I never flat-out told her one.

Never.

All those things I told her about growing up, about moving around and not being able to make connections, about loving baths, about *knowing* how she felt, were all *very real.*

I pull my hand out of my jacket, the metal of the single most valuable item I own digging into my palm. It helps solidify what I have to do, what I have to say to her. Along with her mother's words from earlier, insisting that I keep trying, I know I have to keep pushing even if she pushes back.

"You know exactly who I am." Without thinking about it, I step forward, allowing my dog tags to dangle from the chain so she can see them. "And so do I. That's why I keep these on me at all times. So that when I questioned why I was doing something, when I felt gut-wrenching guilt about keeping things from you, I could hold them and remind myself that it was for a reason. So I could remind myself that I *am* this man, and that every single thing I've done was to *protect* you, like I was trained to do."

My voice breaks, my emotions making it difficult to get out what I need to say even after I begged her to listen.

"I'm the man who helped you when that douchebag tried to grab Jade at the club. I'm the man who *enjoyed* it when you threw me to the ground as if I weighed nothing. I'm the man you fought in this ring and fucked in that locker room. I'm the man who drew you baths and took care of you. I'm the man you made love to last night—"

She cringes again and shakes her head. "No. No, no, no, no, *no*."

Such a simple word might as well be a dagger slicing into me each time she says it, and she paces away from me, putting more physical space between us like she doesn't trust me to be this close to her.

Bishop probably wishes she could forget all the things I just mentioned, that she could go back to the first time we met and make a different decision. Throw me out and ban me from the club forever because then none of this would've happened.

I wouldn't have fallen for her, and she wouldn't have opened up for me.

She wouldn't have had to feel anything.

She could have kept living a life for other people instead of for herself.

And that's the most terrifying part of all this.

The fact that that's what she wants.

She *wants* to go back to who she was before us. She wants to go back to that person who couldn't truly enjoy anything, who couldn't relax, who couldn't laugh or find joy because she was always so worried about everything and everyone else.

That's *easier* for her, to revert back to that person, than it is to look me in the eye and be reminded of what she discovered with *me*.

It's easier for her to *run*.

I watch her stalk around the ring, shaking out her hands and rubbing at the back of her neck. "Why didn't you just stay away?"

God, I wish I knew...

That same question has rattled around my head since that first night, since the moment I felt that thing, that spark of energy flash between us. I had grabbed these dog tags when I walked in, hoping they would ground me and prepare me for approaching Gabe, but it all changed in an instant.

If those drunk assholes hadn't been there, if they hadn't needed more drinks, if they hadn't crossed a line with the dancer, if Bishop had been closer and capable of intervening herself, if any *one thing* had been different...

So would we.

Even if I had worked my way into the Hawke Enterprises

world, even if I had been able to get a job that would have required me to see her every day, I might have been able to grasp these tags and remind myself to stay away.

But the moment she pinned me to that floor, I was a fucking goner.

I know I should have stayed away.

I've trained myself to stay cold and calculating. I've learned the hard way through years of experience that letting down my guard, giving in to my emotions, would only result in pain for me and those around me. Losing brothers in arms, watching them die and having no way to help them, all of it became a reason to shut down the way Bishop did.

And I allowed myself to go through life like that until I met her.

Seeing her struggle made me realize I had been doing the same thing. Taking on the weight and responsibility of things that were beyond my control. Trying to protect everyone by risking my own happiness.

I didn't want that for her or me.

Nor do I now.

I slowly walk around the ring toward her. She put it between us intentionally, to have a physical barrier, but I'm not going to let her do that. I'm not going to let her run until she hears *everything* I have to say.

"I knew what I was doing was wrong, that it was dangerous, and not for the reasons you think. Because I knew from the first moment I saw you where we would end up."

Her tear-soaked eyes flash with her agony. "In bed together based on lies?"

I shake my head. "No, in love with each other."

My statement hangs in the air between us.

Bishop just stares at me like she didn't even hear it. Her passive expression doesn't fool me, though. Inside, she's raging. She's fighting a battle I can't see and is losing it.

Finally, her bottom lip begins to quiver. "Don't say that."

"Why? It's true. I've been in love with you since—"

"*No!*" Her scream echoes through the empty gym, ringing in my ears and cutting me off with the force of her objection. "You don't get to come in here and say words like 'love' because you think that's going to somehow undo all the lies you've told."

"I don't think that."

But she has every right to feel this way, to believe that what I'm saying now comes from a place of wanting to go *back,* but that's not what I want at all.

I never wanted to lie to her.

I never wanted to put her in this position.

Going back would mean returning to keeping things from her, and I will *never* do that again.

"How did you think this was going to end, Gage?" Bishop remains frozen in place, trembling so violently that I wonder how much longer her legs will hold her up. "How did you see any of this playing out in your head? Because it couldn't have gone on forever, the *lie*..."

Her voice cracks slightly on that final word.

And I know it's going to take a lot more than just my explanation to convince this woman that everything we had was real because she will never believe me.

But she might believe herself, if I can get her to listen to that voice inside her own head she's fighting so hard to drown out right now.

BISHOP

Gage inches toward me.

As much as I want to back away, want to put as much distance between us as possible, want to run the other way and find somewhere safe from his eyes, from his smile, from that *look*, I can't seem to move.

I'm rooted in place, frozen by indecision, paralyzed by fear, because every single one I've made lately has been wrong, especially where this man is concerned.

I trusted him. I let him in. I showed him things I never shared with anyone. I *changed* because of him. And he didn't just *let* it happen. He pushed and pushed and *pushed* for it. He did all of that knowing he was keeping this massive truth from me, that he was *lying*.

How did he expect this to end?

Certainly not with me finding his secret lair and discovering he wasn't who he said he was—or that he was in *name* only.

And he hasn't answered my question.

"*Tell* me, Gage. Tell me how this was *supposed* to go. Because you've had *weeks* to come clean, to tell me what you were really doing here and why you needed access to the Hawkes. But you chose to keep that secret. You chose to maintain the lie rather than come clean with me."

The tears brimming in my eyes threaten to fall, but I swipe them away before they can. This man has seen me cry enough, more than anyone else in my life ever has, and that's given him far too much power that I need to take back.

Gage stops a few feet from me, his eyes wild, as if he's teetering on the same edge I am—about to completely lose his grip on his emotions. "How did I see this going?" He sighs, shaking his head. "When I met you, all I was thinking about was how much I wanted to be around you, how I couldn't stay away. The incident with Jade was a foot in the door I hadn't expected, and I took it—both for the mission and because I was being selfish for the first time in my life and wanted to feel what I did around you."

His gaze stays locked on mine, as if he's afraid to look away, afraid I might run if he does.

"I definitely never thought I was going to fall in love with you. By the time I realized I had, it was too late. But I thought that once I figured out where McDonald was and if I could track down Satriano for you, that maybe, just maybe, it would be enough for you to forgive me for keeping everything else from you. That maybe making you and your family finally safe would buy me some..."—he searches for the word—"understanding. But I know I was wrong."

He steps closer, so close now that the leather and spice scent hits me, and I hold my breath to avoid pulling it into my lungs any further.

I can't even trust myself with *that.*

Because that scent has become so synonymous with happiness. With relaxing in his arms, lying on his bed, being held...

Gage overwhelms me without even touching me, and if I give in to any of the pull I still feel toward him, I won't get back out from it.

"I would've told you everything, Bishop, and I would've begged you to forgive me and to believe that everything that happened between us was real, just like I'm doing now." Another half-step brings him within reach. "You *know* it was, Hellcat."

Dammit.

Damn him.

I close my eyes as every moment we've ever spent together rushes through my head. A bright, vibrant video playback of all the things that made me fall in love with him.

That chuckle when I had him pinned to the club floor...

His grin when he turned over...

The "standing offer" he gave me to do it again anytime...

Watching him box with Atlas and so easily get along with Astrid...

Our date in the park when he called me out on my unhealthy workaholic behavior...

The way he had my back when Satriano appeared and refused to just walk away from a fight that wasn't his...

His insistence that he knew what I needed that night and what he gave me by taking control...

All the days and nights since...

One after another, they just keep coming. A tidal wave of memories and feelings that I've been trying to suppress all day, that I've tried to wall off strictly in the "lies" category because the alternative was so much worse.

"I know what you're thinking, Bishop." His voice is soft, calm, even closer than it was only a moment ago. "You're allowing yourself to spiral. You're trying to go back to that place where you live behind a one-hundred-foot high wall and keep everyone on the other side of it. You're trying to shut down the memories of us so you can shut me out...when all I want is for you to let me back in."

When I reopen my eyes, a single tear I can't contain finally trickles out of the corner and down my cheek. "You took everything I've always hated about myself and made me love it. You took all the things I prided myself on and showed me how they were killing me. You made me feel things that I only thought existed for people like my cousins, for people who could be that open. You did all that in a span of only a month. You read me like an open book, knowing you were going to close it."

He tentatively takes another step forward, and my back stiffens. "No. I *cherish* that book. It has been what has kept me going. *You* have been." He raises his hand, and when those rough calluses gently brush against my cheek, I shiver, wrapping my arms around myself. "You know who I am, Bishop. I'm the man you spent the last week with. I'm also the one who has been looking out for you, who's been protecting you from the shadows, even when you didn't know it. Who has been bending over backward, trying to figure out how to keep you and the rest of the Hawkes safe. I will *always* protect you, Bishop. Always. Even if you hate me. Even if you never want to see me again."

My lip trembles, those damn tears threatening again. "Why?"

His gaze softens. "Because anything worth living for is worth dying for."

It doesn't matter that he stole that line from the book in his nightstand, my heart still stutters all the same.

That part of me that I thought was dead forever this morning.

The source of so much agony.

It starts to beat again.

He brushes a tear from my cheek, and I have to look away from the intensity in his gaze, from the very heavy emotions he's trying to convey that I'm not sure I can handle.

"Please look at me, Bishop."

It isn't a command this time.

It's a request.

Somehow, that makes it so much worse.

But I comply.

"I love you, Hellcat. None of this was fake. None of what we have is. It's the most real thing I've ever had in my life, and I think it's the most real thing you've ever had, too. Don't throw it away because I've hurt your pride, because you want to go back to that place where you're an island. Let me back in, and I promise I'll never hurt you again. I promise that if I even *try*, you can bring me back into this ring and have your way with me."

The corners of my lips twitch despite how angry I still am with him.

Probably because the person I'm really angry with is myself.

Not for trusting him. Not for believing him. Not for

ignoring that first initial gut reaction that told me there was something off about him. But for not being able to see the truth until this very moment.

Gage Newhart isn't a stranger.

He isn't a liar, either.

He's a man who fell in love and let that become the most important thing to him over a mission that he knew was going to get very complicated.

He is the person I've fallen in love with.

"I'll do anything, Bishop, anything to prove it to you, to make you trust me again." He pulls my face between his palms, forcing me to look him in the eyes and see the love there. "Anything. Just name it."

"I honestly don't know what it will take, Gage." I swallow through my tightening throat. "I don't know how we move past all this."

His thumb sweeps across my cheek, wiping away another tear as the tiniest of grins pulls at his lips. He slowly drops to his knees, pleading up at me with so much pain in his gaze and unshed tears shimmering there. "I do. With you in control."

A laugh that sounds completely wrong slips from my lips. "Haven't you been trying to get me to let go of that?"

He nods, squeezing my hands. "I have, but I'll tell you a secret that isn't such a big secret. I'll do anything for you, Hellcat. Anything."

I tug him back up to his feet and press my hands against his chest to feel the steady beat of his heart beneath my palm again. To ground myself the way he does with his dog tags.

This man has bent over backward to take care of me, to protect me, to give me whatever I need, whenever I need it. And he dropped to his knees for me, promised to ensure my safety even if I never take him back.

All those reasons I had for hating him, for not trusting him, were my anger about my loss of control. And he's giving it back to me.

"You can pin and straddle me anytime, and I will truly be a happy man." He lowers his mouth to mine, feathering a tentative kiss across my trembling lips. "*Anything* you want will make me a happy man, as long as I'm in your life to experience it with you."

Only an hour ago, my world had fallen apart.

All the pieces of myself I had shown only to Gage and learned to embrace through his love were scattered in the wind, and I never thought I would find them again.

I was ready to go back to being that renegade who rejected all the attempts anyone made to break through my walls.

But he's somehow found those pieces, reminded me how safe they are with him, and rebound them into the story of us.

It took a rogue to do it, but my renegade is finally tamed.

Sort of.

EPILOGUE

TWO MONTHS LATER

BISHOP

The party storms below me.

A swirl of color, laughter, and music.

From my hawk's eye view up in the old choir loft of the Marigny Opera House, I can see absolutely everything.

The couple examining the silent auction items and placing bids...

The mayor and his wife chatting with Savage and Gabe near the stage...

The rest of the family spread out at various tables and chatting up other invitees at the biggest fundraiser of the year...

It all feels so familiar, so normal.

Not at all what we should be doing right now.

But of course, my suggestion that we postpone was dismissed without even having to take a vote.

I would have lost anyway.

Tonight is too important to the Hawke Foundation and all of us. This one night will raise enough money to fund not only the free medical clinic, but also dozens of other community outreach projects we always have in the works.

They wouldn't have cancelled it for anything short of another Category 5 hurricane, and even then, I'm not so sure.

Everyone is enjoying themselves, busy playing their roles, which means I'm not partaking in the festivities.

I'm working.

"I have to say, Hellcat..."—Gage's voice floats over to me above the din from below, and I glance behind me to the top of the staircase where he leans, his heated gaze raking over me—"I like when you get dressed up for these things."

I push up from where I was leaning against the railing and turn to face him, and his eyes skim from the coiled twist of my braids at the back of my head, down over the black pant suit that fits me like a glove, lingering on the deep *V* of nude skin the jacket shows off.

"You're not disappointed I'm not wearing a gown like everyone else?"

He smirks as he pushes off the wall and makes his way over to me, looking positively sinful in his tux. When he reaches me, he bites his bottom lip in a way that makes my insides go molten. "Hellcat, you could *never* disappoint me."

Damn him.

If he keeps saying things like that to me, I might actually wish I weren't working tonight.

He tugs me into his arms and kisses me deeply, a little groan falling from his lips as he presses his growing cock against me. "What are the chances we could have a quickie up here before anyone notices?"

I grin against his lips. "Pretty slim, considering I've never known you to be particularly quick."

He chuckles and nips at my bottom lip. "I'm going to take that as a tremendous compliment instead of a rejection."

"You should."

Our kiss lasts longer than it should, his mouth moving over mine greedily, as if he hasn't tasted me in years when it's only been a few hours since we left the condo to come here.

When we finally come up for air, he rests his forehead against mine for a moment before taking an exaggerated breath and retreating a step. "So, how's everything going?"

I sigh and take up a spot next to him at the railing. "As well as can be expected, I guess."

"No sign of our friends?"

I shake my head.

In the months since Gage came clean about who he really is and why he's really in New Orleans, he's doubled down on his efforts to locate his old mentor McDonald, and our old enemy, Satriano.

It seems that the explosion at the club either scared both of them away or was only a precursor to something much bigger, something that's taking time and planning. Something that's building...

But the point that was made before the opening of the second Hawke Hotel tower rings true just as much now as it did then.

We can't put our lives on hold.

All we can do is our best to protect each other, to watch each other's backs, and knowing we now have the support of the federal government helps ensure that.

Still, I would love this shindig to be over already so we can go home and relax.

Gage glances toward the front door of the event space where two armed guards stand at the ready, only a fraction of the force we have both mingling with the guests and outside surrounding the building.

Always in pairs, so no one is ever alone.

Since we still haven't determined who might have assisted McDonald in gaining access to Gabe's car, it meant a clean sweep of our entire security team and rebuilding from scratch.

It should quell my fears to know we're covered in every possible way, but it doesn't.

"You really think he'll show up tonight?"

I peek over at him, knowing full well which *he* Gage means. "He did last year. Waltzed right onto the dance floor with Wren and acted like he belonged here."

"He wouldn't try that again."

Snorting, I shake my head. "You don't know Satriano the way I do…"

"But I do know you, Hellcat, and I know you've got this. Stop looking so worried and try to enjoy the party." He shrugs, a grin playing on his lips. "I don't know, maybe dance with your boyfriend."

I raise a brow at him. "Is that what you are?"

He wraps his arms around me and pulls me up against him again. "I sure hope so. Otherwise, it makes what I did to you in our bed last night seem *very* inappropriate."

Good God.

My entire body heats at the memory, and I squeeze my legs together against the throb deep in my core.

He nuzzles my ear, his scent invading every breath I take. "I got to tell you, Hellcat…"—his hand slides around and grips my ass tightly—"being *here* was one of the greatest experiences of my life. I haven't been able to stop thinking about it."

"Me either." I press my hands against his chest, digging in my nails. "But if you keep talking like that, we're going to have to leave the party early."

He pulls back, brows raised. "Is that an option?"

I shake my head. "No."

"Damn." He grins. "I'll just have to wait until we get home then."

"I guess you will."

Footsteps sound behind us, and I glance over Gage's shoulder as Atlas and Wren make their way up onto the balcony.

Atlas releases a sigh. "*There* you are."

"You were looking for me?"

He nods.

Gage chuckles. "You sure you weren't just coming up here for a quickie?"

Wren's cheeks heat bright red, and she ducks her head and rests her hand over her growing belly.

Atlas barks out a laugh. "Did someone see us last year?"

I gape at him. "Are you serious?"

How the hell did I miss that *happening on my watch?*

He nods, and I cut my gaze back to Gage, who can't stop grinning.

"See, I told you." He winks. "We had plenty of time."

Shaking my head, I brush off his continued flirtation and raise a brow at Atlas. "What were you looking for us to talk about?"

He approaches, his hand wrapped around Wren's. "I was wondering if you've seen Astrid."

Instantly, my stomach drops. "What do you mean?"

He runs his free hand through his hair. "She was at the table with us earlier, but I've been looking for her for like twenty minutes and haven't been able to find her."

I pull out of Gage's hold and move back over to the edge of the balcony to look out across the party, scanning for her familiar pale-blond hair.

There are dozens of blond heads—socialites, friends, politicians, everyone we cram in here every year to raise money.

But not the one I'm searching for.

"I don't see her..."

Atlas offers a concerned look. "She's been...a little off lately.

Quiet. You don't think she would've left without telling anyone, do you?"

Gage shakes his head, all that humor and warmth draining from his eyes. "No. You all stay here and search from above. I'll go look for her."

GAGE

My pounding footsteps echo through the old stone stairwell as I make my way down from the balcony and out into the main event space.

The party rages around me. Hundreds of people dressed to the nines, chatting, drinking, socializing, all here to support the Hawkes and their endeavor to raise money for the good of the city of New Orleans.

It should be a fun night, a night to celebrate all these people coming together for such a good cause.

And ten minutes ago, I would've said that Bishop and I could have slipped out of here without anyone noticing and gone and had a repeat of last night.

But now any of that lightheartedness has disappeared along with Astrid.

I immediately make my way over to Skye where she sits at one of the family tables with Storm and Landon, Angelina, Allie, and Pope. "Have any of you seen Astrid?"

They shake their heads, and Skye narrows her gaze on me.

"No, but Atlas was looking for her earlier." Her brow furrows. "Is something wrong?"

I try my best to keep my rising concern out of my voice, so I don't panic her. "I don't think so, but if you see her, tell her I'm looking for her."

Skye nods. "I will. I'm sure she's just in the bathroom or talking with someone in a quiet corner."

"You're probably right." I force a smile. "There probably isn't any reason to worry."

But as I move away from the table, my gut tightens and that nagging suspicion in the back of my mind starts to move toward the forefront.

It's that instinct I developed in the Rangers when the shit was about to hit the fan.

I hustle toward the main doors where two of our armed security team members stand. "Have either of you seen Astrid come through?"

They shake their heads.

The team lead dips his head closer so I can hear him better over the music coming from the live band. "No, sir, but we just moved onto this rotation about ten minutes ago, so it's possible she went outside before we came."

Shit.

I glance at my watch.

The shift change was ten minutes ago. Essential to make sure the men stay alert and on their toes, but also an opportune time for someone to slip in or out.

Why would she, though?

I push past them out into the warm evening air. The smell of honeysuckle and magnolias fills it as I step out toward the security team standing a few feet away. "Have either of you seen Astrid?"

They shake their heads, brows furrowing.

The larger of the two men instantly begins scanning the area immediately outside the door. "No, why?"

"I can't find her. No one inside has seen her for a while. I'm wondering if she slipped out to get some fresh air."

One of them points to the back of the building. "Is it possible she went into the garden?"

I nod. “Maybe...”

And it’s possible one of the many other teams might have escorted her and stayed with her.

Since every Hawke is under strict orders not to ever be alone, no one would have allowed her to wander off alone. And she wouldn’t have ignored the order. Not Astrid.

She’s the rule follower, the sweet, kind Hawke, who always looks for any way she can to assist anyone else, who dedicates her life to tutoring employees at the various businesses to try to help them achieve their ultimate dreams.

What she is not is a rule breaker.

That knowledge helps relieve a little of the tension in my chest, but until I have eyes on her, I can’t be confident she’s safe.

I jog toward the corner of the building and turn, almost slamming into two more of our security officers who are out on patrol.

“Mr. Newhart...”

“Have either of you seen Astrid?”

The taller of the two motions absently behind him. “She was just out here getting some air not that long ago.”

“When?”

He shrugs. “I don’t know, maybe twenty minutes ago. A member of the security team was with her.”

A member...

Not two.

My hackles immediately rise. “What do you mean?”

After the realization that McDonald had someone on the inside who got him access to Gabe’s car to plant the bomb, we created the new team and ensured no team member would ever work alone. That way, everyone always has at least one set of eyes on them, monitoring what they’re doing.

Confusion furrows his brow. “She was with someone, a man, broad shoulders...his back was to me, but I assumed it was one of you or one of the team.”

"But you didn't see his face?"

He shakes his head. "No. She was talking casually with him. There wasn't any reason to believe she was in any danger. I—"

"Fuck." I shove my hands through my hair. "What did the man look like?"

"Dark suit, maybe a tux, light hair, blond maybe."

My blood immediately runs cold. "Could it have been silver?"

He tilts his head as if considering my question for a moment and then nods. "Maybe. It was dark and I couldn't see much from where I was standing. But yeah, could have been white or silver."

Fuck.

I race around them into the open grassy space that is less a garden and more an empty side lot that serves as additional space for wedding receptions and other events and scan the entire area, but it's deserted. If Astrid was here, she's gone now.

Maybe she was just with Gabe...

A chat in the garden with her father alone would make sense.

I take a deep breath, then run past the confused guards again. "You two, scour every fucking inch of the property and around it. Look for anything out of the ordinary, any signs of where she might have gone."

They nod and take off as I reach the guards outside the front door. "You two, don't allow anyone in or out and radio the rest of the guards. Tell them to canvas the property and lock it down."

"What's wrong?"

"Astrid's officially missing."

Ducking back into the party, I relay the same information to the guards on duty inside, then rush across the dance floor, dodging happy couples twirling to the lively music.

Gabe stands near the stage with Savage, chatting with the

mayor and his wife. By the time I reach them, I'm out of breath and probably look like a lunatic.

The last thing I want to do is cause a scene, but this isn't something that can wait until it's polite to interrupt.

Gabe immediately senses something isn't right. "What's wrong?"

"Were you outside talking to Astrid?"

His brow furrows. "No. I haven't left the party at all since we got here. Why?"

"Shit."

Savage's jaw tightens. "What's going on?"

I glance up to the balcony to where Bishop stands, watching everything, concern etched across her beautiful face as she speaks with someone on the radio. By now, she knows I haven't been able to find her.

Turning back to Gabe, I try to remain as calm as possible. "Astrid's gone. No one's seen her in at least twenty-five minutes. And one of the guards outside said she was in the garden with a man with light-colored hair."

I see this exact moment that both Savage and Gabe follow what I'm suggesting without having to explicitly say it in front of the man who runs the city and his wife.

Gabe pales. "Satriano?"

"Who the hell else could it have been?" I scan the space, hoping against hope that Astrid will appear and we can laugh this off. "I already locked down the entire event. We'll question everyone. Determine what everyone saw. Check any security footage."

But it won't matter…

Because deep in my gut, I already know it's too late.

Astrid is gone.

TWENTY MINUTES AGO
ASTRID

The light scent of the honeysuckle and magnolias that cover most of the properties surrounding the Marigny Opera House grounds would be calming under normal circumstances.

I breathe it in, hoping it will stop the way my hand trembles.

But it doesn't work.

I'm not sure anything could at this point.

Not tonight.

A twig snaps somewhere behind me in the darkness…

I hope you enjoyed *Renegade Hawke.* The final showdown with Satriano comes in Astrid's story *Resolute Hawke,* the final book in the Billionaires of New Orleans: The Hawke Family Second Generation!

Get your copy: books2read.com/ResoluteHawke

To stay up to date on news, sales, and releases from Gwyn, join her newsletter here: www.gwynmcnamee.com/newsletter

ACKNOWLEDGMENTS

This book has been such a long time coming. When I planned out the second generation of the Hawke Family, I knew that Bishop's love interest was going to have to be a special kind of man who wouldn't let her walls stay up. Gage became that and so much more thanks to my fabulous beta readers Patricia and Renee and my amazing editor David Michael. But Bishop truly came to life thanks to my amazing sensitivity reader Crystal Grizzard Burnette. Your comments meant the world to me. Thank you for helping me make Bishop exactly who she was meant to be.

ABOUT THE AUTHOR

Gwyn McNamee is an attorney, writer, wife, and mother (to one human baby and two fur babies). Originally from the Midwest, Gwyn relocated to her husband's home town of Las Vegas in 2015 and is enjoying her respite from the cold and snow. Gwyn has been writing down her crazy stories and ideas for years and finally decided to share them with the world. She loves to write stories with a bit of suspense and action mingled with romance and heat.

When she isn't either writing or voraciously devouring any books she can get her hands on, Gwyn is busy adding to her tattoo collection, golfing, and stirring up trouble with her perfect mix of sweetness and sarcasm (usually while wearing heels).

Gwyn loves to hear from her readers. Here is where you can find her:

Website: http://www.gwynmcnamee.com/

Shop: http://www.gwynmcnameeshop.com/

Facebook:https://www.facebook.com/AuthorGwynMcNamee/

FB Reader Group: https://www.facebook.com/groups/1667380963540655/

Newsletter: www.gwynmcnamee.com/newsletter

Instagram: https://www.instagram.com/gwynmcnamee

Bookbub: https://www.bookbub.com/authors/gwynmcnamee

Tiktok: https://www.tiktok.com/@authorgwynmcnamee

OTHER WORKS BY GWYN MCNAMEE

The Billionaires of New Orleans: The Hawke Family

Savage Collision

Tortured Skye

Stone Sober

Building Storm

Tainted Saint

Steele Resolve

START THE SERIES FREE AT ALL RETAILERS:

books2read.com/SavageCollision

A Hawke Family Christmas

(novella that bridges First Gen and Second Gen)

AVAILABLE AT ALL RETAILERS:

Books2read.com/HawkeFamilyChristmas

The Billionaires of New Orleans: The Hawke Family Second Generation

Night Hawke

Ruthless Hawke

Reticent Hawke

Relentless Hawke

Reckless Hawke

Rebel Hawke

Restless Hawke

Renegade Hawke

Resolute Hawke

START THE SERIES FREE AT ALL RETAILERS:

Books2read.com/NightHawke

The Sweetest Lie Duet

My Sweetest Agony

My Sweetest Obsession

AVAILABLE AT ALL RETAILERS:

books2read.com/MySweetestAgony

Lumberjacks in Love

Billionaire Lumberjack

Billionaire Lumberjack's Baby

Billionaire Lumberjack's Bride

Billionaire Lumberjack's Beauty

Billionaire Lumberjack's Bargain

AVAIABLE AT ALL RETAILERS:

books2read.com/BillionaireLumberjack

McBride Brother Lumberjacks

Beneath the Mountain Sky

Beyond the Mountain Sky

Bigger Than the Mountain Sky

AVAILABLE AT ALL RETAILERS:

books2read.com/BeneaththeMountainSky

The Fury Family Series

Dirty Pucking Player

Fabulous Filthy Friend

Sinfully Shameless Chef

AVAILABLE AT ALL RETAILERS:

books2read.com/DirtyPuckingPlayer

The Inland Seas Series

Squall Line

Rogue Wave

Safe Harbor

Anchor Point

Dark Tide

START THE SERIES FREE AT ALL RETAILERS: books2read.com/SquallLine

---

The Scarred Heroes Series

Dead Reckoning

Off Course

Clean Slate

START THE SERIES FREE AT ALL RETAILERS:

books2read.com/DeadReckoningGM

The Deadliest Sin Series

(also available in individual novella formats)

Finding Sin (prequel novella)

Wrath Collection (books 1-3)

Envy Collection (books 4-6)

Lust Collection (books 7-9)

Pride Collection (books 10-12)

Sloth Collection (books 13-15)

Greed Collection (books 16-18)

Gluttony Collection (books 19-21)

START THE SERIES FREE AT ALL RETAILERS:

books2read.com/FindingSin

The Slip Series

Dickslip

Nipslip

Beaver Blunder

START THE SERIES FREE AT ALL RETAILERS:

books2read.com/Dickslip

The Supernatural Love Stories in the Absurd

(Written as D.P. Payne)

Parched

Cursed

Spirited

Loched

START THE SERIES FREE AT ALL RETAILERS:

Books2read.com/ParchedDP

CO-WRITTEN SERIES

The Crowned Hearts Duet

Royally Complicated

Russian and Royally Complicated

AVAILABLE AT ALL RETAILERS:

books2read.com/RoyallyComplicated

The Warren Family Holidays Series

Holiday Terminal

Holiday Bridal Wave

Holiday Fake Date

AVAILABLE AT ALL RETAILERS:

books2read.com/HolidayTerminal

Small Town Spicy Bites

Christmas Eve Casanova

Spicy Spring Fling

Filthy Fall Flirt

AVAILABLE AT ALL RETAILERS:

books2read.com/ChristmasEveCasanova

Find out more about Gwyn's books at her website:

www.gwynmcnamee.com

Order ebooks, signed paperbacks, merch, and book boxes from her shop:

www.gwynmcnameeshop.com